BRIGHT MORNING

BRIGHT MORNING

An Anthology of Hopeful Tales

In Honor of Vonda N. McIntyre

Edited by Deborah J. Ross

Evennight Books
Cedar Crest, New Mexico

BRIGHT MORNING

Copyright © 2021 by Evennight Books

This is a work of fiction. All of the characters, organizations, and events portrayed in these stories are either fictitious or used fictitiously.

Evennight Books
P.O. Box 1644
Cedar Crest, NM 87008

www.evennight.com

ISBN: 978-1-952653-08-7

First Edition Jan 2022

To our teacher, friend, and colleague,
Vonda N. McIntyre

Bright morning stars are rising

Bright morning stars are rising

Bright morning stars are rising

Day is a-breaking in my soul.

—*Appalachian spiritual*

Contents

Introduction

Once upon a time, a writer named Vonda N. McIntyre got together with a bunch of other writers to create a shared, ongoing project. Then she died and everyone was very sad, for she was the heart and soul of that gathering. Eventually various members went their separate ways, but some of us started hanging out in a virtual treehouse together. Which was especially nice during the Covid-19 pandemic when we couldn't meet in person. Not that we did much of that, living as we did on several continents. After a time, when we were missing Vonda very much, one of us said, "Hey, let's do an anthology in her honor. And because she gave so many of us hope, let's make that the theme." We also decided to make the anthology a benefit for Room to Read, a charity that promotes literacy for children all over the world.

And so, *Bright Morning* was born. The title comes from an Appalachian spiritual collected by Alan and Elizabeth Lomax in 1937, dating at least to the 1830s.

We all had Vonda stories: How we met her. How we said goodbye. The first Vonda story we read. The last. How we bonded over salmon dinners. How she treated us as equals and inspired our careers. Her humor and her kindness, and our grief at her loss. Here are a few of the many, many Vonda stories.

Hope can mean a lot of different things, especially in today's world. A happy ending is only one kind of hope. It can also mean persistence, finding small gems of joy in the rubble, and believing that things can, against all reason and expectation, get better. That love can prevail. And heal. That we are more than the sum of our experiences.

That together, we can achieve magnificent things.

These pages contain a tremendous range of stories, something for every mood and taste. I hope they give you joy. And hope.

—Deborah J. Ross

Remembering Vonda

Pati Nagle: I first met Vonda N. McIntyre (never omit the "N."!) at the Nebula Awards in Santa Fe, New Mexico in 1997. She was all excited about this new Internet thing which she planned to use to make live reports of the award results, a first-time experiment. She was not that tall, had a mop of curly hair, and wore a really cool, colorful kimono jacket. Vonda was a bundle of energy, but in a quiet, gentle way, not in an overwhelming way.

I didn't encounter her personally again for some years, although her fiction had inspired me from my teen years onward, with many memorable stories including *Dreamsnake* and *The Moon and the Sun*. Her success helped me believe that my own was possible. Always, Vonda was a presence in the fantasy/science fiction field. To me she was one of the "masters" whose genius set the bar.

In 2008, a group of female F/SF writers began talking about joining forces to help each other gain visibility, and Vonda was among this group. We explored numerous strategies, one of the most important becoming the creation of a website/blog/bookstore to feature all the members. It was Vonda who gave this bookstore and the organization (which eventually became a cooperative) its name: Book View Café.

For the next decade and more, Vonda was my colleague in BVC. She and I both wound up working on the website, and later on the ebooks that we gradually began to create and put up for sale. The ebook self-publishing revolution enabled this group of women (and, eventually, men) to present their work to an eager marketplace. It kept many of us afloat who might not have fared so well in traditional publishing, and we took quiet pride in the fact that we cared how each other's books looked. We had high standards for production quality—higher, we believed, than many traditional publishers.

Vonda gave tirelessly of her time and energy, quietly lending her technical expertise to the production of many of BVC's ebooks. She was the queen of catching stupid quotation marks and other technical flaws. She was always gracious, never pushy. She not only republished some of her own backlist titles through BVC, which lent the cooperative considerable cachet, she recruited Ursula K. Le Guin to join and do the same. Le Guin's presence and generosity in sharing her blog posts with BVC was a great boon to the group, and Vonda was the one who made it happen.

In 2015, Vonda was the guest of honor at Sasquan, the World Science Fiction Convention in Spokane, Washington. BVC members gathered from around the country to honor Vonda at this con, and I finally got to see her in person again. She still had really cool, colorful clothing, and though the hair was more silver now, she was mostly the same as when I'd first met her: soft-spoken, intelligent, gently funny, and more opinionated than she usually let on.

I will always remember Vonda with fond affection and gratitude. I miss her, and yet she's still here. Her work endures, and I can return to it any time I feel the need for a Vonda fix. Her energy shines through her stories, and always will.

Madeleine E. Robins: In 1978 I bought a copy of Vonda N. McIntyre's *Dreamsnake*—the first SF book I ever bought in hardcover. Three years out of college, hardcover books were not in my budget, but standing in the Cambridge Science Fantasy Bookstore I started reading it, decided I had to own it right away: the world-building, the clarity of the writing, the characters, the "never seen anything like this before" completely captivated me. After that I read anything and everything of her work that I could find.

Years later, I met her. We'd crossed paths online, but here was this energetic, ebullient woman in a hotel lobby who greeted me as if we'd known each other for years, and included me immediately in the group conversation. The next time we met I reintroduced myself to her (because why would Vonda McIntyre remember me?) and she said "Of course I know who you are." Which floored me: Vonda N. McIntyre, author of *Dreamsnake* and *The Exile Waiting, knew my name.* I did manage to keep my fangirling on the inside: Vonda wasn't the sort of person who looked to be fangirled.

When we became a part of the online author's collective Book View Café, Vonda did formatting on ebooks—including my early Regency romances. I apologized about asking her to work on such early, minor, non-SF books (my formatting skills are nil: that's why I was the royalties manager), but she waved that away. "I'm having fun with them!" And every time I asked for help—every time anyone in the collective asked for help, there was Vonda, pitching in. She had variable patience—a tactful way of saying she didn't suffer fools lightly—but never failed to give her time and her energy, and as with Clarion West, she was a fierce promoter of the collective.

In 2015, at the World Science Fiction Convention, Vonda was the Guest of Honor. We had a party in her honor, and I made a cake inspired by her novel, *The Moon and the Sun*—with a mermaid on the top. Vonda's work was always rigorously rooted in science—trust her to create a mermaid that owed nothing to Disney or Hans Christian Andersen, and was as alien as any creature from Alpha Centauri. I told her my story about buying *Dreamsnake* in hardcover, and she laughed and said she recognized that impulse, and was honored that I'd spent some of my first-job money on her book. Again. I kept the worst of my fangirling to myself and just thanked her for writing a book I had had to own right that moment.

I wish I'd been a little braver about thanking her—then or later--for the characters she created, the worlds she opened, and, in the real world, the frontiers she blazed for me and for other women in SF. I wish I told her how much her work—with its clarity, humanity, and acknowledgment of the realities of the world and its insistence on hope—meant to me.

∞

Nancy Jane Moore: Vonda was supposed to always be there.

I know all of us will die, and yet I still manage to assume that people I know and care about will be there forever. No amount of logic can unseat this assumption; every time I lose someone I'm close to, it feels wrong and unfair to me. As I get older, the losses get more frequent, yet my reaction remains unchanged. I don't get used to loss. Maybe that's a good thing.

I first met Vonda at a Clarion West party in 1997. I think I mumbled, "Pleased to meet you" and then backed away. Vonda was somebody and I was just another of the current crop of Clarion West students. I didn't want to take up her time. It was a couple of years later, when Vonda helped me do something with my website as part of her volunteer work with SFWA, that I realized she never acted like she was "somebody." The stories of her generosity to others, a generosity that included lots of her time, are legendary.

I didn't get to know her as a friend until some years later, when we worked together on Book View Café. I came to treasure the email exchanges—I perked up every time I saw her name in my Inbox—as well as to appreciate all the hard work she contributed. Over the last ten years, I visited Seattle a lot, so I often got to see her in person. We had Aikido in common as well as science fiction, so we'd go out to dinner and tell each other stories. She showed me some of her favorite places around town. I stayed at her house a couple of times.

She blurbed my first novel and beta read my second. I got to beta read her last book, though I've always felt like that was more of an honor than a way of paying her back for all the favors she did me. (I hope I helped, though.) She left us before I could come close to evening the scales. I hadn't worried about it, because I expected her to always be there. Now the regret creeps in.

But the wonderful thing about writers and other artists is that even when we've lost them, we still have their work. And since the first place I really met Vonda was not that Clarion West party but rather in the pages of books, I am grateful for that. In fact, the first time I met her I didn't even realize that I'd done so.

Did you ever have one of those books or stories that sticks in your head, the one you can't remember the name of or the author of, but somehow the story never lets you go? I had one of those. For years, I kept trying to describe it—a young woman on a future and very dystopic Earth, who puts together an escape both for herself and for others.

When Vonda asked me to do an interview with her as her guest of honor presentation at WorldCon in Spokane, I went back to re-read a lot of her work and realized I'd never read her first novel *The Exile Waiting*. About ten pages into it, I discovered I had read it: it was the book I'd been trying to remember for all those years. I must have read it in the late 1970s or early 80s, when I found myself devouring science fiction after reaching my limit with mainstream work.

It's embarrassing that I forgot the author of a book that affected me so much that it stayed in the back of my head; I do usually remember authors even if I often forget titles. But I chalk it up to being new to science fiction at the time. I told Vonda this story, by the way, because while it's embarrassing to forget who wrote something, it's also important to remember that the words had such a powerful effect on me.

Part of the reason her work affected me so much is that Vonda always wrote women characters who had agency, even if they were stuck in a bad situation. And while many of her characters were exceptional in that they did things that were worth telling stories about, they were not the only women in her worlds who did things.

She created realities in which women got to act. This is even true in *The Moon and the Sun*, which is set at the court of Louis XIV, a time that almost defines patriarchy. These aren't stories about the one girl who manages to do something—usually by disguising herself as a boy—but rather stories in which the women act as fully realized people (even within societal constraints) and do the things that make the story important.

As someone who spent a lot of my youth reading stories in which I identified with the male characters (despite never having wanted to be a boy) because they got to do the cool things and because all the women were stick figures, I was hungry for books that included me. Vonda wrote that kind of book as a matter of course, probably because she, too, was hungry for those stories.

That's not all that Vonda's work did, of course. A proper appreciation would include a detailed discussion of all the themes in all the books, but that in itself would be a book, one I hope someone writes some day. As we honor Vonda's memory by putting more stories out in the world, ones that we think she would have appreciated, and raise funds for an organization that promotes girls' education, a goal I know she would have appreciated, let's remember all the amazing work she left behind her.

As Vonda said on her Book View Café biography—despite every effort to get her to say something more detailed—"Vonda N. McIntyre writes science fiction." The only sad part is that now we have to say "wrote" instead of "writes," but at least we still have the words.

∞

Amy Sterling Casil: Vonda N. McIntyre was my best friend I never met in real life. She held our author publishing cooperative, Book View Café, together with her...oh gosh...here I am supposedly a writer and I struggle to find a single word, because there isn't one. Vonda's relations with others were...

Stellar

Impeccable

Shining

Constant

Unfailing

At all times, she showed kindness, consideration, modesty, and caring for others. She was utterly steadfast in her work and relationships. And she was a great writer.

It brings tears to my eyes to recall how kind and also how honest she always was. If she gave her word, it was done. If she didn't think she should comment on a controversial matter, she had a term that carried a somewhat different meaning in our cooperative than it does in military service: "Above my paygrade." In Vonda's wise parlance, this meant she didn't want to step on others' toes or contribute to a dispute. And she stuck to that and on many occasions, convinced me that I ought to keep my mouth shut as well.

I think she was so powerful, this Vonda. And I know the world is a better place because she was in it. Not only because of her work, which included *Dreamsnake* and *The Moon and the Sun* (a personal favorite of mine) and her Star Trek books, which introduced many to her writing—but because of her. Hers was a life so well-lived.

Her steadfast honesty and integrity inspired me to confess a few ill events I had encountered in the publishing or film/TV industries. And Vonda told me how she had come very close to becoming one of Hollywood's biggest screenwriters. Only now, today, are a few women in the film industry offered any opportunities to write or direct films. Vonda loved seeing the screen version of *The Moon and the Sun* being made, and it starred PIERCE BROSNAN as King Louis.

It hurt me, so much, when Vonda was diagnosed with pancreatic cancer. For that was the disease that also took my mother. I prayed and hoped that she would be well, but she went, too quickly. Although, she did finish the book she was writing—*Curve of the World*.

I feel like a kindergartner writing about Einstein's theorems—

That's how far ahead of me I think Vonda was. And I'm sure she would vehemently deny that.

She had this quality and again—I don't know the word for it—but it was a receptive, modest, respectful quality—she trusted me to do the covers for her books for Book View Café. She didn't know all the steps and didn't feel as though she should control everything. For one of her collections, she sent me a green and jungle-like picture that she said had been taken by her sister Carolyn. I liked the picture and thought, "What jungle-like environment is this?" I thought for ages it was some place in South America that created an "other-worldly" look. But I found the picture in my files after Vonda had died and it turned out to be a place I now know well: the "Ding" Darling Nature Preserve on Sanibel Island near where I now live in Southwest Florida.

I've written a lot about Florida and I can sense how much Vonda's sister, Carolyn, must have loved kayaking through this wild preserve just as I and my daughter did not long ago. I also just learned, heartbreakingly, that Carolyn had also died of pancreatic cancer.

Our lives are made of threads, woven back and forth, and—though I never met Vonda in person, in spirit, we met many times and I will miss her forever.

$$\infty$$

Jeffrey A. Carver: Vonda N. McIntyre. Now, there's a name to be reckoned with in the history of science fiction. My first introduction to her was the short story, "Of Mist, and Sand, and Grass," which later became the novel *Dreamsnake*, one of the most powerful stories in all of science fiction. (But really, why limit its reach to science fiction alone? It stands among the most memorable stories of all kinds.)

I hardly need to point out what a stellar example she set for aspiring young female writers. Well, female especially, but all aspiring writers.

My first real introduction to Vonda the person came in 2007, when we were classmates at the first LaunchPad Astronomy Workshop at the University of Wyoming. (LaunchPad is a yearly, week-long seminar in everything astronomical created especially for science fiction writers by writer/astronomer, Mike Brotherton. For a writer, it was a lot like going to Heaven.) The camaraderie of the group was something amazing, and Vonda and I (along with others!) found lots of time to talk, until by the end of the week, we felt like old friends.

Soon enough, we crossed paths again, online. The self-published ebook revolution was just getting started, and we were both active in it. Many emails went back and forth between us on the finer points of tweaking code to make ebooks come out looking the way we wanted. Eventually, she invited me to apply for membership in Book View Café, which I happily did. It was within that group that I really saw her tireless, tireless efforts helping others. We continued to work together on picky ebook-formatting questions, and on customer support, a job I took over from her. If there was a single person who was most central to BVC, and generous in her time, it was Vonda.

We only met up in person on one more occasion—at Sasquan, the SF WorldCom in Spokane in 2015, where she was one of the Guests of Honor. She was as generous and smart and funny as I'd remembered, and this time my wife finally got a chance to get to know her, as well.

With the magic of the internet, Vonda had become an essential part of my publishing community. I wouldn't have thought that we could get along without her. It still feels that way sometimes.

In my original blog tribute to her after her passing, I placed an image—we've all seen it—of the first photograph taken by astronomers of a black hole. I thought at the time that she would have loved to have seen that image, which I believe was published shortly after her death.

That was followed by the thought that perhaps she had seen it, from wherever she was; and perhaps she was smiling, not because it was an amazing photo, but because she'd already gone out and looked at the black hole in person.

I still have that thought sometimes, and I smile when I remember.

Doranna Durgin: My introduction to Vonda was as a reader; my early friendship with her was as a green writer receiving offhand nuggets of wisdom. Our later friendship matured into swapping horse stories, ranting about dirty code on websites, and then working on ebook code together. She shared her philosophy for doing these things; she shared her tips and tools. Really, she shared…everything.

Of course it started with *Dreamsnake*. And her Trek books. I read *The Moon and the Sun* early on, when I barely knew her—just a few years after my first book was published and I had deeply immersed myself in the writing community at GEnie and then the bolthole at SFF. She was always exploring fun things to do for readers, so she was one of the first to send bookplates around. (Yes, that means I have a gorgeous signed copy of that Nebula award-winning work and I went and hugged it before I typed this.)

If she knew how to do a thing, she was glad to help you learn it, too—or refine the knowledge you already had. Because we had the same sensibility about coding (clean, streamlined, and robust across platforms), I still use her CSS as the backbone of my ebook stylesheets. I use her Word-cleansing steps to prepare my files for conversion. I consider the things she used to find when proofing ebook production—the little things that no one else noticed or even thought to look for.

Maybe you've seen one of Vonda's crocheted beaded sea creatures. I have two of them on my shelves—one, a gift during a difficult time. The other was offered in an auction for something—I don't even remember what. They're beautiful and they have perfect heft and the ruffly beads tickle your palms and fingers. Of course I treasure them.

So here I am with all these mini-legacies—not just memories of common interests, conversations, and quiet confidences, but all these gifts along the way, small and large and still alive in my world. And here my memories sit, in a small but heartfelt collection of similar memories, a macro legacy of kindness and paying it forward that encompasses an entire writing genre and community—quietly, never drawing attention to itself, but leaving footprints of encouragement all along the way.

No little wonder we decided to celebrate that legacy with stories of hope. Thank you, Vonda. You meant the worlds to us.

∞

Gillian Polack: I've read so many tributes to Vonda, and each and every one of them is important. I have only one thing to add. Just one. That one thing has remained with me throughout the bushfires and throughout the pandemic and is still with me today. It helps me to handle all the slights and worries others fling too easily in my direction.

Many writers doubt their work. I have seen so many discussions of 'imposter syndrome' and so many workshops in how to handle it. I was one of those writers. I didn't just doubt words or paragraphs, I doubted my capacity to write.

When Vonda looked at a novel of mine for Book View Café and said, "I will format this for the ebook," she let me know that she valued it and what she valued in it. Vonda didn't make a huge fuss, but in every conversation I had with her and in every meeting I shared, I felt that I had a voice and that I should use it.

Vonda was not the only writer who does this. The other writers in this anthology, for example, share this generosity of spirit. Vonda carried it further and deeper than any other writer I know. She created a positive environment where the difficulties of the writing world were not transformed into impossibilities for individual writers. She demonstrated her respect for our writing in every task of publishing and even in casual conversations. It was a quiet respect and it was an inexorable respect. I'm not the only writer whose life was changed by this.

Chautauqua

Nancy Jane Moore

My wristband pinged. A text from Irene, sent hours back, just now getting through: "Keryn: Bus not running. Lost many to Dorcas virus, but contagion has passed. We need help." GPS coordinates were attached, showing them in the hills outside Coalinga. Two hundred miles from Berkeley.

Without treatment, Dorcas virus kills half the people who get it. It first hit epidemic status in rural areas of Central America. The bus often traveled along the US/Mexico border; likely they picked it up before useful information about it spread online, given the spotty internet in such regions. Before the virus reached the Bay Area, medical researchers had found it was transmitted by bodily contact—not airborne—and that an already developed antiviral reduced the death toll to ten percent. A good public health response had blocked the spread in the Bay Area and other functioning urban regions, but the epidemic had left a horrible toll in more rural parts of the country.

I pinged Naheem at the hospital and Amanda in security to get help putting together a rescue trip. If Irene said there was no contagion on the bus, there wasn't, but the virus could still be active in the area around Coalinga and other places between here and there. And there could be trouble even without the virus. The current drought has wiped out most of the farms and other work south of San Jose, leaving it with a mix of survivalists, gangs, and communes— some foolish, some benign, many dangerous. Best to be prepared for anything.

Fortunately, both medical and security were willing to help, because I was going no matter what. I owe everything to Irene.

∞

We traveled in one of the university's field work vehicles, a boxy truck covered with PV that could travel up anything that might pass for a road. It held an ambulance's worth of medical equipment, sleeping bags and tents, multiple barrels of water, and several weeks worth of freeze-dried food. The university didn't want its people to die if they got stuck outside civilization.

Lin, one of Amanda's security team who was also a paramedic, drove. Since the old federal highway system crumbled from lack of maintenance, people in the Bay Area have stopped driving much. Many don't know how; between expanded public transit and the convenience of bicycling, few find the need. I learned to drive on the bus, but that was twenty years ago. I'm rusty.

We made our way south through Oakland on International Boulevard, which is in pretty good shape—though slow—because of the buses that run along it. It's a two-lane road, with community gardens and mini-parks in what were once extra lanes and parking spots. Solar panels top every roof and each building—residential, retail, old warehouse or factory turned into some combination of the two—has a huge water tank set up to collect run-off from the roof during the rainy season. One of the reasons the Bay Area survived the parade of systemic crashes of the 2040s and '50s was that it had already put in place renewable energy sources and water systems.

Only the four of us went—a minimum crew for leaving the city. The university preferred sending larger teams when people left the safe confines of Berkeley and Oakland, but it was a month to spring graduation and many students and teachers were out in the field finishing projects. They had few people to spare. Still, we had support and permission. I'm not the only researcher at the university with ties to the bus, and I'd reached out to Naheem and Amanda in particular because I knew they'd had crew or students who'd come to Berkeley by way of Irene. That got us to telling stories about her.

"The most intuitive guards I've ever had were people Irene referred to us," Amanda said. "I'm not sure how they developed those skills. I didn't want to ask, for fear I'd find out something the university couldn't ignore."

Naheem laughed. "Yeah. I had two women several years back in the nurse/midwife program who probably got their background practicing medicine without a license. They should have been training as MDs, but they wanted a faster program so they could get back to the people who needed them." He turned to me. "You seem to know her better than the rest of us. How'd you meet Irene?"

"I grew up on the bus."

"You grew up with Travelers?" he said.

I nodded.

Travelers is the name Berkeley anthropologist Grace Wong gave to the various groups who took to moving around the country in old buses and RVs, offering entertainment and education to people who live in the places civilization forgot. She has documented a troupe who travels the Great Plains, another in old Appalachia, some in the Old South and in New England. In Louisiana they are keeping Zydeco and Cajun music alive; one in Alaska documents those among the indigenous who still manage to fish despite the warming waters. These forgotten places have their own culture, their own ways worth saving, and the Travelers collect those even as they entertain and educate.

The bus I grew up on was called the Chautauqua Frontera— "chautauqua" because Irene, who was there from the beginning, liked the reference back to the nineteenth century educational movement of the same name, and "frontera" because a lot of the travel was along the US/Mexican border, though the bus did range up through California to the Pacific Northwest from time to time. Like most Travelers, they brought entertainment—plays, music, storytelling—along with news. They held workshops on everything from computer programming to the latest wrinkles in growing food with minimal water to making wooden toys. And here and there, they collected people who needed help or who had something that should be shared with a wider audience.

The internet continues to thrive and expand, and development of new tech devices and ways to use them keeps many major cities humming. But the underlying infrastructure that keeps the world connected is not well distributed, especially in the places that never got much coverage in the first place. Travelers like Irene and the Chautauqua provided a different kind of network.

I spent ten years with the Chautauqua Frontera. They gave me a life in a time when an orphaned child—especially a dark-skinned one of uncertain parentage—would have fallen through the cracks. Irene and the others rescued many people, adults as well as children, and made all of us feel we were special and loved, no matter what horrors we had seen. They didn't just rescue us because we needed help, though they helped everyone they saw in need; they saved us because they thought—no, knew—we had something to offer to the future.

Irene brought me to Berkeley when I was sixteen and convinced the powers that be to let me start taking classes. I ended up with a PhD in microbiology and a lab where I could continue my work on the interactions of bacteria and viruses.

Irene had faith in me. I've tried to live up to that.

"What was it like, growing up with Travelers?" Lin asked. The truck was moving slowly, and electric engines are quiet, so we could hear each other even though Naheem and I were in the back and all the windows were open to give us a breeze.

I had a lot of trouble answering that question before I became friends with people who were raising children, because I didn't understand how different my life had been from that of people who lived in relatively stable urban areas. Watching my friends at the university who were raising kids in as safe an environment as you can get these days showed me what the question meant.

"A different place every week, studying things as they came up, taking care of the little ones, performing in our plays. Tech tools so far out of date that you wouldn't have believed they would still work. And sometimes the bus broke down in the middle of nowhere and we ran out of food and the grownups worried a lot."

"I think all grownups worry a lot," Amanda said. She grew up in a co-op community in West Oakland where adults outnumbered kids two-to-one and everybody made a point of providing support for each other.

"But not all of them have to worry about breakdowns and a lack of food," Lin said.

"Mine worried about sea level rise," Naheem said. "We were in Alameda and the house kept flooding. We had too much money tied up in the house to move—it kept dropping in value—so we were stuck trying to work with it."

"We had to keep moving because the rent kept going up," Lin said. "I wish we'd had co-ops down the Peninsula back then. Real estate stayed crazy even as the roads fell apart from floods and landslides."

Maybe nobody growing up in the twenty-first century got a stress-free childhood at that, even the ones in the good places. Mine was just more exotic.

"I loved it, most of the time," I said. "It was like being on permanent vacation. And I was too young to realize how much I should worry."

"Did you ever get attacked?" Naheem asked.

I flashed on the image of Adrienna, who had entranced audiences when she told stories, falling off the stage when a self-proclaimed protector of the white "race" opened up with an assault rifle. Blood everywhere, and the local authorities let him get away to kill again. "Let's just say I learned to handle a gun at an early age."

That was something else we had in the truck: weapons. We were peace-loving folk, for the most part, but we weren't planning to be anyone's victims.

Even back when old I-5 still functioned between Berkeley and Coalinga—before neglect, not to mention serious floods in the Central Valley, took their toll—it took four hours to get there unless traffic was unusually good. These days travel time is double or triple that, minimum. There's not much in the way of traffic, but the roads that still exist are small and full of potholes. As we moved out of the urban areas into what had once been farm and ranch country, the road got worse.

Five years back the area had seen a lot of floods, but now we were firmly back in the drought. Even though it was spring, the landscape along the road was brown—a decayed brown, not the golden color that used to come when the rain patterns were something close to normal. There were no animals grazing along the road, and nothing was growing in the fields that had once held garlic or strawberries. The farther south we drove, the worse it got.

The landscape kept us on edge, so none of us was really surprised when Amanda, who had been running a wide-range satellite-based scan of the area as we drove, said, "We've got a situation ahead." We'd just turned down State Highway 25, a few miles south of Gilroy.

"Do we negotiate?" Lin said.

"No. From what I'm picking up they've got the road blocked with something huge. People around here are pretty desperate, and someone must have recruited a lot of folks to block the road that thoroughly. Turn left next chance you get. We're going to go the long way round."

We went east for several miles before the road turned south again. "This will get us back to 25 way south of Hollister," Amanda said. "That ought to do it." But she kept watching the scan.

Nothing happened as we circled around, except that the lack of pavement meant we were going ten miles an hour. No one would take this route out of choice. We didn't talk much.

We got back on 25 a few miles north of Los Pinos. "Look at the land," Amanda said, gesturing to the brown fields and hills in all directions. "It's even worse than I thought down here. No telling what we're going to run into."

The next hour was uneventful, but I didn't relax because it was clear that Amanda hadn't. She continued to watch the scan. Just south of the Pinnacles, she said, "Fuck. There's something a few miles ahead."

"Go around again?" Lin said.

"We can't. None of the roads off of here go anywhere except up to a few houses. I doubt that would be a safe choice." She sighed. "This looks like a small deal. We might be able to negotiate our way through it. It's either that or turn around and go back, see if we can get east over to one of the roads on the other side of where 5 used to be."

Before one of us could point out how that would take hours, she added, "And there's no guarantee we won't run into something similar over there."

Lin nodded. He slowed down. The rest of us reached under our seats for guns. Amanda set a small automatic rifle on the console by Lin. Negotiate, yes, but be prepared for more. The truck was well-armored, but it wasn't invincible and neither were we.

I did deep breathing exercises. As we got closer, we could see that the roadblock was a couple of dead trees piled in the middle of the road. Maybe ten people stood around them, most of them holding a weapon of some kind. Lin pulled to a stop about thirty feet from the barrier.

"Stay put," Amanda said. She got out of the truck, holding her gun loosely in her hand. *We aren't fools*, her gesture said. "What can we do for you folks?" she said.

"That's a fancy vehicle you got there. Think we'll take it."

"No," she replied. "We need it. But we can trade some supplies for safe passage."

"What kind of supplies?"

"Something to treat Dorcas virus. Maybe some food."

"You got something for the virus?"

"Naheem, hand out some of the antiviral," Amanda called. She backed up to the truck, never taking her eyes off the guy who seemed to be in charge.

Naheem held a package out the window. Amanda took it and

walked toward the spokesperson, who was also holding a rifle loosely. She handed it to him. "A sign of our goodwill."

The man took it, glanced at it, then tossed it back to someone behind him. "Get Gail to look at that," he said. "What about the food?"

I had already pulled out a box of the freeze dried stuff. It took two hands to hold it. Amanda pulled out a weapons sling made to hold her gun in a ready position, and put it on, still never taking her eyes off the crowd. She stuck her gun in it, then picked up the food and carried it over.

The man pushed the box behind him and someone opened it. "A lotta stuff here," the person said.

"Good enough," the spokesman said. "OK. You can go by." He turned to his people. "Start moving those trees."

Amanda backed toward the truck as a couple of people began to pull on the barrier. And then, without warning, someone behind the trees fired a shot. Amanda went down.

Lin was out of the truck before I could move. The spokesman screamed, "Get that son of a bitch."

I thought he meant Lin at first, but then I could see a bunch of people piling on somebody back behind the barrier. The spokesman meant to keep his bargain and his people had grabbed the shooter. Lin pulled Amanda into the back of the truck, and Naheem went to work on her while Lin jumped into his seat and gunned the engine. He drove into the ditch, people scattering out of our way, and around the barrier, and sped away as fast as that truck would go.

"How is she?" I was scared of the answer.

"She was wearing Kevlar," Naheem said.

I'd forgotten that. Of course Amanda wouldn't have got out of the truck without wearing some kind of armor.

"I'm fine," Amanda said, though her voice was weak. "It just felt like a bad punch to the plexus."

"Which is why you went out," Naheem said. "The Kevlar just barely stopped it. Where are they getting that kind of artillery out here in the boondocks?"

"We need the scan running," Amanda said. "There could be more trouble down the road."

Lin said, "Keryn, would you give it a try?"

It was fancy new tech, too expensive for anyone but security folks and cops, so I'd never used anything quite like it. But it turned out to be similar to most GPS systems; it just provided more information.

The satellites had been collecting that kind of data for decades, but it had taken a long time—and a collapse in a lot of government oversight—for someone to make a workable portable device.

It took me a few minutes to get the hang of it. "I don't think anyone's chasing us, and there's nothing up ahead in the next ten miles."

"This is probably the best place for us to stop, if we need to," Lin said.

"Don't stop," said Amanda.

"Naheem?" Lin said.

"Stop," he said. "Don't argue, Amanda. I can't check you out for internal injuries while we're rattling around like this."

"I'm fine," she said.

"No point in running any risks, when you've got me here to make sure. We're likely to need you again."

A dirt road came up on our right. It seemed to lead down to a creek bed—bone dry of course. "This should work," Lin said. "Out of sight, but not much of anywhere." He pulled off and turned the truck around so we were facing out. Leaning over the seat back, he asked Naheem, "Do you need any help?"

"It would make things easier, but we might need you to get us out of here fast."

"I can drive," I said. "It's been awhile and I'm sure I can't maneuver as well as Lin, but I know how."

Both men exhaled. It was clear Naheem did want help. Lin crawled between the seats. "You sit there, ready to move. If you see anything on the scanner, yell out and then take off."

I nodded. I stared at the scan, which wasn't showing anything. From the back I heard a slight whir from the portable imaging device. Amanda let out a soft grunt a couple of times as the two men moved her around to check for other damage spots.

I would have sworn we sat there for an hour, but when I checked the time only fifteen minutes had passed when I heard Naheem say, "Looks like you came through OK. No bleeding that I can find. I've taped up the rib you cracked when you hit the ground. Let's get down the road."

I moved over and Lin crawled back through. He drove off without fanfare. I kept my eye on the scan. Once we were a mile or so down the road, with nothing showing up, I asked him, "How come you jumped out to get her instead of opening fire? I was ready to shoot until you did that."

He shrugged. "Instinct. It felt like those folks were dealing fair with us, by their standards. Grabbing Amanda instead of shooting anyone seemed like the right call."

"I'm glad it was."

"Me, too."

We drove in silence for the next hour. The sun set. "How's our power?" I asked Lin, more to be social than because I was worried.

"We're OK. Got lots of sun today and haven't had to pull on the battery too much. And it's not likely to be overcast tomorrow."

No. Not much chance of that.

"We're getting close. Can you check the GPS and see if you can take us directly to their location? I don't expect they're in town and I'd rather not meet any more people."

"Sure." I plugged in the numbers and gave him directions. Twenty minutes later we were driving down a dirt road that didn't seem to go anywhere when I saw our lights flash onto a familiar shape. "That's them," I said. I reached for the door handle—we were driving about five miles an hour—but Lin stopped me. "Wait. Give them a yell first."

I'm sure he was right, and I wasn't wearing Kevlar, but I leapt out anyway. "Irene," I called out, giving it the Spanish pronunciation to let her know it was me. I'd always preferred to call her that, though she answered either way.

"Keryn, is that you?" said a young voice. It cracked a little.

"Yes. Where is Irene?"

Someone stepped out of the bus and stood in our headlights. Short and skinny was all I could make out. "Come inside. She's been waiting for you."

She was in the back part where everyone slept, lying on a bottom bunk, propped up by pillows. A toddler sat beside her, holding a picture book. "I knew you would come," Irene said as I leaned over to kiss her.

Her thin white hair was brushed up behind her on the pillow, as if she'd been too hot and pushed it off of her neck. There was an ashy tone to her skin, turning the light brown to gray. When I'd seen her on the bus's last trip to the Bay Area a couple of years back, her hair had reached this stage of stark white, but had still been thick, and she'd moved with the same vigor I'd always known. I'd realized then she was getting old, but that hadn't prepared me for the shock of seeing her so frail.

The other thing that was different was that there were only the three of them—Irene, the teenage boy who'd showed me in, and the toddler. The last time there'd been at least fifteen adults on the bus along with the usual scrum of kids. I didn't know which frightened me more: seeing Irene so weak or seeing the bus without that teeming community. It was as if everything important from my childhood was disappearing all at once.

In the spring of 2040—thirty years back—I was sitting on the bumper of an ancient sedan on the shoulder of a highway outside of Flagstaff, waiting to flag down the next vehicle that came along. My mother lay dead in the back seat. I thought she was very sick and was hoping that someone would come along to help her. I was five years old.

I'd been there six hours. Four vehicles had passed and all four had refused to stop for a tiny child standing in the road. One had even tried to run me down; I'd scratched up my legs and arms landing on the gravel shoulder when I jumped out of its way. That had reduced me to tears, but I was still determined to get help when I saw the bus lumbering along in the distance. Once again I walked out to the middle of the road and waved my hands. It came to a stop about twenty yards short of me.

The bus had once transported children to school, but any trace of its original mustard yellow color had long been painted over with symbols and pictures. The top was covered with PV panels. There were words on the message board above the driver, but they weren't ones I had learned in the reading lessons I'd had from my mother. Irene got off the bus and walked toward me.

A short woman, with generous curves, her gray-streaked black hair pulled back carelessly, skin a lighter brown than mine. She squatted when she got close, so she'd share my level, and said in gentle tones, "Hello there. What's your name?"

"Keryn," I said—the automatic response of a child to that question from an adult. I grabbed her hand. "Mommy's sick."

She let me drag her to the car. My mother's body had already begun to decay in the warmth of the Arizona sun and Irene knew the truth from the smell before she reached the car. Despite that, she opened the door and took my mother's wrist, to feel for a pulse. I am sure she did this for me. Then she led me back toward the bus, where some of the others had raised a shade and unloaded some chairs. She sat me down and explained that my mother had died, and then she held me while I cried and cried and cried.

Others from the bus took my mother's body out of the car,

examined and washed her. Someone stitched together two sheets of canvas to make a shroud. Others dug a hole in the ground in an area past some stunted trees, out of sight of the road. When I finally stopped crying Irene got me a peanut butter sandwich and glass of water. They let me touch my mother one more time before they lowered her into the grave, covered her with dirt, and said a few words. Then they packed up everything of value in the car—including the solar panels from the roof and the certificate documenting my birth in Houston—and put me and my things on the bus.

I remember all the details of that day with a crisp clarity. My memories of the time before it are little snatches—with my mother in a store somewhere, a scary man, a tiny house where I had a tinier bed in a corner. My memories of the time afterward, with Irene and the others on the bus, make up most of what I know of my childhood. But I do not forget that first day.

I learned later that burying her in that way was illegal, even in the chaos of the Forties, but that they had examined her well enough to conclude she had bled to death after an abortion. Had they called the authorities, I would have been put in an overburdened and badly run child "welfare" system and the others might have been arrested even though all they had done was stop to help. The Forties were not a time when Travelers could trust officials in the areas they passed through, and the people on the bus were permanent Travelers.

∞

Irene introduced me to the young man who had brought me inside, Luis. He was fifteen or so, with dark brown skin and hair that stuck out in all directions. "You probably saw him the last time we were here, but kids change so fast. And this is Becca," she said, patting the leg of the child next to her. The little girl smiled at me and then ducked her head behind her book.

The others joined us at that point. Irene greeted them with thanks for coming to their rescue. "I'm afraid it's the end of the bus. We hit a boulder in the road and bent the frame. I'm not even sure how Luis wrestled the bus this far off the road, but it's not going to move again."

"I'm sure he had great driving teachers," I said, flashing the boy a smile to hide my despair that a child had to drive that behemoth in hopes of getting them somewhere to get help.

The power still worked. Lin figured out that they hadn't had any dinner—it was after eight o'clock—and bustled around the kitchen turning some of our dehydrated food supplies into a meal. "We've been eating once a day," Luis explained. "To stretch things."

Amanda helped Lin. She was still moving slow, but she waved away my offer to take her place. "You sit with Irene."

I did. I sat and held her hand and didn't say anything though there were hundreds of things I wanted to tell her, and hundreds more I wanted to ask.

Naheem gave each of the children a quick exam—eyes, ears, throat, temperature. Blood draws to check for the virus and other more invasive tests could wait for morning. Then he turned his attention to Irene, using the same simple tools. I could tell from his face that he didn't like what he heard through the stethoscope and her blood pressure numbers were extremely high for someone who hadn't moved much all day. He asked her to squeeze his arm and even I could see that her right hand barely pressed against him. When she sat up, she used her left to push herself around.

"You haven't been taking good enough care of yourself," Naheem scolded in the universal tone doctors use to chastise patients for not taking their meds or getting enough exercise.

"At my age, there's only so much that can be done," she replied. "I'd still be falling apart even if I were in your fancy hospital up there in civilization. Me and the bus have a lot in common; we're tough, but even we have limits."

He laughed. Lin and Amanda brought us bowls of rice and veggies, and we sat around, chatting about nothing in particular. Becca, no longer shy, bounced around among us, telling stories and asking impossible questions. But soon she was starting to droop. Luis picked her up. "Time for bed, Boo. All these fine folks will be here in the morning when you get up."

She protested loudly for maybe five minutes, but he was firm. He settled her into a bunk a row back. We could hear him telling her about the wolf cub who saved the other animals from a fire—a story Irene used to tell me—as we sat quietly once again.

Eventually Amanda broke the silence. "I think the best thing to do is pack the three of you into our truck tomorrow and head back north. I hate leaving the bus here, but our vehicle isn't big enough to tow it."

"It's had its day," Irene said. "If we leave it here, maybe someone else can make a home in it. And you can grab some of our panels and batteries."

I tried to keep back tears. If Irene could be calm in the face of this loss, I owed it to her to be stoic. But a few dripped down my face.

She patted my hand. "I've done my mourning, but you need to catch up. This was your place, too."

Naheem said, "I'll run a quick blood test in the morning, just to make sure you're not carrying anything we can't handle. Though I don't expect to find anything."

Irene nodded. "Becca's mother died of Dorcas virus, but the child never got that sick. And Luis and I seem to be immune, for some damn reason. The others...." Her voice trailed off.

Lin went outside to do guard duty as Luis came back in. "You should get some sleep, too, Abuelita," he said to Irene.

"I'll do it soon," she said. "But I need to talk to Keryn first. Why don't you start setting up beds for everyone?"

"Come help us get things out of the truck," Amanda said. They all went out, leaving me with Irene.

"You need to know. We found Luis about eight years ago, wandering around in the desert near Tucson. He'd been alone awhile, but he'd managed to make himself a shelter and even get water out of cactus. If he knows what happened to the rest of his people, he's never told me. But," she stopped to take a deep breath, "but he has no birth certificate, or anything like that."

I nodded.

"He's so bright. Like you as a kid. Always figuring something out. No telling what he'll do if he gets half a chance."

"I'll handle it," I said. "Any kid who can drive this thing and take care of a baby will find a place in Berkeley. And we'll get him into school."

"Don't tell Amanda about the papers. She has responsibilities. It might cause conflict for her."

I nodded again.

"Becca was born on the bus. We did affidavits documenting that. They're with the other important papers. Luis knows." She paused again to breathe. A few tears dropped down her face. "Those two are all that's left now. I don't know which was worse, losing the children or losing people I'd been with for forty years."

I patted her hand and tried not to cry myself.

"Anyway, Becca needs a home. I can't.... And Luis is too young."

"I'll take care of her," I said. "There are other kids in our co-op. And you taught me about taking care of kids just as you've taught Luis. I'm rusty, but I can figure it out."

"I knew I could rely on you. You have always been a rock."

"And we'll get you better soon, so you can hang around and be abuelita to them both."

She let a corner of her mouth turn up. "I'd like that."

The others came back in and started making up bunks. Luis gave me a meaningful look. I got up. "We're all tired. I'll let you get some sleep." I watched as he helped her to her feet and helped her toward the composting toilet in the very back.

Naheem handed me my bag. "She's dying," he said softly.

"But you can help her?" I whispered back. "If we can get her back to Berkeley?"

"I can make her comfortable. If she makes it through the night and we don't have too much trouble on the way back, I can maybe buy her a little more time in the hospice. But I think she only hung on this long to make sure the children got to someone who could take care of them."

I couldn't say anything, but I nodded to let him know I heard.

"It's a tough ending for a good life," he said. "But she did so much for so many. I hope someone can say the same about us when we reach this point." He patted my shoulder and went to set up his own bed.

I lay down and let my tears flow until I fell asleep.

Dog Star

Jeffrey A. Carver

"Don't you think we're coming in just a little fast?" asked a husky voice behind Jake in the tiny spaceboat.

"There's a critic on every ship," Jake muttered, without breaking his concentration.

"Just doing my job, I'm just—*whooo*, that asteroid's really coming at us!"

Jake didn't argue. The gray, potato-shaped object was indeed getting large quickly—which was exactly according to his plan. Its orbit was less than ideal, and he had only one day to make a survey before it caromed off another asteroid. He wanted to find out: Was it a candidate for mining? Was it worth chasing if it got knocked out of the cluster?

"Like I said, we want to get in fast and get out, before it bounces off NEA-238," Jake said. If he was right and this rock turned out to have mining potential, his tagging it could be just what he needed to break out of the ranks of the junior surveyors. A lot of Earth-approaching asteroids had been nudged by robot boosters together into this Near-Earth cluster, but not many of them had been studied in detail yet. He had a feeling about this one. "Look—haven't I logged, like two hundred asteroid landings? What are you worried abou—*oh crap, what's that?*"

An alarm honked, the spaceboat jerked, and there was suddenly a much-too-bright flare of rocket exhaust in his peripheral vision. Jake glanced at the control board, then outside—and was horrified to see a bright jet of flame shooting sideways out of the boat. *Sideways!* He slapped the cutoff, checked for signs of fire—there were none—then hastily rechecked his approach speed. He'd been okay before, but not any longer. He'd just lost his main engine. Without that for braking, he was definitely approaching too fast.

"Rrrr, you just shut off our rocket," Sam said, squirming around behind him. "Why'd you do that?"

"Had to," Jake said with a gulp, trying not to betray the fear that was rising in his throat. *Think fast now!* "Looks like we've got to use the attitude thrusters for braking."

"But they're—isn't that just for emerg—"

"This *is* an emergency!" Jake disengaged the computer from the thrusters. He needed them all firing in the same direction to brake. "Okay—almost—*hold on now!*" The thrusters sputtered, and he felt a push, slowing them. But not nearly enough.

"You aren't doing this to impress me, are you?" cried Sam.

"No!" He shut up and focused on the asteroid swelling before them. *Oh jeez, too fast!* Trying not to panic, he kicked in thrust to the right. The asteroid mushroomed before them, and they glanced in with a bone-jarring *crack*. They bounced in a flat arc, sending a cloud of dust spraying from the surface—and for a moment, he thought they'd skip off entirely. But no...they bounced twice again, before skidding and shuddering to a stop. The dust they'd kicked up arced slowly back down in the feeble gravity.

Jake gasped and slumped in relief. Then he put out a spacesuit-gloved hand to check the readouts on the console—and got a jolt of electricity through his spacesuit glove.

"*Yow!*" He rocked back as sparks shot from the console. "*What the —?*"

He punched the master cutoff—but too late, his console was smoking. It must have been the dust, carrying an electrostatic charge —powerful enough to short out his instruments.

"I need to vent! Are you sealed in?" he yelled. As soon as he heard Sam's *yes*, he popped the canopy and pushed it open. The cockpit atmosphere puffed out, taking the smoke with it.

"Rrr, I'm okay. Are you okay?" came a muffled voice behind him.

He blinked. "Yeah, I'm all right. Dunno about the boat, though."

He poked tentatively at the console and switched the master back on. Nothing. At all. No power, no comm, no nav, no thrusters. Air in his suit was still flowing, at least. Looking out the cockpit window at the surface of the asteroid, he was grateful that the dust had cushioned their impact. But they needed help—and soon. He keyed his spacesuit comm.

"*Mayday, Mayday, Mayday. This is scout EX-71, can anyone hear me?*"

He repeated the call half a dozen times. But there was no answer, and he knew perfectly well there wasn't going to be one. His suit comm didn't have the range.

Turning his head, he squinted through his helmet visor. Earth was about the size of a tennis ball, white and blue against the black of space. It was about ten days away by direct flight, if they had a ship designed and fueled for such a trip, which they didn't. He turned his head the other way to pick out the Big Dipper and Cassiopeia. A bit of directional calculation confirmed that their sightline to the mining survey base was presently blocked by the asteroid. Well, it was sixteen hours away under normal thrust, with a working rocket—which they didn't have anymore.

And just under two days from here—without any rocket power at all—was asteroid NEA-238, on a collision course. "I wish I'd listened to you," he muttered to Sam. Sam had wanted him to stick to his filed flight plan, instead of detouring to follow his "instinct" on this new rock.

"Me, too. Am I being a bad dog if I suggest we get out and check for damage?" Sam said, nudging him in the back of the helmet.

Releasing his harness, he floated out onto the step-down ledge. He bounced a little to gauge the gravity—not much—then turned to help Sam with his harness. The smartmutt's black-and-white face was just visible through the helmet faceplate. When Jake released the buckle, the border collie launched himself up and out of the cockpit, gliding in a graceful arc to the asteroid surface. In his spacesuit with the air and power pack on his back, he looked less like a dog than a small cargo pod with legs. Nonetheless, he managed well in microgravity, and he swung his head around now, assessing the local conditions. He reared up momentarily on his hind legs.

"Not much to hold us here. We should move carefully." He started nosing around the outside of the broken spaceship.

Jake followed.

∞

It didn't take long to tally up the bad news. The main rocket had burned through the side of its combustion chamber and was useless. It was a miracle it hadn't blown up. The thrusters were dead. So there was no way they could fly back to base under their own power. Also, the hard landing had cracked the hull casing under the electronics, and the short caused by the electrically charged dust had indeed taken out all communications, as well as computer and nav.

"Bones," Sam said, sitting disconsolately by Jake.

"Well," Jake said, "at least we *know* the transmitter's beyond repair, so we won't waste time with it."

Sam cocked his head inside the helmet. "Oofff. Are you saying that to reassure me?"

"Not really. Just saying…we need to think of another approach. And we don't have much time. What—two days? No, eighteen hours."

"Butrr—fffff—people will come looking?" Sam's encased tail slapped once, hopefully, in the silence.

Jake's face burned. "When we don't report in, yeah. But they'll look in the wrong place. I feel really dumb now, not calling in the course change."

"Why didn't you?"

"I just wanted to get this first look, without anyone yelling at me, before it was too late. I know it was stupid, but you have no idea how much I want to—"

"Get promoted, so they don't treat you like a kid. I know." Sam swung his head around, pointing with his nose at the flank of the survey boat. "What else have we got in there? Anything that can make a signal?"

"Let's look." Jake started opening the side compartments. "We need to pull the sled out first. Stand back." He yanked a couple of levers to free the cradle arms holding the large sample sled, then slid the unit out until the flat sled stuck out from the hull, a foot off the ground, like a wide gangplank. "I wonder if this thing still has power."

"Thought all the power was dead," Sam said.

"This is separate. It's got a small zeep converter, for its levitator."

"You mean one of those quantum vacuum thingies?"

"Zero point energy. Yeah." Jake switched the unit on and released it from its cradle. The sled—a flat, rectangular pallet with an opening and some gear in the center—sank until it floated, bobbing slightly, about six inches off the ground. A flat plate on the underside provided the levitation, drawing energy for its repulsive force from the virtual particles that flickered continuously in and out of existence in the apparently empty vacuum of space.

"If that thing can float like that, can't we use it somehow to get off this rock?" The border collie lifted his elongated faceplate-covered nose, as though to sniff the thing.

"Thing is," Jake explained, "this is the only thing it's good for— floating just off the ground. It's great for that, because it doesn't need batteries or fuel. But it's strictly a local effect—close to that levitator plate. As soon it gets more than a few inches off the ground, the effect disappears."

"So if we tried to ride it—"

"It'd be a really short flight. We can *jump* higher than this thing can float." Jake turned the unit off and it settled to the ground.

"Rrmmf. Squirrels and bones." Sam started to raise his spacesuited leg to the sled, then apparently thought better of it.

"Anyway, we're wasting time." Jake stuck his head into the compartment. "There must be *something* in here we could signal home with." There wasn't. He opened the next compartment. "A laser of some kind would be nice, like a torch laser. But I don't see anything. This prospecting scanner has a laser inside it, but we'd have to tear it apart to get at it. There ought to be some *flares* or something."

"Any spare communicators?" the dog asked.

"I wish. You know how in the old days, there used to be redundancy?"

"I wasn't there."

"Well, that was the old days. Wait! Here are some flares!" With a rush of hope, he pulled the box out and examined the contents. His heart sank. "For marking landing areas. Probably not bright enough for anyone to see back at base. We can try, though." He set the box aside and pulled out everything that looked as though it could possibly be useful. "We'd better take stock..."

∞

The shadows were already long; soon, the sun set and they paused to rest. The inventory was bleak. The little boat was meant for short-range surveys, close to the base-station. Jake had taken them a little further afield than the boat really was equipped for—which would have been all right if the crash landing hadn't taken out so many of the onboard systems. They not only had to worry about a collision in fifteen hours with asteroid NEA-238, they also had dwindling power. Oxygen and water weren't immediate worries, but their power was limited mostly to the packs that recharged their suits. The boat's fuel cell was producing only a trickle, which put the last nail in the coffin of any hope of getting away on the boat.

"We're going to have to tap whatever power we can get from the sled," Jake muttered, "and see if we can cannibalize that laser." The asteroid had a slow rotation rate, and they had some time yet before the base-station would come up over the horizon. At that point they would try to signal with the flares, with a makeshift laser, or with anything else they could manage.

While Jake worked by the light of a small lantern, Sam, with his border-collie can-do spirit, determinedly kept at his job; he was going to keep Jake's morale up by pummeling him with questions. At first he quizzed Jake on what he was doing, but Jake growled at that, and the dog switched tactics. "So, is that nice girl in Analysis ever going to notice that you like her? She treats me real nice. Wufff."

Jake looked up from a tangle of wire and glared. "If we get back alive, you can introduce us." He cursed at the useless hardware in his hands. "Sometimes I think you dogs were more useful *before* we gave you speech."

The dog bobbed his head away and looked out at the stars. He coughed as if he'd gotten something stuck in his throat. "Okay, no talk about girls. And you don't want me to ask what you're going to do with that wire, even if you do get it hooked up..."

"I'm *trying* to feed power to the batteries, and hope it keeps us from freezing, and maybe lets us fire up a laser."

"Oh." Sam didn't sound convinced.

"Talk about something else. Distract me."

"Hoo—hmmm. You want to talk about the elections coming up back home?"

"No!"

"Okay, then." Sam turned his head, as if searching the dark of space around them for ideas. "All right, I got it. I got it. This thing's been on my mind ever since I heard about it."

"Oh yeah, what's that?"

The dog made a whuffing noise. "Well...it's about space. You know how space is big? Really, *really* big?"

"Ya-a-ah."

"Listen, you *asked* to be distracted...and there's something that's always bothered me. About the universe."

"The universe!" Jake looked up. "What about the universe?"

The dog sighed. "It's such a mind-boggling concept, you know? The *universe*. It's so *huge*. We sit here and look out at it, and I can't even wrap my mind around it."

"Maybe dogs weren't meant to think of such lofty things."

Sam snorted in derision. "Like you understand it so well. I may just be a gene-spliced mutt with a chip in my head, but that doesn't mean I can't wonder about the awesome grandeur of space."

"I—"

"Don't even start. Like this crazy business about the universe expanding—"

"It *is* expanding."

"I know that. And it's expanding faster all the time. What's that all *about*, anyway? Even though gravity's sucking on the universe, trying to make it crunch back down?"

Jake glanced up again, frowning. "Well, yeah. That's because there's a force—"

"I know, I know. I read about it. Dark something. Dark emissary? Dark—"

"Energy. Dark energy," Jake said.

"No, that's not it. Wouldn't make any sense. Dark enigma?"

"No. I mean, yes—it's an enigma. That's not what it's called, though."

"Dark *matter*," the dog guessed.

"Dark matter doesn't push the universe *apart*. In fact, dark matter helps hold the galaxies *together*."

"Grrrr. I thought that was strings."

Jake squinted in the dim light at the lengthening line of half-untangled wire in his hand. *I really don't know what I'm doing,* he thought. Finally he reacted to what the dog had said. "No, string theory's different."

"*Grrrrrr.* Maybe dark *superglue* holds the galaxies together, then."

Jake laughed. "Okay, I'll buy that."

"So what is it that's pushing everything apart?"

"I told you. Dark energy."

"*Wullll…*what kind of name is *that*? Isn't energy supposed to be light? Like glowing stuff? And fire?"

"Yeah, usually. But—"

"Bombs. They make a lot of light. And noise. *Ka-boom!*" The dog sneezed. "So how can this other energy be dark?"

Jake finally had the wire untangled. He began stretching it from the sled to the battery bay. "I guess that's the point. They called it *dark* because nobody can see it. They can't even measure it directly. It's too subtle, I guess." Should he connect this wire straight to the battery?

Sam was shaking his head, his ears flapping inside his helmet. "If I say black is white, is that subtle?"

"Um—"

"Subtle as a screen door on a submarine."

"Whoa, boy. Did you just learn that?" The regulator. He should attach the wire to the regulator.

"Never mind. You're trying to get energy out of that wire. If we see a spark, we'll know it's real. But how do we know this 'dark energy' is real, for Pete's sake? I'll bet even Pete doesn't believe it."

"Pete wouldn't believe it if I told him the sun rose in the east."

"It doesn't, on the station. Okay, bad example. But if you're going to give something a crazy name like dark energy, don't you at least have to know it's there? Know *something* about it?"

"We do know something about it. Can you shove those pliers towards me? We know something's pushing the universe to expand."

"But how?" The dog nudged the pliers. "How do we *know*?"

"Because of supernovas, I think."

"Supernovas are pushing the universe apart? I love supernovas! They're so *bright!*" The dog's face widened in a toothy grin inside his helmet.

"Supernovas aren't *causing* it. Supernovas are how we *know*." He paused; Sam looked crestfallen. "They're like measuring sticks."

"Okay. Next fable, please."

"Really—astronomers use this special kind of supernova as what they call *standard candles*. By observing them carefully, they can tell how bright they are."

"Well, rruff. What's so hard about that?"

"Nothing, if the supernova were right next door. Of course, then we'd be toast. But they're not, they're off in distant galaxies. Thing is, there's this special kind of supernova that astronomers know are all pretty much the same brightness *really*—not just how bright they look in our telescopes—and *that* lets them figure out how far away the galaxy is."

"*Woofee!* They know how far away the galaxy is. I'm so excited I can hardly breathe. Can you see me fogging up my faceplate?" Sam was breathing fast, and actually was fogging his faceplate a little.

"It's not that easy to measure, you know. They can't just, like, shine a laser-finder on it."

"Speaking of lasers, how's that thing coming? I've been watching our rotation, and I think the base will be over the horizon soon."

Jake flexed his gloved fists, which were starting to cramp up. He wasn't just wishing he hadn't taken the detour; he was wishing he'd paid more attention in his electrical classes. He had the laser awkwardly hanging out of the survey scanner. It needed juice from the boat's batteries, and right now it wasn't strong enough. "I'm doing my best here. I'm just hoping we can pull enough extra power from that sled to make this laser work."

The border collie leaned in and licked at him—catching only the inside of his faceplate. "You can do it. Anyway, you're not fooling me."

Disconcerted, Jake said, "I'm not trying to fool you."

"About the galaxy distances, I mean. They could figure it out from the red shift, right? So these astronomers have learned zip, the way I see it."

Jake sighed, reaching to loosen a connector. "Dummy. Why'd we ever give you dogs voices, anyway? How can you say they've learned zip. They've learned a lot—"

"Don't call me a dummy. Or I'll call you worse."

"I doubt you even know anything worse."

"Oh yeah? You pink and pukle son of a Jack Russell—"

"All *right.* You're not a dummy. But the thing is, they get a *different* answer from the red shift. Different from the one they get from the brightness, I mean." Jake gestured, making a stirring motion. "They put the two numbers in a big equation pot—"

"What equations? You know I don't like equations."

"Equations for how fast space expands—from the Big Bang and stuff. They stir these numbers all around, and what they come up with is—" He paused, and squinted at the terminal on the battery regulator. Did he have the right one?

"I'm waiting. Earth to Jake. Please continue."

"Huh?" The wire slipped out of his hand, and he swore. "Well, it turns out the galaxies are farther apart than they *should* be, based on how fast space was expanding a zillion years ago, according to the red-shift." He caught the wire again, and started twisting it around the terminal.

"So?" the dog prompted.

"Soooo...after looking at all this, which at first made no sense, they concluded that the universe isn't just expanding, it's expanding faster now than it was before! That's why the galaxies are farther away than they should be." He tightened the terminal nut and looked at the spacesuited dog. "So how could that be? How could the universe be speeding up, when gravity is trying to slow it down?"

"Arrr, that's what I'm trying to ask you—how could it be?" asked the dog.

Jake shook his head. "It's been half a century now, and they still don't know for sure. They call it dark energy, but they don't understand it."

"Who is this *they* person, anyway?" Sam asked, with a little yip in his voice. "It could be aliens behind it all, making us think this stuff is true. Are aliens the *they*?"

"I don't think so. Not unless aliens have taken over all the astronomy departments on Earth and the Moon and Mars."

"Could happen."

"I suppose it could, yes. But I don't think it has. Are you keeping track of our rotation for me?"

The dog snapped to attention and peered at the constellations. He hopped up on top of the cockpit. The inertia of his oxygen pack nearly carried him right on over to the other side. "*Yes*. My friend, if you have laser light, I think we may have a sightline to base." The dog's tail wagged slowly in its encasement.

"All right. I need a little more time. Tell me when it's coming near to overhead." Jake worked in earnest now, testing the connections with gentle tugs. He took a deep breath and turned on the zeep generator on the mining sled. A meter on the battery indicated a slight charge coming in. Good. Jake turned his attention to the laser dangling out of the scanner housing. It was going to be really hard to aim...

"Shine your light now," Sam said.

Jake gripped the unit and aimed the laser up. The base should be one of those points of light just south of Altair. He squeezed the switch. A faint sparkle of green laser light shone through floating dust. When the dust cleared from the path, he couldn't see the beam at all. Determinedly, he swept it around the patch of sky the best he could.

"I don't know if this is—" he began. The power light on the unit went out. He swore.

"Aww," Sam said. "Grrr. Can you fix it?"

Jake pursed his lips and sighed. "Not enough juice. I guess this quantum-energy thing isn't really made to be an electrical generator. It makes enough for its own controls, but mostly it just levitates." He looked up into the black sky, with its sprinkling of stars. "I wonder if anyone saw the laser." He shook his head and picked up the flares. "We'd better light a couple of these." Taking two flares, he hiked far enough to place them on a mound for maximum visibility. He lit the flares and then, unimpressed by their red sparkle, trudged back to the boat.

"We'd better keep thinking," he said, mulling the approaching NEA-238.

While they were pondering, Jake swapped fresh oxygen and power packs into their suits. He thought briefly of trying to tap power from one of the suit packs. But he was too afraid of draining or blowing the packs. It wouldn't do any good for them to be seen if they couldn't last long enough for rescue. They had a quiet meal, of the pasty stuff you ate right inside your helmet. It tasted incredibly good to him right now.

"I've been thinking," Sam said, hopping down from the boat in a graceful arc. He swung his space-helmeted snout toward Jake. "Finish telling me about dark energy, please."

"Look, I don't really think right now is—"

"Please. It won't hurt."

Jake rolled his eyes. "What do you want to know?"

"Tell me what dark energy *is*," said the dog.

"Nobody knows—except that it's an energy field that's pushing against gravity."

"Okay, so it's a sort of antigravity, right?"

"I guess."

"And this energy is coming from…?"

"Well, it seems to come from space itself."

"Like that zero-point stuff you were talking about? Like the levitator uses?"

"I guess. Maybe."

"Uh-huh." The border collie cocked his head and grinned. "Rrrrfffff! You know something? I think we'll get to see the sun rise in the west tomorrow, after all."

"What's that supposed to mean?"

The dog padded over to the sled and put a paw on it. "Zeep—zero —energy. The levitator pushes things apart—*just like dark energy*. Right?"

"R-r-right. I guess."

"Are you thinking what I'm thinking?"

Jake stared at the dog open-mouthed for a moment. "Well, we've been through that. It can't levitate against space. It needs something to *repel*. And as soon as it gets a few inches off the ground, its power falls way off." He shook his head at the dog. "It just doesn't work at a distance."

"Rrrr. It pushes real hard up close, though, doesn't it?" The dog was gazing at him intently.

"Yeah, I guess so."

"Can we try something?" the border collie asked.

Jake shrugged. "All right."

"Raise that sled up as far as it will go, then throw some sand or something up under it. Right up against the levitator plates."

"Um—okay." Frowning, Jake adjusted the sled controls until it was floating six or eight inches off the surface of the asteroid.

"Good. Let's test Newton's laws. Got a shovel?"

He looked around and found a small, flat spade. "All right. Let me get some dirt here." He scooped up some loose dust, then maneuvered close to the sled. "Here goes." Feeling very awkward, he flung the dirt under the sled, trying to angle it up.

The dirt never touched the levitator plates. Instead, it ricocheted down with a force that made Jake hop back in alarm, and sent a cloud of dust out the sides. The sled bounced up a few feet from the reaction force, then sank slowly back down, bobbing as though on a sudden wave.

"Holy freakin'—" Jake began.

"That's it! Rruffff! That's what we have to do! It's just like a rocket!"

"That's amazing! But—"

"There's plenty of dust and loose stuff here."

"True. But we can't just stand beside it shoveling sand under, can we?" Jake whispered.

"Maybe we can. Now bear with me on this…"

Loading the sled with loose dirt was a time-consuming and extremely messy business. But the sled was built for carrying dirt samples, and it came equipped with side panels to hold the loose stuff, and even a transparent tarp to go over it to keep samples from floating away in the microgravity. It had a pulverizing auger aimed down through the square hole in the center of the sled, but the boat's dying fuel cells didn't have enough power to drive it.

In the end, Jake shoveled. Fortunately, there was plenty of loose stuff on the surface. The dirt had almost no weight, but it did have mass and inertia, and when he got it moving upward, it tended to keep moving upward. He lost quite a few shovelfuls before he got the hang of lifting and then redirecting it down into the sled. After a while, he clanged onto rock and metal. (*Metal!* He was right about this asteroid!) He moved the sled to a fresh patch of loose dirt. Gradually, the sled began to fill up with asteroid dust.

"I couldn't dig better myself," Sam said with a woof.

"You'll get your chance," Jake muttered, panting from the exertion. He eyed the slowly growing pile inside the sled. They had a long way to go.

∞

By the time the sled was piled high with asteroid dirt, Jake needed a rest and some food. The sled looked like a loaded cart without wheels, and with a funny-looking post at one end, holding the controls.

"Spare supplies next," Jake said, sucking food paste and water from his helmet dispensers.

"And a name," said Sam. "It needs a name."

"You think about that, while I do this." Jake got busy bringing spacesuit recharge-packs from the boat. He used vacuum-grade duct tape to hold everything to the control post, including the remaining flares. Then he levitated the sled again and used a *lot* of duct tape to secure a couple of clipboards and his shovel at an angle to the unused auger, where it extended downward through the square hole. Jake stood with his hands on his hips, studying his handiwork. The shovel and clipboards were pretty crude; but they only had to withstand comparatively minor forces, deflecting the dirt sideways under the levitator.

"All we really need to do, right, is get off this rock and get headed in the right direction toward base. When we get closer to home, they'll be able to pick up our suit-comms and flares. Right?"

"Right," answered the dog. "And you found iron and nickel here, so maybe they'll forgive you for being so boneheaded." He paused. "Get it? Boneheaded?"

"Yah," Jake said wearily.

"Wouldn't it be funny," Sam said, "if, after all this, they came right here and rescued us?"

"I wouldn't mind a bit," Jake said, yawning. He needed some sleep. They only had about eight hours until asteroid NEA-238 would loom very fast. But they couldn't try anything until *this* asteroid had rotated to the proper launch position, with the base-station above the horizon. So in their urgency to get off this rock, they had four hours to kill.

"I don't know about you," Jake said, "but I'm bone tired. Let's get some sleep, okay?"

"Bone-tired, rrrff," said Sam. "All right, let's rest." That said, he turned around a few times before settling down. A minute or two later, he was sound asleep.

It took Jake a little longer.

∞

In the "morning," they woke to the stars circling overhead, and the sun disappearing behind the asteroid horizon. They ate a brief breakfast of spacesuit-grade paste. "You look like you've been through a mud-bath," Sam said.

"We're not going to be a pretty ship," Jake said, wiping them both down as well as he could. He didn't care so much if the suits looked dirty, but they needed to see clearly through their faceplates. They were depending on the stars for navigation.

"Beauty is in the eye of the beholder, right?" Sam said.

"True. Have you thought of a name yet?"

"Yep."

∞

Sam grew nervous, when the time came to be strapped into place. The dog's tail twitched, as Jake tested the straps, then clipped the tarp down, and finally tightened the cords securing himself to the control post. "It'll work," Jake assured him. "It was your idea, remember?"

The dog was looking around through the clear tarp. "I don't want to go flying off into space."

"You'll be fine. Just do what comes naturally." He surveyed the sled and shook his head. Sam was strapped onto the top of the dirt pile, under the tarp containment. Behind the dog was the opening in the sled.

Jake looked up. The correct star groups were almost overhead. Their trajectory was going to be, to say the least, approximate. But they just needed to get close enough to the base-station for somebody to triangulate on their signals. "Ready?"

"Woof."

"Ready to launch space-sled *Dog Star*. Zero!" He switched full power to the levitators. "Dig, Sam—dig!"

The sled lurched up from the surface of the asteroid on the levitator's repulsion field. Sam dug ferociously, spraying pebbles and dust down through the opening—where it deflected off the clipboards and flew directly under the levitator. The instant it entered the levitator-field, the dust shot downward with a silent *whoosh*, creating a crude rocket blast that billowed out as it hit the surface. The thrust came in gentle bumps and lurches, as the dog shoveled with his feet. The sled wobbled alarmingly and threatened to careen to one side. Jake shifted his weight like a windsurfer. It was precarious, and he nearly overbalanced, but finally he managed to steady it.

"Keeping digging!"

Sam didn't answer, but kept digging. The sled continued wobbling upward—inch by inch, it seemed. "It's working!" They were *climbing*, really climbing, up over and away from the wrecked spaceboat. It couldn't *possibly* work—and wouldn't have, in stronger gravity. But it did work. As the border collie dug, panting audibly, spraying dirt into the repulsion field, they continued their slow, bobbing climb away from the asteroid. Beneath them was a rocket contrail of asteroid dirt.

"We're away!" Jake cried. "We're away, Sam!" Peering past his feet, he could see the spaceboat shrinking. The rounded shape of the asteroid was becoming visible. The sun blazed around the edge, then came into view, forcing him to look away. He craned his neck to focus on the star-patterns above them, and the few recognizable glints of light that were other asteroids in the Near-Earth cluster. "A little more to your left, Sam!"

"Woof!" the dog said, panting happily.

There was a lot of space to cross between here and the base station. But if Sam kept digging, and they didn't run out of dirt, and they managed to steer this thing, and their suit-comms worked, and nothing else went wrong—why, they could be in radio range of rescue by dinner time. Jake felt a rush of confidence. "Good dog!" he crowed.

"*Hree-haw!*" Sam barked, digging as he'd never dug before. And why not? The fate of the *Dog Star* was riding on him.

Emancipation

Pati Nagle

The Custodian of Oporto's Island stood in the darkness of his house, listening to the growing murmur of voices in the Grove of Malamalama outside. It was not a feast day, when a large attendance might be expected at Nightfall, but the woods were full of people.

He knew they had not come just to watch him perform the evening ritual. How he wished his father still lived; his father had loved the ceremonial aspect of the office of Custodian, while he himself dreaded it.

He donned his green robe and the tall feathered headdress that weighed on him so. A tight knot of fear was growing in his stomach, for he alone was ultimately responsible for the sacred rite of Maintenance, and that responsibility was about to be challenged. He went to the door of his house, and as he stepped through the curtain that covered it, the drumming began.

Malamalama, the island's axis, glowed bright with captured sunlight, its near end terminating in a shielded pole in the center of the ceremonial clearing outside the Custodian's home. Dancers—men and women in the traditional garb of the hula kahiko, their hair and arms decked in the leaves and flowers of the island—waited around the pole, ready for Nightfall to begin.

Among the ti trees at the Grove's edge and back into the woods beyond were the island's people, dozens upon dozens of them, more than he had seen at any ritual in months. The Custodian glimpsed his counterpart, the Governor, among the growing throng, and his belly tightened at the sight of her.

How often had he silently wished for her presence at Nightfall—his favorite hour—the beginning of the time when lovers could tryst in shadowed groves and not be observed by curious eyes from across the island's sphere. How often had he dreamed of dancing for her alone, then taking her hand and leading her among the waterbelt's gardens with the gentle night to cloak them.

It was not to be. She did not come as Hoku, the sweet, laughing playmate of his childhood, but as Governor of the island, in the people's name, to put an end to Night.

The Custodian took his place at the foot of the dais that held the Focus, and the rolling drums burst into rhythm. He chanted an ancient prayer to Pele, his hands echoing the words while the dancers swayed in the clearing surrounded by tall palms and bushes heavy with fragrant blossoms.

When Pele had been duly honored, the ipu players began a faster rhythm and the Nightfall dance began. It was centuries old, one of many dances that kept alive the sacred heritage of Maintenance on Oporto's Island, or Moku Wina as the island was called in the chants.

Through graceful gestures the dancers told the story of Moku Wina's creation, how Oporto enticed Pele to come away from Earth and hollow out an asteroid, filling it with all the best things from Earth for the pleasure of his Guests. Dancing hands told how the great mirrors outside caught light from the distant sun and fed it into the island through Malamalama, source of all blessings, and how Oporto had decreed the order of days and nights. As his hands led the story, the Custodian's eyes watched the Governor standing at the clearing's edge, waiting.

The chant ended and a hiss of gourd rattles began; the dancers knelt while the Custodian came forward to perform the ritual of Calibration. He kept his eyes on Hoku as he danced up to the pole and turned the key that sent beams of light shimmering toward the four sacred shrines around the clearing.

His green robe flowing around him in graceful folds, he danced to each one in turn—Hi'iaka, Poliahu, Laka—passing his hands through the light and verifying its centering in the target on each shrine. As he came to Pele's shrine he looked up, thinking a silent, hopeless prayer to the goddess whose rituals he had faithfully performed, and in whom he had never believed.

She did not answer him. Shadows flickered over her image as his hands danced through the light, then he turned away, returning to shut off the Calibration light before approaching the Focus.

The music intensified as he climbed the steps. Before him was the Focus that brought light into the island and sent it glowing along Malamalama; a large, ornate lever, completely unnecessary in a mechanical sense, but vital as a symbol of Maintenance. As the Custodian stepped toward it the drums suddenly stopped, and he heard what he had been fearing since the ritual began.

"Wait, Manuel."

He turned to face Hoku, the Governor, his life-long friend, who had come up behind him. She did not smile, but stepped between him and the Focus, her red robe brushing the grass-covered dais.

"The Council has made a decision," she said, turning to face the people crowding the Grove. Her formal tones carried easily through the clearing and beyond. "Oporto's Island has been dominated for centuries by the rituals of Nightfall and Dayrise. We treasure our heritage, but we are not savages, or children. We do not need lies to control us, or darkness to inspire us with fear. We are an enlightened people.

"Nightfall is a wasteful practice. Every time the Focus is shifted away from Malamalama, precious light is spilled into empty space. We can use that light to better our lives."

The Governor turned to the Custodian, and he saw that her eyes were hard. "The Council has voted to eliminate the process of Nightfall, effective immediately."

The crowd roared approval, and the Custodian felt a sinking in his chest. "That would violate Maintenance procedures," he said over the din. "The Manuals clearly state—"

"The Council consider the Manuals open to interpretation," said the Governor. "We have the right to reevaluate procedures when the good of the people is in question."

"The Manuals were given to us by Oporto," said the Custodian. "To deviate from their instructions will place the island and its people in peril!"

"The Council has debated this," said Hoku, her face a careful mask. "We have concluded that to take the Manuals literally can place us in danger of misunderstanding their metaphorical intent."

"Maintenance must be performed," said Manuel, hoping he sounded firm despite his growing desperation.

"Manny," said Hoku, her voice dropping to a whisper, "don't make it hard on yourself. You haven't got a choice." For a moment her eyes poured warm sympathy into his, then she raised her arms, the folds of her crimson caftan sliding down to her golden shoulders as she turned to the people now crowding into the clearing and called out, "Henceforth, we live in light, not in darkness!"

A cheer went up among the people, and the Custodian's courage crumbled. He gazed out over the crowd in worry. Here and there a mournful face stared back at him, mostly dancers or his acolytes, the Maintenance technicians. He was their spiritual leader, and they looked to him for guidance in this crisis, but his heart was empty. He had said all he could think to say.

The Council ruled the island, and he must bow to their authority. He turned his eyes away from his followers and watched in numb despair as Hoku placed a hand on the great lever of the Focus. She borrowed two gestures from the dance; "light" and "forever." The cheers grew louder.

Hoku beckoned to a Watcher—one of the guards serving the Council—and posted her on the dais to prevent any attempt to shift the focus. Then the Governor stepped down from the dais and passed into the crowd, touching the hands they reached out to her, moving away under the continuing daylight.

The people followed, all but a few faithful who watched the Custodian expectantly as he slowly descended the steps. He stopped in the middle of the clearing and gazed at them, sensing and sharing their fear.

"What will happen, Manuel?" a young dancer asked him, her worried face framed in the leaves and fresh flowers of her headdress. "Will Pele punish us?" Her eyes pleaded for reassurance.

Others gathered around with soft and frightened voices. The Custodian raised his hands to ward off their questions.

"I will appeal to the Council," he said.

It was inadequate, he knew, but it was all he could offer. His followers exchanged doubting glances. He spread his arms in the wavelike gesture of blessing, which seemed to comfort them a little.

"Go home," he told them. "Close the curtains on your windows and doors. Bring night into your homes, and Pele will know you are faithful."

"Thank you, Manuel," they answered, the words rippling in a whispering wave through the small group as they drifted out of the clearing toward their homes.

He watched them go, their hands flashing in the spaces between leaves, speaking in silent, worried gestures. When they had passed out of sight Manuel went into his house and changed his ceremonial garb for light cotton, then went out—barefoot so he could feel the island with each step—through the Grove and down the path that led to the waterbelt.

It was his custom to walk along the belt every evening after Nightfall, enjoying shadows and the soft sounds of water as it traveled endlessly around the island's center; here a trickling stream, there a clever waterfall, lakes like jewels, some with stars flashing underfoot through view—bays lapped by their blue-black depths. The stars were barely visible now, obscured by the continuing daylight.

Manuel stopped and glanced up at a view—bay overhead just as the sharp glint of a mirror's edge passed it. Malamalama glowed steadily bright with the light which should have been diverted for night, some to replenish the great storage cells, the rest to pour off into space.

Music began somewhere nearby, and wild shouting; the people celebrating their freedom from darkness. Suddenly Manuel needed to sit down.

He went to the nearest bench and lowered himself onto it with the weariness of a man many times his twenty-four years. A jasmine bush caressed him with its heavy scent.

How had it come to this? He was Manuel, descended from a long line of Manuels, the Custodians of the island since the time of the Separation, when Pele had returned her attention to Earth where Hi'iaka was making war on her.

It was then that Oporto's children had lost contact with the children of Earth. It was then that Oporto had created the Council, and set into law the Days and Nights of Moku Wina. It was then that the first Manuel had accepted the lifetime post of Custodian, and pledged to train his successor so that the island would always be cared for. And so it had been, until now.

Manuel searched his heart for the source of his failure. He had studied and preserved the Manuals in whose honor he was named, faithfully performed all of the Maintenance rituals—of which Nightfall and Dayrise were the most important—listened to his people and striven to answer their needs. He had tried to hide his own doubts, yet despite his best efforts, the people had begun to question the old ways.

Some said the gods were not real, that Pele would never return to the island to reclaim her lost children. A growing number said the only true power was the people's own, and that no ancient system should dictate to them. Such ideas weren't new—Oporto himself had faced opposition, as had Custodians through the centuries—but never before had a Custodian failed to perform Nightfall. Manuel knew the vital importance of the ritual, of Maintenance, for the island's continued well-being, but he did not know how to impress it on those who saw Maintenance merely as superstition.

"Manny?" came a soft voice behind him, and his muscles tensed.

He didn't answer, but listened to the sound of sandals on the path, the swish of crimson cloth. A hand touched his shoulder and he flinched, then looked up at Hoku, unable to keep a stab of resentment from his eyes.

"I thought I'd find you here," she said. "May I join you?"

"Shouldn't you be at the celebration?" he said bitterly, hating himself as the words left him, for of all the people on the island, Hoku was the one he least wished to hurt.

She gave him the fleeting smile that always made his pulse a little faster; Hoku, heart's friend and gentle leader, daughter of Governors, descendant of Guests as shown by the reddish sheen of her hair. Though most everyone on the island was of mixed blood, the Governor's line still bore the distinctive features of Oporto's heritage.

The Council were children of Guests also, while Manuel's night-black hair proclaimed his descent from Staff. The two groups—Guests and Staff—had shared the governance of the island since the time of Separation; their children ruled after them and kept their names alive, each following his or her parent's path. Dancers and technicians fulfilled their birthrights, Hoku performed her function, and Manuel, until today, had performed his.

Hoku sat beside him on the bench, her hand still touching him, gently making circles on his shoulder. A tiny shudder went through him, despair mingled with release of the tension knotting his back.

"It isn't you, Manny," she said, bringing both hands to bear on his shoulders. "I swear it isn't. You've done everything you should. We have simply outgrown the need for night. Like you always said, these rituals are just symbolic—"

"Night is not just a symbol!" said Manuel, turning to face her. "Night is the time of rest, of replenishment—"

"On Earth, yes. In primitive societies, yes," said Hoku, "but we're beyond that. For centuries people have worked through the night—on Luna, on the stations, even on Earth—and still lived happy lives. There's no need for us to huddle in darkness half the day when the sun's light is available to us all the time."

"If there hadn't been a need for Night, Oporto wouldn't have built the Focus," said Manuel. "He wouldn't have created Nightfall."

"He made Nightfall for the Guests from Earth, so they would feel at home," said Hoku. "And as for the Focus, we control the flow of light, it doesn't control us!"

Her eyes were beautiful, full of righteousness and something else —something dangerously like pity—that stung him and made him turn away. "I don't want to argue with you," he said.

"No," she agreed softly.

They sat in silence for a moment, Manuel acutely aware of the warmth of her hands on his back. He had loved her from childhood, wanted her from youth, but the Custodian and the Governor were counterparts, working together from a distance, living at opposite ends of the island, close and at the same time standing apart.

Never since the island's creation had a Custodian and a Governor joined. It was thought that such an alliance would threaten the balance of power.

Manuel glanced at Hoku. Perhaps she was right. Oporto's people were enlightened; perhaps endless day would enrich their lives, and it was only his selfish love of starlight that made him long for the night. If so, then the skeptics who denounced Maintenance as superstitious nonsense were justified, and the Custodian's function was meaningless.

Except it wasn't meaningless. It was necessary. Beneath the rituals were the foundations of the island's vitality.

Rising abruptly, Manuel paced a few steps away. "I wish to address the Council," he said.

"They won't change their minds," said Hoku.

"It is not for the Council to interpret the Manuals," said the Custodian formally. "Their meaning requires study—years of study— for which I have been trained and the Council have not. It is my duty to advise them." He turned to face the Governor and saw a sadness in her eyes; his words had built a wall between them.

Hoku sighed and stood. "Very well. I will inform the Council of your wish. You may address the next meeting."

He nodded silent agreement, gazing at her with an inner ache that was all too familiar. She raised a hand to her heart in the gesture of family-love, gave him a sad little smile and turned away, her sandals whispering on the path, red robe flashing through the leaves as she left him in the sharp light of day.

∞

Lehua came for Dayrise, and Manuel was both glad and sorry. He had not spoken to her since before the last Night. Hoping to resolve the conflict, hoping he could make the Council see his viewpoint, he had gone to their meetings and reminded them of Oporto's word, which threatened dire consequences if the people failed to perform proper maintenance.

His words had disappeared like raindrops into a lake; the Council would not be convinced. His failure to reach them weighed on his spirits, and though it pleased him to see Lehua among the sparse group gathered in the Grove of Malamalama for Dayrise, he did not look forward to speaking with her.

There were only a handful of dancers this morning, and the flowers they wore were a bit brown at the edges. One musician beat out the Dayrise dance on the ipu, and Manuel chanted words of joy without much enthusiasm. It was hard praising the return of light when Malamalama was already shining brightly.

He finished the song, moved to the Focus where the Council's Watcher stood silent guard and pantomimed shifting the great lever upward, then turned to watch the worshippers drift away. Lehua waited for him by his house, the whiteness of her hair as it brushed her shoulders making her cotton Maintenance garb seem dim.

Lehua—Chief Technician of Moku Wina, mother of Lehua and Manuel—was a grand old dame, stout as a nut and just as tough. No one cared to cross her. Manuel wished he had inherited some of her tenacity; no doubt he would have dealt better with the Council if he had.

He remembered her strong hands around his waist, lifting him up to a Maintenance shaft for the first glimpse of the systems that were his heritage. The hands were gnarled now but still strong, and she held them out to him with a smile.

"You look tired, Manny," she said.

"It's hard to sleep. Come inside, share my breakfast."

Manuel held the curtain aside for his mother and followed her into his house. It was dark; he had formed the habit of keeping the windows covered. He pushed aside a curtain to let some light in, and brought cushions and fruit to Lehua.

"We haven't seen you in Operations lately," she said as she settled herself.

"I've been busy," said Manuel, cutting slices from a ripe mango. He handed her a piece and ate one himself, let its musky sweetness fade on his tongue. "You would send for me if there was any problem."

Lehua bit into a date and chewed slowly. "Have you been down at the Hotel?"

"Not since the last Council meeting."

"What has kept you so busy, then?"

Manuel laid down the knife and wiped the stickiness from his hands with a napkin. "I've been—searching."

"For?"

"A way to make the Council hear me. A way to...."

"To believe in what you are doing?"

Lehua's voice was gentle, but the words cut. Manuel had never been able to hide his true feelings from her, but she had not said a word about it ever before.

Always loving, always accepting, Lehua. Now even she saw the danger that lay in his failure. He could not look into her eyes.

"What would my father have done?" he muttered.

"Your father never faced this kind of challenge."

"You mean the Council."

"I mean the doubt."

He straightened and looked at her, and the pity in her eyes was worse than all the rest. Manuel hid his face in his hands, but the smell of mango clung to them, inescapable as the daylight. He got up and went to the window.

Outside children were playing tag in the ceremonial clearing, something that would never have happened when he was young. The place had lost its holiness, or the people had lost their sense of it. Or perhaps it had never been holy.

"Why did Manuel III make Maintenance into ritual?" he said angrily.

"You know why," said Lehua. "The people were losing interest, and he feared the procedures would be forgotten. He set them to music and dance in order to preserve them."

"He made them a religion, and now we may lose them altogether!"

"Merely because you lack faith? No, Manny. The island is more important than your personal crises."

Like a slap in the face, the words sobered him. He turned to his mother, who sat quietly watching him.

"It seems hopeless, I know," she said. "But you will find a solution."

"You believe that?"

"I know it. These are good dates." She leaned forward, helping herself to another. "Do you remember Hoku's woman-day?"

Caught off guard, Manuel blinked. "Yes"

"She gave you her ti lei. All the boys on the island were courting her, and she gave it to you. I see you still have it," she said, gesturing to where the dried loop of twisted ti leaves hung from the wall above his bed.

"I don't think—"

"She loves you, Manny. Why don't you marry her?"

"The Governor and the Custodian can't marry," said Manuel, more sharply than he'd meant to.

"Can't? I never heard that. You young people place too much importance on your functions."

"You were just telling me my function is more important than my beliefs!"

"Well, that's true," she said placidly, reaching for another date.

Frustrated, Manuel began to pace, the woven mats beneath his feet creaking softly. "How can I go on lying to the people I'm supposed to serve?" he demanded. "It's hypocrisy!"

"Maintenance is not a lie, Manuel. You know that."

"But it's all tangled up in mythology! How can I expect the people to believe what I don't believe myself?"

"They don't need to believe. They need to have faith." Lehua got up and walked to the window, where she stood watching the children outside with a soft smile. "They need to know in their hearts that they aren't alone, that there's a whole universe beyond the island," she said.

"What if we are alone?" said Manuel.

"Why do you still do the Communications ritual, Manuel?" said Lehua. "We haven't had a signal from Earth in four hundred years."

"That doesn't mean we'll never get one."

Lehua's smile widened. "Exactly. You know we might get a signal someday. You know we are not alone. You don't believe it, you *know* it."

She turned from the window and reached out a hand to comfort him, a gesture that sent him back to boyhood. Manuel came to her and sighed as her strong arms enfolded him.

"That's what faith is, Manny," she said into his ear. "It's knowing. Believing is worrying that something might not be true; faith is knowing it's true even if you can't see it. You've got faith, my son. You just have to decide in what."

Manuel gave an exasperated laugh. "Any suggestions?"

"Yourself?"

Lehua leaned back to smile at him, then patted his shoulder and started toward the door. "I'd better get over to Operations. Akamu and Keoni keep arguing about when to reschedule rainfall."

"Lehua—"

She stopped, and Manuel caught her hands in his, squeezing tight. "Thank you," he said. "I hope your faith in me isn't misplaced."

"Of course it isn't," she said, kissing his cheek. "You're Manuel."

"It's just a name, Mother."

"Is it?" Lehua's hand pulled back the curtain over the door. Light spilled in, framing her so he couldn't see her face, setting her hair aglow. "You know, they say a Manuel once saved the Earth," she said.

He could hear the smile in her voice, and smiled back as he watched her walk down the path to the clearing. She patted a child's head, gestured her respect to the four shrines, and disappeared into the trees.

Manuel turned back to his empty house. The uneaten fruit lay on its plate among the cushions. He walked past it to his bed and took down the ti lei from the wall, imagining its making years before, Hoku's pretty hands folding and twisting the long ti leaves into a supple, glistening rope on the morning of her womanhood.

He remembered the glow in her face as she had proudly danced alone that day, the ti lei gleaming between her small breasts, and the voices of dozens of boys begging for the gift. And he remembered his feeling of silent triumph as she had tossed it into his hands.

The lei was dry and brittle now, lifeless, faded with age. He wondered if the same thing had happened to their love.

It was not a trivial question. They both needed successors. Adoption was a last resort for those who truly could not have their own children; it was everyone's duty to pass on genetic heritage as well as function. Perhaps Lehua was right, and it didn't matter that a Governor and a Custodian had never married.

He raised the lei to slip it over his head, but it had dried too narrow, hanging on its peg, and he didn't want to break it. Such a fragile thing now, though it had once been strong enough to bind a man's hands. He hated what had happened to it, just as he hated the change the Council had imposed. Sometimes he even felt he hated Malamalama, source of all blessings.

Bad thoughts. Manuel shook his head to get rid of them, but he knew they would not go away.

He was angry, he realized, not just at the Council but at Hoku personally, for standing against him. She had chosen to oppose him, and none of his arguments or entreaties seemed to move her.

He reached up to hang the lei back on its peg. Its faded green was only a little darker than the grasses of the wall. In time, it would blend in completely. Manuel wondered if he would someday forget it was there.

∞

"You must check the systems again," said Councilor Haveland, fanning himself vigorously in the heat of the Council Chamber. "There is clearly a malfunction."

"There is no malfunction," said Manuel. "All environmental systems are operating at peak capacity—"

"Nonsense!" said Councilor Gary, wiping moisture from his brow with a fine kerchief edged in Councilor's yellow. "If the systems were functioning properly the island wouldn't be three degrees hotter than normal!"

Manuel's fist tightened around a handful of his robe and forced himself to reply calmly. "It is increased demand that is causing problems. Continual day is placing strain on our cooling systems—"

"Then increase their power," said Councilor Petra. "We have the light, let's use it!"

"It's not quite that simple," Manuel began.

"Manuel, we understand your wish to make a point," said Councilor Haveland testily, "but you've made it. The island needs its Custodian to keep the systems in order. You and your descendants will continue to have a place of honor. Now fulfill your function—get the island back to normal!"

"The island can't be normal without Night!" said Manuel, his hands emphasizing his statement with the gesture meaning "night."

"Do the Manuals say night is necessary?" asked Gary.

Manuel clenched his teeth. He'd been expecting that question; he'd spent hours searching the Manuals for just such a reference, hoping to use it in support of his arguments, but he'd found none. The Manuals were written by the Oporto and the Investors, children of Earth, who took night for granted.

"Not in so many words," he said, "but references to nighttime functions make it clear—"

"I know of no functions that cannot be as easily performed in day," said Gary, stifling a yawn.

"The advantages of daylight outweigh the difficulties," said Petra. "We are increasing our quality of life. With continual work shifts we have more space for our workers, we can produce more food and allow people to have more children—"

"All of which will increase the demand on our physical systems," said Manuel, "and they're already overburdened!"

"Manuel," said Hoku, who had been silently observing the discussion, "is it possible to increase power to the physical systems?"

Manuel turned to her, frustrated by her neutral mask. "Yes, but—"

"There!" said Gary in triumph. "He admits it! I move the Council require the Custodian to increase power!"

"We can't maintain an increase indefinitely!" said Manuel, but his protest was lost in a chorus of agreement from the Councilors.

"So ruled," said Hoku, her voice putting an end to the clamor. "Manuel, you have the Council's instructions." Her eyes were hard, and Manuel swallowed angrily, then turned and left the chamber without another word.

Outside the Hotel the air was oppressive; hot and damp, as if the island had been doused in the steam from a battle between Pele and her sister Hi'iaka. A slight stink of rotting vegetation made Manuel frown.

He stripped off his robe, under which he wore Maintenance garb—light, close-fitting cotton for the sacred work of Holding Up The World—but even this thin clothing seemed too much in the heat of the endless day. Manuel glanced at the nearby pole of Malamalama, terminating in the Civic Plaza, exactly opposite to the Grove of Malamalama.

Across the plaza was the Governor's house, flanked by ti trees and stately palms. Oporto himself had once lived there. Now it was Hoku's.

Feeling a sudden tightness in his throat, Manuel turned away and started back toward Operations, on his side of the island. He jogged most of the way back, passing fields of flourishing new crops and others that seemed pale and withered.

Workers looked up at him, some with weary eyes; he was not the only one having trouble sleeping in the constant light. Feeling helpless against their misery, he jogged on past the fields and between flowering shrubs that had dropped their blooms, strewing the path underfoot with flashes of faded color.

Arriving at Operations with a sheen of dampness on his skin, Manuel slowed to a walk and wiped at his face with his robe. He would need a fresh one for Nightfall, and wondered how much time he had before the ceremony.

It annoyed him, having to check. Ordinarily he would have known by instinct how many hours of light were left, but he couldn't count them now, no matter how closely he shuttered his rooms against the incessant daylight.

He strode into Operations with the robe slung over one shoulder and headed for the control room, where he found a cluster of technicians gathered. "What's the status, Lehua?" he said, joining them.

Lehua glanced up from her console, grimacing as she wiped perspiration from her face with a brown hand. On the screens around her frantic images conveyed stress on the island's systems.

"We're at maximum on environmental control," said Lehua. "Power use is up thirty percent, ambient humidity up eighteen percent, water use up seven percent. And the temperature's still rising," she added unnecessarily.

Manuel leaned toward the screen, knowing what he would see. Though the Council blamed the island's woes on system failure he knew there were no malfunctions. He and his technicians had been searching the complex environmental systems for day—seven for nights, though he disliked putting his staff on the continual shifts that the Council promoted—trying to find a problem to correct, but there were none.

The Custodian rubbed his sweating chin, thinking of Oporto's warning to his children of the consequences of failing to perform Maintenance: crops withering, lakes drying, fighting among the people. He had not thought such plagues would actually occur, yet without doubt they were beginning, and only weeks after the Council had first denied his pleas to reinstate night.

"What shall we do, Manuel?" asked Kaleo, a young tech whose dark eyes were tense with worry.

Manuel glanced at Lehua. "I've been given orders by the Council," he said. "We must make a change."

He gathered the technicians into a circle and led the chants of purification that preceded all major Maintenance functions. Feeling Lehua's eyes on him, he hurried through the song, his hands weaving the air in the gestures of blessing.

Then he looked up at Lehua. "Increase power to environmental systems by ten percent," he said.

One of the techs took a sharp breath. Lehua moved toward her console, pausing to look back.

"We'll be drawing on reserves," she said.

Manuel nodded. "I'll inform the Governor," he said, glancing at the screen. "After Nightfall."

He stepped back, breaking the circle, and as he glanced at them the techs avoided his gaze. Their silence followed him away down the hall.

Few people paid any attention to the Nightfall and Dayrise rituals anymore; even his own technicians had lost faith. Often as not he performed the ceremonies alone, but he did so without fail. He was Manuel. If he stopped performing the rituals, he would cease to be Manuel.

As he strode down the corridor he heard the surge of new power into the environmental control system, sensed the change of air pressure as fans picked up speed, felt a breath of coolness as he passed beneath a vent. Welcome as it was to his body, the change only increased his anxiety, for now the physical plant was supplementing the fire of Malamalama with stored light from the great power cells. When their reserves ran out, the island would have no other source to meet its demands.

He went to his house and permitted himself the luxury of a shower. The water was lukewarm, slightly stale. Donning a fresh green robe and his ceremonial headdress, he went out to the Grove of Malamalama and found the clearing empty.

No dancers, no singers, no drummers. The only person in sight was the Council's Watcher, standing on the dais between him and the Focus. With a sigh Manuel walked to his place at the foot of the steps, and stood alone in the silence.

Closing his eyes, he listened to his own breathing and the distant sounds of activity muffled by the woods. He could almost imagine a miracle, a crowd of followers waiting breathlessly for him to lead the ceremony. He laughed at himself; easy with eyes closed.

Easy to mumble incantations and trust in omnipotent gods to take care of you, but he believed—no, he knew—that Moku Wina's people were their own caretakers, and he was responsible for seeing it was done.

Manuel opened his eyes and stared at the shielded pole that marked Malamalama's terminus. Above where the shielding stopped, at a level distant enough not to damage the eyes, the axis gleamed with brilliant daylight. Malamalama, source of all blessings, was after all just a machine.

Sometimes he thought of going through the Manuals and removing all reference to ritual and worship, but when he tried to picture himself performing the functions of Maintenance without the gestures of blessing and reverence, it felt wrong. He was his father's son. He had spent his life training to perform the rituals of Moku Wina's heritage. His feelings, even the Council's decision, didn't matter. Maintenance must be performed.

In a voice barely above a whisper he began the chant to Pele. He did not believe she was creator of Moku Wina, or protector of Oporto's people. He remembered arguing with his father over the dedication to Pele. His father had told him it didn't matter what he thought; Pele must be honored because that was part of the ritual, part of Maintenance.

He danced alone, chanting softly, hands flowing through the air and his bare feet gripping the soft earth of the island. He danced not for Pele, but for his father.

He followed the dedication with the Nightfall dance, then in silence he performed Calibration, his hands cutting knife-like through beams of light. One of the mirrors was slightly off-focus, and he sent a command signal to its driver to adjust. Every bit of light was needed now.

Finally he shut off the Calibration light, and ascended the dais to stand before the Focus. He stared at the lever, carved with symbols no one believed in any more.

"Manuel," said the Watcher, startling him. It was Puna, the woman who had first been posted on guard over the Focus.

"Yes?" he said.

To his surprise she stepped aside. "I think you were right," she said, her eyes bright with worried tears. "The Council shouldn't have stopped Nightfall. Please complete the ceremony."

Manuel caught his breath, and reached out his hand shivering with an instant's joy at the thought of shifting the lever and plunging the island into Night. Instead he grasped the Watcher's shoulder.

"Thank you, Puna," he said, "but the Council would see it as an act of war. There must be a better way to bring back the night."

"How?" asked Puna.

It was a question that had filled him with despair for many days. "Pray," he said helplessly. "Pray for guidance."

It was the best answer he had, and it was not enough. Feeling defeated, he turned away to descend the steps.

"May I pray with you, Manuel?" Puna asked.

Surprised, Manuel stopped halfway down the steps and looked back at the Watcher. Her eyes pleaded, and Manuel returned and took her hands, then began the chant he thought she was most likely to know; a chant to Pele, a simple song, one of the first learned by every child on the island. Puna sang with him, stumbling over some of the words, but when the chant was finished she smiled.

"Thank you, Manuel," she said, looking up at him shyly. "I would like to sing with you again."

Touched, Manuel nodded. "Tomorrow, we'll sing again."

"Thank you," she said as he stepped away. "Thank you, Manuel!"

Puna's voice followed him through the clearing and into his home. As the curtain fell closed behind him he suddenly realized he'd been doing everything wrong. He had been working alone—shutting himself away in solitary darkness, shielding his technicians from responsibility, trying to fight the Council single-handedly—when what he needed was to add the people's voices to his. It was not his faith that mattered, but theirs.

Even if Pele was just a symbol, she stood for Maintenance, and he knew beyond doubting that Maintenance was necessary. Night was necessary too, and there were others who wanted its return.

If he could win back the people's support, the Council would not be able to ignore him. How many days in the unending day he had wasted! Tossing his headdress onto the bed, he caught his long robe in one hand, went back outside, and began to run.

The first people he encountered were field workers, tending new crops. "Nightfall has passed," he told them. One or two sneered, but he ignored them. "I know your work shift kept you from attending the ceremony. I came to offer a prayer for those who wish to join me."

They stared silently at him, and Manuel could feel the heat rising to his face. "Maybe some of you miss the Night, as I do," he said. "Maybe you would like to have it back."

"You won't get it back," said a worker, turning away.

"Maybe not," said Manuel, "but I will pray anyway."

The workers looked at each other, then one put aside her shovel and came to him. Others followed, and Manuel led them in the same children's chant he had sung with Puna.

"We'll sing again at Nightfall tomorrow," he said. "Everyone is welcome."

Moving on, he made the same offer to everyone he found awake, Staff and Guests, at work or at play. Some ignored him but many did not, and each time he joined hands with a new circle and began to chant, he felt the strength of the people flowing through him.

He walked all through the hours of night, returning to the clearing for Dayrise. When he reached it he found a small crowd of people waiting for him, many of those he'd sung with in the last few hours. Among them were a dozen or more dancers, decked in wreaths of fern and flower woven by their own hands, and musicians enough to perform the Dayrise chants. Manuel led the ceremony, then sang the children's chant again with the people and sent them into the day with blessings while he continued his mission.

He lost track of time as he walked all the paths of the island, seeking to sing with as many of its two thousand people as he could persuade to join him. He surprised his technicians by leading them in a chant of celebration he had not sung since the beginning of endless daylight, and laughed inside at their astonishment. They must think he had gone mad, and perhaps he had, but at least he was doing something.

His legs and feet were aching with weariness by the time his wanderings brought him to the Council Chamber. It was empty; the Councilors were busy elsewhere, and he stood in the Chamber's center and chanted a song praising Night while the Watchers at the doorway stared. Then he went outside and crossed the plaza to the Governor's house.

"Hoku," he called, standing outside her window, swaying a little with weariness. "Hoku, come sing with me."

He received no answer, and with a laugh he sat beneath her window. He plucked a leaf from a ti tree nearby and tore it into strips, fingers clumsy as he twisted them together, one end held between his toes and the pungent juice making his hands sticky.

He began to sing, not a chant this time, but a song of love, a courting song. He had sung it softly to himself a thousand times, alone in the darkness of his room, with Hoku's face shining in his imagination. Now he sang it out loud, heedless of who might hear, his hands caressing the air now and then before returning to the rope-weaving.

Manuel had gone mad, the people would say. It might be true, but if so it had happened long ago.

As he sang of starlight on the island's waters he became aware he was not alone. He kept his eyes on the twist of leaves in his hands and tied its ends together as he finished the song, then turned to see Hoku herself, in Governor's red, with the Council behind her.

"Manuel," she said in a voice that matched the sadness of her frown, "what are you doing?"

Rising to his feet, Manuel held out the bracelet he had made. "This is for you," he said.

Hoku's hand came up to take the circle of dark, glossy green. As she looked up at him a flash of regret replaced the frown, and all his anger melted.

"Come sing with me, Hoku," he said softly, taking her hand. "We haven't sung together since we were children. Analani e—remember?"

"Manuel," she said, "you are not yourself. You need some rest—"

"We all need some rest," said Manuel, laughing. "That's what I've been telling you! Never mind, come and sing! All of you, come sing!"

He beckoned to the Council as he led Hoku by the hand down the path toward the far pole and the Grove of Malamalama. They followed, probably with the idea of preventing him from doing anything they disapproved. It didn't matter to Manuel. He squeezed Hoku's hand as she walked beside him on the path.

"I love you, Hoku. I don't think I've told you that in years," he said softly. "It's more true now than ever."

Hoku didn't answer, but neither did she pull her hand away. She walked on beside him, gazing at the path beneath their feet, the bracelet in her free hand.

They crossed the waterbelt on Manuel's favorite bridge, and long before they reached the Grove they began passing through a great crowd, hundreds of people, more than Manuel remembered seeing all together in many years. The people reached out their hands to him as he passed, and he touched their fingers with his own.

When he reached the ceremonial clearing he led Hoku up to the steps before the Focus, with the Councilors close behind. The voices of the people filled the clearing, some questioning, some cheering Manuel. He smiled, then held his hands up for silence.

"People of Moku Wina," he said aloud, smiling, "many of you have sung with me today, and my heart is filled with gladness. Sing again with me now."

He led the same song—the children's chant to Pelea song with no significance toward day or night. It was the voices chanting together, the hundreds of hands moving in unison, that mattered. He heard Hoku's voice join the others, and saw her lovely hands rise in gestures of happiness and love, the bracelet of ti leaves circling one slender wrist.

At the end of the chant the people cheered, and the ipus began to play the rhythms of the Nightfall dance. Voices from the woods joined Manuel's in the chanting; he saw the hands of the people echoing the dance.

Those who didn't know the song chanted "Po, Po,"—calling for Night, Night—and kept up the chant while he performed the dance of Calibration.

The voices rose higher as he approached the Focus. The Council clustered on the dais, and he faced them, smiling, with open arms.

"Councilors," he said, "you honor your people with your presence at the Nightfall ritual." He saw Councilor Haveland ready to speak, and continued. "I thank you for what you have taught us in the time since the last Night. You have shown us what we can accomplish by using all of Malamalama's blessings. That is a good thing, but now we are using more light than Malamalama can give us. Now we are using the reserve power from our storage cells. The island needs to sleep, just as we need to sleep."

A roar of agreement went up from the crowd, so strong it surprised Manuel. He glanced at the people, then at the Councilors, who looked uncomfortable. Manuel went on.

"You have given us the freedom to work through the hours of Night. Now I ask you to give us the freedom to rest. Can we not offer our people both choices?"

Hoku was frowning slightly. "What do you propose, Manuel?" she asked.

"Change is a good thing, as you have taught me," said Manuel. "On Earth the days change in length. I propose a new system that will allow us to have longer days some of the time and longer Nights some of the time, as on Earth. Then we can still achieve more without exhausting our light completely."

The Councilors exchanged glances. "We must discuss this," said Councilor Gary.

Manuel nodded. "I will bring a plan to you tomorrow," he said. "My staff and I will determine the most efficient use of the energy at our disposal."

"Agreed," said Hoku, glancing at the Councilors. "Meanwhile—"

"Meanwhile," said Manuel, lowering his voice so that only the Councilors would hear, "we're depleting our reserves to run the environmental control systems. Let us have a Night to allow them to recover. You can call it a holiday if you like."

He watched their faces anxiously. The Councilors did not look pleased. "Shall I ask the people what they wish?" he said softly.

Hoku glanced at him with sharp amusement. "I don't think that will be necessary," she said. "Councilors, the Custodian's words make sense. Any opposed to declaring a holiday?" When none spoke, she turned to the waiting people and raised her arms. "People of Moku Wina, your Custodian has made a wise suggestion. The Council will meet tomorrow to review a new plan for the use of Malamalama's blessings. In celebration of this, we declare a holiday from now until Dayrise. Let torches be lit to honor Pele, and let Night fill the island so that the torches can be seen by all!"

A cheer broke from the crowd, and accompanied by the roaring of drums, Manuel stepped up to the Focus, placed his hands on the ornate lever, and shifted it downward.

Darkness surrounded him, a black so deep he felt an instant's primal fear of blindness. Then the light of stars penetrated the view-bays, and the cheering rose higher as torches were kindled and began to dance through the woods, scattering away from the clearing. Manuel stood gazing at the stars for a moment, then turned away from the Focus.

His eyes were still adjusting, but he knew the shadowed figure standing still before him was Hoku. He smiled at her through the Night.

"Well said, Governor. You are very good at your function."

"And you are good at yours," said Hoku. "This will be a good change, I think."

Manuel could see Hoku's hand, pale against the shadows of her robe. He reached out to take it, and led her slowly away from the others, down the steps to the clearing.

"I have another change to propose," he said. "Won't you walk with me by the water?"

In Search of Laria

Doranna Durgin

The filly, at three days, was as perfect as a foal could be. After that she outgrew herself, and none of her parts ever matched. Her rump went high one day, her back long the next, her hocks straight on yet the next. Her ears turned too small…her head entered an extended phase of amazing coarseness. No one outside the master's barn gave her a second look unless it held pity.

The girl, at thirteen years, was small and refined, and when she grew, it was with perfect harmony of self. Her legs lengthened gracefully to the perfect limber proportions of a born rider. She never turned clumsy, never tripped over herself. Her figure remained lean and modest, and her menses came promptly and without pains.

But on the inside, she felt as the filly looked. Where the Master's other young riders sought improvement and acknowledgment, she yearned for perfection, always falling short. Knowing, as they all knew, that their every moment was weighed and measured against the very ideal she sought.

Fate assigned the girl and the filly together. The girl cared for filly's every need, taught her proper stable manners, and finger-combed her silky mane and tail twice a day. In return the filly trusted the girl with her heart. And while the girl's own heart was often too full of sharp-edged needs—*approve of me, praise me*, see *me*—sometimes she could quiet it, and then she could hear the filly's, simple and equine and open. *Lean on me, I like you. I can't get that fly—would you?* And most important, *You and I are Us.*

As the filly grew older, as the demands of her training increased, so did her pride and fiery sense of self. She would not be forced or bullied. She would not suffer fools who asked without the confidence to insist politely. She said not *I accept,* but *I allow.*

The girl's name was Dal.

The filly's was Laria.

As Dal, too, grew older, she learned the delicate balance of request, allow, and insist. She created of them a team. *Dal and Laria.* But in falling short of her self-imposed perfection, Dal nonetheless remained incomplete. Hollow in her deepest self, where it truly mattered. And where Dal was not enough for herself, *Dal and Laria* could not hope to complete. Despite their progress, their true excellence, part of Dal yearned always for the unattainable.

On the day Laria turned eight—grayed-to-silver with dark dapples at her knees and a mane and tail still shot randomly with black—Dal found a new halter hanging by Laria's thrice-daily picked stall. Rich black leather with rolled cheek and nose pieces and bright brass hardware.

The touring halter. And beside it, the ceremonial long knife, gleaming and sharp and sheathed in pale leather. The one that was never to be drawn outside the touring routines, during which it would connect with the others for a finale of spiraling light and magics.

For each spring the master chose his seasonal touring troupe, those who traveled from estate to estate, from performance to performance, showing the patrons that which they should support, and that to which they should aspire. Otherwise, they might send their fine horses elsewhere for training. Or worse, they might bring in trainers who claimed to do in a season what took the master years. After that, even the master could only improve them, but never quite make them what they might otherwise have been.

Touring. Honor and responsibility and the scrutiny that came with it. The thrill of the teams coming together for performance, and the fiery flare of the final light magic—proof of equine trust and steadiness.

Dal and Laria would be the best, Dal vowed as she cleaned the hand-stitched performance bridle that emphasized the refined nature of the mare's matured features. Still not a delicate head—no, never that, with that strong, straight nose, the flat planes of her jaw, the wide flare of her expressive nostril. Not delicate, but a thing of strong and wild beauty. Between the two of them, surely they would earn the acclaim she sought.

If deep want could outweigh the nature of things, Dal and Laria would have soared to perfection. But they were in truth no more than first year tour partners. Not unexpectedly, tension crept into Dal's back and legs, causing Laria to hesitate during those moments she should step out most boldly. And Laria herself had moments of distraction amidst the brio of her passage and piaffe—although Dal was as a horseman ought be, and blamed all of Laria's mistakes on herself.

And yet her deep want grew deeper. The intensity of her desire turned cutting-edge sharp. She pushed onward for perfection, ever marking the goal.

Halfway through the season, the Master took Dal aside and spoke kindly, meaning well. He worried that Dal's perfectionism would affect the mare's joy in the work…that it would leave Dal bitter and used up, her potential wasted.

Yes, he meant it kindly.

But Dal, taking the mare from the performance ring to the stable, felt only humiliation. *I'll show you. And I won't give up!* She walked apart from the others through the narrow, sandy alleys of this coastal estate, moving stiff-shouldered and tenser than ever while Laria's hooves plodded into the sand behind her. And though Laria's heart spoke of contentment, Dal was alone in her misery.

Or not quite.

They'd seen Dal leave the ring. They'd seen Laria's apparently docile demeanor. A mare of her breeding would line a man's pockets with gold and fill his pasture with foals.

They found a place to cut Dal off.

"Hand her over," they said, their long knives out. And when Dal stood frozen, Laria snorting and jigging in the suddenly menacing night beside her, they said more. "We won't cut you. We'll cut *her.*"

Dal, for all her lack of perfection, was a true horseman and could not let that happen. And so, hands trembling, she extended the reins, already silently vowing to find and reclaim the mare.

No one had counted on Laria.

She struck, snaking her elegant neck, snapping wicked teeth, breaking fingers. A second swift strike; she clamped down on a wiry biceps, flinging the man against the hard stone wall trapping them in this narrow alley.

But there was a third man, still behind them. Quaking, Dal snatched up the forbidden ceremonial blade, wrenching it from a resistant scabbard and past all safeguards. But when it finally came free, her hand filled with more than the wrapped metal coil of its hilt, and more than the weight of simple metal. Sensation snapped around her, seeking…seeking…

Finding.

Finding Dal.

The long-bladed knife spoke to her. In an instant, it crept inside her, filling all the empty crevices of her soul. Her confidence surged; the blade guided her. She drew quick blood, came back to do it again.

The men didn't want the mare so badly after all.

As Laria snorted and calmed and slowly lowered her high-held head, Dal quietly tucked the forbidden long knife into its scabbard and led Laria onward, her fingers twitching with guilt and relief.

When Dal woke the next day, she found only a hollow memory of her confidence, her competence, her sense of completion. The quiescent knife lay in its scabbard, tucked neatly beside her boots.

She reached for it—but trembled with sudden trepidation, and withdrew. What if her long-sought confidence had been only a transitory thing, a terrible taunt of what life could be? What *she* could be?

For a moment, she didn't dare find out. But then she didn't dare not to.

Her hand closed over the hilt.

The knife spoke to her.

∞

The evening's performance…

Magnificent.

Relaxed, confident…Dal released her tight back and let Laria's fire flow through them both, channeling it into brilliant piaffe, fiery passage, precise one-tempi canter lead changes, a crackling sweep of dancing light for the finale. The audience gasped and pointed, and the Master was speechless.

Dal didn't mind. She didn't need the man's praise. Not anymore.

She knew they were the best.

At the next estate, Dal and Laria dazzled the audience anew. For three nights running. After that, the Master allowed them the same individual recognition as the seasoned performers, and the contrast of Dal's youthfulness drew them even more accolade.

Always Dal wore the long knife. Always she walked Laria back to their stabling alone, one hand on the knife hilt and the other on Laria's withers, not mindful of or needing the praise she now accepted as due. Some thought it was modesty, but in truth it was simply that she already knew.

The best.

Most importantly, Laria was happy. She nuzzled Dal soft greetings; she coyly arched her neck when she offered treats, lipping them gravely from her palm. She reached for the bit when she held out the bridle. And she spoke to Dal with her heart. *I'm important. Let's dance together.* And, in the most intense of moments, oblivious to the audience around them, *You and I are Us.*

She never said *no.* She always said *I accept.*

Until one night Dal walked Laria back to her stall and her thoughts were too full of her own success to allow room for Laria's contentment.

For Dal knew what she was. The knife told her. The knife filled her.

The best.

The next day, after a shortened warm-up, Laria trotted into the performance distracted, disconnected from the *us* of them. And Dal forgot to ask.

Dal *told.* She *demanded.* She *ordered.*

After an instant of surprise, Laria offered more than she'd ever given before. More than her heart, more than her will. Not smoothly, not gracefully, but then…then she gave Dal her power. For that moment, she gave Dal her very sense of self.

Afterward, the Master inquired of Laria's well-being. She was young, he said, and wondered if the strain of maintaining her own brilliance had tired her.

Dal ought to have said, "It was my fault." She ought to have said, "I'll take care of her."

Dal said, "She got lazy. She'll behave for the next show."

And Laria did. But in the following show, she said *I'm not sure* in an honest equine question, and Dal told her *do it now.* Laria's tail flicked and her ears wavered, but she re-balanced herself through dint of will alone. Their finale lacked its now usual brilliance.

As time passed, Laria's willing joy under saddle slowly dulled. Her lovely, once-relaxed tail showed ever more of her wringing temper. And yet the patrons saw only her movement, and marveled over such an accomplished young partnership.

The Master saw the tail, the irritation often displayed in Laria's finely expressive muzzle and nostrils, a flare of protest muffled by the etiquette of her training. *You shout at me,* she was saying. *Your legs and hands are rude to me.*

And I cannot feel your heart any longer.

Sometimes, Dal heard her. And sometimes late at night she wondered at the changes in herself. But in the morning, the knife would speak to her, and she would forget her doubts.

"Laria seems unhappy," the Master said, before an evening performance. "Are you well, Dal? You are yet young; perhaps I have asked too much of you. You strive so hard, when you must simply allow yourself to be. And Laria, to *be*."

But Dal had no idea what he meant.

The very next evening, Laria went out to dance, sorrowful that she and Dal were no longer *they*. Tension coiled in her hindquarters, prevented her from reaching under herself for the lateral work; lacking support from behind, she was unable to lift and free her shoulders.

She tripped.

She hesitated.

She said, *I can't do it tonight. Please hear me.*

she needed Dal to hear her. To restore her trust. To heal their partnership.

Dal said

Do it.

And Laria said *no.*

In front of them all, she said *no.*

Dal, pale and tight-lipped, rode out the explosive denial. She sat deeply as Laria leapt high, as she plunged across the performance ring, wild and untamed and blazing through a score of steadfast horses—as if in their obedience, they could balance Laria's fierce and deliberate defiance.

But no one blamed Laria. They saw her desperation, her trust and love scattered across the ring along with their carefully choreographed patterns.

Laria said *no.*

She finally stopped before the Master, stiff and horrified and yet ready to do it all over again if Dal asked for so much as a step from her.

"Dismount," the Master said quietly, nodding at the orchestra. It sprang back to life, reviving the performance. Dal, disbelieving, hesitated.

"Dismount," the master said again. "Stable her. Instruct one of the handlers to tend her. Not you. Ask nothing of her along the way. Nothing, do you hear?"

"I hear," Dal said, though she didn't. She led Laria from the ring and outside the ornate performance hall—Laria steaming with the heat of her distress, Dal cold and angry, far too certain the mare had failed her. They trod an exquisite path of crushed shells to the stable, together and apart at the same time, until uncertainty caused Laria to plant her feet.

Dal jerked her onward, the bit rattling in her offended mouth. Laria reared high; the reins snapped taut between them. Their eyes met—astonished human eyes, feeling the first surge of personal betrayal. Enraged equine eyes, unyielding, edged with fierce despair. Then, as Laria's feet lightly touched ground, she most deliberately whirled away, cracking the reins like a whip and tearing them from Dal's grasp.

And then she was gone. Nothing left but fading hoofbeats and the stinging pain across Dal's palm.

The Master found her that way, regarded her sadly. There was little need for discussion; there were no words immense enough to apply to this loss. Finally the Master said, "You may accompany us until the end of the season."

Dal shook her head, one white-knuckled hand on the knife hilt. "I need to find her."

The Master shook his head, too. "Come with us, and I will give you severance. It will give you a chance in this world."

"I won't give up. I *don't* give up."

The Master looked at her for a long time. "Dal. This is not a thing you can do. You have not been riding her with the correct heart, and so she would not be ridden. Just as she will now not be found."

Dal made no reply. She looked at her stinging palm and opened and closed her fingers. She could barely feel the imprint of Laria's reins beneath the sense of a coil-wrapped hilt.

And so they left her. The Master exchanged discreet words with the patron and then packed up the horses, their gear, their riders— and left Dal in a strange coastal town with nothing of her own but an obsession.

Dal grew hungry fast. No matter her confidence. No matter that she and Laria had been the best, not in this fishing town with plenty of young men and women already mucking out stalls. When Dal got hungry enough, she cleaned gutters for pennies. When she got cold enough, she stole into the corner of a barn loft on a rainy night. During the days, she ranged the beaches, finding old hoof prints and learning about clams and tides and what the sun would do to one's cheeks and nose.

No Laria.

With fall settling in as a cold, whipping wind, no Laria. The knife reassured Dal, filling her empty spaces. She would not fail. She would find Laria. She would never stop looking, never acquiesce to failure.

As the wind grew colder, as the fishing boats put to port for the season, as her boots wore thin and her clothing thinner, Dal looked. Driven by hubris and borrowed confidence, too certain of her ability to secure winter quarters, she hunted Laria. Until she was gaunt, ragged, hair wild and hopelessly snarled, she looked.

One day she abruptly sat in mid-step, staring stupidly at the circling gulls, realizing how hunger clawed her and cold stiffened her. Realizing that she had no food, and no likelihood of finding it.

Seeing, finally, that she might just have nothing. Looking back along her sandy footsteps as if to discover the answers there, in some decision of her past.

Only then did she see she was not alone. Had not *been* alone. Laria stood on the beach slope behind her. Not near, not far. Up to her knees in the wind-blown, still-green beach grasses—the bridle still on her head and short, broken reins dangling, but the saddle long gone from her skinny ribs.

Beach grass agreed with her no more than tidal creatures agreed with Dal.

"Laria," Dal whispered, coming up to her knees. Laria took a step closer, ears pricked. Listening. "*Laria.*"

But words of love and longing collided with the knife's twining interference and caromed around in Dal's head to become *Laria, how could you? Laria, how dare you? I made us the best—*

"We were the best!" Dal roared.

Laria snorted, threw up her head, and whirled away.

Astonished at herself, too astonished to do anything but stare in horror at the retreating tangle of Laria's tail, Dal gaped after her a long moment before crying wordlessly into the wind.

The wind blew the sound back at her.

Laria! How dare she! Dal keened a sudden wail of denial and fear, as mindless and gibbering as any soul pushed over the edge. *How dare she?*

How could she? Dal was worth so much more than that, was so better than that, so much better than the others, than the Master, than Laria—

Dal blinked, quite suddenly, facing the utter nothingness of her life there in the sand.

Better than Laria? Truly?

So unfair, so unjust. Better than the Master who left us here, better than—

"*Us?*" Dal clawed at the knife, tearing shirt and skin and pants. "*Us?*" Yanking the blade from its scabbard, she dropped it from numbed fingers to thud into the sand, waking the knife anew—hollow promises and beguiling whispers and new understanding.

This was not success. This was not confidence. It wasn't even real. She had in fact given up, giving herself over to the knife. She had made of Laria a sacrifice. Made of herself, that same sacrifice.

But the wind still bit into her very being, her empty being. And the knife still whispered promises. *Whispered…*

Slowly, with an ancient's bones, Dal bent to pick up the blade. It held no grudges. It flooded her with warmth and wrapped her in pride. She caressed it, ran her clumsy, cracked fingers along its planes and edges. How it spoke to her! How it promised her—

Promised her—

Dal lifted her head to the whipping wind, looking out on the empty beach with newly sharp eyes. She'd lost her home; she'd lost her life's work. She'd betrayed Laria.

With this blade, she'd betrayed her own heart.

An agonized cry tore from her throat. Dal staggered upward, pushed herself to a wobbly run, and careened down into the water. Up to her knees in the frigid surf and then further, bracing herself against buffeting waves, she threw the knife to sea. As hard as she could. As far as she could. It arced far above the water, carrying the last of her strength with it.

Dal returned to the sand and fell to her knees, where the next wave licked at her toes and shins. She whispered into the wind, her voice a broken thing. "Come back, Laria…"

There was nothing but the lap of water against the shore, the wind in the grasses, the gulls overhead. Dal felt herself break in two, right in the middle of the void left by the knife. She covered her face with roughened hands and sobbed like a bereaved child, reliving memories—Laria from foalhood, Laria under first saddle, Laria's head resting against Dal's chest, Laria's quiet way of speaking from her heart.

You and I are Us.

Dal understood, then, that she'd never been able to hide from Laria.

She tipped her face to a wan sun and felt herself to be empty. *Was* empty. And for the first time, truly alone.

Breath gusted against her ear. A velvet muzzle nibbled at her hair.

Dal tottered to her feet and threw her arms around Laria's neck, hiding her face in the wind-knots of Laria's filthy mane. Filling herself with the truth of herself. When she finally lifted her head, it was with purpose. *Shelter. Food.* She would go back to the patron, and perhaps they could survive.

She put a hand on Laria's withers, a gesture of old. "Walk with me?"

Laria stood rooted, chin stiff, until Dal removed her hand, and then arched her weedy, once elegant neck. *You. May walk with.* Me.

Dal struggled with those empty inner places—the places the talisman had filled, the places she had always demanded that Laria fill. The crevices they had both learned no one could fill but Dal herself.

The knife had been giving up.

This was pushing onward.

With an inner wrench that made her knees quiver, Dal accepted herself. She replaced a trembling hand on Laria's withers, waiting. *Waiting…*

Laria swished a gentle tail, gently flapped her mane. And they walked together, Laria and Dal. *Being.*

A Plague of Dancers

Gillian Polack

"Stop jostling," Robert grumbled. "She'll be here soon enough."

"I can't see past your big country shoulders," Margery complained. "How can I see the train if you're in my way?"

The fact that Margery had washing-strengthened muscle and ate the good food of both castle and farm was irrelevant at that moment. Robert was certainly bigger, and he was the only one of the young people standing in her line of sight. Adam would have been in her line of sight intentionally, and she would have followed her usual custom of standing on his toes as hard as she could, but Adam was flirting with every young lady he could find. It had been a scarce winter and spring, and this summer he was ready for romance.

Besides, Margery wanted an excuse to nudge Robert, which she would not normally do in church. She didn't have the excuse that most of the others had, of making sure he knew they wanted to negotiate for his woodwork skills, but she was still bent on catching Robert's eye and bumping into him "by mistake." The two knew they'd get married in the usual way, when she was pregnant or both of them had enough money, but the church pretended not to know this, and so within those walls they both behaved as if they were innocent youth.

One effect from the many tragedies of the last year, they'd be married soon. Robert commanded extra wages and Margery was not only paid more, but was permitted to work almost anywhere. So many of their friends and neighbors had been lost that their lives were opening up sooner and more richly than they had expected.

Good came from ill, sometimes.

She'd heard from travelers that not everyone was so fortunate. This made her very grateful for God's gifts and very determined to work hard for them. If there was a time in her life when Margery's true self showed, this was that moment.

Margery felt guilty at her relief at avoiding having children for a little while longer. She loved children and wanted a family and had been willing to force the new priest to marry them, as was customary, but to have time to set up a household was such a great and unexpected blessing. Margery looked around, guiltily, hoping that no one had seen that she was happy. With all the loss, she should not be. From shore to shore people had died, said the first peddler to appear after the crisis. No one knew how many were dead, but everyone who still lived had the blessing of God. It wasn't real happiness, she convinced herself. It was accepting small joys in a difficult year. With the blessing of God.

Father Matthew hadn't made an appearance yet, and Mass was probably going to be late. Margery knew that the fault for this was almost certainly Isabella. "Ma Dame" to Margery when she was at the castle. "Isabella" when something went wrong and one of them sought help from the other. Margery didn't mind working there, but calling Isabella "Ma Dame" was…odd. They'd hardly talked privately for years. Isabella was married and ran the castle and was very much "Ma Dame," no longer able to join most village pursuits. It still felt wrong to Margery. They had played together when Isabella had escaped her staff and sought a friend. It was always Margery she sought.

Everyone from home to the next market town knew Isabella was going to wear the dress with the long train today. That meant full service of the best possible kind. The first in so very long. The priest knew it as well as the villagers. The church was bursting at the seams with visitors from any number of villages, and Margery would have laid a bet on Father Matthew peeking out from his room and waiting until the optimal moment.

Before that thought had completely left her mind, the lady herself appeared, walking past them all, three of her people holding the beautiful green train just off the ground until she reached her adult friends near the altar. Her adult friends were all tightly bound to the family and most were kin. "Near the altar," everyone called it, but it wasn't that close.

This was the signal for service to begin. Margery was certain that the lady intended walking in at that precise moment to make it seem as if she controlled church time. She surely didn't wear that dress just to provoke *that* sermon? The sermon that was delivered without fail whenever she wore a dress with a train. Adam might have intentionally provoked the priest. Isabella was more likely to set life up to revolve around her. Adam's provocation had targeted the previous priest, now Margery stopped to think about it. Isabella enjoyed setting herself against the new priest. He was old and wise, everyone said, and his sermons often told her how to do her duty. Isabella would provoke him whenever she could, for she held the land for God. Not for the priest.

Mass was everything it usually was. Always was. Margery didn't pay much attention. She was there for the sermon. It was the single big advantage their new priest presented, in her mind.

"A year ago," Father Matthew began, "the head of the northern church, our very own Archbishop Zouche, told us to beware the mortalities, pestilences, and more. We have survived. On this feast of St. John, we celebrate the Baptist and the ending of a quarter of the religious year. This year we celebrate something more: we celebrate God having granted us life."

Margery wanted to feel happy at this, but she couldn't. She looked around the uncomfortably-full room. Margery could see almost everyone she knew from miles around. They should not be able to fit. Not even close. She had a future, but too many of her friends had gone on ahead.

"The Feast of St. John the Baptist, the very feast we celebrate today, is the day last year when the Great Mortality reached our shores, or so I am told. It is a time for quiet contemplation concerning the soul, of preparing ourselves for whatever comes next to inflict us, not for the wearing of...of..." The priest lost his words, trying to find a way of describing the horror that stood in front of him. He resorted to old thoughts, things he had said uncountable times. "The reason her ladyship needed three bearers to carry her train was because of the tiny devils cavorting on that train. Invisible to you, those devils are dancing as if their position in Hell depends on it. Holding onto her pride and rejoicing in it. Pride is a sin. Pride is one of the worst of the sins, and..." He lost it again. When he found more words, he finished quickly.

"Not as good as usual," said Robert, thoughtfully, when the service was over and they were outside, in the graveyard. "Although it's pleasant to know he knows we're dressing up again and celebrating being alive. Isabella did us all a great favor by wearing that dress today."

"He hates it," added Margery. "The dress and the happiness. He's a walking misery, that priest."

"Father Bob was kinder," agreed her love. Father Bob had died almost a year ago, of course, so it was safe to remember his kindness and very easy to dispose of the memory of his rages.

"Where's the dance?" asked Henry, who lived so far outside the village that he was often said to belong to the next one. With him was his sister, Catherine, almost jumping out of her skin with excitement.

"Here," said Robert, his arms taking in the whole of the churchyard, with its graves and its trees and its space. "To make it easier for the visitors."

"I'll spread the word." And Henry walked straight into the crowd as if his soul were gone forever.

"Do we have enough musicians?" asked Margery.

"One to lead each trail of dancers. If most people stay, we might have long trails. I wish we could ask the musicians to play together or add a drummer to the rear of each group of dancers, but there are so many of us..."

"First dance since all the deaths. We need each other," commented Margery. "It's not going to be easy."

"It's not, but..." and Robert put on his stalwart voice, "It's going to bring us all back into our world, and we'll be able to live again."

"Robert," interrupted William-the-Baker, "would you help me set up the crowd so that we look sociable and so that the priest and his people don't know what we're doing?"

William was very young to be a baker, but he was the only one of his family who had survived. He'd married, and his first child was on the way. This night was to be a charmed moment when he could be with his friends and pretend the world was not on his shoulders. His big shoulders. William was one of the shortest men in the village and one of the strongest. Not even Robert with his height and muscles could carry what William carried. Margery looked at William's flustered brown hair and thought of the burdens of St. Christopher. Christopher was a saint she never wanted to become, and it hurt her to see William with all his burdens.

"Weren't we going to wait until they were asleep?" Robert looked puzzled.

Margery lost patience with her stupid friends. "Don't they know anyway?" she asked sharply. Too much dwelling on what had changed for them, and each bit of dwelling hurt. She was determined to put it behind her. Be Adam, not Margery.

"Oh," said William.

"I'm not sure he can stop us tonight, even if we start earlier," Robert said, comfortably. "All the young people from all the parishes —we want to be here. And how many of us do what he says outside the church?"

The conversation moved on to something more important. "The drink?" asked Henry whose land was so close that he always looked harried when he came to church. Today was no exception.

"Hidden on the other side of the church. Not near your land, so you won't be blamed for it," Robert said. "Guarded. Leave it there. Ale and graves and merriment do not belong together, remember? Last time we brought ale into the churchyard, we all had to do penance."

All was ready. Everyone had brought bread and cheese and other portable food, and they sat in the churchyard, eating and drinking and pretending decorousness so that no one would throw them out too soon. It was a bonding time. The first time that so many of them had come together since all the deaths.

They didn't talk about the past, but they relished the company.

Adam spent this whole quiet time either mimicking the priest or mimicking Lady Isabella. As Isabella, he waddled with his shoulders pulled back. You could almost see the demons sitting on her train, trying to drag her backwards, head-first into Hell. None of them could actually see the demons, even on Isabella's actual train. Margery put her hand over her mouth, afraid to laugh. Imaginary demons waddling exactly like Adam waddled.

It was dusk, or thereabouts. No one checked on the priest or asked about the hour. The dance began when a musician was ready for it to begin. The crowd quietened to listen to the strings playing a carol. One at a time, two at a time, young people joined behind the musician, following where she led and tracing the rhythm of her strings with their feet. When the trail of dancers was so long that the music couldn't be heard, another musician sprang up and started playing the same tune, attracting his own line of dancers.

"It'll be slow dances all night," Margery commented to her companions. One of her hands was in Robert's and the other held Adam's. The dance was so gentle that conversation was simple. All she had to do was have her palm upwards and fingers gently curled for Adam and the other hand resting in Robert's.

"The price we pay for numbers and carols," Robert said.

Adam laughed. "We can always make it more interesting." He gambolled and frivolled and pretended the dance was one of those that were full of leaps, all the while keeping his hand in Margery's on one side and holding Catherine's hand on the other.

Robert was in that line, along with Henry and William. Isabella joined them quietly, just as soon as she'd come back from changing into a dress she could dance in.

"I thought you'd wear that dress and dance with the train in one hand or hooked into your girdle," said Margery, as they snaked past each other in a carol.

"Not tonight," Isabella answered. "Metal and my most expensive garment would have led to disaster, and honestly, that train is too heavy to hold in one hand. Besides, I wanted to show off that I have more dresses and I wanted to be able to enjoy the dance and I wanted…"

"To be able to play with your old friends as if the castle didn't exist," said Robert.

"It always existed," said Isabella, "but I'm to be married again soon and then all of this will be gone." Her arms spread to encompass not only the castle, but the village and her friends. Her land, her duties, her people.

"They found you a replacement?" Adam was looking for ways to tease the most important woman in the crowd, as if he had no interest and as if he had a chance. "What do you do to them all?"

"Just stop it, Adam," said Robert. What was funny over a year ago was no longer a joke.

"I can't hear the music above your chatter, you know," said Margery, and the lines continued to ambulate through the green grass more quietly, step after step of walking into a bright future.

After a few dances, Margery needed a break. The dancing was slow, but the paths were sometimes narrow. She'd kicked her right foot against a tombstone three times. Each time she'd muttered a "sorry"" to the tombstone and kept dancing, but right now she needed a break. Her excuse (should anyone ask) was that her right shoe was rubbing against her little toe.

Margery wasn't the only one to stand watching. She found herself next to the priest.

"Father," she said politely and nodded her head.

"This will lead to woe," said Father Matthew, gloomily. He always said that. He'd come to them after all the deaths. For his sake as much as theirs, the archdeacon had explained. The young priest they were expecting had been sent to York, for the larger congregations had to be filled first and there weren't enough priests. The rumor from the castle was that they had a priest where others missed out because this priest was incapable of the pastoral side of his job. This was when Margery had discovered that the deaths weren't local. The whole of the north had suffered. Maybe even the whole of England. Margery joined in the laughter over the jokes played on him, but she also treated him as a lost soul.

"Don't stop it," said Margery, urgently. "We need it so."

"You need to dance your way to Hell?" The good father was perturbed. "I couldn't stop it last time. I wish I knew a way of stopping it this time. I do not want to see another of my congregations doomed."

"Another?"

"Last year, on St. John's Eve." That was all he said, as if she knew all. And she did.

"The coming of the illness. We are so few compared with then. It's…I'm glad we're through it." It was easy enough to dwell on in her mind, but Margery found words very difficult when the death of so many people she knew was the subject.

"Nothing," said the priest. "Pestilence is nothing. If I had to handle that, there would be time to give proper rites to most people, to send them to heaven. Dancing leads men and women straight to the Devil. I saw it. I was there. When I came here, that was all I could think of. Everything I do here is to prevent it happening again." He sounded so angry. She wondered if he even thought that God was listening. All he did was talk. Why was dancing such a problem?

"I cannot see it," said Margery, politely. She hoped her face didn't show that she thought he was a madman. Inside, however, she felt a despair. Ma Dame's train was one thing—this attack on their pleasures was something far more worrying. A priest who didn't allow his people to be human and to enjoy life would be a priest who led to despair, and despair now, when finally they were all pulling through, was inconceivably awful. At least he didn't pretend he could order them around. Something had cured him of that.

She saw that Father Matthew was watching her, not the dancers. The skin around his eyes crinkled sympathetically. She frowned, just a little, and this prompted him to speak.

"What happened to my congregation is not what you're thinking."

"I'm sorry," Margery said, and spread her hands to show she meant her apology. "There must be something I don't know."

"There was a dance," he said. "It began like this. Quiet. Refined, almost. I stayed indoors and rested, because I was called on at all hours. So many people. So much illness. So very many deaths. I will say, when I'm upset, that I gave everyone due time, but at the height of the trouble it wasn't possible to spend enough time with them to help them in their final steps. We dug big graves and lined up the bodies, with respect, and we prayed for them, and I prayed with as many as I could prior to their death. I was the last priest left in the town. Everyone received last rites. Everyone. So I slept when I could. I ate…sometimes."

"The night of the dance," he continued, his voice so solemn it invested the word "dance" with a feeling of death, "I had said farewell to three of my best congregants. Holy. Devout. Comforting. They all died in a single afternoon. I was alone."

"When the dance started, I was exhausted. I rested and, eventually, I fell asleep. I don't know how long I slept. Maybe hours. Maybe days. When I woke up, I didn't know how many services I had missed or how many people died alone."

The dance line Margery had left looped around on itself, and Adam tripped William. William fell and so did Isabella and Henry and Catherine. Adam bowed in charming un-apology, and Robert sent him to the back of the line, where he could cavort all he liked but was reduced to following.

"Right now," the priest said, quietly, "this is different. Or maybe it was the same at the beginning."

"At the beginning?"

"The beginning of the dance. When I woke up it was full night and St. John's Eve. I went outside to see why the music lingered. Half the town was still there, dancing as if there were no tomorrow. They had been taken by evil."

"Taken by evil?"

"Friends and family called their names, and the dancers did not hear them. Some were forced to drink water, but most danced and danced and danced without food or drink or rest. I called on them, on St. John, then on the Lord himself. No one listened.

"The musicians played and did not stop even though their fingers bled. The lines danced after them.

"When I pulled the musicians out, the dancers kept dancing. No music. Dancing. And dancing. And dancing. A line of unholiness that started on St. John's Eve. Three days they danced. Then some danced more. So many died. So many were injured." He drifted off.

Margery found her eyes telling history for him, replacing the people in front of them with the memory of the dead. Her deaths were not from dance, but her friends and family were still gone. Ghosts dancing on their own decaying bodies.

Margery's body froze. It felt as if the priest was sending the evil forth by watching the dance. Whether it could happen here or not, she had to do something. She kept her voice light, even as her hands clenched into fists.

"I wish my voice were louder," she said, ruefully. "We must make sure your dance of death doesn't happen here." She couldn't bear to see how much he hurt. And she had to prove to him and to herself that her people were not possessed. But the pestilence had changed her, and she no longer raced into crises or lost her calm over them.

She walked briskly up to Robert and moved her feet to the music to stand next to him. She told him what the priest had said, and he kept dancing. She told him what he should do. "Father Matthew needs it," she said. "He's hurt beyond anything I've seen. And we need it. To prove to ourselves that we're not possessed."

"Not for me to instruct the village, my love," he said, and kept dancing. "I know my place."

Margery stopped, and the dancers slowly swirled past. Her lips pressed together, bottling all the emotions that wanted to explode from her. Her feet were frozen with fear. She thought, "St. John's then and St. John's now. Maybe they will all die." Then she thought, *Too many are already dead. These are my friends and the rest of my life. I can prevent death and I can cure the priest.*

Margery shouted, "Quiet, everyone. Stop dancing. We need to talk. There's ale! You can dance afterwards. Quiet!" she shouted, "Stop dancing!" She heard her small voice fade against the night. She needed someone louder.

She asked Father Matthew if he would call out and stop everyone. "Just for a prayer," she suggested. "We need a prayer of thanks for being alive after this awful year."

The priest looked at her, his eyes bleak and his posture despairing. "I can't do anything," he said. "I tried last time and no one listened. It was just like you, shouting to the night. It won't work."

Isabella had taught Margery the perfect word for moments like this. "Damnedeus!" she said, as if she were swearing. Of course she wasn't. Calling on the Lord God was hardly offensive. It felt good. Very good. It emboldened her. She said it again, "Damnedeus!"

She tried talking to Adam the way she had with Robert.

"Get lost," he said, cheerfully.

There was a stick by one of the graves. She picked it up and whacked Adam's knees with it.

Adam stopped dead in his tracks, pulling Robert out of place and stalling the line behind him. Margery grabbed his forearm and pulled him out. The dance continued without him, and Adam stomped heavily on the ground, letting his annoyance travel deep into the earth.

"You're treading on a grave," said Margery, amused at the place he chose to stomp.

"Well, don't do that," he said, irritated. "Don't whack me when I'm dancing. I didn't hurt anyone when I tripped William, you know. You don't need to revenge yourself. Besides, Robert wasn't affected—"

"I know," she said, "But I need you. And Isabella. How do I get Isabella? You can do something wicked, you know, just as long as the priest doesn't see it."

"Easy," said Adam. "And I shall fulfill a dear, dear dream."

He went up to Isabella in the dance, just as Margery had with Robert. Instead of talking, he edged closer and closer until he was touching her. He kissed her, then danced away, out of reach. Isabella dropped her dance companions and chased him, furious.

When Isabella had calmed down, Margery explained the problem. Isabella only half believed her. "I shall talk to the priest," she said. She came back to them quite quickly, and very melancholic. "What do you want us to do?"

"I want you, as Ma Dame, to lead a small prayer of thankfulness when there's even a hint of what Father Matthew is scared of. That will stop everyone and give them time to catch their breath or to have a drink or go home. And it will remind us why we're here. This is a celebration."

"And me?" Adam looked plaintive.

"Do you think that shouting is going to stop anyone, at all?"

He looked across and shook his head. "Not tonight."

"You're essential, then. Whether Father Matthew allows you or not, you're going to ring the bell. Over and over. No one can hear music above the bell, and they'll all have to stop until Isabella has the attention to lead her prayer."

"How long do I ring the bell? I can't see what's happening out here from in there."

"It's like measuring time to cook, except that you're measuring time to lead a prayer."

"I don't know how to cook," retorted Adam.

Margery sighed. "You choose a song that's the right length, and you sing it in your head."

"I know the exact song," crowed Adam. "You know the one I sing in church. It's perfect for bell ringing. Religious and everything."

"A prayer?" asked Isabella. "Which one?"

Margery laughed. "I know the one. Isabella, you avoid being near him on that day, every year."

"That's not a prayer," Isabella said, firmly. "No song is a prayer when the chorus goes, 'Hee haw, Mr. Donkey.'"

"It's better than that," said Adam, reproachfully. "Much funnier. And holy. Oh, so holy."

"I'd rather the good father led the prayer," said Isabella, mildly, changing the subject.

"He's a mess," said Margery. "I asked him if he'd lead a prayer, and he refused. This is up to us." The other two, looking at the way he stood like a thundercloud, arms crossed and face dark, had to agree. "Besides, if we can make this work, it will change how the Church talks to us. Whenever he wants to rant about devils on trains or…almost anything, in fact…all one of us will have to do is start whatever prayer you lead us through tonight. Not the donkey one. And dance a step or two. We're good Christians, and we know it."

"And if we lead the prayer, then it's our village, not his." Margery could see Adam planning dance steps to use when the priest needed reminding.

"I wouldn't go that far," said Margery. "I was thinking about the blessing of the field he did when he first arrived. How he tells us that Rome is more important than everything we know and how the fields remain unblessed. How he said Mass without using a bit of the field to be blessed and the way he kept the procession inside and didn't take it around the field."

"You want less talk of devils and more of the old stuff?" Isabella was thinking it through as she spoke.

"The entertaining stuff," said Adam. "Processions to keep storms away and stories from the Bible and alcohol. Lots of alcohol."

"They have the Easter plays in town," Isabella said, wistfully.

"We've always had our own ways. Special prayers. Special ceremonies," said Margery. "We've lost too many people, and this new priest comes from somewhere folks don't do anything interesting. If we ring the bell all night, we'll cure his melancholy and we'll earn ourselves all the good things."

And so it was. Every time Adam rang the bells for the length of time that it took him to sing the most indecent religious tune he knew, all the dancers stopped, and Isabella led them in a quiet prayer. At first the priest was bewildered, but as the evening passed he left the dancers to their own devices. Late at night he joined them when the bell rang, and followed Isabella's quiet prayer. He didn't try to lead. Not once. He didn't even join in. Margery asked him about it.

"I made my decision earlier," was all he said. Margery wanted to know what that meant, but didn't dare ask more. The priest looked as if he'd built a wall around himself, and she was too tired. She'd done enough. The wall would have to wait. Or it would have to be dealt with by the clergy. She gave a small smile when she realized that in his self-imposed solitude, the priest had missed entirely the group of young men who, instead of praying, went to the back and drank ale.

And this is how Adam became the bell ringer and Isabella became a force to reckon with when anyone tried to obliterate custom and why Margery was treated with more respect by the priest than anyone else in his parish.

Years later, Robert told their children, "Bell, ale, and carol is more effective than bell, book, and candle at getting rid of demons." He never told them that his part was the ale.

They eradicated the invisible demons quietly and without fanfare. Just like a carol, in fact, a dance of grace and gentleness and many twists and turns.

Sanitizing the Safe House

Leah Cutter

Paper burns differently than wood. Particularly when you're dealing with bound items, like weekly planners, old yearbooks, sheaves of letters tied together with pink ribbons. It takes time to destroy all that evidence of a life well lived, time to build a fire hot enough to burn through all the photographs and old recipes.

Time I didn't have. My client had been compromised, and I had to get him the hell out of Dodge.

Or Topeka, actually, where my current charge had been living.

This particular safe house was a really nice place, well taken care of. It had been built back in the early fifties—a brick rambler with a stand of pine trees to block the winter winds whipping across the prairie. Backyard was wide open, just a short wooden fence to mark the property line. It would have been a great place to raise kids, with more trees just past the fence, as well as a small creek.

Idyllic, really. Norman Rockwell come to life.

Except for the meth lab that had sprung up at the neighbor's.

The area was now crawling with ATF, FBI, and every other three-letter acronym department you could think of, as well as a few you've never heard of.

Officers hadn't started looking hard at my client. But they would. And while my team was good, even they made mistakes. Some official would find something and come to question my guy. And me, I was just a contractor for one of those three-letter acronyms, so my boss preferred for us to fly under the radar at all times.

Better for the authorities to just not find my client.

So I had to move him. Give him yet another new identity. Remove all the evidence of his former existence. Sanitize the place while still leaving behind enough debris to make it look as though he'd just moved, not like a professional had come through.

Luckily, it was still spring. Burn bans only happened late in the summer, when the sun had baked the weeds to dry husks and the dirt the combines threw up made the air hazy. I wasn't the only house on the road with a bonfire in the backyard that afternoon—the sun was shining for the first time that week, even though the wind still blew cold.

I stirred the ashes with a long, pointed stick, spreading out the pages so they'd burn more quickly. I'd dumped the boxes of paper on top of the wood already piled in the backyard pit, figuring that the wood would burn eventually.

"Why, look at what my favorite firebug is doing."

That voice. A smoky alto. Caramel cream, threaded through with cherry brandy. At least half my dreams featured that voice. It also starred in a similar number of nightmares.

It was complicated.

"Hello, Angela," I said without bothering to turn around. If she wanted to shoot me, she already would have.

"Hello, Frankie," she replied, coming to stand beside me. She wore a practical outfit: heavy black work boots that probably had steel-reinforced toes, sturdy cargo pants, and a navy blue windbreaker with a three-letter acronym on it.

A contrasting reflection of what I wore—flannels and jeans, baseball cap from the local feed store, nothing to make me stand out. Just a regular guy, mid-thirties, Hispanic.

After the silence had dragged on, I finally dared to look at Angela's face. She still looked like an angel to me, though her blonde hair was pulled sharply back and she wore "workday" makeup—a touch of mascara, pink lipstick, and only the wind adding color to her pale cheeks. Her nose turned up the slightest bit at the end, and I could still see the pictures of her as a kid with long braids and freckles on that cute nose.

"You look good," Angela said cautiously. "You taking care of yourself?"

I heard the word *finally* tacked onto the end of that. I *was* more fit than the last time she'd seen me—five? No, six years ago. I was eating my veggies and working out again. Free weights had broadened my chest and slimmed my waist. I'd had to buy all new pants as the old ones had started falling off my butt.

"Whatcha want?" I asked instead of replying. Wasn't about to tell her that going to the gym was a sure sight better than trying to drink away my regrets, as I had the first few years after she'd left.

"Who's living here?" Angela asked. "Your latest insurgent?"

"My, ah, *client*, has already moved on," I assured her.

"And what was he, she, hiding from?" she said.

"Hmmm. Let's call him Larry, as in Larry the Lounge Lizard," I told her.

"You always did hang out with a certain class of folks."

"What does that say about you?"

She rolled her eyes. "Get on with it."

"Seems like ol' Larry made some accounting errors for some important people. Now, Larry tried to prove that they were just honest mistakes, until someone found Larry's *other* bank account. You know. The one overseas."

"I see," Angela said. "And I suppose your boss, being the generous guy that he is, decided to help ol' Larry out?"

I beamed at her. "You got it! And since Larry hadn't signed anything like a non-disclosure agreement, all the intel he gave about his old operation was legal and everything."

"Riiiight," Angela said. "So you wouldn't happen to know where ol' Larry is right now, would you?"

"Not a clue," I told her cheerfully while I poked at the fire. More paper caught, burning brightly. "I'm just a cleaner."

"I know, I know. Your hands are never dirty," Angela said. She shook her head. "You wouldn't mind if I searched the place, now, would you?"

"Only if you have a warrant," I told her. "I am a law-abiding citizen, and I expect my police force to be just as law-abiding."

"Fine," Angela said. "Will there be anything left for us to discover?"

"Nope!" I lied. "Though…the ashes might still be warm."

"Thanks for the warning." The sarcasm could have been cut with a knife.

She paused, looking out over the yard. Then she sighed, loud enough for me to hear over the wind and my pounding heart.

Looked like we were about to get to the meat of things.

"I recognize the yard," she said softly. "From the pictures you sent."

I stopped poking the fire and looked up, trying to see what she did. The trees in the far back had been a lot smaller, but maybe the fence was the same.

"A lifetime ago," I finally said.

"Many lifetimes ago," Angela replied. "When there could have been a 'we'."

Before our choices led us down different paths.

"I'm sorry I never came to visit before now," she continued.

"As you said, many lifetimes ago." I was proud at how casual my voice remained. "Now, officer, unless there's something else?" I didn't want another fire between us: it would burn me to a crisp this time.

"Nothing, citizen," she said. "Happy cleaning."

"Thanks," I told her.

It had been a bad idea to stick ol' Larry here. I hadn't known what to do with the place, though. I couldn't sell it. Not without giving up all hope of…her.

When the police had first come knocking on his door, Larry had called me immediately, demanding to be moved. I'd assessed the situation and had agreed.

However, there was something fishy going on. Larry was all packed up by the time I arrived a day later, which he couldn't have been, not given the timeframe.

Plus, he must have been in contact with someone from his old life. There were too many pictures from his previous life, too many letters and old books. He couldn't have accumulated this much even after a decade.

He knew it was against the rules, but Larry also wasn't the sharpest knife in the bunch.

Was Larry trying to figure out a way of sliding back into his old life? Did he really think his old boss was the type to forgive something like embezzlement? Not to mention working for the government now?

Something else was going on. And I didn't have time to figure it out.

I thrust my stick into the ashes, frustrated. Picked up one of the boards buried underneath the boxes of paper and heaved it upward.

Huh. More paper was trapped underneath the wood already piled there.

Mapa de Costa Azul caught my eye. Plus other tourist brochures.

Crap. Just what had Larry been up to?

I hadn't been lying to Angela. Technically, I didn't know where Larry was when she'd asked about him. Pat was one of the best on my team: a big-boned Irish woman with red curly hair and laughing green eyes who I never would have bet against in a bar fight. She'd stashed Larry in a hotel along one of the barren stretches of highway leading away from the city, a truck stop that had high turnover and wouldn't think twice about somebody paying cash.

I took extra time cleaning out the house, wiping down finger-prints, removing DNA traces, then planting false clues in case Angela was stubborn enough to send a team through.

It was close to midnight by the time I finished. When I finally left the house, the sky was clear and full of stars—more than I ever saw in the city. The air felt chilled and crisp, with just traces of smoke from this afternoon's fire. A single car raced by on the country road, the sound echoing across the empty fields.

If I'd moved here with Angela, as we'd planned so many years ago, I would have planted more trees out front. A grove thick enough to block what little traffic noise there would be, while not giving good enough coverage for surveillance or snipers.

I shook my head. That was a dream best left burned in the backyard with all the other memories of our past lives. She liked being a cop too much. While I could have left my job—it wasn't a vocation—we were never sure whether it would actually let me leave. Too many officials knew my number and weren't afraid to call day or night. I wasn't a fixer, but I frequently did clean up messes.

Still. I would have made a go of a new life with a job I could have talked about, if she'd been willing, if she hadn't backed out at the last minute, after I'd already bought this place.

I zipped my jacket up higher, ignoring the chill I felt creeping across my shoulders. I turned to look, but no one was there, watching me. Nobody but my ghosts, anyway.

Then I yawned. God, I was tired. An entire day of hard cleaning left me wrecked. Despite all the work at the gym, I wasn't twenty anymore. I had enough cash saved up for a long retirement if I was careful. I just didn't know where I wanted to go, what I wanted to do.

Or as Angela would have put it, I still didn't know who I wanted to be when I grew up.

No one was on the highway as I drove out to it. I sat in the drive-way for a little while with the lights off, staring, making sure that no one was there, hidden and watching me. And no car lights imme-diately came up behind me once I started down the road.

I knew I was being paranoid, but that caution had saved me more than once.

I called Pat while I was driving. She gave me the address of the truck stop hotel, along with a cheery "Hell, no," when I propositioned her as usual.

I didn't mean it. She knew that. It was a game between the pair of us.

She could probably see that my heart still belonged to Angela, and always would.

The truck stop hotel was perfect. The smell of diesel fuel and burned grease hung in the air. Lots of traffic all hours of the night. Tons of semis parked in the back. Too many people coming and going for some clerk to pay attention to a short, balding, accountant like Larry.

Of course, there were also too many cameras to hide from, but we weren't doing anything that wasn't above the board.

Pat had told me the room number. Third floor, in the back, close to the stairs. The hotel smelled dank, like the spring rains had molded the carpets. Dim lights, but no one else was in the narrow hallway.

I knocked on the door. Nothing complicated—we weren't some sort of spy team with fancy codes.

"Door's open!" came Larry's cheerful voice.

I shook my head. Larry was far too trusting.

"Now, Larry, you know better" I said as I walked through the door. Stopped.

Two single beds in the center of the room. Larry sitting on one, looking pleased.

Couple of goons on the other bed. One goon with a gun pointed at Larry, the other, now, pointed at me.

"Sorry! Wrong room," I said, immediately starting to back up.

"Stay right where you are," commanded a more familiar voice.

From the small bathroom came, let's call him Mouse. Larry's old boss. Face like a rat, only softer, squishier, so Mouse fit him better. Gray fuzz covered his chin, two-day-old stubble that was probably supposed to make him look tougher, but just rounded his face out more, like a homeless bum. Wore a blue denim work shirt and black pants, so clothing a little nicer than his goons who were dressed like the locals, in flannels and jeans.

Mouse also had a gun pointed at me.

"I don't want any trouble," I said, closing the door behind me.

Maybe that was a mistake, cutting off my easy getaway. But I didn't want any innocent bystanders getting shot, either.

Though given the paper thin walls of this place, any bullets would probably go straight through and end up in the parking lot.

"Sit," Mouse ordered, indicating the bed next to Larry.

"Larry, what did you do?" I asked as I complied.

"Mouse here is giving me back my old job!" Larry said with a huge grin.

"And you believed him?" I said.

"Got me an insurance policy," Larry bragged. "Better one than last time. Gonna get out for good, go south and stay there."

"Then why are they here with guns pointed at you?" I said, indicating the goons on the bed opposite us. "Is it because they trust you?"

Larry blinked owlishly at me for a moment. Then he looked at the goons, looked at Mouse, then back at me. "They're not just pointed at me!" he said, sounding like a bratty boy.

"What do you intend to do with me?" I asked. I didn't want to know what they intended to do to poor Larry, didn't want to be an accessory to the crime. Ol' Larry was on his own this time.

"Ransom you back to your boss," Mouse told me cheerfully.

I blinked, surprised. Then I laughed. Couldn't help myself. "I'm an independent contractor," I told him. I knew the agency who'd hired me sure as shit wouldn't pay anything. They'd probably gleefully cancel the contract, happily so if I ended up not being able to send them a bill.

Mouse narrowed his eyes at me, then turned to glare at Larry. "This is the guy, right? The fixer?"

Larry nodded vigorously while I just shook my head. "I'm just a cleaner. I've spent all day cleaning up the house where this guy was living. I'll help him move, again, but then I'll just go back to cleaning again."

"He's a *fixer*," Larry insisted. "He makes people disappear."

"Only metaphorically," I said.

Larry gave me a blank look.

It was probably too big of a word for him. "I give people new identities," I translated. "New lives. They disappear from their old lives, only to start new ones. I don't kill people. I don't even carry a gun."

Technically, that was true. My gun was in my car, as usual. My boss gave me grief about that, and I didn't care.

Always easier to talk yourself out of a situation if you weren't carrying.

Mouse nodded. "They'll still pay to get you back," he said.

I shrugged. "So you plan on kidnapping me and holding me for ransom?"

"That's right! Larry did say you were a bright guy," Mouse agreed. "POLICE!"

The door came banging down.

My avenging Angel came through, leading the charge.

Angela and the others hadn't been following me, not exactly. They *had* been following Mouse, and were quite interested when our paths intersected. When I got him to admit to a crime, they decided to act.

Or Angela had, regardless of the chain of command.

Though Angela's three-letter acronym department had made the bust, the inter-departmental squabbling was interminable. And giving me a headache.

I sat in the back of the operations vehicle watching. We were located close to where I'd started, one of the farmers loaning his field to the officials, most of whom were here for the original meth lab bust that had sprawled out.

It surprised me how much grief Angela's CO gave her, busting her chops in front of everyone.

Finally, after sworn statements and sworn secrecy and at least one phone call to my boss, the officials turned me loose. My head was pounding and I was bone tired, but I still waited an extra hour until Angela came walking out from under the tent as well.

"Buy you a cup of coffee?" I asked, falling easily into step with her as she walked out into the open field. The stars were starting to fade and the horizon had an orange glow to it. The air had gotten much colder, making me pull out my gloves.

Angela glanced at me and kept trudging toward her rental car. I knew it had to be a rental—she'd grown up in Wisconsin and never would have voluntarily bought a white vehicle, a moving snow bank as she called them.

"What's your CO got against you?" I said as she beeped her car open.

Angela sighed and finally said, "You."

"Me?" I asked, surprised. I didn't know the woman, had never met her.

"She knew me back…before," Angela said.

I nodded. I understood what she meant by before—that time long ago when there had been an us.

"She couldn't believe I was going to give up my career, give up everything, for some guy," Angela said. "She was the one who talked me out of it, eventually. And she's never forgiven me for even considering it."

"That was ten years ago," I pointed out. Suddenly, the realization hit me. "And you're still on the bottom rung of your department, aren't you? She's never let you advance."

Angela took a deep breath, then let it all out in a loud sigh. "I hadn't wanted to believe that she would sabotage me, my entire career, but she has."

"So what do you want to do about it?" I said cautiously. Though it was growing lighter by the minute, it still felt as though a huge pit of darkness lay before us.

"I could fight it. Fight her." She shrugged. "I'm not sure it's worth it, anymore."

"The career? The badge? The job?" I asked cautiously. I couldn't kill the hope rising in me.

Slowly, Angela nodded her head.

I didn't want to get burned to a crisp. I was older, wiser.

I still didn't care. This was Angela. My angel.

I turned and casually leaned against her car, looking back over the east, toward the rising sun and my farm. Pink clouds now lay streaked across the sky. The smell of ashes was far away.

"So what do you want to do?" I asked as Angela also turned and leaned against the car beside me. She wasn't close enough to touch, but I could still feel the heat of her body all along my side.

"Sleep for twelve hours? Drink some coffee, have a really good meal, then sleep for another twelve?" she suggested.

"And then? After that?"

In a broken voice, Angela replied, "I don't know. I don't know what I want to be when I grow up."

I blinked, surprised. "Neither do I," I told her.

My heart pounded so hard I was surprised it wasn't making the empty car I leaned against echo like a drum. My fingers were both cold and sweating inside my gloves. The coffee I'd had earlier was burning its way through my stomach as well as threatening to come back up.

But it was now or never.

"You want to go someplace and maybe try to figure it out? Together?" I asked, the words hardly above a whisper.

"Us?"

"Us," I said. "We."

Angela shuddered as though ice water had just been dripped down her bare neck. She stood still for so long I had to glance over to see if she'd been frozen in place, or possibly even died of shock.

She still stared straight out at the horizon. She didn't look back at me, but I felt her hand brush against mine, then our pinky fingers intertwined.

I stared back out at the horizon with her, watching the sunrise.

"So, have you ever been to Costa Azul?"

Smiley the Robot

Amy Sterling Casil

Don't tell me that love isn't true.

"This is a song?" Smiley the Police Robot asked.

"You like it," Gia replied. "I can tell. You're smiling."

"I always smile, Miss Gia."

"Keep calling me that," she said, drawing her cable-knit fisherman's sweater close to her neck. It had been fifty years since anyone had called her miss. "You'll go far."

Just then, a kid on a sleek, bright orange skateboard sped past Gia's street-front apartment where Smiley stood, and Gia leaned out the window toward him.

"Stupid robot!" the kid cried, skidding to a halt, and making a ridiculous face.

"Go safely," Smiley said.

"Stop that!" Gia cried. "You little monster! I'll tell your mother!"

The boy was about eight. "I ain't got one!" he replied.

Gia shook her fist at the kid. "You little liar!"

"It is all right," Smiley said to her. "They do that all the time."

"Smiley, don't you just want to whack the hell out of him?" Gia smoothed her scarf and again worried at her sweater. She was cold—always so cold. But poor Smiley!

"I am" Smiley said, and he paused, turning to watch the kid as he disappeared down the street. After a moment, he turned back. His face was unchanged, but there was something in his measured, slow, utterly gentle and reasonable voice, that told Gia that he was not unaffected.

"I do not like it when the children tease me," he said. "I do not like it when I go on a call, and they try to hurt me. A woman hit me with a broom last week."

"Oh, Smiley," Gia said. "And you're always smiling."

The song played on. Instead of answering her, Smiley said, moving a bit back and forth as if he was about to dance, "I like the beat."

Gia grinned. "That's the idea. They don't know what they're listening to these days. The kids have all turned into a bunch of unholy geeks. Maybe they wouldn't be so horrible to you if they knew you liked music."

Smiley shrugged, or something like it, with his blue-clad mechanical shoulders. "Who sings this song? Woman or man?"

"You can't you tell?"

Smiley made a little clicking noise. "I'm a robot cop," he said. "Not a music critic."

"One time, the real cops used to come and have coffee with me at the end of their shift. They thought I was gorgeous. They wanted to—"

"Marry you?" Smiley asked.

"Not hardly," Gia said. She leaned inside from her window box and grabbed her coffee. "Would you pretend that you can drink it just for a while, Smiley?"

"Of course, Miss Gia," he said. He said that every time. He always pretended to drink the coffee.

"Go on saying that, dear," she said. Miss Gia. Oh, dearie. Well, let me just get some stale Lorna Doones and lemon drops for you, dearie. How in Christ's name had she ever gotten so old? Not gray hair white. And the face of a half-boiled plucked chicken.

"Saying what, Miss Gia?"

"Miss Gia. It makes me feel young again. Everybody else calls me ma'am. Do you know when they started that, Smiley?"

"What is the difference between ma'am and miss?" Smiley asked.

"About twenty years, if you're lucky," Gia said. "I was lucky. They started in when I was about 35. And that was when I thought I was getting old."

"You're not that old, Miss Gia."

"Oh, Smiley," she said. "The kids tease me just like you! Can't you see the difference between me and those girls next door?" Gia gestured toward the two-story stucco apartment block on the other side of her courtyard.

Smiley's head swiveled all the way around. Gia watched the fake brown hair on the back of his stainless steel head whip like fine grass in the breeze as he scanned the apartment building. Smiley, much like the Man of Steel and Ray Milland in that old movie, had X-Ray vision.

"I don't know, Miss Gia. They're still in there sleeping. You have more energy than they do."

"I always had more energy!" Gia snapped. "But they're young, and gorgeous. I used to—"

"Your bone structure is wonderful," Smiley said.

Gia set her coffee cup down on the windowsill with a clatter. "Somebody said that when I was thirteen years old," she said.

"Did they have X-ray vision, too?" Smiley asked.

"Maybe it's true," she mused. The sun was very bright. The mountains were sharp in the distance, mottled gray and purple with veins of basalt and quartz; at this time of the year there was just a dusting of snow at their peaks. How she had loved them. As she had done often in recent days, she said a little prayer of thanks that she could still see them. And to herself, thought, "Goodbye, if I don't wake tomorrow. Goodbye."

For Gia was eighty-five years old, and when she stood too quickly, her heart fluttered in her chest. Everything hurt. All of the time. Her jeans hung on her hips as if the bones were clothespins. Once upon a time, she'd had gorgeous breasts, but she couldn't put that name to the things that had replaced them: flesh-colored baggies filled with Jell-O.

Did Smiley notice? Was he sorry for her, or repulsed, as so many were? She saw it in their faces. But they hated Smiley, too, she thought. They didn't like the way he looked, either.

Instead, she said, "Smiley, I used to love to dance. This is Madonna. She was famous."

"I know who that is," Smiley said. "I download *People* all the time. She died last year."

"Yeah," Gia said. "Smiley, don't remind me!"

"You could have had cosmetic surgery like she did," Smiley continued in a practical tone. His perpetual grin made it all sound so appealing and wholesome. "You have good bone structure. This is what they say she had."

So Smiley had "metal structure" and Madonna had gone out looking much like her idol Evita Peron, just a ninety-year old wax model from Madam Tussaud's. It was something like *Reanimator*, or Frankenstein's monster with real Scandinavian blonde hair implants.

"I like myself the way I am, Smiley," Gia said, swallowing painfully.

Was she going to cry? In front of this robot: how many times had he seen people cry?

She guessed that it didn't matter. He kept her happy.

"It's 11:30," Smiley said, checking his watch. He had an internal clock, but he wore clothes just like any cop. He told Gia that it helped him get along better. Made him more like a real cop. "I must go downtown now and patrol during the lunch hour. There has been some vandalism. Rollerblading ruffians."

"I heard," Gia said. On the city council feed. Two of the council members were the grandchildren of friends she'd known years ago. Smiley, don't go, she thought. Don't go. Every Tuesday and Thursday, he came. And for some time, he had been the only…person, she thought, foolishly…thing, with whom she spoke, or had any contact.

"I will see you next Tuesday," Smiley said. "If things are quiet, of course, Miss Gia."

Then he turned and walked away. He almost walked like a man.

"I thought today was Tuesday," Gia said, but Smiley was already at the end of the driveway, starting down the sidewalk.

Four days. Friday, Saturday, Sunday, Monday. She could wait.

On went the song. Don't tell me that love isn't true, it's just something that we do.

Haven't you had enough lovers, Gia? Enough flowers and candy? You weren't in Madonna's class, but then she wasn't that pretty, was she? They called you the most beautiful woman…the most beautiful…

Gia saw half her face reflected in the paned window as she shut it, shivering. Good bone structure. Very easy to see. Nobody needed X-ray vision. God, so cold. Always so cold. When the last man's been dead ten years; what is that? Three thousand six hundred fifty days? And every one of them a lonely waste.

"A mayfly dies in a day," she whispered. "But while he's at it, he's beautiful."

Let it fall by the way, baby…

She would have sung, she really would have, if her voice hadn't been such a godawful crone quaver.

"Smiley," she said instead to herself, "Smiley, how can a horrible old hag have feelings for a robot?" And asked herself, too, could a robot have feelings for anything—

∞

On Monday, Gia woke and padded to the kitchen, taking down her coffee canister. After a minute of fighting with the screw-on top, she broke down and searched the junk drawer for the plastic "round tuit" some politician had sent her. "Seniors vote for me!" was what it had said, or something like that. No self-respecting person would keep something like that. A flashing memory of her trying to open the aspirin bottle with her teeth, and her lower right molar shattering came to her. She used the "round tuit."

"Oh, no," she whispered. The jar was empty.

"Smiley's coming," she said. And she had no coffee. It didn't matter that Smiley couldn't and wouldn't drink it. It was the fact of offering it to him. She had to have coffee.

She logged on the net; they weren't due to deliver the groceries until Thursday, but maybe they would send the boy by today.

The fat man in the checkered apron appeared, just as always. "Good morning! It's Monday, January 22. How can we feed you?"

"I'm out of coffee, fat man," Gia said. Wait Monday. Monday! But it was Tuesday. Smiley was coming. It was Tuesday, wasn't it?

"Your delivery is scheduled for Thursday, January 25," the fat man said. "You are on the Senior Flex Plan. You will have..." He paused and the digital feed flickered in and out. He began to list the thirty-one items on Gia's weekly grocery delivery.

"Can't I get coffee today?" Gia asked. "I don't need the rest until Thursday."

The screen flickered in and out. "You are on the Senior Flex Plan," the fat man repeated. "Your delivery is scheduled for—"

"Oh, shit," Gia said, then she slammed her fist on the control pad. That hurt.

Senior Flex Plan. That meant she got what the government said she could get, once a week, at the exact same time. It was kind of like the way they used to give away Government Cheese and Butter. Only a boy brought the bags to your door and Gia had to stick her thumb on his nasty ID pad, just so Uncle Sam knew it was her. Sometimes the boy even carried them inside and put them on the counter for her. There was no way she could afford an extra delivery. It wasn't just the price of the coffee; fifteen bucks a pound or whatever it was now it was that they'd deliver "non-authorized" regular coffee like Folgers or something instead of USDA coffee, and that it would cost...she didn't know. On the city council feed the other night, people were complaining that deliveries were going up like crazy. What would it be? Thirty, forty bucks?

"Where's my purse?" she muttered.

Under her bed, of course.

And in her wallet, behind the pictures of her daughter Kathy and the kids, behind her ancient Red Cross blood donor card and her Official Member, Republican Party card, was a tightly-folded bill. Gia prized it out, and unfolded it.

Twenty dollars.

And Gerrard's was just up the street. Just up the—

Gia realized that she wasn't sure any more just how far Gerrard's Market was from her apartment. This was because it had been…

Two Christmases since she'd been out of the house. Not driving—God, no—not that. They took your license at seventy-five whether you wanted them to or not, but she hadn't walked outside for more than two years. The most she'd done was lean out of the front window, talking to Smiley. And staring at the passing people and cars.

She was getting mighty tired of staring at teenaged boys wearing pastel-colored polyester jumpsuits and girls in prairie dresses.

There was nothing wrong with her legs. She could walk. All she had to do was put one foot in front of the other. It would do her good, she thought. The fat man had said…Monday. Yes! Smiley was coming tomorrow, not today. She had all day. She could stop and rest under some of the big cypress trees she remembered, up on Center Street, on the way to Gerrard's.

By the time she got dressed, Gia was feeling less confident. She wrapped a striped silk scarf around her neck and tied a little bow. That looked ridiculous, like a wizened Katharine Hepburn trying to do Shirley Temple. She tucked the ends of the bow inside the scarf. There, that was better. More like just plain Katharine Hepburn. She toyed with the idea of bringing the scarf higher under her chin, and tying it around the top of her head. *Lion in Winter* Katharine Hepburn. No—more like somebody with a toothache. How had that old bag gotten away with it? With great care, she drew herself a mouth and painted it with her last decent lipstick. The last thing she wanted was one of those horrible old lady mouths, where they missed their lips by half an inch on either side.

The cane was in the closet behind the broom and dustpan. Gia got it out, and realized she was trembling from the effort.

Chin up! If she tied the scarf on her head the way she'd considered earlier, she couldn't help but have her chin up, so she did it. And then she was out the front door, fumbling with her keys. The keys were hanging on a hook by the stove. They were dusty and greasy.

The first block went well. Gia's chin was up. The morning air was sharp and clean. She didn't feel as though everyone was staring at her from their passing cars. It was after nine; there were no other walkers on her side of the street.

But by the time she reached the corner to turn toward Gerrards, she was out of breath, and her heart felt like a tiny vibrating sac of jelly in her chest. Her knees ached; her hips were making a frightening popping noise.

And she looked up Center Street and realized that it was ten or twelve blocks, instead of six. All uphill.

She crossed to the other corner, her small heart fluttering. As she went past the mortuary on the corner, a battered white truck pulled to a stop beside her.

"Where you going, lady?"

He did not look like a nice man.

"I'm out for a walk," Gia said, and she moved her legs faster. She gripped the head of her cane and held her purse close to her chest with her other hand.

"I'll give you a ride," he said, creeping along beside her in his rusted old bucket of a truck.

Gia stopped, lifted her cane, and said, "Fuck off!"

His watery blue eyes widened; the truck rattled as he gunned his engine and sped off.

After that, Gia felt better.

She was on a mission. She had to get coffee for Smiley. And it was good to walk, to be out in the fresh air. To see the pretty houses along the way. The trees, the well-kept lawns. My goodness, some of them even had little robots out there mowing. Weren't there any real gardeners anymore? When had that happened?

While she'd been sitting at home, rotting into nothing, was when.

Sometime later—it was after ten, so it meant that it took her more than an hour to get to Gerrards—she reached the market. About a block from the corner where the market had always been, Gia had become suddenly terrified that the store would be closed. Out of business. With the fat man and home deliveries, maybe nobody went to the market any more. Maybe they just—

But the lights were on; there were many cars in the parking lot.

The automatic doors opened and Gia stepped inside. She looked at the carts for a long moment. No you don't need a cart, she told herself. You have twenty bucks and you'll be lucky if you can afford a bag of coffee.

"Hello!" said the man who was piling bananas in the produce

department. Gia didn't recognize him, but he acted like he knew her.

"Hello," she said back, and her voice didn't even sound like her own voice. "I'm afraid could you tell me where the coffee is?"

The store looked different. All gourmet stuff. Weird a whole pile of silvery dried fish next to the apples. They still had their heads. Now the banana man was stacking blue spiky fruits that looked like something from Mars.

"Coffee? Well, it's next to the Sim Stim and Energy Drinks. Aisle Eight."

Sim Stim? Energy Drinks? People actually drank that, did they? She'd seen the commercials.

Gia's knees felt like they were going to buckle. Someone had abandoned a cart right beside her, so she grabbed it and took several deep breaths. Aisle eight. She could do it. Why, if she put her purse and the coffee in the cart, she could take it home that way. It was all downhill

Bag lady!

Never!

Aisle Eight started with the Super Ovaltine, then continued with a display of twenty different kinds of sugar (mostly calorie-free), then got into the Energy Drinks and Sim Stim. Yupi, Yogi, Vigor, Metabolite, Metaborama…it was endless. There was even one called Suck It Up. With an exclamation mark.

Down at the end of the aisle on the bottom shelf was the coffee. Gia saw the prices. The cheapest was a half-pound of Folgers. Twenty-two dollars.

She leaned over the cart. She wasn't going to cry. Maybe there was a display somewhere else. Maybe she could get a quarter-pound.

The banana man went by at the other end of the aisle. She called after him, but he didn't seem to hear her.

Then, after a moment, she saw him coming back the other way.

"Excuse me!" she called. "Is this all the coffee you have?"

He nodded.

"I don't have enough money," she said, swallowing hard.

He looked at her, puzzled, then said, "Why don't you use your card?"

"My what?"

"Your EBT card. I thought all older folks had a—"

Gia shook her head. "I don't know what that is," she said. That wasn't precisely true. She was pretty sure that she'd gotten one in the mail five years before, but she'd cut it up, just like she did every other credit card.

"You use it for a senior discount. Half off everything," he said. Then he laughed. "In fact, I was a little surprised you were in here today. Tomorrow is Senior Discount day. Every Tuesday. It's packed!"

"I get my groceries through the net," she said. "The fat man—"

"Ah," the banana man said. "Well, that's very convenient. But if you run out, then what will you do?"

"I did run out. I ran out of coffee. I'm expecting a guest tomorrow. I really wanted—"

"Oh my gosh," the banana man said. Then his face changed. "Ma'am, has it been a while since you've been, uh, shopping?"

Gia nodded. A lump had come up in the back of her throat. She was afraid that she was about to cry. He was so nice. His eyes were very kind. And she realized, aside from Smiley, the grocery boy, and the nasty truck man, this was the first person she'd talked with for months. Truth be told…years.

"Are you married?" she blurted. Then she covered her mouth.

"Yes, ma'am," the banana man said. "Twenty-two years. Two boys and a girl."

Gia smiled. "What a coincidence! That was my second marriage, almost that long. The…coffee costs twenty-two dollars. I only have a twenty. I guess I'm out of luck."

"You have grandkids, ma'am?" he asked.

Gia cleared her throat. "Uh, yes. Two. They live in Florida."

"Oh, that's a long way. I suppose you fly out to see them?"

Gia shook her head. "No," she said. "Never have." Kathy was on Welfare. It had been at least six months since she called. Kathy had never been much of a writer or a reader, either, so that was that for e-mail.

"Gosh, it is expensive," he said. "If you don't have the EBT card and all; senior discount's seventy-five percent now, I hear."

Why in the hell had she cut up that card? Why hadn't anybody told her what the card was in the first place?

"I…I think I got that card," Gia said. "I cut it up. I thought it was another credit card that I didn't need. I only get seven hundred a month."

The banana man's eyes widened. "What?"

"I said I only get seven hundred—"

"My gosh, ma'am," he said. "Everybody went up to fifteen hundred two years ago. What in the heck happened with you?"

Gia fumbled with her purse. Maybe if she showed him her ID card, he'd see how…no, then he'd see exactly how old she was. She straightened her scarf instead.

"I don't know," she said. And that was the truth.

"You should have an advocate," he said. "My mom's seventy-five and she swears by hers. Don't you have somebody who comes and visits? Makes sure you have everything you need and your benefits are straight?"

"No," Gia said. She'd never heard of such a thing. Nobody came. Nobody visited. Except…

"There is somebody," she said.

"Well, sure," the banana man said. "All older people have one."

"He's a police officer," she said. "He comes every Tuesday and Thursday. That's why I want the coffee. He's coming tomorrow. I always like to have coffee for him."

The banana man nodded, then his eyes narrowed. "He's a cop? You should have your EBT card, ma'am, and be getting twice what you've got. Why, I can't imagine how anybody'd be able to get by on seven hundred. Fifteen hundred's bad enough these days!"

"I can see," Gia said. "With coffee twenty-two dollars for half a pound!"

"Let me tell you something," the banana man said. "You tell that officer friend of yours to take an interest in your affairs. And look here," he said, picking up one of the nicer packages of coffee, at forty-five dollars. "You take this home with my compliments. We aim to take care of our older customers here."

"I…can't," Gia whispered. She pushed the shiny bag of coffee back at him.

"Yes, you can," he said. "I don't like to see older people doing without."

He didn't want to see an old hag suffering? Gia couldn't speak. She reached in her purse and took out the twenty.

"Here," she said. "For the coffee. Maybe you can break up the package. I don't—"

"You're taking it," he said, laughing. "For heaven's sake, keep that little bit of money you have. You might want a bite to eat on the way home."

He put the money in her purse firmly, then he put his hand in the small of her back and gave her a gentle push toward the front of the store. The three women who were checking smiled at her and waved. Gia was smiling, too, by the time she left. Her legs didn't hurt quite so much as she got to the edge of the parking lot. She paused by the concrete wall that surrounded the lot and looked back at the store. The banana man had stood near the door, watching her, but he was gone. After she caught her breath, she started out of the lot, but then she heard something coming up behind her. Fast.

Whirring wheels. A scraping noise. Loud voices.

She never saw the two coming up behind her, but she saw the fat boy and his ugly friends right away. And got the fat one with her cane, right across the face.

One of the skinny, ugly ones with him started laughing. "She's just an old lady! You let an old lady whack you!" He started to skate around her, fast.

Gia slashed viciously at him with her keys and cane, missing by a foot. The keys were in her hand, laced between her fingers.

"Fire!" she screamed. "Fire!" But her voice wouldn't carry. Couldn't carry. She was eighty-five years old and a hundred yards from the store. With all the people. People who might...

"Gimme that," the skinny one snarled. He lunged at her.

She held her purse close to her chest, and the bag of coffee. She couldn't let them have the coffee!

"What you got in there, Preparation H?"

"Ensure?"

Then she heard giggles behind her and realized that there were more of them. What Smiley said...these were the rollerblading ruffians! They looked ridiculous to her, in their pastel blue, yellow and pink polyester jumpsuits and big black skates. The fat boy looked like he had some money, with slicked-back orange hair and big, shiny skates with rockets on them. She had hurt him. He was kneeling, holding his cheek.

"Goddamn old bitch!" he said. He sounded like he had a speech impediment.

The others were circling around her, like they were waiting for something. Maybe for her to cry, or beg for mercy.

"Come on, lady, just hand over your junk. We won't hurt you," the thin, acne-covered one said.

"Screw off," she said, but she was trembling. Then she yelled "Fire!"

"Shut her up!" the fat one said, struggling to his feet. "Somebody's going to come out of that store and see!"

The skinny one lunged at her and this time, Gia could not strike out, because her cane had gone flying. He had her purse, tugging viciously. If she could just hold her ground, maybe he'd fall. Her heart felt like a bird trying to fly out of her rib cage.

"No!" she cried.

He gave another tug and Gia felt her legs giving. Her shoulder hit the ground hard, then her hip.

Something crumbled.

"Smiley, help me!" she cried.

Through tear-blurred eyes, she watched the others lean over her. Five or more. Somebody kicked her. They were laughing, screaming things that she couldn't understand. Her purse flew away, up into the air. Dimly, she realized that her arm had snapped, and that there was blood. A lot of it. Something was coming out of her arm. Out of her sweater.

She closed her eyes. She was no longer afraid, not particularly, but she wished that it didn't hurt so much. She wished they'd just finish and go, but by the time she heard footsteps and raised voices from somewhere beyond the circle of her torturers, she was no longer able to see, even when she opened her eyes.

The skates scraped roughly all around her. She heard the roar of the fat boy's skate-rockets. Smelled something burning.

"Smiley," she whispered.

"My God," she heard somebody saying. "Those bastards! If that was my son, I'd kill him."

"Call the cops!"

"Jesus Christ on a stick, call the MedicAlert!"

"The poor little gal," she heard somebody saying. She thought it must be the banana man. "The poor, poor little gal."

Then everything was black and quiet.

It was like one big dream. And it went on and on. Sometimes Gia was interrupted by a stranger with food; and that horrible monster of a nurse with a mustache who wanted to "bathe her." At these times, she remembered that she'd been terribly hurt, and that something awful had happened to her, but mercifully, these times were brief, and she slipped back into the happy dreams she had. Mostly she thought about her favorite lovers, and sometimes her friends. She went bowling. She bathed Kathy, and dried her hair with a soft towel while the little girl giggled. She ate a grilled cheese sandwich, and it was buttery and crisp, the cheese oozing out the sides.

So bad for you, she thought. So very bad to eat so much grease and fat all at once.

Then she ate a grapefruit. Some of it struck her in the eye. Steve, her second husband, the one with the thick, curly red hair, wiped off the juice, then he kissed her. He slipped his arms around her waist and she wanted to cry.

Her eyes fluttered open a brief moment.

She heard voices from somewhere outside her room. It was a madhouse, of course. She was in an asylum, and they'd drugged her up and tied her to the bed. She couldn't move either her arms or legs.

"I am here to see Miss Gia," somebody said.

"I'm sorry, it's family only," came the curt reply. A woman's voice: cold and careless.

"Her family is far away. I have contacted the daughter. The daughter will not come." Gia thought she recognized the voice. There was something about it. Strange, low and measured. Too calm. A very odd voice.

"We still can't allow you to see her," the nasty woman's voice replied.

"I will obtain a warrant," the first voice said. "I will return to search the room."

"Well!" the woman exclaimed. "I never!"

"Sorry to have upset you, ma'am." Gia heard the woman's footsteps receding.

Gia drifted away into more dreams. She heard a man calling her. "Miss Gia…Miss Gia…"

She was eating papaya and squirting lemon on it. A bird flew past her window. Then a ball. Kathy was playing outside.

There was something cold on her arm. Again, her eyes fluttered open and she looked up to see a smooth, blue metal face smiling down at her.

"I have come to see you, Miss Gia. The youths who attacked you are in custody."

"I…see…" she croaked. Who was this creature? Some nut in a Tin Man suit!

"Help!" she cried. It came out sounding like somebody was crumpling paper.

"I am here," the creature said. "You are safe."

"Help!" she cried again, struggling in her bed. My God, they had strapped her arms down! And legs, too!

"Miss Gia, it is me, Smiley. Officer Smiley."

"You're crazy," she said in her dry, half-whisper. "There's a crazy man attacking me!"

Now there were two smooth metal hands on her shoulders and the strange metal face was grinning at her, right in front of her face. She shut her eyes.

The slow, calm voice continued. "Six teenagers attacked you. The rollerblading gang. I have apprehended them. They are in custody. They cannot hurt you anymore."

Gia tasted something nasty in her mouth. She heard the rush of a rocket, saw a faint flash of black skates. Then she remembered a fat, ugly face, with bright orange hair. Boys, wearing awful polyester jumpsuits, skating around wildly. Hurting her!

"Why did you walk to the store, Miss Gia? Why did you not tell me you needed help? You could have called any time. I am on duty twenty-four hours a day."

She opened her eyes. The face was still looming, and still grinning. She remembered.

"Smiley," she whispered. And at once, her whole body hurt. She felt a deep stab of shame. Why, she hadn't even remembered the right day—she hadn't had to go out for coffee at all. Not then. Not on that day. "I wanted to get you coffee," she said, voice full of remorse. "The man at the store told me so many things. I didn't know—" her voice trailed away. Her throat was raw agony.

"I obtained a special warrant from Judge Morris to see you. I am supposed to search this room," Smiley said.

"Judge…Morris…" Gia whispered. Could that be her Judge Morris, who she'd known once upon a time, forty years before?

"He told me that he knew you once, long ago," Smiley said. "He told me to look after you. You are famous, Miss Gia. Your picture is on the netfeed even today, because of what happened."

"Famous like Madonna," Gia said.

"Yes," Smiley said. "Just like Madonna."

"So go ahead and search," Gia said.

Smiley did not reply. Instead, he pulled a gray plastic chair close to her bed and sat down. Then he took her hand and stroked her palm lightly with his cool metal fingers.

"There is a nurse here," he said. "The nurse stated that you should be dead."

Gia turned away from Smiley. "I remember," she said. "Why am I still alive?"

"I told the nurse that she did not know you. You are a strong woman, Miss Gia. That is why you are not dead."

"Smiley," Gia said into the pillow. "Smiley, that sounds like something a person would say. Not a—"

"Not a robot?" he asked. "Miss Gia, I want to say so many things to you."

"We had good talks," she said.

"Yes, Miss Gia," he said. His hand gripped hers. It hurt, a little, but that pain was nothing compared to what she felt in the rest of her body. Her arm...she saw the big white cast. And her body was in a cast, too. She must have broken her hip. When the kid knocked her down. She remembered well when her arm had snapped. And there was something funny about her head, too. She guessed they'd broken her head, too. How on earth had she survived?

She forced herself to turn back to Smiley. He was still grinning that idiot grin. In a sharp bit of pain that had nothing to do with her body, and everything to do with her heart, she saw him for what he was now, a blocky, shiny, blue metal robot with an absurd, ever-smiling face. Just a robot. What kind of lunatic would think that a robot would make a fine friend? Even...fall in love...with a robot?

Tears stung her eyes. Tracked viciously down her cheek and into the corner of her mouth.

"I'm a pitiful old woman," she said. "I lived...lived in a crazy fantasy world all my life. My own daughter doesn't even care about me."

"No," Smiley said. "You taught me many things, Miss Gia."

"Smiley," she said, her voice quavering. "Let me be. I just want to get out of here" and she looked around the ugly gray-white hospital room, turning her head painfully.

Then, from somewhere deep inside, she cried, "Go tell that nurse to unplug me! Get me out of here! Give the bed to somebody who needs it!"

"No," Smiley said. He was out of the chair. His hands returned to her shoulders. "You should stay. There are machines. Nanos. They can make you young again. Heal your broken parts. You can have the surgery that Madonna had. She could have lived forty or fifty years more. She just forgot to take her—"

Gia stopped him, remembering the story. "I would forget to take my pills too, Smiley," she said in a calmer voice.

"I would help you remember," he said.

"Smiley," she whispered. "Smiley, you're a robot. And I'm very old. I don't want to be something I'm not."

"Miss Gia, I have so much to learn. You were teaching me. You can't—"

"I just want out," she said. "People aren't like you. We don't have parts that can just be replaced."

"Miss Gia!" Smiley was now leaning all the way over her, looming. "Yes, they do. Yes, they can. I earn fifteen thousand dollars a month. This is a Federal law. Robot cops must be paid the same as all other officers, including overtime."

Gia had to admit, it was a lot of money. "You work all the time," she said. "What on earth do you spend this on?"

"Nothing," he said. "I am a rich robot. I can spend as I choose. And I choose to spend this money on you."

Gia laughed. It was very painful. Then she looked at the thick black straps tethering her arms. There were more beneath the covers, holding down her legs.

"Smiley, don't waste your time talking about money," she said. "Just let me loose."

"What? Let you" His head swiveled. He hesitated.

"Undo these straps. They're hurting me."

"Yes, Miss Gia," he said. In a moment, her arms were free, though the one in the cast lay uselessly on the covers. She lifted the arm that would cooperate, and brushed her fingers against his smooth metal cheek.

"You're very sweet," she said. "You make me feel better."

He shook his head.

"If you do care about me, you'll help me," she whispered.

"I don't understand," he said, very slowly. "If I pay for these procedures, you will be well. You can look young again, Miss Gia. You're not like me. You can change."

Something stuck in her throat. Hard and unyielding. She found it difficult to swallow, and even more difficult to speak.

"I don't…don't really want that. I just want to—" She thought for a long while. Fought for the words.

"I want to feel like a human being again," she said. "You don't know what it's like to feel like you're not even human any more, and that no one in the whole world, not a single person, even cares if you're alive or dead. I want to feel like a human being, with someone near me who cares."

Smiley was silent. He slid one of his strong metal arms beneath her shoulders, and lifted her up in the bed.

Then he leaned close, and pressed his cool metal cheek against her face, like a child. "I do know how that feels, Miss Gia," he said. "I am a robot. And only you ever cared what happened to me or what I did."

"Smiley," she cried, and her chest felt warm and cold, all at the same time.

After a moment, he raised one hand, and wiped the tears from her cheek. "I will do as you say," he said.

"Take me out," she said. "Carry me out, and lay me in a bed of roses. I want to see them. I love them."

"I will," Smiley said. "They will not stop me."

And she knew that he meant it.

"I want to tell you something about life," she whispered in Smiley's ear. He was so strong. Gia, who had been carried over the threshold or hurled into a bed or onto a couch many times in her life, had never been carried in quite such a way, by quite such a powerful man. And that was how she saw him now—a man made of metal, certainly. Her Smiley.

"I want to see the roses," she said.

"Yes, Miss Gia."

"I wish you could smell them," she said.

"I am a robot," he said. "I cannot."

"You're a man, too," she said. "And a man could."

He paused just before the elevator. "Thank you, Miss Gia," he said.

Behind them, the nurses clamored. Gia had paid no attention to them whatsoever except to glare at the mustachioed nurse who had tortured her with "bathing."

"We've called security! You may have had a warrant, robot, but you can't do this!"

"I am doing this," Smiley said, turning slightly toward them.

Then, to Gia, he said, "I wish to smell the roses."

She nestled her head against his huge metal bicep, smiling. They entered the elevator. The nurses hung back; Gia realized that they were afraid of Smiley.

When the elevator doors opened, two hospital security men greeted them, their service revolvers drawn.

"I'm releasing myself from the hospital," Gia told them.

"We're going to have to ask you to take her back," one of the men said to Smiley. "We don't want to hurt anybody, but you're breaking all the regulations."

"What's got into you, tin man?" the other one demanded.

Smiley merely strode forward, brushing the one on his right aside if he was a mannequin. The man sprawled on the floor, eyes wide. The other one turned, keeping his gun trained on Smiley.

"If you discharge your weapon, you will probably injure Miss Gia. I cannot allow that," Smiley said. He paused. Then, he said, "You will certainly not injure me."

"Stop right there, robot!" the security man called.

Smiley shifted, putting all of Gia's weight on one arm. It hurt—a lot—being held this way. She heard an amazing popping sound. Had the gun gone off?

The man screamed. Gia realized that Smiley had simply crushed the gun in his left hand. That had been the popping noise. Parts flying off.

The one on the floor was scrambling to his feet. Aiming his gun. Good Lord, the fool wasn't going to shoot, was he?

"You may follow us," Smiley said. "But have some respect. I am taking Miss Gia to the roses."

"Damn!" the first officer cried. "Damn it all. They'll send you back to the bit-bucket, you crazy robot!"

"I am prepared to defend my actions," Smiley said. "I am aware that there is a review process."

"Tony, call the cops!" the second officer yelled. "We can't do anything with him."

"I'll melt you down myself, you stupid robot! You dumb piece of shit—they'll come down here and pull your plug."

Smiley was nearly at the exit. The big automatic sliding windows opened.

"I did not draw my weapon," Smiley said, turning back to the two security men. "You drew yours."

Gia saw a good-sized group of nurses coming out of the elevator, along with other people—orderlies and even a couple who looked like they were from the kitchen.

"There they go!" one of the group called out. "Where's he taking her?"

The whole crowd followed them into the parking lot. Gia noticed with pleasure that they stayed quite some distance back. Far enough away that no one could hear what she said to Smiley, or what he said to her. It was getting difficult to see, and she was one mass of agony from head to toe.

"Smiley, I don't feel very well," she said softly. "You should hurry."

"Yes, Miss Gia," he said. "I will try. Where are the roses? I did not see them coming in."

Gia had been to the hospital more times than she cared to think about, in the years when she was still getting out of the house. That was where nearly all of her friends had died, save those few who slipped and fell at home, or had a heart attack in bed. In the back, there was a big rose garden, with dozens of plants all in neat rows. The first bloom should have come on them. She prayed this would be so.

"There's a garden behind the big building," she told Smiley. Then she closed her eyes and tried to dream the pain away, but she couldn't. Dozens of people made a lot of noise walking around, even if they were fifty yards away.

"Smiley, I wish they would go away," she said as he strode steadily around the side of the hospital.

"They will not," he said. "You are a famous person because of the attack."

"Like Madonna," she said.

Smiley made a little coughing noise. For a moment, Gia could have sworn that he laughed.

"I see the flowers," he said.

"Are they…blooming?" She thought that she could smell them.

"Yes," he said. "All colors."

"Name them for me," she said, because it was too difficult to open her eyes.

"They are yellow, Miss Gia. White. Red. Pink."

"Can't you do any better than that? Use that brain they stuck in you!"

"Miss Gia," he said. And there was the strangest sound in his voice. "I will try."

∞

And Smiley spoke to her of the roses. Gia was very weak now. His voice came to her as if from a distant room. He told her of the pink ones, with yellow edges, the color of a sunrise over the mountains, and of the pure white ones, like a soft dove's wings, and the deep, crisp red ones, the color of a young girl's heart.

"That's Mister Lincoln," she whispered.

"Mister…"

"The darkest red roses are always Mister Lincoln," she said. "And the white ones are John F. Kennedy."

"They are Presidents," Smiley said. "They both died when men shot them."

"Yes," Gia said. She felt something changing. Her body shook. The world seemed like it turned upside down for a moment, and in a great burst of pain, she opened her eyes. Smiley was kneeling beside the rose garden. She was resting on his lap.

"I have never shot a man," Smiley said. His silver hand reached out to pick one of the roses. A pink one, so lovely, with pale yellow barely brushed on the tips of the curling petals. He brought it close to her face, and the perfume came to her.

"When a person dies," he said quietly, "Do they plant a rose for them?"

Gia heard, but could not see, the crowd gathered behind them. She did not want them there. Only Smiley. He seemed to understand what she was thinking. "They cannot see you," he said. "I am covering you. Protecting you."

She sighed.

"Miss Gia," he said. "There is something inside of me. It feels strange. It…hurts."

"The robot's doing something to her. He's gone crazy!" someone from the crowd yelled.

"I have never shot a man," Smiley said, much more loudly. He said this to the crowd, Gia realized. "I do not plan to do so now." She heard noises; they were moving away. In the distance, there were sirens.

"Smiley," she whispered. "Just be with me."

He was grinning down at her. "I am trying…not to smile…" he said.

"But you must," she said. "That's the way you were made."

"That is not the way I am," he said. "I am not smiling inside. Inside, Miss Gia, I am crying. Like when they yell at me, and when they hit me."

"Men don't cry," she said.

"I am not a man," he said. Then, his hand rose in a flash. She saw the metal fingers form into a fist. And he hit himself, square in the jaw. He looked down at her, and she saw that one corner of his mouth had fallen.

"Smiley! You hurt yourself!"

"It does not hurt there," he said. "It hurts in here." And he pressed her head against his chest.

"My God," she said, wondering. "Smiley…"

His fist flashed again, and he struck himself once more. Now both corners of his mouth pointed downward. It looked so strange; he had damaged himself very much. It would cost a lot to repair, she thought. Oh, poor Smiley! With the last bit of energy she had, she reached upward, so slowly, with so much pain, and put her fingers against his broken mouth.

"The crazy robot's hitting himself! Now he's going to hit her," a man's voice cried. The people were closer. She smelled them. Heard them.

"Stay away!" Smiley said in his most commanding voice. He lowered his head, brushing his face against her fingers, and she realized that with his broken mouth, this was how he was able to kiss.

"I will miss you," she said. She felt sleepy. There came a rushing in her ears. And there were roses all about her. She felt covered with their rich, sweet scent, felt the softness of the petals.

"I have made the bed for you, Miss Gia," Smiley said.

She looked up at him one last time, at his crazed, crooked face—no trace of a smile remaining—and closed her eyes.

"For you, I will cry," he said. "I do not yet know how, but I will learn. For you, I will plant a rose. I will drink coffee."

"Always to learn," she said. "That's what life is, Smiley. Coffee will rot your insides."

"Yes, Miss Gia," he said very quickly and his voice sounded so strange, and far away. "Love is something that we feel. Hurt is something that we feel, and to be alive is to feel."

And she felt his metal hands gently caressing her, lifting her.

"I must take you back now," he said.

"No," she muttered. "No."

"Yes," Smiley said.

He lifted her, and she was covered with petals.

"I am taking her back," Smiley said. Gia understood that he was not speaking to her. They were amid the crowd. The people parted. Smiley strode through, and Gia's eyes fluttered open.

There was a cop there, a real one, and his revolver was drawn. "Put the old lady down," he said. His partner was right beside him, half-crouched, with a shotgun.

"I'm not," Gia whispered. Not an old lady.

"I am taking her into the hospital," Smiley said. "I have done nothing wrong."

"Put her down, Officer, or you'll be decommissioned right now." But the cop's voice was softer. Gia could barely see his face, but she thought that something about his expression had changed.

"We don't want to shoot you," the second cop said. "Just... whatever's going on...you've got to let the old woman go." He was much younger, and gentler, than the first one.

Then the first cop relaxed. "What did you do to your face, Officer?" he asked.

"He's crazy!" a man yelled from the crowd. "He smashed his face. He was going to—"

"That's enough!" the first officer cried, silencing the man.

"What happened to your face?" the second officer said, very softly.

"I could no longer smile," Smiley said.

"He was trying to kill the old lady!" the insistent man in the crowd said.

Gia felt Smiley tightening. Hardening. His head turned. "You will stop calling her that. Her name is Miss Gia. She is a human being."

"Yes, she is, Officer," said the first cop. "And you could have killed her."

Smiley relaxed. At that moment, the first officer lowered his revolver. He nodded toward the second officer, who pointed the barrel of his shotgun toward the pavement.

"You're in a lot of trouble," the second officer said.

"I had a search warrant," Smiley replied.

The officers looked at each other, amazed.

"Now I will take Miss Gia back. She will get better. She will take treatments. I will pay for them."

"What kind of treatments they got for being a hundred and fifty?" said someone in the crowd. Gia tried to see who it was, but she could not.

"She wanted to see the roses," Smiley said to the first officer. "I did as she asked."

The officer nodded. Gia thought that his face looked very strange, as if he was thinking, very hard, and it hurt him to do that. "Let's all go back," he said. He put his hand on Smiley's arm.

Smiley was still hard and unyielding. "I will not leave her."

"Officer," Gia said, and it felt like she was barely making any sound, "I would like a rose. For my room."

Smiley started to turn.

"No," she said. "The other officer." And she inclined her head toward the young cop with the shotgun. He stood awkwardly, not moving.

The first cop turned toward him. "Pick one, Dave," he said. "Make it a nice one."

"Pink and yellow," Gia whispered. But he did not hear her. She saw him moving toward the red roses, then hesitating, and reaching for a white one.

"She says pink and yellow," Smiley said. At that moment, four more cops came trotting up.

"What the hell is Dave doing?" one of them demanded.

It hurt too much to smile. Laughter was impossible, but Gia nestled in Smiley's arms. The older cop shrugged and the new arrivals stood, hesitating.

"He's picking a rose. For the lady," the first cop said.

"Dispatch said Smiley's gone rogue," one of the group said.

"We're escorting her back upstairs," the first cop said.

"The crazy bucket of bolts!" one of the others cried, stepping forward. His revolver was still drawn.

"Put that down!" the first cop commanded. "This isn't the shootout at the hospital parking lot. We're going to escort this lady back inside. Us, and the officer here."

"Thank you," Smiley said. "I am not a bucket of bolts."

The cop glared at him. "You're writing the report," he said. "Or I'm kicking your tin-can ass!"

"Don't listen to him, Smiley," Gia whispered as she and Smiley and the group of cops made their way through the crowd. "Your ass is cute. I always liked it."

"You are better already," Smiley said.

"Smiley, I wanted to die," Gia said.

"I know, Miss Gia," he said. "And now I will tell you my secret."

"What?" she whispered. They entered the elevator. The cops piled in, and in the jostling, Smiley leaned close to her and spoke very softly.

"Until today," Smiley said, "So did I."

"What was that?" the first officer asked.

Smiley waited a moment. "I told Miss Gia that today I thought that I could touch the sky."

"Pretty damn poetic," the cop said, clearing his throat. The younger officer leaned close and put the pink and yellow rosebud on Gia's chest.

"Pretty poetic for a robot," Gia said.

"I was thinking it was pretty poetic for a cop," the officer replied.

"God damn it!" Smiley cried. "I can't smile."

"Yes," Gia said. "Yes, you can."

And that was all.

More Lasting Than Bronze

Judith Tarr

Zachariah Frazee stopped to breathe. The hill was not the worst he had climbed on this journey without apparent end, but each new escarpment of this brutal country took a greater toll of his failing strength. He clung to the mule's pack saddle and wheezed, and did his best not to despair.

The animal ignored him, cropping the pungent greasewood that grew in patches on the hilltop. He had regrets about the horse he had left in Tombstone, sold to the livery stable for a price even his innocence knew was criminally low. But a horse was an extravagance he could no longer afford, unlike the mule, who could survive on thin forage and scant water, and still carry such odds and bits as Zachariah needed to keep body and soul together while he hunted down a myth.

The Indian women at the spring had told him he was close. Their men were out God knew where, massacring settlers for all he knew, but the band of women and children had welcomed him without fear or apparent hate. They refrained from laughing openly at his attempts to speak Apache, and assured him in perfectly adequate English that "the mother of iron" was no more than a day's walk.

The one who spoke for them added, "She hides herself well. Look for the cloud over the mountain, and the earth that drops away."

He had been trudging for hours toward the peak that wore a lens of cloud like a lady's hat. His breath was nearly gone. He would have to stop, regardless of either urgency or the day's heat, and hope that once he had, he would be able to start again.

As if in response to his thought, the mule, which had pulled ahead of him while he dithered, stopped abruptly. Its long ears were upright and quivering.

He looked down. And down and down.

It was just as the woman had said. The earth opened at the mule's feet. There below was a deep cut, a gash in the barren earth. But through it and past it he saw light, and a shimmer of green.

∞

Without the mule he would never have reached the bottom, or half stumbled, half clung to the pack saddle down the length of the canyon. At the end of it he looked out on the impossible.

The green was the green of this desert West, true enough, yellowed with dust and relentless sunlight. But there was so much of it. He stared down an alley of cottonwoods in full leaf, standing along the bank of a stream that bubbled up out of the earth. It meandered along a sandy trail toward a structure that would not have looked out of place in the wealthier enclaves of Boston or Philadelphia.

The wall that surrounded it looked as if it had grown in this place, rooted in the stony earth, rising sheer like the mountains that rimmed the desert. Parts were built of the native stone, dun and gray with a hint of rusted iron. Parts put him in mind of the pueblos he had seen scattered around this country, some inhabited by the living, some only by dust and ghosts.

In the center nestled the most modern of mansions, a veritable painted lady, blue and gold and mauve and ocher, as intricate as a house made of gingerbread. Its windows gleamed in the old-gold light of late afternoon. A weathervane rose from its cupola, a raven perched on an arrow made of black iron and pointed, it seemed to him in that astonished instant, direct toward his heart.

Movement drew his eye back to earth. A—person—had come round one of the many corners, moving a little too smoothly, a little too fluidly, with a faint whirring of gears and the faintest metallic clanking.

It was a mechanical, beautifully made, in a black frock coat. Its smooth metal face regarded him with blank equanimity. The voice that issued from its speaking grille was as smooth as the face, genderless and perfectly modulated. "Welcome."

Zachariah's mind was blank. He had taken care to have no expectations, but now he faced the great flaw of his planning: he could not imagine how to respond.

The mechanical's face was not designed to show emotion, and yet the lift of its hand and the tilt of its head spoke to Zachariah of understanding. "Come," it said.

He stayed where he was. The mule tugged at the rein, straining toward a patch of rye grass.

"She will be tended," the mechanical said.

Still Zachariah hesitated. The mule jerked the rein out of his hand and settled to graze.

That was clear enough. He paused to slip the bit and loop the rein out of the way, then turned toward the mechanical, which was standing perfectly still. "I'm ready," he said.

The mechanical turned without a word and led him up the steps toward the door of the house.

∞

Coolness wafted toward him, blissful after the heat of the day. He breathed deep of it, forgetting for a moment why that was inadvisable, before the air caught in his failing lungs and tore.

He sank down with eerie slowness. He felt the hands that raised him, felt the movement as they carried him, saw a dance of shadows and whispers. His body drifted away, gasping and wheezing and coughing blood as dark as wine.

A faint thread bound him to it, but the rest of him wandered through a maze of rooms and corridors and ramps and stairs and, here and there, a ladder leading upward or downward into darkness or sudden light. There was no end to it, and no logic that he could discern, unless it were dream logic.

Sometimes the stairs led to new levels of the house, and sometimes to a blank wall or empty space. Doors opened on nothingness; windows looked inward to a room without a door. Once he entered an elegant parlor, looked up and saw open sky.

Everywhere he went, he seemed to be alone. But shadows flitted on the edge of sight, and whispers tantalized him with words he could not quite understand, fragments of verse or song in languages he barely knew.

At last he came to a place that was almost painful in its mundanity. It was a room of some size, with bare walls of the mud brick that was so common in this country, and dark beams holding up a smoke-darkened roof. All around it sat and stood and lay the impedimenta of a mechanist's workshop.

There were machines in all stages of construction, and mechanicals both complete and incomplete, the former arranged in glass cases like an exhibition at a museum. Zachariah might have paused to examine them, but the dream swirled him away, depositing him in the center of the room, where the mechanist himself bent over his labor.

As soon as Zachariah had thought that, he realized his error. The heavy apron concealed much of the mechanist's form, but the hair caught up in a net that gleamed like woven steel was a thick knot of braided black and silver. The cheeks beneath the welder's goggles were smooth, and the hands at work amid the tangle of wires and gears, while not particularly small or delicate, had a lightness of touch that was rare among the male of the species.

He could not tell what she was making: it was much too small for the usual run of mechanical servants. A pet perhaps, such as had been all the rage in Boston when last he was there. He had seen the most delightful little bronze sausage of a dog, which—

He reined himself back from that flight of fancy. The mechanist fit wire to wire and gear to gear, meticulously, even her breathing matched to the movements of those long skillful fingers. It was mesmerizing, though he understood not at all what she was doing. It drew him in, captivated him, till the whole world was wire and gears.

The fingers drew back. A soft click echoed in the silence. One by one, in a dance of brass and copper and steel, the gears began to turn.

They seemed to draw the light to them, capturing and holding it with a most peculiar buzzing hum. He spun in the center of it, faster and faster, until he shrank to a speck and abruptly went out.

$$\infty$$

Zachariah's body was dying. That was nothing new: it had been fading before he came West. But when he opened his eyes on a room in a stranger's house—and not for the first time, if he acknowledged the truth—his reckoning had shifted sharply. He would not leave this place as a living man.

The mechanical that had welcomed him at the gate was sitting by a window through which slanted a long shaft of golden light.

"Evening again?" Zachariah asked it.

It bent its head. The light gleamed on the polished bronze of its skull. It rose with peculiar grace and helped Zachariah to sit up. Then it held a cup to his lips.

He paused for an instant, but shook his head, half rueful, half heedless. If the thing had come to poison him, it would have done so while he was insensible. He yielded and drank.

The elixir tasted of flowers and honey and, to his surprise, wakefulness. His body's lassitude was no less, but his mind came sharply awake. He saw the dance of dust in the sunlight, caught the faint scent of oil and warm bronze, heard the light firm tread of the woman who came to stand by his bed.

On his long journey he had composed a pretty little speech full of careful compliments, with meticulously calibrated doses of admiration for achievements that were, in certain circles, renowned, and rounding off with the reason for his coming, the humbly bold request: "I am a journalist, a mere and plebeian scribbler, but I have some small pretension to scholarship, and a sincere devotion to truth. It would be my honor, my very great honor, to tell your tale to the world. If you would but spare me an hour of your time—"

The words never passed his lips. The oddity he had come to find, the lady of legendary wealth and pedigree who chose to immure herself in a remote canyon of the wild and desolate West, in a house that she had built and continued to build and would never cease building, because to stop would be to tempt forces that even rumor could neither imagine nor define—now that he was here, in her presence, he understood too much, and nothing at all.

Her eyes were the color of blued steel, in a face to which beauty was irrelevant. They fixed him with a clear and steady stare.

He bowed as best he could, and said, "Zachariah Frazee, madam. At your service. And you are, I believe, the Honorable Hypatia Folger-Meddowes?"

"Not of late," she answered in a voice of remarkable depth and sweetness, with an accent somewhere between Boston and Windsor. "What would you be, then? Process server? Adventurer? Thief?"

"Scribbler," he said, shocked into matching her directness. "Journalist, if you will, madam. I came to find a story. A rumor, legend—this house—"

"Thief, then," she said, but without apparent ill temper, "come to steal my peace. Who betrayed me?"

He set his lips together.

As did she, but still without anger or great annoyance. "Ah," she said. "Well. It doesn't matter, does it? The world will hardly beat its way to this door."

"It is a long and trackless way," he acknowledged. "Which is remarkable, considering" His hand took in the house, the furnishings, the mechanical standing mute by the wall.

"Perseverance is a virtue," Miss Meddowes said. She sat in a chair that had not been there an instant before, nor had it or the mechanical moved, that Zachariah could see. But time was stretching oddly, perhaps from the drug, perhaps from his nearness to the next world.

The drug, and that nearness, loosened his tongue. "I heard that you built this house for the spirits, to atone for the sins of your ancestors. I heard that you tend a spring that confers immortality, and that you guard the gates of the sacred cities of Cibola, and that you are the last true heir of Mr. Babbage and Lady Lovelace. I heard so many stories, tumbling over one another, as if one name could take on the power of any fool's fancy. So I came," he said, "to find the truth of it. Because when all else is gone, when life and death themselves have shrunk to nothing, all that is left is the truth."

The flood of words receded abruptly, leaving him gasping, wheezing for what breath was left him. She sat still. His clouded vision could not make out her expression, but it seemed to him that the silence had a certain edge of weary indulgence. Or perhaps amusement.

At length she spoke, and her tone was wry. "Of Cibola I know little enough, though the people of this country say there are pueblos to the north that had a great plague of Spaniards, all of them hungry for gold. The spring you passed by if you came from the southwest. It nourishes the people and animals of the region, and it never runs dry. But I never knew anyone to come away from it with eternal life."

Zachariah could attest to that. He had drunk from the spring, and found the water cold and sweet. But his life was fading all too quickly.

"The other, then," he said, faint but carefully clear. "Mr. Babbage —Lady Lovelace—"

"Indeed," she said.

He peered at her through the crowding shadows. "That is the most wondrous of all the tales. And this—" He tilted his head toward the mechanical "is a wonder of the world."

"It is," she agreed with a serene lack of humility.

"Can you tell me what—how—spin me the story? If you will, madam?"

She understood what he was asking, he thought. She would know that he was not leaving his house. Nor would he be writing the story, let alone sending it to his paper. Not now, and not from here.

But he would know. He would have what he came for.

"You came for the truth," she said, as if he had spoken his thoughts aloud. "But what truth is that? Do you want simply to know? To understand? Or do you want to live forever?"

"No one lives forever," he said, "except in spirit."

"That is true," she said.

The way she said it was so strange that he forgot himself and tried to sit up. But his body was past that. When the storm of coughing had passed and she had sponged away with her own hands the blood and worse, he lay as still as the rattle of his breath would let him.

"Would you?" she asked. "If you could?"

She spoke with peculiar intensity. Her eyes were fixed on him. He saw in them a kind of hunger.

It was not that she would devour him, but that she wanted something. Something uniquely valuable. Something—

He had heard a rumor once, a whisper in a shadow, back in Boston, and then again in Philadelphia. Because he was what he was, he had laid it away in memory, but given it little thought. It was preposterous, like one of the novels his sisters were so excessively fond of.

And yet here, in this place even stranger than he had dared to expect, he began to wonder. Could it be true?

He answered her question at last with a question of his own. "What are you asking me? Whether I would want my name remembered? That's the ancient poet's immortality, right enough."

"Do you have time to be disingenuous?" she responded with a hint of sharpness.

That stung the truth out of him. "Be blunt, then. Tell me what you mean."

"Your body is dying," she said. "There is no saving it. Your spirit, however…"

"My soul is immortal, or so I've been told. Is there something here that might alter that?"

"Quite the contrary," she said. She paused and drew a breath. He would not have called her agitated, but she was possessed of some deep emotion. "There is a way. It's more theoretical than practical, but the mechanisms are in place. I have ventured the experiment with lesser souls, and with one of our own kind who offered herself freely for the advancement of science."

Zachariah lay still. He had little movement left in him in any case, but her words seemed to interrupt the turning of the world.

The mechanical who had waited on him stirred slightly, hardly more than the drawing in of a breath had it been a living thing. His eyes turned toward it. There was nothing about it of the female and only a sketch of the human. And yet…

He had come here for mundane if noble purpose. He was a

journalist to the end. The story was life, and the truth was the soul that animated it.

This was more than he had ever hoped for. But it was a conundrum. He took pride in telling the story straight and pure. To insert himself into it, to become it—

"'If this is true," he said, "if it is possible, the ethics—the morals—the ramifications—"

"Yes," she said.

"And yet you would do it."

"I am a scientist," she said, "and, in my way, a humanitarian. Imagine the possibilities. Bodies too broken or worn to endure, but souls still strong, still vibrant. Still yearning to taste of what life has to offer."

"But is it life?" he asked, his eyes on the mechanical that had gone still again, its blank face unmoving, its eyes flat, empty. "Without breath or blood or sense of touch, no taste, no smell, only the simulation of sight and hearing. What joy can it know? What pleasures can it take? Can it only yearn for all that it has lost?"

"The same might be said of the bodiless spirit," she replied.

"Ah, ghosts," he said. "The earthbound, the doomed and damned. But they say Heaven is everything that life was and more."

"And Hell is everything that life fears and hates. Would you gamble on your destination?"

His response was drowned in coughing, with the copper taste of blood, and pain that tore at the roots of his lungs. There was no fear in him. He was past that. He could let go. He would know, then, what no living man was given to know.

And yet…

"I cast the dice," he said, "between Heaven and Hell."

∞

The mechanical carried him with effortless strength through the maze of the mansion, gliding as smoothly as a boat on still water. The warmth of its body surprised him. It was not human warmth, not quite, but neither was it was cold of lifeless metal.

He had so many questions, but there was no time. Each breath he struggled to draw came shallower than the last. Darkness was already closing in. And pain. No one had warned him that this death would hurt so much.

Time now was slipping, catching on itself. One moment he floated through a shadowy corridor. The next, he lay on a table in the workshop that he had seen in his dream or vision.

Miss Meddowes bent over him. Someone or something else arranged his limbs with brisk gentleness. The corner of his eye caught the gleam of the mechanical.

"If all goes as it should," she said, "you will slip painlessly into sleep, and wake…elsewhere. Are you ready for that? Do you consent?"

"Yes," he said. Whispered. Thought.

She must have heard, however faint it was. She inclined her head. And time stopped.

He had dreamed like this before, wandered these halls, taken in the wonders of this workshop that was unlike any other he had seen. This time, however, the thread that had bound him to his physical self stretched thinner and thinner and ever thinner. He hovered above the broken, shriveled thing on the table. He felt nothing, looking down at it, but a kind of distant pity.

A little distance from it, on another table, lay a shape that, for size and substance and number of limbs, bespoke the human. With the sight that was given him in this dreamlike state, he could not see it clearly. It did seem less forthrightly mechanical than the one that stood by it, assisting Miss Meddowes as she moved through a dance of arcane and yet oddly beautiful science.

There were wires and cables and a globe that sprang into sudden light. The glory of that radiance captivated him. It lured him; sang to him. Tempted him with supernal sweetness.

And yet he held still. It was not the only light in this place. There was another, dimmer and more distant, but somehow even stronger. In between the two, he understood more than his mortal frame could have sustained. He knew all there was to know. He saw the turning of stars, and flocks of galaxies. All of creation was contained in him; he was without limit, beyond death or time or mere existence.

It was not fear that drew him back. Never fear. But curiosity—there was that. And a lingering sense of obligation, a memory of what he had been and what he had hoped to be.

The earthly light swelled around him. It was warm; to his wonder and growing delight, there was a fragrance about it, like sunlight and new grass. It filled him as water fills a cup; he tasted something like honey, and something like wine.

The spirit remembers. It was not a voice, not precisely, but he heard it as if it were Miss Meddowes who spoke. He let himself sink deeper into the light and the fragrance and the taste that grew to fill the world. Honey and wine, and bright metal without the taint of blood.

It was probably a sin in the old Papist sense, to sit up in this world that had changed forever. The body he inhabited was a thing of metal and glass and polished stone, a work of art as perfect as anything he had seen in the museums of Italy. His skin was bronze, his eyes ivory and obsidian.

He had a heart, a clockwork mechanism that beat in its proper place in his breast. He breathed, a working of subtle bellows, animating his body, fueling it with the power of the air. He could eat or drink if he chose, and make use of the nourishment, though it was not a necessity.

He was a wonder and a marvel and a monster such as he could never have imagined, more dreadful and impossible even than Mrs. Shelley's celebrated creation. That had been cobbled together from human flesh, after all. There was nothing human in him, except the soul that contained his essential self.

This was nothing that he had prepared for. He had no goal, no plan. He was a shell filled with light, and a flood of questions, and a tide of pure wonder.

That wonder lifted him to his feet. He stood swaying as his balance found itself, face to face with the mechanist who had wrought him.

She made no move to touch him. Her expression was as blank as that of the mechanical who still stood where it had been while he was still in the mortal body.

She was horrified, he thought. She had made him; she had given him life. Now that he was real and not a mere scientific possibility, she could not bear the sight of him.

This was how the world would look on him. This stunned silence. This bone-deep revulsion.

Then she stirred. She breathed. She laid her hand over the beating of his clockwork heart. "Marvelous," she said. And then: "Can you speak?"

"Yes," he answered. His voice had a lovely timbre, both deep and clear. "I can see and hear. Feel. Taste. Smell—how?"

"Science," she said. "Study with me, and I can teach you. If you wish to learn."

"I do." He did not have to pause for thought. Part of him knew it was mere practicality. Here he had a place. In the greater world, if it would ever be ready for such a thing as he had become, it would by no means be soon.

He had time. That much he was sure of, even as new as he was.

All the time in the world. And all the world to understand what he had done and how, and the full scope of the why.

He stretched, aware of the smooth oiled movement of his mechanical limbs, and the air through which they moved, and the strength that slept in them. It startled laughter out of him. Of all the things he had thought he would feel, the last, and the most welcome, was joy.

Panacea

Pati Nagle

See, it all started one night when we were sitting around the campfire, stinking drunk. It was November and we were three days into a two-week dig that was originally scheduled for September. The ground was hard, on the way to frozen, and we'd worked until dark because the sun was going early and we were on a short schedule. Our water buffalo, promised by the university for day one, had not yet arrived. We were tired, cold, and filthy, and our camp was a hundred miles—half of it of rough dirt road—from the nearest civilization, a tiny town that rolled up its only sidewalk at 5:00 p.m.

Fortunately, I had a good team for this dig. Rob was my assistant as usual, and we'd worked with Jacob, Berto, and Evie before.

We had two students along, a skinny white kid named Steve and a mostly non-verbal Latino with the tragic name of Juan Tomas. They got to do the scut jobs and take the heckling that was all part of their dues. I'd started them off with my standard warning that if they even looked at Evie the wrong way I would kick their asses if she didn't do it first. Neither of them had tested that edict. They were okay, both of them, and if they stuck with it they'd make good archaeologists some day.

That night they were huddled with the rest of us around the fire, and apart from making the fresh fish bring more wood, we didn't harass them. It had been a long, hard, cold day and we were all pissed off from being short on water. We were short on beer, too, so after we killed two six-packs I broke out a bottle of whiskey. That was when it began.

"Say, I wonder if this stuff will get the red out," said Berto, looking from the bottle in one hand to the fingers of the other, which he pensively rubbed together.

"Don't you dare," Evie told him, grabbing the bottle. She took a swig. "This stuff's too precious for washing."

"So's the water," said Jacob, holding out his hand for the bottle. Evie took another swig before passing it.

"I called the U," Rob said. "The truck hauling the buffalo broke down in Springer. They're sending another one."

"Great," I said, trying to sound upbeat.

Berto was still staring at his fingers. "I been on a lot of burial digs, and this ocher is the worst I remember for sticking."

"It always sticks," said Jacob. "Stained the heck out of my white shirt when I wore it."

"Serve you right, wearing white to a dig," said Evie.

"Hey, it was my first time!"

"Yeah, but *this* stuff sticks worse than usual," Berto said.

"Why do so many ancient cultures use ocher in their burials?" asked Steve, who'd been gnawing at the back of his thumb.

The others all gave him a Look, except for Juan, who was poking what was left of the fire with a stick, sending up sparks and a spiral of cedar smoke.

"Well," I said patiently, "that's an excellent question."

"Yeah, you can do your thesis on it," Evie added.

"Early cultures all over the world did it," Jacob said, passing the bottle to Juan.

"Might be they thought it was good medicine," Berto put in.

"There are a number of theories, but no one has really reached a conclusion," I said. "It's worth researching, if you're curious, Steve."

"They used it for other stuff, too," Jacob said. "Some tribes painted themselves with it."

"Some tribes still do," Evie said.

"I think I found where they dug it," Juan said. He handed the whiskey to Steve, who stopped chewing on his thumb to accept the bottle and sat staring at it.

We all looked at Juan. He hunched a little, then picked up his stick and poked the fire again. "I was walking up the arroyo at lunch. Found a deposit of red clay on the side, in the wall. I brought some back."

"Where is it?" Evie demanded.

"Put it in the tent. I'll get it."

He stood, leaving his stick on the ground, and headed for the small tent he shared with Steve.

Steve started coughing and handed me the whiskey. Might have been his first swig—he came from a dry town, one of the few left in the state. The first few times the bottle had gone around the circle, he had just passed it on. I put a steadying hand between his shoulder blades until he caught his breath, then took a pull at the bottle and handed it to Rob. Steve continued to cough, though he was getting control of it.

Berto put the last stick of wood on the fire and huddled closer to the heat. "I'm getting too old for this shit. Maybe I'll retire."

"To a desk job?" I said. "You'd hate it."

Berto grimaced.

Juan came back with a sample bag full of dirt. He gave it to Evie, who whipped out her flashlight and examined the bag, then opened it and took out a pinch.

"Yup," she said, rubbing her fingertips together. "It's the same as what's in the burial."

"I thought they had to trade for it!" Jacob said.

"Coastal tribes had to. It's found inland, usually in marine sediments. Good spotting, Juan." Evie handed the bag back to him. "Add it to the inventory in the morning. Rob can help you record it."

"I—was going to keep it," Juan said.

"You can get some more," Evie said, holding out her hand for the whiskey.

Berto passed the bottle to her. "What do you want it for?" he asked Juan.

"My mom makes pottery. She likes to make her own glazes."

"Let me see it," Jacob said, holding out his hand. Reluctantly, Juan handed him the bag.

Steve coughed again, still suffering from the whiskey. He was back chewing his thumb.

"Why you sucking on your thumb, boy?" Berto said to him.

Everyone looked at Steve, who hastily removed his knuckle from his mouth. "I cut it."

"Well, put some of that ocher on it. You can test its medicinal properties."

"It's generally not a good idea to ingest minerals," Jacob said.

"So paint it around the cut. Here." Berto took the sample bag from Jacob and got to his feet with a grunt, then limped away toward the supply tent. His bum hip had been bugging him since the first night—the cold was getting to it. He'd been grumbling about it for years, but now he was starting to talk about maybe getting a hip replacement.

Berto came back a minute later with a tin cup, stirring whatever was in it with a small paintbrush, one of the tools we used to clear soil away from artifacts.

Jacob grabbed the bag of ocher back from him. Berto went around the fire circle to Steve.

"Hold out your hand."

"No, that's okay," Steve said.

"It's in the name of science," Jacob said, standing and joining Berto. "Come on."

Steve gave a small, unhappy cough, but allowed Jacob to take hold of his forearm and peel back the cuffs of his coat and sweatshirt. Berto used the paintbrush to dab sludgy ocher above and below the cut, then covered the back of Steve's hand as well.

"Hm. Nice color."

Steve coughed.

"You need some on your chest, too," Berto said.

"No, that's okay," Steve said, alarmed.

"It's just the whiskey," I added.

"Yeah, but maybe it'll help," Berto insisted, on a roll. "Worth a try, right?"

Jacob proceeded to pull up Steve's jacket.

"Guys" I said, but they were fast. Jacob had the kid on his back, torso bared, and Berto was already painting him with ocher. Steve went into a fit of coughing. Jacob pinned his shoulders, holding him still while Berto decorated his chest.

"That's enough," I said.

Berto glanced at me and backed off. Jacob released the poor kid, who sat up, still coughing, and pulled his shirt and jacket down over the ocher smeared all over him. I'd make Berto pay to clean the jacket, I decided, as he and Jacob returned to their places.

Evie had quietly passed the whiskey bottle to Juan during all this. Juan now handed it to Steve, who defiantly took a pull before handing it to me.

"Hey, you're not coughing," I said.

Steve shot me a sullen glance. "Cleared my lungs."

I took a swig from the bottle and held onto it. Berto and Jacob had maybe had enough. I looked at everyone around the circle, evaluating their state of inebriation. I was responsible for them, and while things hadn't gotten too out of hand, I felt it was time to put on the brakes.

Besides, the fire was dying down and the whiskey was almost gone.

I took another generous pull and gave the bottle to Rob, who followed suit. As A.D., he was entitled to polish it off, and he did.

"Better pack it in," I said. "We'll be up at dawn."

"*Before* dawn," said Rob, who acted as a whip.

There was grumbling, but they all dispersed to their tents. I broke up the fire and put a couple of shovelfuls of dirt on the coals to smother them, then stood staring up at the sky. Cold stars—a million of them—gleamed like mica particles in the depth of space.

Juan came and stood beside me, staring up at the sky. "I'm sorry, Boss," he said. "Didn't mean to cause trouble."

"It's okay," I said. "No harm done. Good find on the ocher deposit. Show me where it is, tomorrow."

"Okay."

In fact, he wound up showing all of us where it was. Curiosity, maybe, or just the novelty of looking at something other than the burial site we were working on. After we ate our lunch—same sandwiches as yesterday and the day before—we followed Juan to where a generous vein of vivid, dark rust-red marred the lighter-colored sediment halfway up the wall, right at a bend in the arroyo.

"It was mined, for sure," Berto said. "See how it's been hollowed away? That's not from water."

I nodded. He was right. No one except Juan had been at it recently, but the deposit had been scraped out at its widest point, and it wasn't erosion. I rubbed a fingertip along it, finding the ocher to be harder than the less colorful soil above and below it. I'd seen hundreds of clay deposits, but few of such intense color.

"Right. Make a note of the location, Rob. We'll add it to the report. Okay, lunch break's over. Back to the site."

With minimal grumbling, the crew turned back toward camp. Steve stayed staring at the ocher deposit, wearing a pensive frown.

"How's the thumb?" I asked.

"Yeah, well, the cut's closed up. It's pretty much healed."

"Overnight? Let me see."

He showed me his right hand, still stained with ocher. I'd expected to see a paper cut, but instead saw the line of what must have been a nasty gash, at least an inch long, on the side of his thumb. As he said, it was closed now. The ocher had slopped over it, I noticed.

I glanced up at him. He was watching me, watery blue eyes looking for a response.

"Interesting," I said. "Come on, let's catch up."

We were a few minutes' walk from the camp. Ahead of us, I could hear Berto and Jacob bantering.

"You know, it actually would make a good thesis topic," I said.

Steve kept silent.

"What did it feel like? Any sensations?"

"Felt warm," he said. "My chest did, after they painted it."

I frowned. There'd been no hot water in the camp.

"Definitely worth further study," I said.

If Berto had used urine to mix the paint—but no, I'd have smelled it. The ocher itself didn't have much of a smell. He must have just used a splash from one of the water jugs. It should have felt cold.

So there was maybe some chemical reaction going on. That was odd. I'd have to get myself a sample and do some testing.

Ahead, Rob was nudging the team back to work. He shot a look back toward us. "Hey, Stevie-boy, get a move on."

Steve jogged away. I picked up my pace a bit, too, and before I returned to the dig, I went into the supply tent for a quick look around.

There was the cup Berto had used, sitting on a corner of a table with the paintbrush still in it. I frowned. Bad form, Berto. Always take care of your tools.

Of course, he *had* been stinking drunk.

I picked up the cup, took a quick look and a sniff. Nope, no urine. Just a faint, coppery smell. The bristles of the brush were bent in the dried ocher. I put the cup back. Rob would find it, and probably chew Berto's ear off before making him clean the brush.

The water buffalo arrived mid-afternoon. Much rejoicing ensued. Rob permitted the crew to pause and fill canteens and our water jugs, then drove them back to work.

"You can wash after dark," he said. "We've got three more hours of daylight, and we're going to use them."

I couldn't argue with that. We were racing time already. By my calculation it would not be physically possible to complete the dig in the time we had, so we'd just have to get as far as we could. I was already composing my request for an extension in my head, while I logged bits of pottery and bone.

I was in the tent I shared with Rob, getting out my canteen, when I heard Jacob yell. I ran out and followed the increased shouting.

Jacob was on the ground just beyond the dig site, and the others were all there or heading there. I arrived in time to see Evie wielding a shovel like a spear. With one massive thrust, she stabbed it into the ground.

"Got it," she said, eyes a bit wild and her dark hair coming loose from her braid. She looked at me and added, "Rattler. A little one."

She'd decapitated it with one blow. Berto limped over and picked it up by the tail.

"Watch out for the head," I said. "It can still bite."

"I'll bury it," Evie said, and started digging.

Juan was on his knees next to Jacob. "Did it hit you?"

"My ankle," Jacob said, struggling to sit up.

Rob and I exchanged a look. "Just lie still," Rob said, pulling a marker out of his pocket and checking his watch. "Juan, go get the first aid kit."

Juan ran for the supply tent, and Berto limped after him. Rob found the bite and circled it with the marker, adding the time. I squatted next to Jacob, shading his face with my body.

"You'll be okay," I told him. "We'll get you to a hospital."

The nearest one was in Springer, a three-hour drive at least. The sun would be down by the time we got there, if we had to drive.

Rob had his phone out, talking to 911. Nearest helicopter was probably in Las Vegas, over 200 hundred miles away.

Berto brought a knapsack for a pillow, and he and I got Jacob settled more comfortably. Juan came back with the first aid kit. I rummaged through it—no antivenom. There was an epipen, which we might need. I pocketed it.

"Where's it hurt?" I asked Jacob. "Is it spreading?"

Jacob nodded. "M-my ankle hurts. And it's going up my leg."

"Just relax," I told him. "Keep still as much as you can, that'll slow it down."

"It was just a little one, right?"

I nodded, not adding that young snakes were more dangerous, because they hadn't learned restraint. They spent all their venom in one bite.

Rob got off the phone. "No medevac in Las Vegas," he said.

"What?!" I frowned.

"It's down for maintenance. They're sending one from Santa Fe. Hour and a half, probably."

I gritted my teeth. Jacob might lose some toes, maybe the foot. Worst case, the leg.

Rob started questioning him about his pain, writing more data on his leg. The bite was just above the ankle, which was starting to swell a little. I handed Rob the epipen, in case it was needed, and stood up to get Jacob some water. Steve was watching a few feet away. As I passed him, he looked at me.

"Ocher," he said.

I paused, frowning.

"Paint it with ocher."

I ran through the snake-bite "don't"s in my head. Don't use a snake-bite kit, don't try to suck out the venom, don't use a pressure bandage or tourniquet, don't take pain relievers.

"It might help," Steve added.

"Or it could make it worse."

"How?"

"I…don't know."

I started for the supply tent. Steve came along. I filled a cup with water, and grabbed Berto's ocher cup, still there with the paintbrush. I put a splash of water in it and gave it to Steve to carry.

As we walked back I thought through everything I knew about viper venom. It interfered with blood-clotting. Maybe the clay would counteract that? But would there be risk of internal bleeding? Would it trap venom in the tissue, or leech it out?

Jacob was starting to sweat. Berto propped him up while I gave him the water. Steve squatted beside him and started telling him about the ocher and his healed thumb, stirring the ocher with the brush while he talked. He showed Jacob his thumb.

"When did you cut it?" Rob asked.

"Yesterday, late afternoon. It bled for an hour."

"Why didn't you bandage it, dope?" Berto said.

"I did. The bandage came off when I was getting firewood."

Steve stirred the ocher. "You don't have to try this, Jacob. But it might help. We could paint it around the bite, might help the pain."

"D-do it," Jacob said, handing me the empty cup. "Can I have some more? Thirsty."

I fetched a canteen while Rob lectured Jacob about how he'd be responsible for the decision if he let Steve put ocher on his leg. Ass-covering. The business side of me agreed, the practical side of me hated it. My gut told me the ocher was worth a try.

Steve was painting Jacob's ankle when I got back. He carefully painted around the wound, leaving Rob's markings exposed. The medics would need that information.

"That helps," Jacob said. "Paint up my leg."

"How far up is the pain?" Rob demanded, touching a few inches above the ankle. "Here?"

"Not that high. Paint it. Paint up to my knee."

Steve painted his leg up to the calf before running out of ocher. He looked at Juan. "A little more?"

Juan took the cup and headed for his tent.

"Oh, man. Yeah, that helps," Jacob said, after downing another cup of water. He leaned back and closed his eyes.

In the end, Steve painted his leg up to the knee and did his whole foot for good measure. The swelling had stopped; we didn't need the epipen. Rob marked the limit of the pain over the dried clay. By the time the helicopter arrived, Jacob was relaxed and had stopped sweating.

I went with him in the chopper to the County General in Clayton, while Berto drove to meet us. I had taken a photo of the dead snake, for identification purposes. The doc at the hospital looked at it and decided the bite had been minor, because Jacob's symptoms were unusually mild.

"What's the red stuff?" he asked me.

"Just some clay. We thought it might help the swelling."

"Guess it did. He'll be fine. We'll keep him overnight for observation, but it looks like one dose of antivenom should do it."

An hour later Berto arrived with a change of clothes for Jacob, who was on his cell chatting up his girlfriend when Berto came in.

"Hey, you're not limping," I said to Berto.

He shot me a look. "Ocher."

I blinked. "Okay."

"You're looking good, buddy," Berto said when Jacob got off the phone.

"I feel good." He looked at me. "Thanks, Boss. That stuff's amazing!"

"It was your call. Glad it worked out." I held out a hand and we shook. "Get some sleep. We'll check in with you in the morning."

On the drive back to camp, Berto and I caught each other up. He'd left the crew helping Evie tan the skin of the rattler, using ocher.

"Says she's gonna make a hatband out of it. Too small for a belt."

"So Jacob's response made you decide to put ocher on your hip?"

"Yeah. I asked for help since it was hard to reach, and that *pendejo* Steve painted my whole ass."

I laughed. "Turnabout is fair play, *amigo*."

"Stuff gets *hot*," he added.

"That's what Steve said. I wonder what causes that."

"I dunno, but I think we better figure it out."

In the morning, we all rose before dawn and went to the arroyo with shovels and garbage bags, and proceeded to dig out the entire vein of ocher. We split it into seven shares—one for Jacob—which gave us each several pounds of clay.

Juan gave half of his to his mom, who's made some amazing pottery with it. He gave me a mug she made as a souvenir.

Steve is now doing a deep dive into the literature on ocher use in early cultures, to be followed by interviews with cultures who currently use ocher in the Americas, Australia, and Africa. He's planning his dissertation already, even as he's starting to map out his thesis.

Evie and I are in the midst of chemical analyses, which we're conducting in our spare time. We haven't figured much out yet, except that the ocher from our vein, which is darker and more intense in color than our control samples, is also more chemically volatile. It's not the water that makes it heat up, it's the contact with both water and flesh, and we're still working on isolating the reaction. Ordinary ocher doesn't heat up the same way.

Our ocher is effective on just about everything, from paper cuts to gastric distress (when applied externally) to arthritis. Berto canceled his plans for hip replacement and stopped talking about retiring from field work.

Jacob's snake-bite incident gave me the perfect reason to request an extension of the dig, which has been granted for the spring. Between now and then, Juan and I will be scouting in the area, looking for more burial sites.

And more ocher.

From the private journals of Ada Byron King, Countess Lovelace

> *…My hand shakes so from mere contemplation of the impossible. Not dead, not dead at all. Not merely the echo that haunts my life, but in existence still, mad, bad and dangerous to know, waiting curled and coiled in dread suspension until he may walk abroad again. It cannot be so. It must not be so. I will prove that it IS NOT so.*

But a negative cannot be proved. If Fletcher was not in all ways insane, if he still exists in some form, which of the others might also live? The poet Shelley, so fantastically drowned and with his body burnt upon the beach with only my father and one other as witness? What of Mary Godwin, whose hand wrote of the dead brought back to life? Oh, God in Heaven! What did she know? And Polidori? Failed doctor, failed author, so in love with <u>him</u>? What did they truly do in that year of darkness on the shores of Lake Geneva?

I must know. Madame M. Must be called into action. Fraser as well. Wretch he is but clever, quick and useful.

I am resolved. I will begin with the doctor. But where can he be? After all these years, with a whole world in which to hide himself?

The Soul Jar

Steven Harper

The iron spider clicked across the table and delicately dropped the sugar cube into my cup. I stirred, careful to keep my cuffs away from the crumbs that littered my plate.

"They're wrong, every one of them," said Victor Kalakos from across the table. "From Archimedes to Newton."

"I don't see how." I sipped. The tea was nicely sweet, but had gone lukewarm. "The laws of physics are inviolate. Two objects cannot occupy the same space at the same time. If that weren't so, my spider wouldn't be able to walk across the table. It would sink into the surface instead."

"But the physical laws ignore what makes it walk in the first place, and that invalidates even Newton!" Kalakos exclaimed with more enthusiasm than accuracy. His own cup was long emptied, as was the silver flask standing next to it. The spider skittered to the edge of the table, paused, and turned left. "There! You see? It turned left. Based on what? I'll tell you, my boy: the sum of its experience. And there is no physical law to explain that."

"Like John Locke claimed."

"Exactly. We are the sum of our experiences. Let me give you an example. If you were to pull one leg from that spider and replace it, would it be the same spider?"

"Of course." I turned the spider, and it clicked back toward the teapot.

"What if you replaced all eight legs?"

"More or less."

"Would that spider turn left or right at the edge of the table?"

I shook my head and glanced out the car window. The train wasn't moving. Clouds darkened above the River Liffey as the sun set, and Dublin lamplighters were making their rounds. One of our girls had already attended to lighting the car's hanging lamps, which now shed a soft yellow glow.

Ringmaster Victor Kalakos had an entire train car for himself, a house on wheels. He had a large bed, comfortable chairs, two wardrobes, a small stove, full bookshelves, and a perfectly functional bar.

The wealthier performers usually lived in small wagons—we rolled them into the boxcars when it came time to move—while the poor ones pitched small tents behind the main one. I lived in a wagon myself, but as the ringmaster's chief assistant, I came and went from Kalakos's car as I liked. We usually took a late tea together after the Kalakos International Emporium of Automata & Other Wonders had shut for the evening.

"There's no way to know which way a rebuilt spider would turn," I said. "It would have different experiences and might make a different choice. Or it might not."

Kalakos leaned across the plates a little unsteadily. He always got philosophical when his flask was empty. "There might be a place that does know which choice it makes. And I think you hold the key to it."

"Me?" I was so startled, I forgot my hard-earned grammar. "How so?"

"You see the future."

"I don't, sir," I reproved gently. "I sometimes see the choices people make and what will happen from them. Sometimes."

"In other words," Kalakos said with a vigorous nod, "when a man stands at a crossroads, wondering if he should turn left or right to get home, you can see that the right turn will take him safely to his family but a left turn will take him into an ambush of bandits."

Automatically I looked down at my hands. My left has six fingers on it, but living among circus performers had long ago driven out any hint of self-conscious feeling. "That oversimplifies the case, but yes."

"I maintain," Kalakos continued, "that the man turns both ways. That in one place…call it a universe…he turns right and arrives safely home, while simultaneously, in another universe, he turns left and dies. The two universes exist, side-by-side, invisible and insensible to one another, but they exist nonetheless. Before the man makes his choice, there is a single universe. The moment he decides, the universe splits into two, one for each choice, each with its own set of physical laws, occupying the same space at the same time. This happens a million times, a billion times, every time something different could happen."

"No, sir." I shook my head again. "When the man makes his choice, the other possibility ceases to exist. I know."

"Except you exist in *this* universe," Kalakos said triumphantly. "So you are automatically unaware of the other universes and their outcomes. But you can see each universe a split-second before it is created. You—and your counterparts in the other universes—see the potentials."

"Rubbish!" I cried, then added quickly, "Sir."

"Have you ever held up two mirrors so they reflect each other?" Kalakos said mildly.

"Yes. It makes me dizzy." As did this conversation.

"I've often thought that's what it must be like for you." Kalakos picked up the spider and idly flipped it over. It was the size of a saucer, with spindly legs. A key stuck out of its back, slowly unwinding. The legs quivered as if in fear or protest. "You stand in the middle and see infinite reflections stretching in both directions, but each one is a tiny bit different."

"I wish you wouldn't do that, sir," I said, growing a little tired now. "The spider gets upset."

"How so?" Kalakos brandished the little automaton. "Is it alive? Conscious? Did you give it a soul?"

I shuddered and wrapped my six-fingered hand round my cup. "You know I didn't. I meant I'll have to reset the flywheel, and it's bloody difficult. What brought up all this talk of other universes, anyway?"

Kalakos returned the spider to the table and leaned back in his chair. He was a tall man, and rangy, appropriate for a circus ringmaster. His black hair had gone grey at the temples, and he wore the expected enormous moustache and sideburns. He probably used to be quite handsome in his youth, but the lines acquired in his forties weren't kind to him, and I sometimes wondered if I would meet a similar fate, though I didn't much look like him. I was shorter than he, with the lean, compact build of an acrobat. At twenty-one, I kept my sandy hair short and my face clean-shaven because with facial hair I looked like an idiot.

"I'm remembering another time, I suppose," Kalakos said as the spider skittered round in a circle. "And wondering how things might have been different if I had made other choices. Have you ever been to Geneva, Dodd?"

"No, and you keep asking questions you know the answer to. Why is that?"

He chuckled. "Perhaps it's my own way of determining the future."

A knock sounded at the door. Kalakos cocked his head, and I sighed. It was always something. No doubt the elephant had broken down. Or the wirewalker had gone into a whorehouse and needed bail money. Or the Great Sabatini had got drunk and made someone disappear again. I glanced at the car door and felt a familiar sensation steal over me as my talent opened. My talent came and went as it pleased, and I never quite got over the unease it gave me. When I looked at the door, I expected my talent to show me a series of choices stretching out before me as it usually did.

My hand jerked spasmodically round my cup. It leaped from my grasp and shattered on the boards even as Kalakos called for the visitor to enter. Before I could react further—or even speak—the door opened and in strode a stranger—tall, broad-shouldered, in his late twenties. He had deep red hair under a high hat, a wolf's grin, and wide blue eyes that sparkled in the lamplight. His long black overcoat hung open, revealing a white shirt, black Hessian boots, and a fashionably-cut brown waistcoat.

Kalakos's face went instantly pale as milk, and he bolted to his feet. "Joseph Storm! As I breathe, can that be you?"

The man's grin widened. "It can. I've just perfected a clown act, and I need a circus position. You can provide one for an old friend, I trust?"

"In the name of our Holy Lord and Father of us all, Joseph," Kalakos said in a strangled voice, *"where is your brother?"*

"Am I being rude? Then, Mister Victor Kalakos," said Joseph with overmuch formality, "allow me to present my brother, Nathaniel August Storm."

Into the car came another man, one completely identical to Joseph. Red hair, blue eyes, tailored clothes, everything was exactly the same. Except this man wasn't smiling. He kept his eyes down, and his posture was uncertain. I, for my part, found myself dizzy and confused, as if I were watching events through a funhouse mirror.

Kalakos inhaled and exhaled with quick and shallow breaths. He looked ready to faint. I didn't feel much better, and I coped by focusing on something else.

"Mr. Kalakos?" I managed to say. "Are you ill?"

Kalakos seemed to remember that I was still in the car. "I...I'm fine, Dodd," he stammered. "Perfectly fine. Would you excuse us?"

"Of course." I snatched up the spider and all but bolted for the railcar door. In my haste, I tripped on an uneven board. A pair of solid arms caught me, and Nathaniel Storm pulled me upright.

"Sorry," I muttered.

"Certainly." Nathaniel's breath came warm in my ear, and I found myself flushing. Confused, I fled out the door and down the three steps, the spider tucked under my arm. The two larger spiders that waited near the steps rose and skittered after me like obedient puppies.

One always had to consider a lifetime of hard labour in the most disgusting of prisons if we got caught following our natural inclinations.

The Irish summer evening was damp and cool, with a smell of coal and sulphur. Trolleys and horses and carriages clattered past in the street. Merrion Square, the park we had rented within Dublin, was already growing trampled and muddy from our presence, though the Emporium had only arrived last week. In the near distance, the Tilt rose up like a canvas tomb. Smaller tents huddled round it like gravestones. Behind me stood the train, a sleeping iron dragon with the Ringmaster's car as its tail.

Merrion Square was an ideal spot for a circus, since a rail spur ran right past it. In a few days, when the audiences began to dwindle, we would pack everything into the bright boxcars and clatter on to another town. Belfast, perhaps, or even London.

I moved a few steps away from the car, still feeling unnerved and trying to sort out what was happening. When I looked at the door just before Joseph and Nathaniel Storm's entrance, my talent had shown me two futures, but the power and fear in both had smashed me like a hammer and blinded me to the final outcomes in both. I did know I had seen both devotion and destruction, inextricably intertwined, and I couldn't sort out which of the two futures would come to pass, or even which one to choose. I was a wirewalker balanced between two extremes, and I feared that I would fall at any moment. The shock of it continued to unsettle me, and I rubbed my extra finger with my left thumb.

"What should I do?" I asked the spider under my arm. It waved its legs without answering. On the ground, its brethren scuttled about my ankles. If they had no specific orders, they tended to run in circles. I had no idea why. It wasted the energy stored in the winding spring, but I couldn't find a way to make them stop. If I changed the Babbage engines that controlled their actions and removed the tendency, they stopped working entirely.

"Dodd!" Kalakos stuck his head out of the railcar door. His face was still pale, but his nose was red with drink. "Mr. Storm parked his wagon near the Tilt. Have it moved to Clown Alley. We're adding his clown spot to the main show."

"What?" I said, startled. "We already have a full show. Who are we to drop from the schedule in order to—"

"Just see to it, Dodd." And he slammed the door again.

All the next day, the ringmaster hid from everyone, admitting only the Storm Brothers to his locked train. Once in his presence, they remained with him every moment.

"Who the hell are those two?" asked William Myrtle, our strong man. He was barely thirty, but was aging rapidly and looked closer to forty. Myrtle probably thought this was simply due to his nature. I knew differently.

"I have no idea," I said, "but they open with us tonight."

The show that evening was a near sell-out. The stands were crowded with families and courting couples and a few single people looking for companionship—the usual sort. Kalakos, in his red-and-white striped shirt and top hat, strode out of his wagon with a tempestuous expression, and no one dared ask him about the Storm brothers, who were nowhere to be seen. Once everyone was lined up outside the ring door curtains, the calliope started playing, and the Emporium processed into the ring.

We began every show with a parade. Kalakos stonily marched up front, waving his cane in time with the music. The great iron elephant followed, its heavy feet thudding on the packed earthen floor, then a rainbow explosion of clowns, then the brassy mechanical horses and their slender girls in white feathered dresses, then the muscular acrobats in their tight red shirts, and more. I strode in with my twelve spiders cavorting about my ankles. The smallest, painted purple, could sit on my hand, and the largest, painted red, was the size of a collie. The Storm brothers were still nowhere to be seen. Strange—most new performers want to be in the opening procession.

The audience applauded and cheered. Children pointed at the elephant. Everyone and everything marched thrice round the ring, and then the human performers scattered to do small spots for the crowd while the mechanical animals continued round the circle. My spiders amused the crowd with small tricks—plucking handkerchiefs from pockets, "kissing" girls and babies, making backflips upon command—while I answered questions. The young men always asked how they worked, and the young women always asked about me. I used to give them small paper flowers, but that annoyed their young men, so I've stopped the practice.

One young man with coal-black hair leaned toward me over his cane and murmured in my ear that he would love to discuss certain…automatic functions with me, if only I could meet him after the show? I considered the offer, but abruptly found myself remembering Nathan Storm's arms around my body in Kalakos's wagon. A bit flustered, I told the young man I had other plans and quickly moved on.

At last the automata pranced out and we performers cleared the Tilt so Kalakos could introduce the Flying Benjamins, our opening trapeze act. I waited outside with the other brightly-dressed performers, who stood or sat in silence or conversed in low whispers so their conversation wouldn't carry into the Tilt. I rewound my spiders. Henry Wells, the chief ring groom, opened the side of the elephant to ensure the boiler was stoked properly. The smell of coal smoke mixed with a wet breeze from the River Liffey. My eyes strayed, searching for Nathaniel Storm but not finding him in the press of people. How had he and Joseph forced Kalakos to give them a spot without so much as an audition?

"Presenting," Kalakos boomed from inside the Tilt, "the amazing Storm brothers!"

Two men darted through the ring door curtains into the Tilt. I ordered my spiders to stay and hurried round to the main entrance. Martha, the ticket girl, nodded at me as I dashed past her and found a place in the shadows near the grandstand.

Joseph and Nathaniel Storm had already leaped into the ring. Here they showed another oddity. In a clowning duo, one was usually a joey in whiteface makeup, and he dominated the other, who played the "smart" fool, or *auguste,* who wore makeup of simple wide circles round the eyes and mouth. Joseph and Nathaniel, however, both wore makeup in the *auguste* fashion.

The men wore identical baggy red polka-dot shirts, sagging blue trousers, and floppy purple shoes. They had artfully tousled their red hair, so there was no need for wigs. The only difference between them was that one twin wore a canary-yellow coat. I couldn't tell Joseph from Nathaniel, and I was surprised at how much I wanted to. Both men cut handsome figures despite the clown makeup. For a moment I felt Nathaniel's arms on me back in the railcar, and the crowded Tilt grew warm.

Joseph—I assumed he was the dominant one—paced about the ring, preening in his ludicrous jacket with obvious pride, then looked round in puzzlement and dismay. He had no mirror to see his fine clothes in! He turned to Nathaniel and, tapping one floppy foot, held out his hand with comic impatience. Nathaniel pulled an impossibly large hand mirror from one baggy pocket—and dropped it. The glass shattered.

Joseph furiously chased Nathaniel round the ring, shoes flopping, clothes flapping. Eventually, he caught his servant, trounced him soundly, and sent him away for another mirror amid laughter and scattered applause.

"They're good," murmured William Myrtle. I jumped—I hadn't noticed the strongman sidle up to me. "I've never seen an act like this one. Did they invent it? Where've they worked a ring before?"

"I've no idea," I said distractedly.

Joseph returned to his preening. A moment later, there was the sound of breaking glass behind the ring curtain, and Nathaniel slunk back into the ring with a horrified expression on his face. He was carrying a full-length, empty mirror frame. Nathaniel bit his nails and shot fearful glances at Joseph, who hadn't yet noticed what was going on. My heart filled with pity for him, and I had to remind myself it was only a clown spot.

An idea seemed to strike Nathaniel. He set the frame down and hurried out of the ring. A moment later, he reappeared—wearing a duplicate of Joseph's jacket. Once again, the clowns looked exactly alike.

Nathaniel picked up the frame and set it down with a thump behind Joseph, who jumped and spun round. In a flash, Nathaniel let go the mirror frame and duplicated his brother's pose, as if *he* were the reflection. Laughter rippled through the audience, and I joined in.

Joseph narrowed his eyes, seeming to notice something was wrong. He leaned forward to get a better look at the mirror, but Nathaniel was ready for that and he copied the gesture perfectly. Joseph—and Nathaniel—shrugged and turned his back, whereupon Nathaniel stuck out his tongue over his shoulder. The audience roared. William guffawed and slapped me on the back with a heavy hand.

Joseph whirled round and pointed accusingly at the mirror, but Nathaniel was ready for him and pointed accusingly back. Still suspicious, Joseph wiggled his left hand while making a silly face. Again, Nathaniel simultaneously duplicated each move. As the spot continued, Joseph's movements grew more absurd and more complicated, but Nathaniel copied him so well that I found myself wondering if there really were glass in the mirror after all. Abruptly, both clowns picked up the frame and, holding it between them, whirled round, faster and faster until I completely lost track of which twin was which. Finally, in disgust, the pair thumped the mirror down, straightened their respective collars, and stalked off in opposite directions. At the last moment, both looked back, waved to the mirror, and exited to thunderous applause.

"I've seen my share of good joeys," William said over the noise, "and these two are fantastic. The mirror work is brilliant. First new bit I've seen in ages."

I stared after the brothers without answering, then ran backstage to find them. Joseph was already towing Nathaniel back to Kalakos's railcar, and my own spot was coming up soon. In that moment, my talent opened up, and I saw that chasing after them would only end in humiliation. However, I did have another choice that would be less frustrating—at least for the moment.

I scrawled, *Plans changed. Meet bhnd main tent aft show re: automtc fnctns* on a calling card, handed the card to my littlest spider, and pointed out the young man with the coal-black hair. My spider scuttled away on its errand, and the other choices vanished. Some time later, a very intense discussion began behind the main tent. We were quite discreet, of course—Irish law was strict. The discussion ended in my wagon, as I knew it would. In the morning, the young man was gone.

I knew that would happen, too.

∞

"Ferrous," I said, "wake up." Then I smashed him on the head with a sledgehammer.

The blow rang with the clang of a church bell. The great iron dragon's eyes cranked open. He sucked in air and expelled soft steam through the horns on the top of his head. His boiler fires were banked, which always made him sleepy, and the blow I had dealt him was barely powerful enough to get his attention.

Ferrous was a huge black beast, a combination of dragon and locomotive, with wheels instead of claws and iron skin instead of scales. His strength was powerful enough to pull the massive circus train, and his codex complex enough to negotiate the maze of railways that snaked through the British Isles and the Continent. Kalakos had coded his cards, but I had modified them several times.

"Yes, Dodd?" Ferrous hissed. His mouth was fashioned just above the cowcatcher, giving him the appearance of possessing a beard.

It was two days later, a Monday, and the Emporium was closed. The Storm brothers had performed four more times—matinees and evenings—to great success, but they always vanished afterward to the ringmaster's railcar. Today, however, things had changed. Kalakos remained closeted in his railcar with Joseph, but I'd caught Nathan strolling toward the wagon he shared with his brother. On impulse, I had asked if he wanted a tour of the Emporium. To my relief and pleasure, he most certainly did. Since the day was fine, both of us were wearing flannel trousers and pullovers, with the fisherman's caps so common here in Dublin.

The headlamps that made up Ferrous's eyes were now staring down at us as we stood on the track before him. Nathan—he preferred that name over Nathaniel—stepped back. I took him by the shoulder and gently brought him forward again. He took off his cap.

"Ferrous," I said, "allow me to present Nathaniel August Storm. He's just joined the Emporium and will be riding with us. With your kind permission."

The eyes swiveled down in Nathan's direction. Nathan swallowed but remained still. Ferrous stared at him, then swung his gaze back to me. "He is trustworthy to ride?"

It was his standard question. One quirk of Ferrous's Babbage engine was that he never allowed strangers to ride with him, so all new employees of the Emporium needed to be introduced before their first transport. "He is," I said.

"And you are close to him, Dodd?"

That question startled me. Ferrous had never asked it before. "I...I feel he is worthy of—"

"Very well." Ferrous yawned. "I will go back to sleep now." And he did so.

"That was...quite amazing," Nathan said in a quiet voice.

It was then that I noticed my arm still lay round his shoulders. Nathan hadn't drawn away, either. My face grew hot with embarrassment and I quickly pulled back. Nathan continued to stare at Ferrous's sleeping form as if the little affair between us had been perfectly unremarkable. My eyes stayed on Nathan. His hair, red as an autumn leaf, was slightly tousled from removing his cap, and a few freckles sprinkled his nose.

"Well," I said with a slight cough, "now that you've seen—"

"Does he have a soul?" Nathan asked, his eyes still on the iron dragon.

An image of a strong man strapped to a table flashed through my head. Metal helmet. Electric wires. Leyden jars. My mouth dried up.

"What makes you ask?" I said.

"There are stories. Rumours that an automaton can become complex enough to house a soul, one stolen from a human being. Or that they even create their own, spontaneously."

I laughed, but it sounded forced. "The church doesn't like that sort of talk."

"I've seen automatic locomotives before, but never one complicated enough to speak," Nathan said. "Does he really think?"

"I don't know," I said. "John Locke claimed that any living creature that is aware of its own thinking must have a soul, but that was long before the first Babbage engine. Ferrous's codex is very limited. It doesn't go much beyond timetables and the type of coal he's given."

Nathan put out a cautious hand and touched the sleeping dragon. No reaction. "So this isn't magic."

It had been a statement, not a question, but I answered it anyway. "No," I said, on safer ground now. "It's science. All automata are animated through a combination of electricity, mechanics, and a bit of chemistry."

"I've seen real magic, you know."

Another image flickered. Cold thin fingers caressed my cheek and a soft voice whispered icy words in my ear.

"It's rare and difficult," I said woodenly, "but it's out there. Where did you encounter it?"

"China, Borneo, Japan." He glanced at me with a small smile that made me hunger to see more.

"I've never been that far East. What's it like?"

"People are much the same, though customs are very different. In many cases, certain ideas that make people angry here are ignored or accepted there."

He looked at me with guileless blue eyes, and I couldn't break away. Was Nathan thinking the same way as the young man with coal black hair? I wasn't quite sure, and there were so many risks in finding out. If I made a mistake with a total stranger, a fistfight might erupt, but we would ultimately part company. Nathan I would see every day. And rejection from a stranger meant little, while rejection from Nathan would destroy a billion branching universes.

At that moment I wanted very badly for my talent to open up, but the wretched thing had abandoned me completely.

"I see," was all I could say. I felt stupid and foolish. "Um…you've seen the rest of the Emporium. Do you want to see the Black Tent?"

Nathan looked a little disappointed, or perhaps it was only my willful imagination, and I was seized with an overwhelming desire to grab him by both shoulders and ask obvious and powerful questions. But I didn't.

"Yes," Nathan said. "Very much."

We threaded our way through the complex of tents and wagons that made up the Emporium. Cooking smells mingled with scents of animal manure and sawdust. Monday might have been a day off from performing, but that only created a day of maintenance and rehearsal. Ida and Mary Edgewood tried new additions to their wirewalking routine on a low rope they had set up. Carl Greene, a.k.a. the Great Sabatini, stood near his wagon, talking to an invisible audience as he pulled brightly-coloured handkerchiefs out of nothing. Aleksandr and Maksim Danylchuk coaxed Natasha, the World's Biggest Automatic Elephant, onto a tiny iron platform. Barbara Bellington Jones sat beside her tent with a plate of food, tossing titbits to the dozen poodles sitting in her ample shadow. Henry Wells supervised his two sons as they scrubbed and polished the six automatic horses that cantered in perfect circles for every show. All the performers except the children looked rather older than they were, and all of them except the children had a faintly mechanical air to their movements, a vague listlessness that only vanished when they entered the ring. Outsiders simply assumed the circus life was a draining one. I knew better.

Our progress through the Emporium was slow—several people stopped Nathan to praise his performances. Nathan accepted their words with an embarrassed flush. They all smiled at me but instinctively avoided engaging me in conversation because of my connection with Kalakos. I was long used to this and barely noticed.

"Where did you learn to clown like that?" I asked after William Myrtle stopped Nathan for congratulations, the fifth person to do so. "I've never seen anyone perform the mirror spot so well."

"Joseph and I are very close. He's been obsessed with that spot his entire life, so we do it."

The thick, sugary scent of caramel wafted by, mixing with the smell of soap as we passed old Margery Mays, who was kneeling behind a tub of water and indifferently scrubbing a bright blue shirt against a washboard.

"What are you obsessed with?" I asked, a little playfully. "What do *you* like to do?"

Nathan halted and looked at me.

I stopped, too. "What's wrong?"

"No one's ever asked me that before," he said. "I like it."

I felt discomforted, but in a way I enjoyed. His eyes were so blue. Cloth continued to slap against water as Margery did her washing. "So what's the answer?"

"You should know," he replied. "You see the future."

Now it was my turn to stare, but in shock. "Who told you that?"

"My brother. Or perhaps it was Mr. Kalakos."

I couldn't respond. Nathan noticed my distress, and his expression became instantly contrite.

"I'm sorry, Dodd. I didn't mean to hurt you. Really." He put a brief hand on my shoulder. His touch, light as it was, seared my skin through the cloth like a branding iron fresh from the forge.

Henry, the ring groom, led the two newly-scrubbed mechanical horses around one of the tents. They snorted steam and smoke as they passed. I tried to keep the memories back, but Nathan's touch and the smell of coal smoke broke barriers. Sudden loneliness washed over me, even though Nathan stood not a foot away, and I didn't want to keep anything from him.

I held up my left hand, the one with six fingers. "I see things. Not just the future, but also…*things.*" My eyes lost their focus and I forgot where I was. "I started life as a climbing boy, back before automata put the chimney sweeps out of business. My friends and I squirmed into tiny spaces with little brushes, and Scar—the man who owned us in all but name—forced us to scrub them clean. The chimneys were narrow and black as night. It was hard to breathe. Sometimes you got stuck. Trapped in the black bricks with no way to move."

Nathan shuddered. "It sounds horrible."

"And then there was the Thin Man," I whispered.

"Who was he?"

"I still don't know. Sometimes I think he was just a figment created by my own mind, a personification of the terrible futures I saw for my friends. Sometimes I think he really existed."

"But who was he?"

The whole world faded away now. For a moment, I felt poised again, held between devotion and destruction as I had outside of Kalakos's wagon, unnerved and unsettled. Nathan stood before me, solid and complete, and I turned my focus on him, ignoring the other sensation, refusing to examine the choices. Nathan's blue eyes and sunset hair became my universe. Words poured out of me, desperate for something to connect with. Nathan drank them in for me, and I felt grateful for his presence.

"The Thin Man killed you," I said. "He hid in the dark places and made you slip and fall three stories into a stone fireplace. He loosened bricks that crumbled under your knee so you dropped downward a little and became wedged in place until you suffocated. He started chimney fires that roasted you alive. All the climbing boys told stories about him, but I was the only one who could see him. I was the only one he talked to in the dark. Finally he burned one of my best friends to death, and I realized running away was safer than staying. Just before I scarpered, the Thin Man begged me not to go, so I knew it was the right choice. Maybe he only existed because I could see him. I haven't seen him since.

"In the meantime, I had to eat, and climbing boys make good

thieves. We can get into all sorts of places. I never got caught, either —I knew when the mingers were coming. But I was still living in shadows. Then I came here, to the Emporium, looking for something to steal. Kalakos caught me, but instead of beating me or arresting me, he put me to work. I swept his forge and cleaned his workshop and even learned to be an acrobat. But with the automata I found my true talent." I remembered where I was and shook myself free of the memories and of Nathan's blue gaze. "Sorry. I ramble sometimes."

"You needed to. I like listening to you, Dodd."

He was so ingenuous, so calm and carefree. I envied and desired it at the same time. "Come along," I said. "I'll show you the Black Tent."

The Black Tent was always erected some distance from the main Emporium due to the risk of fire. It was called the Black Tent not for its colour, which was canvas grey, but because Kalakos and I did a fair amount of blacksmith work there. I held the flap aside for Nathan, my eyes on his face so I could catch his reaction.

Nathan didn't disappoint. His expression lit up with wonder, like a josser in the front row. The Black Tent was lined with machines of all shapes. Gears spun, keys twirled, steam puffed, whistles peeped, wheels whirled. The half-completed elephant head I was working on opened and closed its mouth. The iron cat batted at the bars of her cage. Other animals—goats, dogs, rabbits, frogs, even a small dragon —lay on the ground or on shelves, waiting to be repaired or activated for a performance, but a few pairs of eyes summoned the energy to swivel sleepily in our direction. Most were prototypes—the working automata were housed elsewhere in Henry's care.

Worktables, benches, storage cupboards, trunks, and tool racks occupied the central area of the Black Tent, and a serviceable forge with a carefully-designed chimney took up part of one wall. Beside it stood a tall rack of Leyden jars, each labeled with letters in Kalakos's careful handwriting: WM, CG, MD, HW, AD, though several jars along the bottom were left blank. Beside that stood a long table with an electrical apparatus attached to it.

My windup spiders, all twelve of them, skittered across the ground and various work surfaces to greet me. The two smallest clambered up my trousers into my arms like small children wanting a kiss from Papa while the others leaped and cavorted round my ankles. I reached down to pat the big red one and give it a windup.

"Hello, Red," I greeted it.

"I always miss the main show," Nathan said. "Joseph runs us back to Kalakos's railcar or the wagon."

"Why do you stay in there all day?" I asked.

Nathan hesitated just noticeably enough. "Joseph isn't sociable. I finally persuaded him to let me out for a while. Do your spiders perform?"

A pointed change of subject, and I couldn't resist showing off. I said, "Juggle spot three!" All the spiders but Red rolled themselves into little balls. Red snatched his brothers up with his forward legs and juggled them. He bounced them off the ground or off his own body, and they leaped back into formation. Ten of them linked themselves into five balls in mid air, let Red toss them about again, and they split back into ten.

"End!" I said, and they all dropped to the ground. "Bow!" The spiders turned to Nathan and bent their legs.

"Amazing!" Nathan applauded, and I felt more pleased than if I'd received a standing ovation from the Royal Court. "And you invented them?"

"I did." An idiot grin spread across my face at his enthusiasm.

"You're a genius." Nathan put out his hand and a spider scuttled toward him to investigate, its key spinning merrily. "What are all those jars on the shelf for?"

At that my face hardened. "They belong to Kalakos. They store… electricity. I prefer spring and steam, myself."

"And this one?" He reached for the lynx-sized cat in her cage. Quick as a flash I grabbed his hand and yanked him away. The cat lunged, her sharp iron claws swiping the air his flesh had occupied a split-second before. She hissed angrily and lunged again. The metal of her flesh rattled against the scratched and battered bars of her cage. Nathan went pale.

"What happened?" he asked, backing away.

"Kalakos created her years ago, but she became more and more unstable," I said. "Now she threatens to disembowel anyone who opens the cage."

"Why not destroy it?"

"It's… complicated." In that moment I realized Nathan's hand was still in mine, warm and strong. Our eyes met, and he made no move to withdraw. I started to do so myself, then my choices opened up in front of me. If I pulled away, I saw myself frightened and alone. If I kept his hand, I saw myself frightened and *not* alone.

I kept Nathan's hand and squeezed it. Nathan squeezed back, and the other choice vanished. We didn't say a word about our new arrangement as I went on explaining different aspects of the Black

Tent—the forge where Kalakos and I created our own gears, the ink-stained tables where we drew plans and made calculations, the intricate workings of half-built difference engines of the sort first built by Charles Babbage and perfected by Ada Lovelace. He kept my hand throughout, and I thought my heart would burst from that tiny gesture.

"But what's it all for?" Nathan finally asked.

"For?" I echoed. My mind was mostly on the fact that I was still holding his hand.

"Why do you build these machines for a circus? Surely you could find a position at a large shop or even a university." He touched one of my spiders with his free hand, and it bobbed up and down for a moment. "The same applies to Kalakos. Why does he spend his time here?"

"I never thought about it. Kalakos has always been here. And he took me in and educated me, and so I stay. Without him, I'd still be dodging mingers."

"What's Kalakos dodging?"

I pursed my lips in puzzlement. Nathan had the disconcerting habit of asking simple questions that required complicated answers. "I've never—"

"I want the other half now, damn it!" The tent flap burst open and Joseph Storm strode in, closely followed by Victor Kalakos. I dropped Nathan's hand as if it were poisonous and stepped away from him.

"And I'm telling you," Kalakos replied, "the procedure should be spread out among at least three sessions. Doing it all at once creates an enormous risk."

"I don't care. Do it all *now*."

"Mr. Kalakos?" I said uncertainly.

"And you," Joseph growled at Nathan. It continued to astound me how exactly alike they looked. "I've been looking everywhere. Didn't I tell you to go to the wagon?"

All of Nathan's earlier charm and inquisitiveness drained away. "I...I didn't..."

"As for you—" He stabbed a finger in my direction. "You will do as you're told and help Kalakos."

My mouth dropped open at his audacity. "Remember your place, Mr. Storm," I snapped, "or perhaps you'd like to find another position?"

"Would that please my brother?" Joseph countered in an oily voice, and my blood chilled. "There's so much you don't know, Dodd, so keep your mouth shut and remember *your* place as street trash."

My fists were already up. The spiders, sensing my agitation, surrounded me like a pack of iron dogs. Their claws clicked in a sinister chorus that didn't seem to bother Joseph in the slightest. He snatched up the smallest from the ground and held it pointedly before him. The spider struggled in his grip like a kitten, its delicate legs waving impotently in the air. I froze.

"Joseph," Nathan pleaded, "don't."

Kalakos, apparently ignoring us, had moved behind the table near the Leyden jars. "Mr. Storm. If you please?"

I turned to stare at him. His deferential tone frightened me more than the possibility that Joseph might destroy my beloved spider. Kalakos, meanwhile, took up a blank Leyden jar from the bottom shelf and a fountain pen from the drafting table. A cold draft washed over my body as he wrote "NS" on the label. I now knew what Joseph Storm meant when he said I would "help."

"No," I said. My teeth were chattering.

"Yes, Dodd." Kalakos replied, his eyes boring into me. He hadn't spoken to me in that tone since I was a youth. "I will perform the procedure, and you will assist, just as Mr. Storm says."

I moved toward him, my spider forgotten. The other spiders hovered between me and Joseph, uncertain what to do as I grasped Kalakos by the elbow. "You promised you wouldn't do this anymore," I whispered hoarsely. "You know what it does to people. Leave Nathan alone."

"I brought you up from the gutter, Dodd," he said.

"Please!" I was begging now. "Not him. I…I care about what happens to him."

Kalakos's eyes softened. "I know." Then they hardened. "Now do as you're told or I'll put you on this table as well."

I wanted to refuse him. I looked to Nathan and then to Kalakos, caught between them. I remembered Nathan's hand in mine. But I also remembered the way Kalakos rescued a street thief worth less than the clothes he wore.

Woodenly, I accepted the Leyden jar Kalakos handed me. I connected it to the casing while Kalakos had Nathan remove his pullover and shirt, exposing a sleekly powerful chest and abdomen. He lay down upon the table and let Kalakos strap him down. Joseph watched, still holding my spider. Nathan accepted the treatment without comment, obeying his brother here just as he did in the ring, but with none of the sly digs. I wanted to ask why, but I couldn't even bring myself to meet his eyes.

"The jars all contain the souls of your performers, is that right, Doctor?" Joseph said.

"Doctor?" I asked.

"They do not." Kalakos drew a buckle across the smooth skin of Nathan's chest. "It isn't easy to remove a soul from a human being and house it in something else, either organic or automatic. Most say it can't be done."

I glanced involuntarily at the cat in her cage. Kalakos took up a helmet-shaped device made of copper netting and fitted it over Nathan's head while I took a metal plate and pressed it against his breastbone. Nathan looked at me with that strange child-like acceptance in his eyes, and I looked away. I had wiring to connect.

"You said your device can do it," Joseph accused.

"It can," Kalakos replied. He set straps round Nathan's ankles. "A soul is nothing more than a form of electromagnetic energy. Babbage and Lovelace's difference engine allowed us to calculate the exact frequency for the soul. A sufficiently complicated electrical device—" he gestured at his machine "—has the power to move a soul from one place to another, just like we can move current from a generator to a Leyden jar."

"I like that you keep their souls in jars," Joseph said pleasantly. "It's a brilliant way to keep them under your thumb."

"I told you those aren't souls," Kalakos said. "They're pieces. I once had a machine in Geneva that would transfer a complete soul all at once, but that device was destroyed. I did rebuild, but without the proper inspiration—"

"His name was Georgie Byron, as I recall," Joseph interrupted. I stiffened and turned to stare at Kalakos.

"—without the proper inspiration, I couldn't get it right," Kalakos continued as if Joseph hadn't spoken. "My new machine failed to transfer the subjects properly, and they were…damaged. Then I realized I could simply dial back the voltage and not take the entire soul. It does no immediate harm to the owners, though they tend to age faster and die sooner. And it does make them more pliable. I don't worry about them snooping among my machines. Or asking questions about my past."

"I've noticed. How did you get them on the table in the first place?" Joseph said.

"I tell them I just need a small reading for an experiment. Afterward, they don't have the wherewithal to ask further."

"Since I'm not so accommodating, I will ask—what do you use the soul pieces for?"

"Why do you think my automata work so well?" Kalakos countered.

Joseph nodded. "One soul bit per automata these days then. So what about your sweet little cat?" Joseph pointed at her with his free hand. She made a metallic hiss. "Do you call her Patches? Or Legion? What a terrible experiment that turned out to be."

"A sad miracle," Kalakos said grimly. "More than a dozen souls inside will drive anything mad, I know that now. She needs no power source, for all the good it does her. My penance is to look after her."

"And what about this spider?" Joseph brandished the little automaton, and his tone grew suggestive. "Whose partial soul does it house? That strapping strong man? The sword swallower?"

I didn't dare speak. Anger made my hands shake, and I found it hard to keep connecting wires.

"Dodd doesn't need my machine," Kalakos said. "He doesn't even know how to operate it. *His* Babbage engines are beyond brilliant. Sometimes I think his automata generate little souls of their own." He went to the control panel on the casing, which was covered in switches and dials. Opening it, he thrust a hand inside to check something, then withdrew it. "Dodd, I don't need you for this part. Go now."

I looked at Nathan, strapped shirtless to the table, wires sprouting from his head and chest. "Will it hurt?" he whispered.

"A bit," I murmured. "You'll convulse for a moment, but it'll be quick."

"Go, Dodd," Kalakos repeated. "Out."

I turned on my heel and strode past the brothers, refusing to meet Nathan's eyes, my spiders trailing after me. Joseph's voice stopped me at the tent flap.

"You forgot one." He held up the littlest spider. I reached for it, but he deliberately bent one of the delicate legs backward with the thin screeching sound of tortured metal. Then Joseph tossed the creature to me and turned away. Caught between fear and anger, I snatched my twitching creation out of the air and left.

The long, chill Irish twilight had descended over the Emporium. Lamps and candles glowed within tents and wagons. I walked quickly, dodging tent stakes and heavy ropes that smelled of tar and refusing to think about what was happening on that table in the Black Tent, refusing to see Nathan strapped to table, refusing to look at the future pathways that diverged before me. My troop of spiders kept pace. I set the broken one on Red's back for him to carry.

The wagon Nathan shared with his brother loomed ahead of me like a wooden beast. Perhaps my feet had taken me to it of their own volition. I glanced at the other wagons parked in the vicinity. No one seemed to be looking, and I doubted anyone would have the temerity to say anything if they were. I climbed the short creaky steps to the rear door. The wagon was boxlike, and brightly-painted with large wheels. Two hooks hung at the top of the door, which was locked. A snap of my fingers brought one of the spiders to me.

"Open!" I ordered.

The spider climbed the wood to the doorknob. From its underside extruded a set of small tools that served a multitude of functions. With a *click*, the lock scraped open and I was inside.

"Light!" Two spiders produced phosphorescent spheres to illuminate the interior. Like all of its kind, the wagon was compact and efficient. A pair of bunk beds took up the front. Shelves folded down from the side walls to serve as tables, and storage boxes with cushions on top created seats. One shelf was currently in the down position. Newspapers and a few books lay scattered across it. A coal stove the size of a hatbox near the door allowed heat or, in bad weather, cooking—most performers prepared meals outside or visited the Emporium's food tent. A scent of cedar hung in the air.

My spiders clattered inquisitively about the wagon as I touched the lower bunk, where I was sure Nathan slept, and noticed something—the bed had recently been altered. The upper bunk was new, as were the mattress and counterpane and pillow. The lower was much more worn, and the blankets were patched.

The bottom of the bunk was a built-in drawer. Inside, neatly folded, lay clothes that smelled like Nathan. I pressed a nightshirt to my face, seized with the overwhelming desire to run for the Black Tent, snatch Nathan up, and run with him until the Emporium vanished beyond the horizon.

But would Nathan go? Leave his twin brother and pieces of his soul behind?

My talent opened up, and several reflections stood before me, mirrors within mirrors. In all of them I asked Nathan to run away with me, and in all of them he said—

I slammed my eyes shut and clapped my hands over my ears. I didn't want to see. I didn't want to know. Eventually the vision faded, and I blinked down at the half-open drawer. Something at the back caught my eye. Uneasily, I extracted a rolled-up canvas tube. A painting. I unrolled it, and my spiders gathered round as if they, too, wanted to see.

At first it seemed to be a singularly well-done portrait of Joseph—his proud expression gave him away—dressed in a fine suit with an old-fashioned cloak draped over his right shoulder. As the painting unrolled further, revealing more of him, my skin prickled and my breath tightened. Arching downward from the side of the man's stomach was Nathan. His body lay face-up, his arms dangling like fleshy tubes, his blue eyes vacant. A bit of silver drool ran from his open mouth. His single leg went round Joseph's chest while the other remained buried in his brother's body, as if he had tried to escape but didn't quite make it. Nathan was naked, his ribs gaunt, his red hair unkempt.

At the bottom of the painting was a sign: THE BROTHERS LAZARUS AND JOANNES BAPTISTA COLLOREDO NOW ACCEPTING VISITORS. ENQUIRE WITHIN. The top of the painting had two grommets in it, ready to hang on the two hooks I'd seen outside on the door.

Fear chilled my stomach and made my bowels watery. My heart thudded hard. I had encountered dozens of freaks in my time, but this one made every bit of my flesh crawl.

"I've seen real magic, you know. China, Borneo, Japan."

I shoved the painting back into the drawer and fled, barely remembering to lock the door behind me. The moon lit my way as I ran all the way back to my own wagon with my heart in my mouth.

Nathan was sitting on the steps. The horrible painting rose in my mind, and my first response was to turn away from him. Instead, still standing, I embraced him where he sat in the silver light. He pressed his face to my stomach and wrapped his shaking fingers in mine. The spiders formed a half-circle guard of honour round us, the injured one still on Red's back. I stroked Nathan's hair, and felt surprise at how powerful such a small thing could feel.

"I'm sorry about what Kalakos did to you," I said hoarsely. "He won't do it again."

"It's not your fault," he replied. "And I don't mind."

I backed up and stared. "How can you not mind? He strapped you to a table and put a piece of your soul into a jar!"

"My soul doesn't belong to me." Nathan rose. "It never did."

"Don't give me that shit about souls belonging only to God," I said, pushed into cursing. "The church uses that lie to keep idiots under—"

"My soul is Joseph's," Nathan interrupted. "And he wants it back."

I want the other half now, damn it!

My legs weakened, and I grabbed at Nathan for support, which he gave. "I don't want to talk out here," I said. "Let's go inside."

My wagon was much like Nathan and Joseph's—bed at the front, fold-up tables, tiny stove. The spiders stayed outside, and I locked the door. For the first time, we were completely alone and in a place where no one could walk in unexpectedly. I was aware of Nathan's scent and the heat from his body as I lit a lamp and we took up seats.

"I know your real name is Colloredo," I said. "And I know what you used to…be."

Nathan looked down. "You think I'm a freak."

"No!" I grabbed his hand. "It startled me, yes, but I'm past that. How did you separate?"

Nathan dropped my hand and breathed hard. "It's difficult to talk about. Even with you."

"If you can't, I under—"

"No, no." He waved my objections away. "We were born attached to each other like that, but Joseph was fully formed while I was…not. It was as if I were some sort of parasite, draining the life out of him. I only had a rudimentary consciousness and no intelligence to speak of. I flopped next to my brother and drooled while he tried to go about a normal life. People mocked him when we were children until our mother hit upon the idea of covering me with a heavy cloak. Old-fashioned, but it worked. Still, there was no way for him to learn a trade. Eventually, Joseph was forced to travel the country, exhibiting himself to any who came to look with coin in hand. He did quite well, actually—Joseph is very intelligent. He's had dinner with kings, you know. But through it all, he wanted a life of his own, one without a parasitic brother growing out of his side."

"You're not a parasite," I said earnestly. "You're a person."

He nodded grimly. "Still, Joseph deserved to be free of me. Doctors said it couldn't be done, not even with the help of automata, so he looked to magic. It was easy enough to find magicians—Joseph had exploited his contacts at court very well, and sorcerers were fascinated by us in any case. But none in this hemisphere could help. We travelled to the Orient, to India, China, and Japan. Eventually we came to Borneo, and there we found a circle of witch doctors." Nathan's eyes grew hard. "For three days they did terrifying and painful things to me—to us. In the end, they drew us apart and brought my body to full strength. But powerful magic always comes with a powerful price."

"Which was?" I didn't want to hear, but knew the answer would come.

"The magicians said we shared most of a body because we only had one soul between us. No man can live long without his soul, and rather than leave one of us to die, they cut our soul in two, leaving half for each."

"Dear God," I whispered.

"If either of us strays more than a few miles from the other, it means instant death for us both. When one of us dies, the other will follow within weeks."

"Did the magicians tell you that?" I asked sharply. "Or did you hear it from Joseph?"

A small bubble of laughter burst out. "You're as intelligent as he is. The magicians told us, actually, after they pulled us apart. And I can feel it. It hurts when we separate too far, like I'm tearing in two."

"So Joseph is hoping Kalakos and his machine can restore him," I said.

He nodded, and I wanted to gather him into my arms. Something held me back, however. Old habits? Fear? I wasn't sure. This conversation, confession, felt a little off. "How did Joseph even know about the machine? How did he meet Kalakos?"

"That happened years ago, in Italy. Joseph was exhibiting us, and the man you call Victor Kalakos befriended us. He had an iron cat, half a dozen Leyden jars, and a machine that barely worked. You can imagine my brother's interest when we ran across him here in Dublin, though he'd changed his name—and profession."

"What was his name then?" I asked. "Joseph called him Doctor."

"His name was John, I think. John Polidori. He was heartsick over a poet, or something."

"Polidori," I repeated, tasting the name and trying to attach it to the man I knew as Victor Kalakos. He had lied to me for years, and I felt betrayed. You lied to the flatties in the audience, not to other circus folk. Not to me.

Nathan sighed. "I love my brother, Dodd. I wouldn't even exist without him. All his life, I held him back, dragged him down. I have to give him what he needs. He deserves that."

"Your brother wants Kalakos to hand him your soul piece by piece," I scoffed. "No one deserves that much."

"There's so much you don't know, Dodd." Nathan took a deep breath. "Kalakos did it all at once. My soul is already gone."

A crushing weight slammed over me and the cold returned. I tried to speak, but my voice wouldn't work. Nathan took my hands in his. They were warm.

"He didn't," I finally croaked.

"He did. Kalakos put my half of our soul in that jar. The machine will recharge soon, and then he'll give the soul to my brother."

"But you'll die!"

His voice grew soft. "Then we should make the most of what time we have." He leaned forward, intending to kiss me. My hands shook and my heart raced like an overwound automaton as I leaned toward him, smelling his scent. A coppery taste came to my mouth. Our lips brushed—

—and he broke away. Nathan shot to his feet and turned his back.

Sudden anxiety made me ill. Had I done something wrong? "What's the matter?"

"It still doesn't work." He was shaking all over. My first thought was that he was weeping, but I quickly saw he was holding in silent laughter. I couldn't understand why. Then things fell into place and I felt dropped into a tub of ice water.

There's so much you don't know, Dodd.

"Joseph!" I said hoarsely. "You son of a whore!"

He turned. Nathan's gentle tenderness was gone from that handsome face, replaced by Joseph's sneer.

"Remember your place, Dodd," he said, "or perhaps you'd like to find another…position." His kick slammed into my stomach. The unexpected move caught me by utter surprise, and the air burst from my lungs, leaving me gasping on the hard wagon floor. In an instant, Joseph was sitting atop me, my arms pinned beneath his knees. A straight razor flicked open in his hand and he set the blade against my neck. My eyes went wide. I tried to control the terror that made my heart jerk beneath his weight.

"Do you know what it's like to share your soul?" he hissed. His eyes had gone hard and flat as blue glass. "All my life I've wondered what it is to think as other people, *feel* as other people. I've lured people into my wagon on the pretence of gawping at me and then done fantastic things, intense things, trying and trying to understand what they *feel*. But it never worked. Now I've taken my twin's soul for myself and kissed his catamite, and I still feel nothing. Something's wrong."

"I don't doubt it," I gasped. The blade pierced the skin on my neck and I flinched. Warm blood oozed round the razor. "If you're going to kill me, just do it."

Joseph shook his head. "It would be too hard to explain your disappearance. And I don't need to kill you. Not while I have a firm hold on you." He reached behind himself with a free hand and grabbed my groin in a strong fist. The leaden pain that twisted in my lower gut made me cry out. "I know what you are, and I know what you want. You'll do everything I say, now and forever, or I'll reveal your filthy nature to the world. You'll spend the rest of your life chained to a prison treadmill, letting the guards fuck you for a chance to see the sun."

"What do you want?" I wheezed.

"Nothing at the moment," Joseph said. His tone had turned pleasant, as if we were discussing automata gears. "But when I come for you, you'll be ready. Just as Kalakos was."

He gave me another hard squeeze, and then he was at the door. "I have my brother's soul," he said over his shoulder. "You can have his body." And he was gone.

I lay gasping on the floor for several moments, then sat up to press a handkerchief to my neck. Fear and pain wound iron bands around me. Then I thought of Nathan, and I was out the door, rushing through the early night to the Black Tent, my spiders behind me. The flap already lay open, and I burst inside.

Nathan was gone. Kalakos sat on the empty table of his machine, face long. Beside him stood the Leyden jar with the stark initials NS inscribed upon it. The tent smelled of ozone.

"I knew you'd come," Kalakos said. "Nathan's in his wagon, if you want to know."

Enraged, I rushed across the tent and grabbed him by the lapels of his jacket. "Tell me Joseph was lying. Tell me Nathan still has his soul and I'll let you live!"

"I'm sorry." Kalakos was limp and soft in my grip. "I'm not proud of it, Dodd, though the fact that I extracted Nathan's entire soul without harm to him should be—"

"Without harm?" I cracked my fist across his jaw. The cat yowled appreciation from her cage. "How's *that* for 'without harm'?"

Kalakos rocked back on the table and put a hand to his face. "I deserved that. You may hit me again, if you like. I won't stop you."

I pulled back my fist again, and dropped it. The anger drained out of me. "Why did you do it?" I asked instead. "Why didn't you just refuse him?"

"After all these years, I thought I'd left Dr. John Polidori behind me," he said. "Dr. John Polidori and his gambling debts and his failed experiments and his involvement in that young baron's death and his wonderful faked suicide. But Joseph Storm remembered me. He has letters in my own hand confessing my love for a…certain awkward person and detailing our more intimate moments. I expect he stole them when we first became friends and held onto them all these years."

"The awkward person was George Byron?"

He looked even more pained. "I hope you, of all men, can understand. At any rate, Dr. Polidori is wanted for questioning by a number of courts—or he would be if anyone found out he was still alive."

Trying to remain calm, I picked up the Leyden jar as if it were a priceless jewel. It was strangely light. "He'll never let you alone, you know. Blackmailers never do. Once you do this, he'll want something else, and then something else. You may as well put this" —I brandished the jar—"back into Nathan's body. I *need* you to do it. I can't operate your damned machine."

"No."

The anger swelled again. "Why not?"

"I'm weak, Dodd." He looked close to tears. "I face life imprisonment at hard labour if I don't obey Joseph Storm."

"I know the same secrets," I said cruelly. "What if I tell you to restore Nathan's soul or *I* go to the police?"

Kalakos snatched the jar from me. "Don't talk nonsense." He set the jar behind him and grabbed my shoulders with both hands. "You're like a son to me, Dodd. Your machines are more brilliant than mine, and you see into universes I can't comprehend. You'll go further than I ever did, and what father doesn't want that for his son?"

It was the first time he had ever said such things to me, but rage overwhelmed tenderness. "What kind of father destroys his son's chance for happiness?" I snarled.

He turned away from me then. "Trust me, Dodd. Go now. Go to your friend and tell him how you feel. Things will look different in the morning."

"Do go, Dodd," Joseph Storm agreed, from the open tent flap, and I wondered how long he'd been standing outside, listening. Had Kalakos known he was there? "The good doctor and I have a process to finish."

Resolve filled me. "I'm not leaving without that jar."

"Then I'll go to the police."

"I'm not Kalakos," I growled. "I don't care about the police."

"Dodd," Kalakos interjected feebly, "please."

"In that case" Joseph gestured and two large men in black coats entered the tent. One of them had a metal arm with claws on the fingers, the other wore a large eyepiece which I recognized as a small codex that would enhance reflexes. "Perhaps my friends here can persuade you."

The two men moved toward me. I pulled a whistle from my pocket and blew. Instantly, my spiders swarmed into the tent. "Defend!" I ordered.

The spiders leaped. Red knocked the man with the metal arm flat on his back, and the injured spider attached itself to his face. He screamed. Eyepiece-man glided aside and flicked one attacking spider to the ground, but two more swarmed up his coat, and a third bit the back of his neck. The man grunted and snatched the biting spider, intending to fling it away, but it wrapped all eight legs around his wrist. Blood ran down his neck. The cat screeched in her cage. I reached for a heavy lead weight.

"Stop!"

I spun. Joseph was standing over the Leyden jar with a hammer.

"I'll smash it," he said.

"That might kill you." I said, though my mouth had gone dry. "Or send Nathan's soul back to his body."

"It might send Nathan's soul to eternity. Let's find out." He raised the hammer, and my talent crashed over me, showing destruction and devotion again, and I couldn't tell them apart. Cold fear tore through me. I didn't understand what I was seeing. Worse, I didn't know what would happen if the futures were resolved, but Nathan was clearly bent on resolving them.

"Don't!" I cried.

Nathan paused, and the vision vanished. "The spiders, then."

"Come!" I ordered. Instantly, the spiders left the struggling men and surrounded me. Shuddering, the man with the metal arm got to his feet while the eyepiece man wiped blood from his neck and glared murder at me.

"Shut them down," Joseph ordered.

Hands shaking, I pressed the switch on each spider that disengaged its spring mechanism. They went still.

"Hold him," Joseph said to his men.

"What are you doing?" I gasped as iron-hard hands grabbed me on both sides.

Joseph towed an unresisting Kalakos to the table. "You're going to watch the final process. You deserve it, Dodd."

I fought again, but the men were too strong. Joseph lay on the table and Kalakos, working alone, connected man and jar to the machine. When I tried to close my eyes, my captors pried them open. Joseph grinned the entire time, even when Kalakos threw the final switch and he convulsed hard. The jar snapped with current, then went quiet.

I vaguely remember howling like a dog. The hired men shoved me out of the Black Tent and tossed my dead spiders after. I stumbled to my feet, feeling numb inside. By now it was nearly midnight, and barely enough yellow gaslight leaked into the Emporium from the street lamps to illuminate my way. Someone shouted in the street, and a hiss of steam gushed wetly from a distant pipe. A few sallow faces looked out of wagon windows doors or peeped through tent flaps as I ran past, but no one spoke, and I ignored them. Nathan drew me inside the wagon he shared with his brother and shut the door. The smell of cedar surrounded us.

"How do you feel?" I demanded.

"Much the same," he said, and I touched his face. Then his chest and his arms and his hands. I thumped his sides, gently and first, then harder and harder. I slammed his shoulders. I beat my fist upon his body until he caught my wrist.

"I'm here," he said. "I'm real and solid."

And then he was kissing me. I kissed him back, and our arms went round each other for a long, long time. His large hands ran down my back and pulled us together. My heart swelled up and I pressed against him, trying to go into him, *through* him. Occupy the same space.

"We don't have much time left," I said when we separated. My breath was coming in short gasps. "In a few weeks, you'll age and die."

"I know."

I felt strangely free of a sudden. "We should do something fun. Fuck Kalakos and fuck the Emporium and *fuck* your brother."

"Do you know what I want to do?" Nathan asked with a mischievous air. "I want to go into town and get drunk and kiss you with ale still in my mouth and then I want to go with you into a room with a big bed and watch you take your clothes off one bit at a time."

"Mr. Storm!" I kissed him again, and licked his teeth. "You took the words out of my mouth."

We stole two live horses from the stable tent and rode up Merrion Street to Westland Row and turned down George's Quay on the River Liffey. The cobbled streets were deserted except for the occasional carriage or pedestrian, but the closer we got to George's Quay, the busier the city became. People and horses and automata crowded the streets and walks. Light and music and drunks spilled out of open pub doors. A circle of people cheered as four men fought a brass automaton. Deep-cleavaged prostitutes called out to us. Scents of garbage and manure and piss all mixed with the wet smell of the Liffey. I guided us down a side street, where I happened to know of a series of inns and pubs that catered to men of a certain type.

Fuck that. They catered to men like me. And Nathan.

I paid a boy to watch the horses and led Nathan into the common room of the Standing Stone. The drinking was in full swing, and smells of stout and sweat hung in the air. Sailors from ships in dock mingled with tradesmen and well-dressed gentlemen in booths, at the bar, and at tables. The wooden floor was sticky, and conversation was loud. Nathan drank it all in like a boy allowed at his first grown-up party, and I loved that about him. I wanted to show him the whole world so I could see that joy cross his face every day.

I found two chairs at an already-crowded table and ordered a round for everyone seated there, which made me popular. Nathan sat down, and I flung an arm across his shoulders. He grinned.

"I'm Dodd," I said, "and this is Nathan. We're going to get drunk because he doesn't have a soul."

"Hell, I don't either," said a man sitting across from us, and with a start I recognized him as the man with coal-black hair. "Priest took mine years ago in a confessional."

"And I left mine with that boy in New York," said an older sailor. "Cheers!"

We all clanked mugs and drank. Nathan kissed me with the taste of Guinness still dark in his mouth, and the others roared their approval.

An hour later, the two of us stumbled upstairs together. In a room with a big solid bed, Nathan had everything he had wanted, and so did I. At last we lay back sleepily, our bodies dimly reflected in a cloudy mirror that hung over the wash stand. Nathan smiled in the soft light, his arm heavy across my chest.

"I never want to leave you," he murmured. "For the rest of my days."

∞

In the morning, I woke up and rolled over. The mattress beside me was empty, and Nathan's clothes were gone. I sat up, holding my head. It throbbed only a little, but it hurt with more than a hangover. So much for promises.

The door opened and Nathan came in, fully dressed, with two mugs of tea. Behind him, the mirror showed his back. "Get up, lazy!" he said. "I want to see more city."

I smiled so hard, my face was like to split in half. "There's a performance tonight. We should be there."

"I'm quitting," he said. "What's Joseph going to do to me? In a few weeks, I'll be dead anyway." He set the mugs down and jumped on the mattress. "I want all the fun I couldn't have before. Starting with this." He kissed me, and the tea he'd brought went stone cold before we managed to leave the bed again.

While I was dressing, I said, "Your brother told me about Borneo and everything else. How much do you remember of your life…before?"

Nathan was looking out the window at the noonday sun as if he had never really seen it before. "I remember everything Joseph did, everything he learned," he said. "I suppose that's for the best. I wouldn't know how to speak or read or even walk otherwise. But it's like remembering a dream. Every time I eat or drink or touch you, it's like I'm doing it for the first time." He grabbed me in a rough embrace and lifted me off the floor. "I'm so *alive* when I'm with you, Dodd. I know I'm going to die, but that's all right, as long as you're here."

When I got my breath back, I said, "There's another option."

"What do you mean?"

"The machine. It could still save you."

Nathan shook his head. "Joseph won't give any part of the soul back. There's nothing left for me."

I laid his hand on my chest. My heart beat beneath his palm. "I'll give you half of mine."

A moment passed, and Nathan looked at me for a long time. His fingers closed over mine. "No, Dodd. You'd age faster, and if you ever left me, you'd die. We'd be chained forever."

My stomach dropped. "Don't you want to be with me?"

"More than anything," he laughed. "That was never a question."

"Then why?"

"Because *I won't have a choice*. Do you see? It's the difference between *wanting* to be with you and *having* to be with you. The mirror's broken, Dodd. The spot is ended."

I opened my mouth to reply, then cut myself off. I didn't want to understand, but I did. "So what do you want to do?" The lump in my throat made it difficult to speak.

Still smiling, Nathan stepped forward and kissed me. Behind us, his ghostly reflection in the wash stand mirror copied the gesture. "Do you know no one's ever asked me that question before? I told you —I want to spend the rest of my time with you. In this city. Because I *want* to. I'll die here because it's where *I* want to die."

With that, Nathan reached out to run a warm hand through my hair. I shivered, trying to soak up Nathan's gentle touch and store it away before—

My talent opened up, and choices echoed in front of me. But this time, I didn't bother to look. I savagely snatched Nathan's wrist in an iron grip, and all other universes vanished before I even saw them.

"Horseshit!" I snapped. "You don't know what the hell you're saying." Nathan's blue eyes widened and he tried to back up, but I refused to let go of his wrist. "That business about being chained is an excuse. The world is enormous. We might find another scientist with a better machine, or a circle of druids with a better spell. Hell, *I* might figure out what to do, given time. You're just afraid of all those choices you haven't been able to make, so you're choosing not to choose."

I released Nathan's wrist. The expression on his face was at the same time apprehensive and accepting of my words. He stared at me for a long time as stale air crept round the room.

"You don't know what it's like," Nathan said at last, his voice all but inaudible. "The mirror is broken. I never know what's going to happen next."

A bark of laughter at the irony of his statement escaped me. We were more alike than Nathan knew. "You can be trapped in that or freed by it," I said. "Come on. Let's find Kalakos and get you half a soul."

Nathan stayed silent for the entire ride back to the Emporium, and I didn't ask what he was thinking. When we arrived, William Myrtle rushed up to us, his large muscles unmistakable, though he wasn't wearing his strongman costume. He was looking more lively, his eyes more energetic. "The mingers are at the Black Tent!" he said. "Mr. Kalakos—there's been a murder."

Cold fear slid down my spine. Without a word, Nathan and I rode hard to the Black Tent. My spiders sat outside where I had left them, their winding keys run down and motionless. We abandoned the horses, and inside the tent we found two constables and a tall, gaunt police detective in tweed. Kalakos stood calmly near the forge, his silver flask in hand. Behind him, every Leyden jar had been smashed, and I knew the source of William Myrtle's energy. Clearly, shattering the jars reunited souls. Had I known, I would have broken Nathan's jar myself.

On the ground lay Joseph Storm, clothes torn, his eyes wide and glassy. A dozen enormous wounds slashed his flesh. Scarlet blood soaked everything. It was dripping down the worktables, it had spattered the canvas, it had splashed the automata. In her cage, the cat was drenched with it, and bits of meat clung to her iron claws. She hissed at me. The smell of a slaughterhouse lay thick on the air.

"There you are, Dodd," Kalakos said cheerfully. A bloody scratch marred his face. "This is Detective Flint. I've already told him who I really am."

"What did you do?" I gasped.

"He's gone off his nut," one of the constables muttered.

"I realized you were right about blackmailers, and decided to end it the only way possible. That cat never changes. Once you open the cage, it all ends." He drank deeply from his flask. "I loved George Byron, and lost him. I loved the baron's son, and killed him. Devotion and destruction, inextricably intertwined."

I stared in utter shock. My thoughts fled all the way back to the moment that terrible and wonderful knock had come at his railcar door. Devotion or destruction. Those unnerving choices, the two I had been unable to sort out, had stood open and unresolved all this time, and I hadn't noticed because I couldn't bear to look closely. Devotion or destruction. Which one would come to pass?

I whispered, "Oh my God."

"Which will *you* choose, Dodd?" Kalakos looked pointedly at his bloody machine. "Which universe will you create and which will you destroy?"

"Sir," Detective Flint said to him, "you'll have to come with me now."

"Afraid not," Kalakos said. "I've one more life to destroy." His breathing became laboured. He dropped to his knees, clutching at his throat. By the time I reached his side, he was dead. A smell of almonds hung in the air.

"Cyanide in the flask," Flint pronounced. "Damn it."

I fell into a haze. The detective asked questions, but they were perfunctory. The bodies were taken away. Hands and arms guided me out of the Black Tent. I came to my senses in my wagon, sitting on my bed with Nathan beside me. My face felt hot, and I knew I'd been crying.

"They hired some women from town to clean up," Nathan was saying.

"Did they cancel the show tonight?" I asked.

"No. Myrtle volunteered to be ringmaster until something more permanent can be decided. News of the murder gave us a sold-out house."

"Mr. Kalakos would be happy about that, I think." I rubbed my hands over my face. "How are you handling it?"

"Perfectly well. It comes with not having a soul, I think. And now I'll never have one." He gave a harsh laugh. "If Kalakos hadn't taken my soul, I'd be dead, do you realize that? Joseph's half would have fled when he died, jerking mine out with it and killing me with the shock. By making me a soul-less automaton, he bought me a few weeks' life."

Kalakos's last words to me played over and over in my head, gnawing at me like a worm. "Nathan, who told you that you'd die if your brother did? Do you actually *remember* the witch doctors saying so?"

"No," Nathan said. "Joseph told me. After we were separated and we stopped sharing memories."

"Except before he attacked me in your wagon, he said the *magicians* told you both. He lied to me." A bit of hope flickered like a small star. "I think he lied to you, too. I think Joseph lied about a number of things."

"And why would he do that?"

"He needed to keep you close, keep your soul in a living jar until he could get at it. But he was afraid you might kill him first. He himself killed easily, and he couldn't see that his twin brother wasn't like that. He couldn't see that you're the same but backward. So Joseph told you that if he died, you died. But it was a lie. Nearly everything he said was a lie. Come on!"

I pulled him from my wagon and all but ran for the Black Tent. The Emporium was in an uproar. Performers rushed about, chattering and shouting with newfound enthusiasm, despite the ringmaster's death. The shattered Leyden jars had repaired their souls. The calliope hooted, and sausage sizzled in the food tent. People plucked at my sleeve, offering sympathy or demanding information. I shook them off more rudely than I intended and kept going, towing Nathan behind me.

The hired women had done a good job with the Black Tent, but the canvas was still stained red-brown in places. The machinery and automata were all clean, except for the cat, who wouldn't let anyone touch her. I avoided treading on the spot where Kalakos had died and headed straight for the table with Nathan at my side. The dials on the apparatus seemed to stare at me.

"Tell me," I whispered.

And for once, my talent opened at my command.

"What do you see?" Nathan whispered.

"Two possibilities." I shut my eyes. "When I was strapping you to the table, Kalakos reached inside the machine for a moment. There are two explanations. Either he made a minor repair, *or he disabled the machine.* If he made a repair, the machine stole your soul and you're going to die. If he disabled the machine, the soul transfer didn't work and you're going to live."

"Which possibility will come true?" His voice was hoarse.

"I don't know." I opened my eyes and looked at him, his face pale beneath autumn hair. "They're both equally possible. Kalakos cared about me and wanted me to be happy, but he was equally frightened of Joseph. In order to find out what Kalakos did, we have to open the case and look. Once we do, the two possibilities will collapse into a single path. You have half a chance of living once we open that case."

Nathan swallowed. "Oh, God."

I suddenly couldn't stand still. I dashed outside, snatched up the broken spider, and brought it back in. A bit of rummaging through the workbenches turned up a spare leg. "Remember when we were talking to Ferrous?" I said.

Nathan was still standing by the table. "You quoted John Locke."

I unbolted the bent leg and slipped the new one into place. "So are you thinking?"

"I'm thinking," he said. "I'm thinking that I love you."

My hand jerked spasmodically and I almost dropped the spider. I recovered myself and finished installing the leg. "I…"

"Can you say it, Dodd?" Nathan asked. His back was to me. "I think the final outcome is based on what you say next."

My mouth was dry, my hands were sweaty. Devotion or destruction. I still hadn't chosen. "I love you, Nathan," I said. "In this and every universe."

Nathan grinned over his shoulder at me, and my heart raced. Then he picked up a heavy hammer from the forge and smashed the machine. He hit it again and again, until it was nothing but a pile of wreckage. Nathan tossed the hammer aside.

"If the possibilities are never resolved," he panted, "what happens then?"

I wound up the spider and set it on the table, pretending nonchalance but unable to keep the enormous grin from creeping across my own face. "It means we'll have to have faith that a man as good and fine as you has a soul, and to hell with any machine."

Nathan strode toward me, and I opened my arms, aching for his touch. But he halted a scant foot away. He raised his hand, pressing the palm to an imaginary pane of glass. Without thinking, I matched the movement. Nathan raised his other hand. Mystified, I did the same. Then a sudden light sparkled in his eyes and he yanked me into his arms, bringing my space into his.

"Ha!" he growled in my ear. "Broke it!"

Beside us, the little spider skittered to the edge of the table, paused, and turned right.

Cuckoo

Madeleine E. Robins

Tannesburg was too small to have an orphanage. When the hired man from Sarah Eamon's place found a baby swaddled tightly in grimy cloth and propped against a tree at the edge of Miss Eamon's property, he brought it with him into town and left it with the doctor. And although the village was not yet connected to the new telephone line, Tannesburg had an efficient grapevine and Miss Eamons had heard all about the foundling and the way it had squalled, tucked under Pete Hargill's arm like a laundry bundle, long before Pete returned to work the next day. Then Sarah called at the doctor's house, justifying her curiosity with a sense of responsibility: Had not the baby been abandoned beneath her elm tree for anyone to find?

Mrs. Pratt, the doctor's wife, ushered Sarah upstairs to the second best bedroom to see "the little stranger," hastily accommodated in a makeshift crib. Mrs. Pratt went on about the child in nursery-room whispers, her voice squeezed high and girlish from her tight-corsetted body, waving her hands with their accompaniments of lace and floating cambric while Sarah looked at the baby. She had expected a pudgy infant with a vapid baby's face, but he was not like that. Even in sleep the tiny face was narrow, bony, with eyes set deeply below dark arched brows, and large elfin ears. Above his high, slanting forehead there was a dark thatch of coarse hair; about him altogether an air of strangeness, of slight deformity. As she looked at him, Sarah felt pity, and that vague wistfulness that sometimes hurt her at the sight of a baby. Then the child opened his eyes and stared soundlessly up at her, and Sarah felt a shock of familiarity run through her. They watched each other for a long moment; the baby's eyes were violet.

"…and so ugly, poor little thing. Who's to take care of him is what I want to know, Miss Eamons. We've no provision for this sort of thing; the Doctor and I cannot be expected—after all, I'm not a young woman anymore, and my health—"

Sarah turned away from the crib. "I'd take him, Mrs. Pratt," she said. "I'd like to."

While the ugly child in his crib slept, the ladies went down to the parlor, and Mrs. Pratt gave Sarah the first of many lectures she would hear on the folly of adopting the boy. What business had a maiden lady, no matter if she was barely thirty and well-to-do, to be raising a child like that, a boy, and a stray, too, parents the Lord knows who?

Sarah heard the words over and over. Tannesburg had a certain pride in Miss Eamons, living in the old white house settled in acres of green lawn; as they would have protected Sarah from ruffians and outsiders, they now tried to protect her from the baby—only Sarah refused to be protected. From the first moment, sitting cool and smiling in Mrs. Pratt's fussy parlor, her determined civility could not be persuaded.

She took the boy home within the week, bought a crib and baby clothes, toys, made arrangements for the daughter of the livery stable to come and help with extra chores at the house. The boy was christened Joseph. Sarah spent hours sitting, watching him, playing with him, looking for the flash of something turbulent in his violet eyes. Two weeks after his discovery, Tannesburg was distracted from the subject of Miss Eamons and her foundling by the incursion of a horseless carriage into the streets; gradually the adoption ceased to be a nine-days' wonder.

Joe grew slowly, small for his age. Neither Sarah's encouragement nor the cook's ingenuity could fill out his frame or plumpen his narrow face. His nose grew long and bony, incongruous in a child's face, and his elfin ears grew larger, pronouncedly pointed. There was also a deformity, twin ridges of bone parallel to his spine that began just below the shoulder blades. When he walked, Joe carried himself hunched forward slightly.

Children in the town, even the gentlest of them, called him names. It might have been expected: his odd looks and violet stare were disconcerting; his voice was harsh and croaking. Sooner or later someone would give in to the temptation to play a trick on the dummy, taunt him, make him cry. When he was old enough to start at school the teasing briefly became worse, and Joe returned from school every day bruised and dirty and stubbornly silent. Just when

Sarah thought she would have to do something, take steps, the boy learned an odd knack for effacing himself, avoiding the trouble-makers, and the trouble lessened.

Through the fights Sarah had watched, afraid to interfere or even comfort too much. Even as a very little boy, Joe had a manner that dismissed sympathy; Sarah had recognized that at once; it was something they shared.

Though Miss Eamons and her boy became a commonplace, they were never wholly taken for granted. Married women from town called at the big white house from time to time to advise her about raising the boy, certain that even the best-intentioned maiden lady could not raise up a boy without guidance.

They came, in complicated afternoon dresses bustled over impor-tant figures, carrying parasols and beaded reticules, and balanced teacups as they lectured. "Boys, Miss Eamons: you can't wrap them in cotton wool. My Teddy, for instance"

They gave her the benefit of their experiences graciously, and if Joe stopped in the parlor for a moment on his way out to play, they smiled generously on him, disconcerted by the tenderness at the corner of Miss Eamon's mouth and the gentleness of her hand on his hair. "Children must take their share of lumps, Miss Eamons," the ladies would tell her when he had left. "You can't be too easy with them just because…"

The 'just because" would drift off uncomfortably, and after a little while the ladies would finish their tea and go, between discomfort and virtue. Sarah Eamons was a maiden lady; what did she know about raising boys? And such an odd boy. It must be such a quiet life for the child. Neither of them would have recognized Sarah Eamons an hour later, running in lunatic circles across the lawn near the wood, playing a ruleless game of catch-as-catch-can with Joe, laughing, breathless, until Joe reached up to overbalance her, knocking her to the ground.

"Mama?" He circled back, just out of reach, to where Sarah lay gasping, a splash of white linen on the grass. For just a moment his eyes were dark and serious, alarmed. "Mama, are you all right? I didn't mean to hurt you."

"You can't wrap your Mama up in cotton wool, Joey," she sputtered, laughing. Sarah got shakily to her feet again. "But I do think it's time for dinner."

By the time they reached the house, hand in hand, Sarah was listening to a story of Joe's; when Carrie, one of the hired girls, met them on the sun porch, they unclasped their hands as if by mutual consent, and Sarah sent him off to clean up for dinner.

In the evenings they sat on the sun porch at the back of the old house if it was warm, with Joe by Sarah's feet, leaning against her chair, near enough so that she could touch his shoulder as they talked, so that he could turn and bump his forehead against her knee, his awkward caress. When the weather turned cold, they moved indoors and sat together on an old red davenport, reading together, inspecting picture books of English castles, Russian mosques, French cathedrals with vaulted ceilings and odd carved figures guarding the downspouts and doorways. Sometimes Joe made up stories for Sarah's benefit, or she would talk about growing up, about her parents, about waiting for something special that had never come.

Once he asked Sarah why she had never married. She thought seriously before she replied; her answers to his questions were always considered. She and Joe were sitting that evening on the sun porch, washed with sounds; the clatter of the hired man carrying coal for the new patent furnace; a rattle of supper dishes from the kitchen; a bird's call from the woods; the silvery click of Sarah's knitting needles. She was making a scarf for the boy; bright blue wool spilled down the front of her long white skirt. On the faded Oriental rug at her feet, Joe sat playing a game with twigs and stones. Sarah looked up at last, past the barn toward the trees that hemmed the north edge of the lawn. She smiled and admitted, "I suppose I never thought the last man who asked me would be the last man who asked me."

The boy accepted the logic of that. "There were lots of them that asked; didn't you like any of them?" He clicked two stones against each other so that one jumped into the air and was lost in Sarah's skirts.

"Oh, well, *like.* I liked some of them. But not one of them special-ly," she explained, still watching the border of wilderness. "They'd come on Sunday to take me buggy riding, or sometimes sit right here on the porch with me, watching the sunset."

"And?" The boy looked up at Sarah, frankly trying to reconcile her with a woman fifteen years younger, a Miss Eamons with beaux and a flirtatious manner.

"And nothing, love. As soon as the sun set Carrie would rattle dishes inside and they'd realize that it was dusk, and me a single lady with no chaperone, and they'd do what was proper and take their leave." Sarah's eyes dropped from the woods to her knitting, from green to blue. "No one ever stayed past dusk," she murmured, more for herself than for the boy.

At her feet Joe nodded again and returned to his game. Sarah, looking down at his stooped shoulders and narrow head, smiled and returned to her knitting. It was as if, she thought, they had to know each other very well, as if each was learning the other even when they were quiet; then it was as if they were hermits, sharing the silence companionably, watching, waiting.

When he was eleven or so, Sarah noticed that the bony ridges on Joe's back were getting larger. The skin over them was stretched tight and dry, patchy red. Sarah swallowed a quick taste of panic; the thought came from nowhere: *So soon?* She sent for Dr. Pratt.

The doctor examined Joe, teased him gently about his thinness, saying over his shoulder, "What's the matter, Miss Eamons? Don't you feed this boy more than once a week?"

Sarah tried to joke back, her voice wavering over the words. "Feed him? Dr. Pratt, Joseph has two hollow legs. If you saw him at table!"

Joe sat pliantly under the doctor's prodding hands, grinned a shy grin that was overshadowed by that beaky nose, and said nothing.

When the examination was done, they left Joe to dress; Sarah took the doctor out to the sun porch and sent for iced tea. Then she turned to him, and her eyes were dark-circled and afraid.

"Boy really could use a few extra pounds, Miss Sarah," Dr. Pratt began easily. "He hasn't complained of any pain? The skin around the —ah—affected parts seems irritated."

"I've seen him scratching at it," Sarah agreed. "But he hasn't said anything. Doctor, what's happening to him?"

Dr. Pratt paused uncomfortably, as if he were genuinely at a loss. "Miss Sarah, I can't tell you what I don't know. We don't know who his folks were, if this condition is congenital, anything like that, and I've never even heard of anything quite like your Joe's case. All I can say is to wait. He's sound, healthy—that is, except for...well, you know as well as I do that the boy's not...altogether normal. This may be part of the course of his, uh, his condition."

"All we can do is wait," Sarah repeated dully.

"It's the only answer I have right now," the doctor agreed unhappily. "You might put some lotion on the bumps to soothe the itch."

Carrie brought the iced tea, and Sarah and Dr. Pratt sat quiet, sipping. When the doctor rose and Sarah had paid him, she offered to have the hired man take him back to town in the buggy, but he refused, insisting the walk would do him good. By the time Joe had appeared, half a cookie in his hand and his smile lined with crumbs, Sarah had calmed down a little and could smile at him.

"It's all right, Mama. I'm fine," Joe told her, and patted her hand awkwardly.

Sarah kept herself from gripping his hand, clutching at him. "You're fine, but too skinny. Where do you keep all the cookies you eat?" she teased, but inside the voice repeated, *So soon?*

After that, Sarah kept a jealous, distant watch on the boy, unwilling to encroach on his freedom but fearful, terrified of the change she knew in her bones was coming soon. Where the intuition came from, she could not have said, and gradually, as time went by and nothing seemed to happen, she began to scoff at her fears, relaxed and let the tension ease from her. It would be a shame, she reasoned, to hem Joe round just to ease her own mind.

∞

She was awakened from deep sleep one night by shrieks. Joe's screams, high and unnatural, like the coarse screech of a crow. Sarah was out of her bed in a minute, trailing her night wrapper around her as she ran. Outside his room the two hired girls stood, hands fluttering near their mouths in mingled fear and curiosity. "Don't sound like nothing human," Bess was saying.

"I'm sure it's just a nightmare," Sarah said hurriedly. "Go on to bed. If I need you, I'll ring." She did not stop to argue.

Joe was tangled up in his bedclothes, whimpering and crying. His skin was fiery hot to touch, and dry; when she turned him over Sarah saw that the bony ridges on his back were enlarged, breaking the skin in places. Sarah left Joe just long enough to send Bess for Dr. Pratt. Then she went back to Joe's room, bathed his forehead in cool water, and held him trying to calm his cries.

The doctor was not much help. He looked at the boy, gave Sarah a powder to bring the fever down, and shook his head, angry at his own helplessness. "I don't know how to fight this. It must have something to do with his back, but I'm damned—excuse me, Miss Sarah. I don't know what to tell you except to wait and do the things we can do for a fever: give him the powder when he gets restless, a spoonful in water. And send someone for me if he seems to get worse."

Sarah nodded dumbly and went back to Joe's bed.

The fever lasted through the night and into the next day, and the white house was filled with Joe's harsh cries. The hired girls and the cook and the hired man felt sorry for Miss Eamons and the boy, but kept as far from the room as they could. Joe began to murmur incoherently sometime that afternoon, the same garbled, incomprehensible sound over and over. Sarah sat by him holding one bony, hot hand in her own, changing the dampened cloths on his forehead, watching him and wishing she could reach him, talk the language of his fever to him. At nightfall he was still delirious, showing no sign of change for good or bad. Bess tapped at the door and persuaded Sarah to take a bite of supper, but she would not leave the boy. A tray was brought upstairs to her.

Toward midnight it seemed to Sarah that Joe was quieter, a little less restless; he cried out less frequently. In the silences she had time to realize how tired she was; her eyes were gravelly red and her head hurt with a dull, pounding ache. When it seemed that Joe was sleeping, really asleep, Sarah went down to the kitchen for a few minutes to make herself tea, a tisane for her headache. There was a certain comfort in measuring white willow bark, chamomile, and cloves into the pot, adding hot water and smelling the rich, calming odor that rose up from the warm teapot in her hands. She took the pot and a china cup with her on a tray.

Joe's door was open. Sarah frowned and cursed herself for carelessness, worrying about the draft. Then she saw: Joe was gone.

"Oh, God." She stood in the doorway, unable to move, the tea tray still in her hands. "No, God, please." Upstairs? Downstairs? Somewhere along the hall? Then she heard the scratchy pad of bare feet on the polished boards of the hall floor and felt a draft. He was at the front door.

Sarah dropped the tea tray and ran for the stairs, took them two at a time. When her shawl caught on something, she pulled at it angrily and a small table crashed down behind her; a vase broke. Sarah ran blindly down the stairs, out the door, calling Joe's name.

He was a pale blur in the moonlight, making his way across the smooth darkness of the lawn toward the north woods. As he walked he was talking, still in gibberish, and his hands flew up in gestures to an unseen listener.

Sarah followed after him. The smooth kid of her slippers skidded on the damp grass and she kicked them off, running barefoot across the lawn, aware of the chill and the brass taste of fear in her mouth. She called to Joe over and over, but the words were jolted as she ran, lost in the darkness, unintelligible. He was almost in the woods; Sarah did not realize at first that he had stopped walking. His small, pajamaed body was framed against the dim trees as he waited for her. When she reached him, Sarah was out of breath, unable for a moment to do more than gather him into her arms. For the first time in hours, his skin was cool to touch.

"Mama," his croaking voice broke the silence. "Mama, look."

Then Sarah looked into the edge of the wood and saw. First the eyes, a dull violet glitter in the dark. The same jolt that had gone through her years before when she first saw the baby in Dr. Pratt's spare bedroom went through her again. Sarah held her boy closer to her, rocking him slightly, crooning, "Baby, baby, it's all right. Joey, come back to the house. It's all right."

The boy squirmed in her arms, twisted around to face the waiting shadows. Sarah thought she saw more eyes, more indistinct figures deeper in the woods.

"They've come to get me," Joe said simply.

Her heart contracted. Sarah shut her eyes tightly for a moment. "Shhh, baby," she whispered, and stroked his long cheek. Like an answer, the creature in the shadows stepped forward into the moonlight and spoke to Joe in a grating stream of language.

"Mama, he's kin of mine. They're my people." Joe's voice was full of wonder, joy; the words said *at last* and *of course*. They cut Sarah to the quick.

She looked at the creature. Tall it was, taller than a man, with a slanting forehead and heavy brow that shadowed his glittering eyes. The creature's body was broad and muscular, his face long and narrow, his nose more like a beak; his ears were large and sharply pointed, twisting an inch or so above his head. Behind him there was a rustle of movement; wings, Sarah realized. Huge, powerful wings that sprang, she was certain, from bony ridges that ran parallel to his spine.

"What does it want?" She asked at last, although she knew.

The creature broke into harsh speech again. Joe listened, seemed to understand.

"His name is Hreu, Mama. He's come for me. It's time. Do you see?"

So soon, Sarah thought.

"They are my kin. I never belonged here, except to you, but I'm one of them." Joe raised one hand ruefully and gestured over his shoulder at the reddened, bony lumps on his own back. "They'll know how to take care of me, Mama," he added softly. He was still holding her hand tightly.

Sarah stared ahead of her at the creature, her mouth set like pale stone. "They will take care of you? Where were they when you were a baby? Where were your kin when you were left in the woods? Joey" she tightened her grasp on his hand. "It's too soon. It's not time yet."

"It's time, Mama. It's how they do, leaving the babies to be found and raised up by others. When the change comes, they know, and they come to get them. It's my turn now."

Sarah dropped down to her knees, holding the boy, and suddenly it was as if he were the adult and she, the child. He spoke to her slowly, in a considered manner, with inexorable reason. "I love you. But this is so strong. I can't not go with them. I have to, Mama. They're *my people*." In those words Sarah heard echoes of years of taunts and bruises.

Then Joe giggled, a high, giddy sound. "In another year I'll look like Hreu. You couldn't explain that in town, not wings!"

Briefly he looked like any ordinary little boy, his face lit with mischief. A profound sorrow washed over Sarah; it took her a moment to control her voice. "I won't ever see you again."

Joe stopped giggling. He looked at Hreu, struggled with broken syllables and his own vehemence, then turned back to Sarah. "Come with us, Mama. Hreu says you can, if you want. There aren't many of us left, but enough. You could come." In the dark his eyes flickered back and forth, from Sarah in the moonlight to Hreu in the shadows. "Please come."

For a moment Sarah played with the possibility. Standing in the chilly night air with dew on her feet, she thought of her years of waiting for the flash of difference that would conquer her, the flash she had seen in Joe's eyes and in Hreu's. Joe was right. Hreu was right: she could not keep her boy with her any longer. At best he would become a prisoner in her house; at worst he might be killed by the people of Tannesburg. She thought yearningly of flight, of adventure, of Joe's voice lingering over the words "my people," making even Sarah an alien.

Very slowly, very deliberately, she said, "If you have to go, go with my blessings, Joseph." Her voice said *darling, baby, little one, sweetheart.* "I couldn't go with you; I'd only slow you down. You'll be learning so much, growing up." Sarah drew a shaking breath and looked over Joe's head in to Hreu's violet eyes. Did they understand what they did to the people left behind? "I love you, baby."

He flung his arms around her neck, tight, and hung on for a long moment, his narrow cheek pressed against hers. "I love you too, Mama. I won't forget you, I promise I won't...."

It was Sarah who pushed him away, gently. There were tears on his face when he turned to follow Hreu and disappear into the wilderness.

Sarah was discovered by the cook the next morning, huddled on the steps in the kitchen, the hem of her robe still damp, ruined with dirt and dew. She was so deeply asleep that the cook was afraid and sent for Dr. Pratt, seeing to it that Miss Eamons was wrapped in blankets and settled in a chair by the fire. When Sarah woke, surrounded by the ruddy concerned faces of the cook and the maids, she began to cry, huge, gasping sobs that echoed softly hoarsely in the kitchen.

"Sweet lord, the boy's died in the night." The cook sent Bess upstairs to see, and in a few minutes the girl was back, as pale as Sarah, to report that Joe was gone, his bedclothes all twisted up and the door wide open. Sarah wept, unhearing.

Dr. Pratt and the cook pieced together what must have happened, the boy's delirium and fevered escape, Miss Eamons's waking and fruitless pursuit. The doctor did what he could; left laudanum for her, and went home to tell his wife.

The forms were observed. Advertisements were placed in the papers, letters to the sheriffs of neighboring counties—but nothing more was heard of Joseph Eamons, and he was at last regarded as dead, gone as mysteriously as he had come twelve years before. Through the fall and winter, Miss Eamons did not mix with her neighbors, and it was said she took the boy's death far too hard, and he only an orphan and not even real kin. Still, people were kind to her and solicitous. Through her veil of grief, Sarah came to realize this and was distantly grateful.

When spring came, she began to go about more, started concerning herself with church work and the library committee. She was again the handsome Miss Eamons, crisp and deliberate in her lawn dresses and cashmere shawls, her civility careful but warm. Only once did she break the calm, when a well-meaning lady from the Women's Auxiliary suggested that Sarah might adopt another boy. Then her smile disappeared and there was only bleak anger when she spoke. "They are not like dolls, Mrs. French. You do not replace one with another."

No one mentioned the idea to her again.

In May, when it was warm enough to spend afternoons on the sun porch, Sarah took her knitting there and sat, looking out at the empty green of the lawn. One afternoon as she sat, Carrie appeared. A man had called and was asking to see her.

"What is his name, Carrie?"

"He says it's Mercier, ma'am." Carrie struggled with the pronunciation. "He's from clear up in French Canada. Should I show him in?"

Her curiosity piqued, Sarah nodded. Carrie returned with a tall man, dressed in a light summer wool suit. He was middle-aged, handsome in a quiet sort of way; his red-brown whiskers brushed the collar of his shirt when he smiled. About his eyes there was a look of tiredness, and something more than tiredness in their expression.

His voice was low, attractively accented. "Miss Eamons? Thank you for seeing me. I realize it may seem strange to you, a man you don't know—you will understand. I think. I read your advertisements."

It took Sarah a moment to remember. "Advertisements?" she repeated blankly.

"Yes, ma'am. And I have been in Tannesburg for a few days, asking questions. I hope you do not mind this, but I think you are the person who can help me. I had a daughter."

Something in the way he said it made Sarah really look at him for the first time. "I see," she said slowly. "Mr. Mercier, may I offer you some tea?"

He nodded gratefully, and Sarah rang for another cup. By common consent they spoke idly about the weather until Carrie returned with the teacup and hot water. When she was gone, Mr. Mercier began his explanation. "Adele, my daughter, was an unusual little girl. We adopted her, my wife and I, when she was only a few weeks old. A foundling discovered near our village. When my wife died, Adele and I became even closer, all in all to each other, you would say. Then, about eighteen months ago, she was taken ill, dreadfully so. I lost her."

"You lost her," Sarah repeated deliberately, considering.

"I lost her," he agreed. "She was different from other children, Miss Eamons. Adele was—"

"Thin and bony with a funny voice and a nose too big for her face," Sarah said, conscious of a mounting excitement. "Am I right, Mr. Mercier?"

He smiled, not happily but as if he had found a resting place after a very long journey. "You are right, Miss Eamons. When she left, I didn't let go easily. I tried to follow after her."

"Did you ever find—"

"No. I'm sorry, Miss Eamons, I never did. But Adele told me before she left that there were others, other children like her, other people like me and you who raised children and loved them and lost them. I have been searching for someone like you since I knew she was lost to me."

They talked quietly for a long time. The sun set, and they sat in the lavender twilight, still talking, while Carrie rattled dishes noisily in the parlor, trying to remind Sarah that it was past the hour when a gentleman could sit unchaperoned with a maiden lady. Finally, Sarah asked Mr. Mercier if he would like to stay for dinner.

He smiled and glanced toward Carrie's officious silhouette in the parlor window. "Not tonight, I think. But I would like to come back again, if you will permit me to." He rose and gathered up his hat and stick.

"Tomorrow. Please." Sarah urged. For the first time in months, her smile was generous and touched her eyes. "We have a lot to talk about."

He took his leave, and Carrie saw him to the front door. From the sun porch Sarah could dimly see him on the path and then on the road, walking toward Tannesburg. When he was out of sight, Sarah sat down again, thinking of Joe without pain for the first time in months. Cuckoos, Mercier had called Joe's people, for the bird that left its young to be raised up in other nests. Cuckoos, a sign of spring.

It was warm enough, but Sarah did not sit outside long. Dinner would be ready shortly. Paul Mercier would be back in the morning.

Unmasking the Ancient Light

Deborah J. Ross

Shadows choked the damp and silent Antwerp street as the young widow Beatrice de Luna, moving stiffly under the weight of an edifice of gold-stitched black satin, climbed the steps of her mansion. It was very late, and she'd just returned from her audience with Queen Marie of Burgundy, Regent of the Low Countries and sister to Charles V of the Holy Roman Empire. Although she felt relieved that the interview which she had postponed so many times was at last over, she already regretted having lost her temper.

When she crossed the threshold, to be met by a bevy of servants, she drew her first easy breath of the evening. Within these walls, Beatrice de Luna, forcibly converted New Christian and court favorite in this year of 1543, no longer existed. She shed the name as easily as her fur-lined cloak and became once more Gracia Nasi, of the house of Hebrew princes.

Gracia waved the servants off to bed, all except for the old nurse who had come with her from Portugal, barely escaping the Inquisition. Once upstairs and wrapped in a woolen dressing robe, Gracia asked Esther to bring wine. "And if Reyna or my sister are still awake, ask them to join me."

Candlestick in hand, Gracia paced her rooms, measuring their length and weight. The outer chamber was spacious, anchored by heavy dark furniture. Shadows, like dampness made visible, clung to the corners. Esther had lit a fire in the sleeping chamber, and the embers gave off a lingering glow. To one side lay an odd little room, small and windowless, the reason Gracia had chosen these chambers for herself, rather than the larger ones her sister used. She lowered the candlestick to a table of ebony inlaid with ivory, one of the few personal treasures she'd salvaged from Lisbon. She could easily have replaced it; her late husband had left her in charge of a spice-trading empire that spanned half of Europe. But the table had belonged to Gracia's mother and to her grandmother before her.

With a gentle tap, the door swung open. Esther entered carrying a silver goblet. Behind her came Brianda, swathed in sable-lined wool, and Reyna. Reyna looked very young, braids tousled and cheeks still flushed with sleep, yet graceful as a willow. She took the goblet from Esther and held it chest-high, advancing with measured steps. "I bid you good Sabbath, Mother."

Esther's eyes glinted in her lined face, strong and brown like well-loved leather. With a fleeting smile, she closed the door behind her. She would stand guard in the hallway until Gracia released her.

Brianda went straight to the fireplace and held out her hands. The Low Country winters troubled her more than they did Gracia; some days, she said, she could never get warm. "You're back late," she said to Gracia. "And our nephew, João?"

"Stayed to dice with Maximilian," Gracia replied, accepting the goblet from Reyna. "You wouldn't have enjoyed the evening. It wasn't like the court in Brussels. As I expected, what Mary wanted was Reyna's hand for old Don Francisco."

"That decrepit old wastrel!" Brianda said. "I'll wager he and the Emperor have already decided how they'll carve up Reyna's estate between them!"

"Mother..." The word came half a whisper, half a cry of pain.

She's like sun on water, Gracia thought. *One moment as solemn as a priestess, the next a mere child.*

"I put them off once again," Gracia said with deceptive mildness. What she'd actually told the Queen Regent was that she'd rather see her daughter dead than married to Don Francisco. Harsh words but true, and in these times, bordering on perilous. The rack waited but a breath away.

"But these troubles will not be resolved tonight," Gracia continued, "or if they could be, others would soon arise to take their place. For now, let us welcome the Sabbath."

If any men had been present, Gracia, as the woman of the household, would have used the usual form of the blessing and lit ordinary candles with a taper from the fireplace. Now the three women came together, each holding her cupped hands in front of her. Softly they breathed the ancient words, summoning the feminine aspect of the divine, "*Brukha ya Shekhinah, elohaynu malkat ha-olam...*"

With each phrase, the air in the little room quivered. The space between Reyna's hands glowed softly, then that between Gracia's, then Brianda's. As Gracia watched, a feeling rose up in her, not any emotion she could name aloud, but a stirring in her innermost heart. Her breath caught in her throat. The light kindled into flame; she could feel it streaming through her, through her daughter's child-soft fingers, from a past that no longer existed to a future she could not imagine.

Yet this Light must remain hidden, passed from mother to daughter in an unbroken chain. Her own mother called it Miriam's Gift, after the prophetess sister of Moses. She'd spoken of other powers, too, of the balance of the ancient forces of Fire and Water, of mastery over storm and wave.

Brightness swelled to fill the room. Of the three, Reyna's burned the clearest, molten white gold, Brianda's a delicate pink, like the petals of an exotic rose. Gracia searched the depths of her own fire and saw only layers of amber light. For a moment, she glimpsed a shape, a flickering shadow. It looked like someone in a short cloak, his face a blur as he moved toward her.

Suddenly Reyna gasped. The image vanished and the flames died.

"What did you see?" Gracia asked.

"A man without a face."

"Perhaps your future husband," Brianda laughed. "I saw water and rows of beautiful colored lights floating above it. It means a voyage, I expect, or some kind of merrymaking on a lake or river."

"Mother? What was yours?"

"I'm not sure." Gracia tried to picture the wavering figure, but it slipped from her mind.

Gracia recited the blessing over the wine, sipped it, and passed it on. Reyna's vision could mean anything, she told herself, from the hand of the Inquisition to a child's uncertain fears. But no, Reyna's power was the strongest of any of them.

Gracia pressed her lips together, thinking. She'd thought to remain in Antwerp a while longer, while she continued liquidating the family assets and transferring them by circuitous routes, gradually moving eastward, beyond the reach of Christendom. Now her own impulsive words to the Queen had cost her precious time.

Brianda took a second gulp of wine and wiped the back of her mouth with one hand. "Well, that's done with. Good Sabbath, both of you. It's too cold for me here; I'm going back to bed."

Reyna lingered after Brianda left. When Gracia held out one hand to her daughter, Reyna rushed into her arms. Gracia, enfolding her, inhaled the faint orange-blossom scent of Reyna's hair. Under the layers of lace and wool, the child's body quivered.

"They shall not have you," Gracia murmured. "I promise it."

Reyna pulled away, eyes huge in the candlelight. Tears beaded her lashes. "What will we do?"

"What we have always done." How could she say more? All her life had been like this, evasions and subterfuge, running, hiding from one threat after another. Yet always the Light endured, the place the outer world could not reach. She remembered asking her own mother, even as Reyna asked her now, "Why call the Light when it cannot save us?"

"We do it to remember," Gracia repeated the answer.

"Sometimes I wish we could forget," said Reyna.

"Don't worry, *preciosa*," Gracia said, putting an arm around Reyna and leading her to where Esther waited to escort her back to bed. "We will find a way."

∞

The next morning, Gracia breakfasted in her sitting room, wrapped in a fur blanket. Outside, a sleeting rain fell in gusts, tapping against the thick, dimpled windows.

Brianda joined her, still in a pique over not being invited to last night's audience. She picked at her sweet bun, her mouth drawn down and brows pulled into a straight line. The pastry was yesterday's baking.

Gracia pushed away a dish of apple peelings. "We'll have to leave Antwerp sooner than we planned."

"Where will we go?" Brianda made a pretty moue. She'd hated the move from Lisbon to London and then Antwerp.

"Venice. I've received word that our assets have arrived safely." Gracia's stomach twisted and she caught a whiff of something salty and rotting-sweet. It was an aftermath of last night, she hoped, and not another bout of bilious indigestion.

"Oh! Venice!" Brianda's cheeks flushed. "*La Serenissima Dominante!*" She clapped her hands together. "It's my vision of lights on the water! The festivals, the regattas, the gala balls! But we won't have to live in that awful Foundry area, what do they call it, *il gheto*, will we?"

"Of course not." They could not afford the slightest public lapse, for to appear to be other than devout Christians would be admitting apostasy. No place lay beyond the hand of the Inquisition. Not Spain, where their family had lived for centuries; not Portugal, where Gracia's husband was now buried. Not even here in the north.

Before Brianda could chatter on, their nephew, João Miguez, came in. He'd stayed behind last night, drinking and gaming with the Imperial heir, and the frenzied glamour of the court still hung about him. But when Gracia called him by his Hebrew name, Joseph, a tension seemed to lift from him, his shoulders rose and then fell. He sat down facing her as he had on so many other mornings when she'd taught him the family business.

"I shall remain here to do what I can," he agreed. "Have you decided how you will get out of the city?"

"I thought to go first to Aix-la-Chapelle, under the pretext of taking the waters for another bout of stomach illness which I believe will strike me soon, then to Lyons instead of Augsburg, the usual route." She went on, ignoring Brianda's aggrieved sigh. "You must be careful, Joseph. Once Charles learns I am gone, he will almost certainly charge me with Judaizing."

"To give him the grounds to confiscate whatever property he can." Joseph nodded.

"You must argue that the prosecution is illegal because we are not subjects of the Holy Roman Empire but foreign merchants, free to travel as we wish," Gracia said, ticking off points on her fingers, "that we are exemplary Christians, that the business belongs to Reyna and to Brianda's daughter, *la Chica*, while she and I have only our own small dowries."

"Much too small!" Brianda said pointedly. Her face reddened at this reminder that her husband had named Gracia the administrator of his half of the business, thus giving the elder sister control of the entire trading empire.

"Some of the coffers that Charles will likely seize are in the custody of German merchants here who themselves have property in Venice, which I will petition the Doge to sequester by way of compensation," Gracia said.

"Perhaps the offer of a substantial loan will put Charles off for a while," Joseph said. "We've already lent him a hundred thousand livres."

"Having an emperor so deeply in your debt can cut both ways." Gracia frowned. "Such people are uncomfortable owing money they cannot repay." In the past, powerful men had slaughtered whole communities of Jews to cancel their debts.

Joseph's eyes flashed, reminding her of how he'd looked when jousting with young Maximilian. "Let me suggest an additional touch, a diversion. We will put about a rumor that Reyna and I have eloped to Venice, with you in pursuit."

Brianda clapped her hands, her mood shifting like quicksilver. "It's so romantic!"

Gracia smiled wryly. "It will certainly give Don Francisco something to think about. But we must be careful. We'd better make sure we're seen attending Mass tomorrow."

Brianda excused herself, on the pretext of looking after the infant, *la Chica*, but actually, Gracia suspected, to inspect her wardrobe with an eye to what might be suitable for the elegance of Venice.

Venice, *La Serenissima Dominante*, Queen of the Adriatic, had already passed her prime as the dominant trading power of Europe. Gracia and her household settled in a small palace in the fashionable *Zeppa* district. Winged cherubs, dancing nymphs, and sea creatures adorned the painted ceilings. They acquired their own gondola, with cushions embroidered with swans and hearts. They rode in it or walked, for horses were forbidden within the city.

Gracia's rooms looked east, past the triple arched windows that reminded her of Moorish Iberia, past the lacework of canals, the arching bridges, and the iron lamp posts in the shape of dragons. East, to Turkey. Already her agents had arrived in Constantinople, preparing the way for her eventual arrival. She tried to imagine what it would be like to live openly, without this constant miasma of intrigue and subterfuge.

The Emperor Charles had brought the predicted charges of apostasy against Gracia, charges that Joseph answered with certificates of unimpeachable Christian observance, interminable legal pleadings, and judicious gifts.

Although Gracia's house in Venice had become a center for the community of Marranos, "hidden Jews", she dared not associate openly with any who openly practiced the faith.

The new year brought another round of festivals, saints' days, and Carnival, the ten days of gaiety that preceded Lent. Not even Brianda, in her wildest dreams, had anticipated the explosion of revelry. Everywhere, strolling musicians played their lutes and *vihuelas*, gondolas sprouted ribbons and the carved heads of griffins and bare-breasted sea maids. On the streets, people went masked, transformed by their costumes into gorgeous birds or figures out of legend, concoctions of feathers and spangled silk. The whole household was soon caught up in the festivities, with invitations to one party after another.

The Doge's gala took place on the lagoon on a series of huge floating platforms hung with paper lanterns in fanciful shapes. The Doge himself held court in the costume of Neptune, with a trident tipped with sapphires and blue topazes. Fireworks arced through the night sky, while servants liveried in red and silver handed out goblets of fruited ice. The Doge had commissioned a piece of music in the new style called *madrigale* especially for the occasion.

Gracia had chosen a mask of peacock feathers rimmed with golden beads. Here on the carpeted deck of the Doge's barge, as on the streets, she found the Carnival regalia bestowed an unexpected freedom, as if in hiding their faces, people felt freer to reveal themselves. In recent years, a custom had grown up of addressing a fellow reveler as "Sior Maschera," without regard to rank or sex.

And here we are, she thought as she tasted her lime ice, *Old Christians and New, true and false, Venetian and foreigner, with only the thickness of a mask between us.*

Then, as if the water itself had turned treacherous, the barge shifted beneath Gracia's feet, sending her stumbling into the man behind her.

His tallness caught her by surprise; she could see nothing whatever of his face or form, he was so completely swathed in black and white. Even the hands holding the precisely folded lace handkerchief were gloved. The black *bautà* covering his head and shoulders and the short *tabarro* cloak were of silk, which only nobility might wear. Behind the flaring white mask, she caught the gleam of eyes.

He bowed to her, an exaggerated gesture as if he were a performer with the *Commedia dell'Arte*, and called her "*Madonna Maschera.*" His voice was deep, with a strange resonance, but that might have been due to the mask.

Before Gracia could reply, a pair of revelers capered between them. When she looked again, the man in black had disappeared. He might have been a liquid shadow.

"Who was that?" Brianda's voice beside her asked.

Gracia shivered. "I don't know."

Brianda's mask hung by its cord around her neck and her cheeks had gone blood dark in the light from the paper lanterns. She prattled on, talking too fast, about the ices, the French wine, the

Commedia performers. It seemed to Gracia that her sister, usually so confident and gay, was gasping, feverish.

"You must not take ill from these night vapors," Gracia said, slipping her arm through Brianda's. "Come now, we'll go home and I'll summon my physician."

"What do you mean, *go home?*" Brianda jerked free. "It's not even midnight! I for one intend to stay and enjoy myself!" She jerked her mask back over her face, slightly askew. Her voice rose in pitch. "You think you can rule everyone, just like you do the business. But the firm isn't yours, half of it belongs to *la Chica*, and should be mine to run!"

"Be still! Such things should be discussed in private!" Gracia shook, whether with fury or terror, she could not at that moment tell. Whatever had possessed Brianda's tongue?

"Go on home! Nobody wants you here!" Brianda's laugh burst from her like the raucous cry of a gull. She whirled and plunged back into the throng of merrymakers.

Gracia trembled as she wrestled her temper under control. She was angry enough to go home alone and yet she could not simply abandon her sister. Around her, the music shifted to a minor key and the masks took on a subtly altered character. The barge's lights looked pale and tinny, the surrounding water immeasurably deep. Were the eyes behind the bulging forehead of *Dottore*, or the hooked nose of *Pantalone*, truly human? Or had they taken on some quality from the sea-depths, the hidden shadows?

Gracia had seen shadows before—in Antwerp, and before that in Lisbon. Sometimes it felt as if she had been hiding from them all her life. Yet the next time she gathered Reyna to kindle the Light, she felt a difference, as if something dark and brooding had seeped into the waters along with the tide.

∞

Brianda slept for the better part of two days, dosed with poppy elixir and attar of roses. Gracia had just finished her morning's correspondence when Esther came into the sunlit conservatory and said there was a gentleman to see her.

"A Count dell'Sarto. He says you've met before, at the Doge's gala."

The half-written letter to Joseph fluttered to the carpet. Gracia found herself on her feet, with no memory of having risen.

She recognized him by his tallness, although not much else resembled the masked reveler. When he bowed, he removed any possible doubt. He wore a high-necked doublet of Oriental brocade trimmed with velvet, slightly padded in peasecod style above Venetian breeches. His hair was clipped as short as an Englishman's, his face clean-shaven. She was surprised to find him slightly homely.

"You are even more beautiful without your mask," he said in that strangely resonant voice.

She stepped behind the chair and ran her hands over its back, tracing the stylized wave pattern. "*Signore,* you presume upon an imagined introduction. I thought it the Venetian custom that neither words nor actions survive the night of masks. As for your flattering words," she raised one eyebrow, keeping her tone light, "I am a widow, and surely my beauty is no concern of yours."

"Speaking frankly, *madonna,* I am here to court your daughter."

"My Reyna?" Gracia's breath caught in her throat. Her skin prickled. "Your pardon, *signore,* the notion took me by surprise. Whatever makes you think I am looking for a husband for her?"

He gestured, shaking back the frothy lace at his wrist. Gracia noticed that the skin of his hand was unnaturally pale and smooth, as if stretched too tight. "It is I who am looking for a wife."

"Then you have made this visit in vain."

"I am well aware she has been sought after by others. But I care nothing for her fortune. You can keep that, give it to the poor, whatever you wish." He sounded impatient now. "I want the girl."

The wooden waves dug into Gracia's palms. Her knuckles went white. Just then, the Campanile in the nearby Piazza San Marco chimed, signaling the end of morning.

The count stepped back, as if repulsed by the sound. Gracia swept around the chair. "I wish you a pleasant day, then, and greater profit elsewhere. Esther, please escort the count to the door."

Dell'Sarto glared at her, eyes rimmed with red-veined white. "You are a rash and foolish woman. I warn you, the time will come when you will give her to me, and gladly." He departed in a swirl of sable-trimmed cape.

∞

Shortly after Joseph concluded his affairs and joined Gracia's household in Venice, invitations arrived for the upcoming festivities of *Martedì Grasso* and the *Festa della Sensa,* Ascension Day, celebrated by the Marriage with the Sea. Haunted by a growing sense of unease, Gracia demurred. The more she hesitated, however, the more determined Brianda became. Reyna, too, complained when at the last moment, Gracia said she felt ill and desired them all to stay at home.

"All my friends will be going!" Reyna whined, sounding very much like her aunt. "And Joseph, too, so it will all be proper! If you don't feel well, you can stay at home with Esther." The three women were sitting in Gracia's rooms upstairs, with the sunlight slanting on the white walls and the wind from the Adriatic blowing softly through the lace curtains.

Gracia considered, saying nothing for the moment. She'd used her fragile health as an excuse so many times she could not always be sure if she imagined the gnawing pain in her stomach. Besides, Venice was one of the few cities where women could attend such events without hindrance. What harm could there be in Reyna and Brianda enjoying themselves?

Brianda's brows knotted together and her lips went sharp. "If I had proper control of my half of the business—*la Chica's* half, I mean—then we would have no need to argue over this. We could go to all the parties we want. Why should Gracia be the one to dictate what we can and cannot do?"

The answer which leapt to Gracia's tongue—that Brianda's husband had good reason to leave her in charge of the business and not his own wife—died unspoken. What purpose would be served by throwing that in Brianda's face? Instead, she said, "We already live a freer, more luxurious life than ever before. All our reasonable needs are met. And you have your dowry for your private use."

"My dowry! A pittance, while you command an empire!"

Gracia shifted uneasily on her divan. "The money is not mine to spend," she said carefully. "I hold it in trust." *And not just for our daughters,* the thought came to her. She blinked, and it was gone. In its place came the vision of the hundreds of her people trapped on the Lisbon piers, without food or water, forbidden to set foot on the waiting ships without submitting to conversion.

Brianda stood up, shoulders back, chin thrust out. Her eyes, which had always been dark, seemed all pupil, like pits of blackness. "I will go to the *Festa,*" she said in clipped syllables, "and I will have what is rightfully mine. And if you try to stop me, sister or not, you will regret it!" With a swishing of full skirts, she swept from the room.

There followed a long moment of silence, during which Reyna twisted her lace handkerchief in her lap. "I didn't realize—"

"Your aunt is uneasy in her mind, that is all," Gracia said with a certainty she did not feel.

"I wish I were like you, so patient and sure." Reyna sighed. "Sometimes everything is clear, I know what I want and who I am. The next moment *tía* Brianda says one thing or my friends say another, and I don't know what to think!"

"Hush, *preciosa*. No one expects you to be wise all of a sudden. You will have years to learn about such things, as well as good advisors, just as I had my husband Samuel and his brother Francisco, and now your cousin Joseph."

"But right now I want so much to see the Doge go out in his gilded *bucintoro* and throw a wedding ring into the sea!" The girl's eyes shone with anticipation. "It isn't wrong to want that, is it?"

"No, of course not, although I think we had better not let Brianda go alone. The pleasures of the world are not evil in themselves, but they can blind you to other things. Do you remember that night in Antwerp when you asked me why we call the Light?"

"Yes, *mama*. And you said we do it to remember. And I said there were some things I'd rather forget. That's the danger, isn't it? And that's why we..." Reyna's sweet voice hushed. Her chin lifted, and her eyes seemed to see beyond the years. "Why the Light shines through us."

"We must hold on," Gracia said with a fierceness which surprised her. "We must remember."

∞

On Ascension Day, the sky over the Piazzo San Marco turned white. The water of the lagoon took on a strange, opaque brilliance, masking whatever hid beneath its surface. The Piazza thronged with the fair that had opened the day before and would continue for a fortnight; traders from all over Europe displayed their wares in wooden booths garlanded with flowers and ribbons. Gracia remained behind on the pier with Esther as the Doge's elaborately decorated boat pulled away, trailing a flotilla of followers, city luminaries, foreign ambassadors, even the papal nuncio. She did not think Brianda could get into any difficulty alone on a gondola with Reyna and Joseph.

Gracia strolled by the ranks of stalls, her gaze skimming the fine brocades, the incense, carved ivory, clumps of myrrh, polished amber, and jade, the piles of grapefruits, pomegranates, and local vegetables from Sant'Erasmo. She remembered how Reyna had smiled when Joseph helped her on board the gondola. Joseph's charm was undeniable. And he was clearly fond of his young cousin, he knew almost as much as Gracia about the family business, and there would be no question of Reyna being lost to the faith…

"You cannot keep her from me, you know," said a resonant voice at her shoulder.

Gracia startled, caught herself. Today he was wearing white satin trimmed with gold. There was something mocking in the way he swept off his plumed hat and bowed to her.

"We have already said everything we have to say to one another. *Buon' giorno, signore.*"

"I think not." He put out one hand, palm up. His fingers curled, first the index finger, then the others, one after the next, in a fluid ripple, like a slow ingathering of tentacles. Gracia's feet froze on the paving. Her nostrils flared at the smell of something rotten, like dead fish. The sea breeze turned sour. Beside her, Esther looked away, eyes filmy, smiling at the capering of a masked performer.

Gracia's heart fluttered against her ribs like a caged bird. She saw for the first time how tightly the skin over his mouth was stretched, as if his face itself were a mask. She could almost trace the outline of his teeth through his lips.

What does he want with her?

"Even now," he whispered. "Even now I can bring them back, the things I have set in motion. It is not too late. Speak, give me what I need. I am not vengeful."

Anger, hot and bright, shot through Gracia. *What you need! Always it comes down to needs—blood, lies, money most of all!* She thought of the families waiting on the Lisbon pier, starved and beaten on the roads, the thousands more trapped in the iron cauldron of Iberia. She thought of all the gold that had poured through her fingers over those years, the gifts, the bribes, the imperial loans that would never be repaid. She saw the flames leaping between her daughter's hands, the pure and ancient Light.

"Look!" a voice behind her cried out. "The Marriage with the Sea!"

Trumpets blared out from the pier. Gracia strained her eyes against the brilliance of the water. The flotilla blurred, motes of shadow against the diamond surface. She could not tell which gondola held Reyna. Such a fragile thing, that little boat, to stand between her daughter and the dark beneath the waves.

A figure stood at the prow of the foremost boat, arms raised, then tossing something into the water—a wreath tied to a golden ring.

"Aaah…" A low cry reached Gracia's ears, more like raw animal pain than any human emotion. Despair mingled with defiance, quickly choked as the wreath disappeared beneath the waves. What a strange reaction to the ancient ritual! She turned, wondering, toward the count. But although she searched the crowd of merrymakers, she saw no sign of him.

∞

Masked, she wandered through *il gheto nuovo*, gazing up at the unadorned facades. It seemed to her like a moated prison, damp and dark, unbearably crowded. The gates, she'd heard, were locked every night. People thronged the narrow streets, Gentiles as well as Jews, many come to do business at the banking establishments or to consult with physicians. She heard the songs of children, the polyglot of languages, Ladino and Yiddish as well as Italian, the chanting from the synagogue. She could feel the vibrancy, the richness of the life around her.

One word, and it would all be gone. Even as she thought it, an icy shiver touched her. She raised one hand to the mask she would take off at the end of the day and the one she would not.

Emotions swept through her, fear and sorrow and more she could not tell. She went home to her sunlit palace and was silent for a long time.

∞

One morning, when Reyna and *la Chica* were visiting friends, Brianda stormed into Gracia's private rooms. Gracia had just refused to pay for an opulent supper-party that Brianda proposed.

"You have made me the laughing stock of Venice!" Brianda cried. "Living on my sister's charity, with hardly two coins of my own to rub together. Do you know what people say about me? That my husband wouldn't trust me with my own money so he left his half to you! You, already richer than five kings put together! You're never satisfied, are you? You must have it all!"

Gracia drew back. Her sister's face was distorted almost past recognition, cheeks flushed, eyes glassy with reflected light. Even her voice sounded strained, barely human. She'd known Brianda would not be happy, but the vehemence of her sister's words took her by surprise.

"Samuel and Francisco trusted me with good reason!" A tight, poisonous shimmer caught in the back of Gracia's throat. Once she'd begun, the words came boiling out of her, all the things she'd kept back over the years. "Do you think they would have given you custody of a single pin, you flighty, thoughtless woman? When have you given the least thought to running the business, to trade markets or travel routes, exchanges or loan rates? Your head is like an old stocking, stuffed with parties and gowns, who has the biggest jewels and how close you are seated to the Doge's table! Have you ever for a single moment thought of anything or anyone besides yourself?"

"That is enough!" Brianda scrambled to her feet. "How dare you say those things to me!"

"How dare *you* say such things to *me?*" Gracia could not remember getting up. For an instant, she caught the faint smell of a dead sea creature. Then it was gone and she a mere fleck on the surging tide of her fury.

"Ungrateful whore!" "Shrew, harpy!" "Scheming, greedy!" "Betrayer!" "Thief!"

Brianda ran weeping from the room. Gracia sank back into her own chair. Her temples throbbed and under her fingers her face felt hot and dry. She wondered if she were going to be ill, truly ill. She glanced up at the ceiling and her heart stuttered. Surely there had been winged *putti*, playing their sunlit harps among the painted clouds.

And that great gray sea beast, that half-seen Leviathan, rising through the spumy waters, where had it come from? Why had she never noticed it before?

∞

Over the next few weeks, life assumed the semblance of normality, with the exception that Brianda took all her meals in her rooms and avoided Gracia's presence. One morning, the household awoke to find she had disappeared, along with her most valuable personal belongings. Gracia calmed the children and began a search. Quickly she discovered that Brianda had established herself in a small but elegant house, far beyond the means of her modest dowry, near the Ponte di Rialto. Brianda refused all overtures from Gracia, even to meet with her in public, and Gracia's agents soon discovered why. By then it was too late.

Surrounded by witnesses of unimpeachable anti-Jewish sentiment, Brianda appeared before the Venetian courts and charged Gracia with apostasy.

Beatrice de Luna, also known as Gracia Nasi, had only pretended to convert to the true faith, her sister avowed. Her real motive in coming to Venice was to prepare the way to Turkey, where she would once more revert to the ways of her ancestors. The move would place the souls of her niece and daughter, as well as their considerable fortune, beyond the reaches of Christendom.

This was the speech Joseph reported to Gracia. She herself had no part in the proceedings, for persons so accused were forbidden to speak in their own behalf. She set aside her own emotions and began her defense, preparing testimony regarding her meticulous observance of Christian rites, strategic gifts, and all the intrigues she had mastered in Antwerp. Before she could set these plans in motion, however, the Venetian authorities stepped in, arrested her, and confiscated her assets. As if this were not enough, the next day, the papal nuncio assumed guardianship of Reyna and *la Chica* and placed them in a nunnery, "to ensure the purity of their spiritual up-bringing."

∞

"Prison" seemed too harsh a term for Gracia's new quarters, and yet not harsh enough. It was not an underground cellar, dank and lightless, with chains on the walls and moldy straw for a mattress, but a suite of sparse, airy rooms with barred windows. The building had once been a nunnery and Gracia had apparently inherited the Mother Superior's quarters. The outer room was furnished with a chair and a large, hideously realistic, wooden crucifix. The smaller room had a cot, a washstand with a cracked ewer, a chamber pot, and another, somewhat smaller cross.

Clearly, Gracia thought as she inspected the rooms, *I am meant to pray for my sins.* A smile hovered over her lips as she unpacked the trunks Esther had sent after her, clothing, linens, brushes, mirrors, soap, candles, and, more precious, books and writing materials.

A priest was sent to hear her confession, which she dutifully gave. But as she recited the litany of minor transgressions, her heart felt as if it were being squeezed in a vice.

Work steadied her over the following weeks, as it always did. But as she sat at her own desk, in her own chair, thoughts weighed on her mind. Greed was a volatile thing—once aroused, it could flare up like tinder, whole families consumed, Brianda herself and *la Chica,* too, the entire Marrano community at risk, the Jews in *il gheto nuovo* as well. The Inquisition waited but an accusation away. Brianda might be flighty and short-sighted, but she was not an utter fool. She knew these dangers, for she'd lived with them all her life. Why had she risked such a thing?

Joseph brought news of how Brianda had been caught in her own trap. Her agent in Lyons had demanded a portion of the proceeds and when she refused, had turned on her, denouncing her. The French king, scenting unanticipated gains, seized their property, thus freezing the very monies Brianda had counted on for her own.

"But we have allies," he told Gracia. "I have appealed to the Sultan of Turkey, describing your plight, the harshness of your treatment here, and the fate of Reyna and *la Chica.*"

Gracia paused, considering. With her trading empire in decline, Venice lived on sufferance from her powerful Eastern neighbor. The Sultan was well-known for his religious tolerance.

"He has already dispatched his *chaus* to negotiate terms," Joseph said. "I suggested in turn that Reyna might make a fitting match for the son of the Jewish court physician."

Gracia's eyes widened minutely.

A muscle in his jaw leapt to hardness beneath his clipped beard. "Reyna and I have discussed matters before. She understands that certain—" his eyes went dark, hidden, "—sacrifices must be made for the sake of the family."

"That may be." Gracia rose to her feet. "But they will not be made by *my daughter.*"

He bowed his head. Something in the movement reminded Gracia of the earnest young man she had taken into her Antwerp house, taught and nurtured, the boy he'd been before Maximilian and all the scheming that had come since then. She touched his hand.

"We will speak no more of it. Besides, I know the Doge. He is no fool. He will take the hint the first time."

Gracia sat up in her narrow prison cot, gasping from a dream of half-glimpsed spectral figures. Beneath the fine lawn of her night dress, her heart hammered against her ribs. She slid her feet to the floor, shivering in the humid air. From the lagoon came the tolling of the marker buoys. Only the faintest moonlight penetrated the window bars, yet the crucifix cast a blurred shadow, its arms no longer quite straight, as if melting under its own weight. As she watched, the dim light took on a greenish hue.

Moving by feel instead of sight, she circled the rooms. The peephole in the outer door was shut, the hallway beyond, silent. Shadows pressed in on her from every corner.

Gracia strode back into the bedroom and pulled the embroidered silk screen across the doorway. Cupping her hands in front of her, she whispered the ancient words, *"Blessed be thou, O Creator of the Universe, Sustainer…"*

The air between her fingers glowed. For a moment, she saw nothing in the flickering light and she wondered if her vision, never as great as Reyna's, had failed her. Then a shape of white and gold wavered into clarity. The flames darkened, streaked now with ashen tones of burnt gold and umber. Once again she caught the outline of a man in a short *tabarro* cloak, moving toward her, one hand outstretched, grasping—

"Dell'Sarto!"

The light flared up, filling half the room. The figure swelled also, to stand within it as large as life. The bright mist fell away and she saw his face.

Gracia raised one hand and smothered a cry. Surely such a creature had never walked the earth. The eyes that met hers were white and bulging, without pupils, blind as if from staring too long into the lightless depths. Skin stretched tight as a drumhead across bones like convoluted shells. There were no lashes, no brows, the ears mere dimples, the nose a doubled slit. The lipless mouth covered rows of serrated teeth, and along the sinuous neck, blood-red gills pulsated.

A stench rose up to gag her, of rotten sea-creature and something else, a perfume seductive and ancient.

Gracia spied the band of gold encircling the neck like a slave's collar, half-hidden by the gills. Above it, the mouth twisted once, twice, then a sound issued forth, rusty as sea-chains or boats creaking in the night.

"Free me, I beg of you!" The creature raised limbs trailing glabrous seaweed to paw at the golden ring. "Free me from this Earth that holds me fast. Use your Fire to melt it away!"

In the echoes, Gracia caught a hint of familiar resonance. Her skin crawled. She'd felt a presence from the moment she'd set foot in Venice, lurking in the fluid dark beneath the canals. Now she understood. Chained to the sea by the ancient *Festa* ceremony, it needed a balancing power of Fire to free itself. Reyna, strong and clear…and inexperienced, malleable. Reyna, now hidden behind the convent walls.

It could not reach Reyna. Now it wanted *her*.

It's what you really want to do, whispered through Gracia's mind.

Peace, find peace in the sea. Give in...

"No!" Gracia pressed her lips together and lifted her chin. The brightness surged in response, white and brilliant purples in kaleidoscoping patterns. Sparks leapt and a smell like burned kelp seared the air, a puff of greasy blue smoke.

"Let us discuss this reasonably, *madonna*," the creature said. "I mean you no harm."

Gracia could not tell if it were pleading or threatening, so subtle and shifting were its tones.

"And I can be a loyal friend. What can you do alone, here in man's prison, your gold in the hands of your enemies, your daughter locked away with the she-priests? Could you not benefit from a powerful ally?"

She felt an inner tug, an aching desire to agree to those suave words. *Oh, Brianda, is this what happened to you?*

"Consider the scope of my dominion," the sea creature continued in its soft, beguiling voice. "The oceans run deep and far, even unto the ends of the earth. With a word, I can drown your enemies, flood their fields, destroy their mighty navies. Consider what we might accomplish together once you have freed me..."

Gracia shook her head. She would bargain her wealth for safety or freedom; she would not bargain with Miriam's Gift.

"You cannot win, O woman. For a time your strength will hold, but then, ah then! it will fail you. Mortal flesh always fails. Only the sea never tires."

Gracia felt a strange fluttering, then a tightness in her chest, a cramping in her belly as if the illnesses that she pretended over the years had come to pass in reality. Her breath caught in her throat. Her vision blurred.

Suddenly the creature made a quick, lunging thrust toward her. She brought her hands up and flames shot from her fingers. It screamed, writhing its long, scaled tail.

"Mortal!" The syllables distorted, merged into a sound like the roar of a sea storm. The creature reared up, claws reaching for her. "Defy me at your peril! I will *take*—"

"You will take nothing!" Gracia's temper flared up like a sword, whetted and ready to her hand. Fire raged though her. She quivered with its power. "I have had enough with *taking*, enough with *bargaining*! Unclean beast, begone! Take yourself from my sight! Rot in hell or the bowels of the sea, I care not—but come not to me or mine ever again!"

The air between her hands, ignited by her fury, shimmered, incandescent. Its brightness pierced her, filled her. The ring around the creature's neck glowed as if molten.

The sea creature shuddered, wavering. For an instant, it seemed to bow down before her, and she thought it might be summoning what powers it possessed against her. But it could not wrest the Light from her; only she could choose to wield it.

And I choose! For my Reyna and for my people, I choose!

"S-s-sooner or later," came its fading whisper, "your power will be mine!"

Gracia blinked, startled. Then she laughed aloud. "O creature of the deep, do you think this power comes from *me*? Do you think it *mine*?"

O Shekhinah, Mystery of Mysteries!

She dropped her hands, surrendering the Light to its source. As the brightness faded, so did the image within it.

"Go where you will, to the very ends of the earth," creaked the rusted-iron voice, growing thinner with each syllable. "I will be waiting…"

The voice failed. For a long moment Gracia stood listening to the silence.

The creature was right. There was no corner of the earth, not Lisbon, not Antwerp, not the Sublime Porte of Constantinople, no human kingdom that could shelter her, nowhere she could hide.

Hide… echoed through her mind.

Gradually her eyes grew accustomed to the dimness. A pale illumination cast twisted shadows from the crucifix. Gracia walked over to it. It was not fastened to the wall, but hung from a row of nails. It was heavier than she expected. She hold of the bars of the cross with both hands and turned it away from her, toward the wall.

"Let this be an end to lies." Her voice, at first a whisper, grew stronger and more triumphant. "From this moment onward, I will no longer hide what I am."

As if touched by prophetic vision, she saw her people huddled on the Lisbon pier, in *il gheto*, in a thousand darkened prisons. She saw them lift their heads, arise, follow. Like Miriam of old, she would go forth. Her dreams would become a bridge, her Light a beacon. And never again would she wear a mask.

∞

The old woman stood at her balcony, looking out over the water. Warm and clear in the Turkish sun, the bay sparkled on the surface and turned blue as sapphires below. Yet always she felt the darkness in the shadows, the brooding hunger. She felt it here in Constantinople and she felt it in Tiberias, in Palestine beside the Sea of Galilee, where even now her agents were building the settlement that was the first step toward a Jewish homeland. She would not live to see the completion of that work; the years held her too tightly in their grasp, even as the sea creature had warned. Yet she smiled as she turned away from the water, wandered through the rooms filled with books printed in Hebrew under her patronage, watched Reyna play with her young daughter. The shadow might be ever with them, but now the Light burned bright and free.

To Kiss the Star

Amy Sterling Casil

Melodie kicked her heels restlessly against her wheelchair footrests. At last he had come. The bare whiff of bitter smoke told her that that John, her Friendly Visitor, had lit his usual pre-visit cigarette on the Mary-Le-Bow Center patio.

How Mel loved the smoke. It reminded her of the bonfire her younger brothers had set on a long-ago, lazy autumn afternoon while she watched from the caned rocker on Mum's porch. Before she had lost her sight.

The leaves, brown and yellow and orange, had fired up with a crackle as the boys laughed madly, the smoke billowing skyward, nearly the same color as the icy gray Midlands clouds.

John's cigarettes, like the burning leaves. He had told her name of his brand. An elegant name, vaguely exciting. Mel wouldn't forget it, because it was like his name: John. Her voiceboard was ready. She hit the up arrow just as she heard his feet padding into the dayroom.

"John Player Special," the voiceboard said.

"Aw, Mel, you caught me at it again."

Mel laughed, honking like a lost gosling. Something was wet on her chin. Drool, she supposed. John's hand touched her chest, then something soft and antiseptic-smelling wiped her face. Her bib.

The damn nurses had bibbed her, and she'd told them no bib, please, because John was coming. Today was her Friendly Visit. Furious at the nurses' betrayal, she kicked at the floor with her feet, rolling her chair back a few inches. John followed.

"You'll get me to quit," John said. "Just keep at me."

"You're too handsome to die young," Mel pressed into the voiceboard.

"Did your Mum call?" John asked.

Mel shook her head. More drool on her chin. "Don't wipe me," she said through the droning voiceboard. No intonation, no fury, just the bland voice with vaguely elongated vowels and clipped consonants, because that was how it made words, from vowels and sounds put together, depending upon how she rolled the smooth plastic ball controller and which of the four arrows she pressed.

"You're twenty-three, you don't need your Mum's permission."

"Twenty-four," Mel corrected. "I know," she added, about the permission.

"This is the chance of a lifetime, Mel. I thought you would have done it by now."

Mel nodded. John was right. She should be getting her implants by now. It wasn't every spastic, blind twenty-four year old cripple who won the lottery to explore the stars. Her number, chosen for the chance to be a probe controller for the ISA, sent light years away to Tau Ceti or Sirius or wherever they needed to send her.

"I thought today might be our last visit, so I brought you this. It's nothing much." John took her better hand, her left, and pressed something into it. Mel felt a delicate chain and small hard cubes that she rubbed between her fingers. A bracelet, with beads or stones, deliciously warm from being in John's pocket.

"For me?" Mel hadn't expected a gift. Especially not anything so personal, like a bracelet. Again, the wetness on her chin. Disgusting spit! Damn rebellious mouth! She heard herself making noises, but she couldn't reach for the voiceboard just then, because John was fastening the bracelet around her wrist.

"It's a W-W-J-D bracelet," he said. The cube-shaped beads had cooled because Mel hadn't any circulation in her hands. Cold hands, warm heart, her Mum had always said. The bracelet was loose. Mel was afraid that it would slip off as she jerked her arms around like a puppet, the way she did sometimes.

"Wuh, wuh, wuh," Mel said, with her mouth.

"What does it mean? Oh, sure—it means 'what would Jesus do?'"

"Thank you," Mel said through the voiceboard. Why had she thought it might be a real bracelet—that the beads might be pearls? Like boyfriends and girlfriends gave each other. She didn't believe at all in Jesus. How could she, after the way she'd turned out? No God she would ever believe in could let people turn out the way she had.

"I love it," she said, glad that the voiceboard was so easy to use for lies.

John steadied her wrist. Mel realized she'd been flailing again. "After you go, we probably won't see each other again. I mean, by the time you get back—" He paused.

"You'll be very old," Mel said.

"I'll probably be dead," John said, laughing.

Mel changed the subject. "How's your song doing?"

John didn't say anything for a moment. "Oh, crackers, you know. Fire it up."

"Is that good or bad?"

"Good," John said. "We're doing the next one right now."

"Viddy, too?"

"Viddy too. And the first thousand are special release. The kiddies get Star Bars with every copy and the first fifty get a T-Shirt."

"Tres Fab," Mel said. "I wish I could see it," she said. She'd heard John's music, but wanted so desperately to see the videos. John was a viddy star musician. Played guitar and sitar. Hana, the morning nurse, had told Mel that John was "A God ... so totally fab."

"Look, Mel," John said. "Don't worry about your Mum. Or your brothers. Just go. If I had the chance, I'd take it in a heartbeat."

Mel shook her head. "I know. You're right," she said. They wouldn't wait forever. She wasn't the only one who could make the trip. There had to be lots of... cripples. Waiting for the chance. Sitting in their chairs and drooling, waiting for their number to come up, for ISA to pick them and make them something like whole again. No. That wasn't it. Not whole, but something... different. Turn the whole stinking, spastic body off. Adapt the brain which was functioning, discard the body that wasn't, and shoot it off to the stars. Live forever and go where no man could ever go. Not a whole one, anyway. Small things like brains could go in hardened housings. Big things like bodies couldn't. Or shouldn't.

"Mel, why on earth are you waiting?" John asked.

Because of you, John, Mel thought.

"I know it doesn't hurt," John said. "I saw a vid, all about it. It's like magic, how they put you in the probe."

Mel flailed until she found John's hand where it rested near her leg. His warm fingers stroked her cold palm. "I'm afraid," she told him, even though that wasn't true. She couldn't possibly say the truth.

"That's natural," he said.

Her head began to roll around, and her chin fell on the damp bib.

"I asked them if I would be able to see again," she continued.

"They haven't answered me."

"I'm sure you'll be able," John said, squeezing her hand. "You'll have better senses than any normal person."

"I guess that's better than having the senses of an abnormal person," Mel said.

John laughed loudly. Mel sensed that his laughter was forced. "That's what I love about you," he said. "You've got a smashing sense of humor."

Didn't all cripples?

"Take me for a walk on the patio," Mel said, folding her hands in her lap. "You can smoke there. I don't mind." John was a very good Friendly Visitor. He put his hand on her shoulder and guided her gently as they went.

Mum brought sandwiches packed in a wicker basket. Mel smelled the sandwiches—pressed liver and spirulina paste, she thought—and also smelled the basket, hearing the crackle as Mum opened it. She'd taken Mel out across the wide field, where the pollen made Mel sneeze, stopping when they reached the small hillock in the middle. The sun burned the part on the top of Mel's head. She asked for a napkin. Sighing, Mum covered Mel's hair and laid out the food.

"Can you chew today, dear?" Mum asked.

Mel nodded. She seldom used the voiceboard with Mum. Mum preferred it that way; she liked Mel to use the baby talk and the grunting which had been all Mel could manage for most of her life.

"How are the boys?"

"Oh, fine. Jack's got a new girlfriend. Peter's still into his electric trains." Mum fed Mel a piece of the sandwich. She had been right: it was liver sausage and stale-tasting spirulina paste.

"How about Davey?"

"Oh, the same," Mum said. This meant that Davey hadn't quit using. Davey was two years younger than Mel. He was tall and athletic, but he'd started in with drugs at the age of twelve and had never held a job for longer than two weeks. Davey was Mum's favorite.

Mum sat by Mel's chair, spreading out her skirt with a rustle of fabric. "Listen," she said. "About your e-mail."

Mel deliberately pushed some chewed sandwich paste out of her mouth and made a choking noise. Mum got up, knees crackling, to wipe Mel's face.

"Dear, I don't think you should do this. It's horribly dangerous. And you'll never..."

"Never what?" Mel said through her voiceboard.

Mum roughly wiped the sandwich paste away, and then stuffed another piece in Mel's mouth. "You know what I mean."

"You mean that will be it once they do the implants and get rid of my body."

"Yes. Don't be smart."

"What does it matter, Mum? What good is my body now?"

"Dear, we've been over it. Don't you think if they can send a ship to another star, they might not find a cure for you? What if you do this, and the next day they come up with an operation which would make you..."

"Normal?" Mel said. "They can give me a prosthesis body now, Mum. But where would the money come from?"

Mum was weeping. "Christ on His cross, Mel," she said. "Why do you always have to throw it in everyone's face?"

Mel said nothing. She thought of John, the way he smelled. She wanted to see his face, all fab, the way the nurse Hana described him. She imagined herself normal, wearing a white seersucker dress, running across the field with John, laughing. John's hair was long— she had touched it. Hana had told Mel it was dark brown and shone in the light. Soft, and a little bit curly. Mel's hair was thin and patchy, a muddy dark blond. It had gotten worse, since she'd gone blind. Before, she had been able to comb it on her best days; put ribbons and bows in it. Now, it was chopped off just below her ears, so it wouldn't fall in her face or get nasty with bits of food or drool. Practical, the way things needed to be at the Mary-Le-Bow Center.

"I'm going to do it," Mel said through the voiceboard, glad of its impersonal drone.

"Mel!"

"Don't argue, Mum." Mel remembered what John had said, about her being old enough. She wished she could have said it with his style, his carefree flair.

Mum's arms were around her. Mel's face was pressed uncomfortably between Mum's breast and her bony shoulder. "I'll never see you again, luv. Not if they send you off on that ship."

Straining to move her arm, Mel got one hand on the voiceboard. "You never come unless there's something wrong anyway," she said, knowing what it would do to Mum.

"Oh, Mel," Mum sobbed. "How can you hurt me so?"

"John says I should go for it," Mel said. The voiceboard droned on. "I think I will," she said, although she did not mean it. Going would mean leaving John.

The ISA counseling specialist was an American. Mel supposed that she should have expected that. The Americans had pioneered the technology for the space probes. No normal bodies could survive the trip to other stars, with the hard radiation and all the other myriad challenges. So, the essential part of people—their brains—had been placed in hardened housings and intimately connected to the probe itself. It was one way to do it. Not the only way—just a way—to explore and discover ahead of the complex and costly generation ships which would follow.

Because of the danger involved, condemned criminals were to have been the initial probe controllers. But that hadn't gone over. Why not give people a chance who deserved it? That was the public outcry, about the time Mel had gone blind. The ISA had decided that people like Mel should be selected, not criminals.

If you were a registered applicant and your number came up in the lottery, you had thirty days to decide. If you declined, your chance went to someone else: another waiting cripple. You couldn't be older than twenty-five. You couldn't be married, and couldn't have any children. If you were under legal age, your guardian had to give permission. Mel knew all this, but it was repeated for her during her orientation. She didn't know why she was surprised when the ISA people came to the Mary-Le-Bow Center. She supposed it was easier to bring the equipment and the specialists to the cripple, rather than transferring her.

The ISA counseling specialist, who had a western twang which Mel thought was very cowboy-like, told her how the implants worked.

"We put them into your cerebral cortex," he said. "Bio-electrical devices. We also implant controls into the main nerve centers which control body function—cerebellum and pons and so-on. The probe will become your body."

"I've never had very good control," Mel said.

He chuckled. "This will be different," he said. "After we start the process, you'll have two weeks to decide if you want out. In fact, you can stop it at any point up until the time we—"

"Get rid of my body," Mel said.

"Yeah," the counselor said. "You got it."

"Can you tell me something?" Mel asked.

"Anything. I'm here to answer all of your questions."

"Before you put me in the…"

"Housing," he said.

"I want to know if I'll be able to see again. Is that part before or after?"

"Oh," he said, drawing in his breath, as if she'd surprised him. "You could see some things, I think. You'll have your visual cortex connected and I suppose we could fix something up. I hadn't thought about it quite that way before. Not everyone we work with is blind."

"Before the final step—will I be able to move?"

The counselor clicked his tongue. "Move? Well, you mean more than you can right now? I'm afraid not. We'll have to shut many functions down. You may not be able to move at all."

"My voiceboard?"

There was a pause. "Possibly. I can't tell until we evaluate you further. With your degree of motor impairment, it's difficult to know. There may be seizures. We are working with your brain, you know."

"If I can't use my voiceboard, how will I tell you to stop?"

The counselor touched her hand. He tapped the middle of her palm with one finger.

"Twice a day until the final step, I'll tap your hand once. You move your fingers, if you want to go ahead. If I don't feel anything, I'll tap twice. Like this." She felt him tap two times. "If you move then, we'll stop. Remove the implants."

"That's good," she said. "Is that it for today?"

The counselor patted her shoulder, impersonally. "If you're tired," he said.

"No," Mel said. "I'm not tired. But today is my Friendly Visitor day. I'm expecting someone."

"Oh," the counselor said. "Well, that's good. Who is she?"

"Him," Mel said. "His name is John. He's a musician."

"Very good," said the counselor. Then, he left.

Mel waited in the dayroom for an hour. No one came. Finally, she wheeled to the door and pressed the call button. She guessed it had been about ten minutes when a nurse finally showed up. It was Hana.

"Yes, luv?"

"Hana, I was waiting for John."

"Oh, he's not here?"

Mel was had to force her exhausted, trembling hands over the voiceboard. "Do you see him?"

"No, luv. I suppose he's not coming today. Let's give you a nice bath. You'll want to be all fresh for those nice ISA gentlemen. How lucky you are!"

"I suppose so," Mel said, hoping that John would come later. It was so unlike him not to come, and not to call. He always called, and he was hardly ever late. After the bath, during which Hana had scrubbed too hard, Mel thought, though she couldn't say anything without the voiceboard, Mel sat by the window in her room, feeling the warm light on her cheeks. Why hadn't John come? Or called? No one knew anything, and it was too tiring to keep asking. She fell asleep in her chair. When she woke, it was cold. She was still by the window, and they were fastening a dinner tray on her chair and tying a bib around her neck.

"Hana," Mel said to the nurse, who was washing something, Mel thought perhaps her water jug, in the sink.

"Yes?" Hana began to hum a little tune, something Indian-sounding. Maybe that was what John's music sounded like. Mel had always wanted to hear it, but John always forgot to bring his recordings. He was so busy.

"Before I go any farther with this, I want to do something." Mel paused, waiting for Hana's reaction. There was none. "I want to smoke a cigarette. Like John's," she continued.

"Oh, luv! The way you breathe? You'll keel over! It's nasty, nasty. Why would you want to do that?"

Mel kept working at the voiceboard. "I want to smoke a John Player Special. I want to eat lobster. I want to feel what it's like to have somebody…" Mel meant John, but she wasn't about to say so. "I want somebody's arms around me. I want to feel a kiss."

Hana turned off the water. Mel felt her sit on the bed, smelled her cologne. Hana's hand, damp from the water, brushed Mel's forehead.

"I think I understand." Hana's warm lips touched Mel's cheek. She took Mel's hand, and rubbed Mel's wrist in a soothing way.

Mel tried to speak with her mouth. "I wuh-wuh-hunt s-s-s-s…"

"You want a bit of life," Hana said. She raised Mel and held her close. "I'm no man, not like what you mean, but I love you, Mel-o-die." Hana almost sang Mel's name. Tears stung in the corners of Mel's eyes.

"I see what I can do about that lobster," Hana said. "My boyfriend's a chef. Have I ever said? He'd be proud to make something up for you. I don't eat meat, but I've heard that lobster is very good. You'll like it. But first, we'll get you dressed, for those ISA doctors."

Later that day, the ISA technicians finished implanting her visual bio-electrodes. The counselor told her that they'd made something up for her: a special visor similar to one which had been developed for cold-fusion technicians, the ones who worked with the magnetic bottles which contained the reaction. The visor was sensitive in the ultra-violet and infra-red, as well as the normal visual spectrum. Whatever she would see through it wouldn't be like she what she had seen before she'd gone blind.

Mel's old doctor had said, brutally, Mel remembered, that she'd really gotten the short end of the genetic stick. Cerebral palsy—a spastic—with a heart defect, and retinitis pigmentosa. It didn't get much worse than that, he'd said.

The ISA counselor arrived, just as the technicians were fitting the visor. He spoke to her, holding her hand while they fitted the metallic piece over her temples and eyes. "I know it hurts. Just stay with us. It's going straight into your optic nerve, which ain't damaged. You oughta see something, but we can't guarantee technicolor."

Mel had shut her eyes. They'd said it didn't matter whether they were open or shut. It was going over the eyes, not into them. The implant went through her temples. The connection was so fine, he'd said, that no one could see it, and she wasn't supposed to feel it. Even so, Mel felt like they were breaking holes in her skull with a jack-hammer.

"You can't move," the counselor explained. "It won't work until you've adjusted thoroughly and the implants have integrated."

Mel realized that they were drilling holes in her skull, not for the implant, but to stabilize the visor. She couldn't say anything. They'd taken her voiceboard away, promising to give it back when they'd finished. She heard a voice, moaning. Hers. Something dribbled on her chin. They whacked the crown of her head, again and again.

The counselor squeezed her hand. His finger tapped, once. She squeezed back. "That's great," he said. "Now, they'll activate it."

Mel closed her eyes. It was as if she had opened them, but she hadn't. A long, mournful-looking face appeared, grainy and hazy, like an antique telly when it was turned on. Big nose, and a wild head of bushy hair. The face smiled, crookedly, showing a mouth full of even, pale teeth. He must be the counselor, Mel thought. Her head was throbbing viciously, but she managed to smile in return. Somebody thrust the voiceboard in her lap.

"I see you," she said. "You've got a big nose."

"That's right, darlin'." The head turned. More shapes—the technicians' faces, appeared. Hazy and wavering, but unmistakably concerned. "Hey, she's got me!" the counselor called to them.

"I haven't seen anyone in six years," Mel said.

"And my good-looking mug is the first! I'm touched," the counselor replied. The technicians were grinning. They were both young, close to Mel's age. One blond-seeming, though colors just didn't look the way she remembered, and the other darker, with a thin, nervous face. Another face appeared. Dark, pretty, soft and round, with large eyes and full lips.

"Hana," Mel said.

"Ah, that's right! You can see!" Hana wheeled a cart toward Mel. The technicians grinned, parting to allow Hana to approach, while the counselor stepped back, crossing his arms. Hana lifted the cover of a metal dish with a flourish.

Mel remembered what lobsters looked like. This lobster was huge, his eyes black dots on long stalks. Mel almost expected him to lift his claws and start snapping at her. He was bright red, she thought, but somehow the color didn't look right. Too vivid, perhaps, as if he was glowing. He glowed with heat, she realized. She saw it, rising in waves from his shell.

Hana removed a claw and cracked it. She worked a piece of hot white flesh from the claw and brought it to Mel's lips.

"Here's your taste of lobster," she said.

Mel took the soft flesh in her mouth and began to chew. It was silken and buttery, yielding to her tongue and her teeth. Beyond delicious. She closed her eyes, but the visor still worked -she could still see. They were smiling at her, Hana looking proud, the technicians nodding. The counselor took a handkerchief from his pocket, and blew his nose, trumpeting loudly.

Mel swallowed the lobster. "I can't close my eyes," she said.

"Yes, you can," the blond technician said. "Tap your temple, on the left side."

Mel flailed around a bit, then managed to slap the side of her head with her thumb. Everything went dark.

Her heart leapt with sudden fear. Had she broken it? "Now I can't see."

"Do it again. Right side." This time, Mel struggled with her bad right arm, and struck a glancing blow against her cheek. Nothing happened. She gritted her teeth, and tried again. This time, she hit her temple. Everyone reappeared, including the lobster.

"It works," Mel told them.

The blond technician slapped his darker partner on the back. "I told you!"

"So," the counselor said, leaning forward, causing his face to expand like a strange balloon. "What would you like to do? We have a day or two before we go further. How about a play? Something at the Globe? Or a museum? Would you like to see some paintings? Sculptures?"

Mel shook her head. "No, I'm okay. Maybe a book. I would like to read, like I used to." Before the RP had gotten so bad, Mel had devoured every book she could get her hands on. Listening to books wasn't the same. It was nice, but not as satisfying. She thought of John. Sometimes he had read to her. Shakespeare; the poems of Elizabeth Barrett Browning. One time, from Alice in Wonderland. She wanted to see John, but she was reluctant to say so, especially with the technicians there.

The counselor shook his head. "I didn't think you'd be so easy to please," he said.

"I already told Hana what I wanted," Mel said.

Hana stroked Mel's forehead. "Yes, and you've gotten your lobster. Go ahead, finish it all. He's five pounds."

The blond technician whistled under his breath. "A fortune," the other one said.

Hana began to feed Mel. Mel gorged, smiling with pleasure. She rested her hand on her stomach as the others began to eat the rest of the lobster, grinning and laughing. She couldn't possibly finish all of it. She was warmly happy, the ache in her head fading, as the others ate.

Mel felt sleepy, and she told Hana that she wanted to take a nap. She thanked the technicians, and the counselor, who shook her hand with a crushing grip, again reminding her of a cowboy. He needed a cowboy hat to complete the picture, but otherwise, she thought that he was perfect. She reminded herself to ask him the next day whether or not he was from Oklahoma, or Arizona, or one of those other cowboy places in the States.

Hana pushed Mel from the dayroom into the long corridor, which was not as long as Mel had thought, now that she could see it. It was lined with dull prints of horses and huntsmen. She wheeled Mel into her room. How small the room was. The bed was narrow, with four plump blue pillows at the head, topped with Mel's teddy bear. There were a few pictures tacked on a cork board to the right of the bed. The boys, Mel realized—how tall they had grown. A sink, where Hana and the other nurses washed things. A narrow window, looked out on the roadway, where she saw rows of blockhouses across the street.

Mel had often heard children playing in the morning. Now she knew where they lived.

She saw a daisy in a small vase on a table by the window. Spit tray beside it. A small closet was open on the opposite side of the room. Mel saw a row of open gowns hanging inside the closet, all the same, striped blue and white. Fuzzy slippers rested below the hanging hems of the gowns, which Mel realized for the first time had teddy bear heads on them. Mum had brought them for her birthday—Mel had instinctively disliked them and thought that the odd shapes she had felt on their toes represented defective workmanship, since Mum was always looking for a bargain. Mel looked down at her feet for the first time since she'd been able to see. She wore pale pink socks. Her feet were turned toward each other, and curled into themselves, like pictures she'd seen of Chinese women with their feet bound. They'd turned that way since she'd been blind. Above the doubled-over pink socks, her legs were the width of a broom handle, and dead, waxy white.

There was a mirror above the sink. A polished mirror, not glass, but steel.

Mel flailed about with her left arm. She couldn't reach her head.

"You take your nap now," Hana said. She left Mel in the middle of the room and went to the bed, getting the covers ready.

Mel stared at the mirror. If she moved a foot or two closer, she would be able to look into it.

"I'm sleepy," she said.

Hana took the voiceboard from her lap and put it on the table by the vase with the daisy. Hana turned back, and something in her expression told Mel that she had sensed what Mel was thinking.

"There's time for that later," Hana said.

Mel pushed the button on her chair which moved it forward, toward the mirror. Even though she didn't want to look, somehow she had to look. She gazed down at her stick legs a moment, then up to see her face in the mirror. Every bit of joy she had felt earlier, to see, and to taste, bled out of her. The visor was the least of it, like a big pair of blind metal sunglasses over her face. Bolted over the strange, barely-human landscape which had been her face.

"Ih-ih-hut-ssss-zzz," Mel said through her slack lips. She saw the wetness on her pocked chin before she felt it. Hana retrieved the voiceboard and put it gently on Mel's lap.

"It's Friendly Visitor day tomorrow," Mel said. "If John comes, tell him I have been taken for more implants," she told Hana. "Tell him

I'm not coming back."

"Oh, luv," Hana said.

"Leave me," Mel replied. Then, after a few seconds, she added, "please." She looked at her wrist and noticed the bracelet. How could John have visited her? Spoken to her? Touched her? On the bracelet were four tiny square beads set among smaller seed beads, like colored pearls. W-W-J-D, she read on the squares.

Goodbye, John. Her lips trembled. She heard herself making noises. Goodbye. She flailed around until she struck her left temple with a strong whack, and everything went black. Tomorrow, she would tell the ISA man to take off the visor, and to stop everything. Part of her wanted to go into the ship, if only to get rid of her horrible face. Another part of her said that the stars would hate her. Recoil from her, and she would wander, cold and alone forever. Somehow, that seemed appealing, but no. She would stay in her place in her wheelchair. That was all she deserved. All that was needed.

She would tell Hana...no. She would call herself. In the morning. She could see to go to the phone now. She would make sure that John knew he was no longer needed.

What would Jesus do? Jesus would weep.

"I won't go," Mel told Hana, when she came to take her to the dayroom. "I'm staying in bed." Mel knew that it was coming out as garbled moans—spastic talk—but Hana seemed to understand.

"I give up," Hana said, after struggling to get Mel to sit up in bed. Mel should have called, tried to stop John. She had just been so tired. She buried herself in the covers, kicking as well as she could until it felt as though she was covered completely. Like a cave. She got part of the sheet hooked around her hand and dragged it over her head, then turned on her side, away from Hana.

"Today's your visitor day," Hana said, trying to wheedle a response from Mel. "And those ISA men will be coming soon, too."

Mel pressed her lips together, forcing herself to think about Mum, and her brothers. She tried to go back to sleep, but fell only into a drowsy half-sleep, vaguely aware of Hana moving about, cleaning things, pottering in Mel's closet.

Mel shivered, as someone touched her arm. "You're still wearing my bracelet." It was John.

She jerked her arm, trying to pull it back under the warm, safe covers.

"I'm sorry to have missed our day." John patted her shoulder through the sheets.

Mel heard herself mumbling. She wasn't quite sure of what she wanted to say. No matter what, he wouldn't understand. God, let him not see her face.

"Mel, please sit up. I've got something to tell you." The bed sank down. He was sitting beside her.

She ground her face into the pillow. "Nuh-no," she said. She tried to call for Hana, then realized that she hadn't heard her soft movements, or her humming, for some time. The traitor had let John in, then left them alone.

John was pulling on the covers. Mel struggled, using her hands as weights, but it was hopeless. The sheets slipped away. She flailed toward her head, trying to cover what she could of her face. Her rebellious hand struck the left side of her head. She could see once more.

"Look, if it's this thing they've put on for your eyes, I don't care. It looks like sunglasses, is all. Big sunglasses."

"No!" Mel said. Desperation made her voice strong.

John grasped her shoulders. He turned her around as if she was a doll.

"Mel, I don't care. I've been visiting you for a year."

Her face. He was seeing her horrid face, and she couldn't cover it. She caught a glimpse of him through her clenched fists. She tried to strike her left temple, turn off the visor, but her arm was completely rebellious. He had her hands, both of them. He drew them away from her face.

A groan escaped her lips as she struggled. John, so fab. His features were fine, almost feminine. His hair was as soft and shiny as the hair of a dark, lovely woman. He had a small beard and moustache, neatly trimmed around his chin and lips. She held herself as still as she could, though every muscle in her body was going wild. Her feet twitched beneath the covers, out of control.

John took her wrist, turning the bracelet. "That visor is nothing," he said, smiling. "I'm glad you're wearing the bracelet." Something shone on John's left hand. A ring—he'd never said he was married. Of course he was married. His wife was probably as stunning as he was.

"Muh-muh-muh," Mel said. She jerked her body toward the table and the voiceboard. John looked uncertain. She moved her shoulders toward the table, and his eyes followed.

"Your voiceboard. Right," he said. He retrieved it. While he walked across the room, Mel thought of covering herself again, but it was too late. He'd already seen her. And he'd been seeing her, for the past year. She had been a fool—a complete fool. She didn't know why he had come to visit her, but it certainly couldn't have been for any of the reasons she'd imagined for so long, in her self-deluded blindness.

When he put the voiceboard in her lap, she said, "It's so kind of you to visit the ugly cripple."

John looked puzzled, as he sat by her once more, then sympathy came over his face. No, Mel thought. Pity. She thought of hitting the visor again, going blind, but he was fab, as Hana said. The most gorgeous man she'd ever seen, she thought—and she had loved to collect pictures of the teen idols, before her eyes had gone. That had been stupid then, just the way this was stupid now. But she loved to look at his face, even as he looked on her with pity, as if she was some trapped laboratory monkey, or a freak from the vids.

"Come on," he said, forcing a cheery tone in his voice, Mel thought, "let's take a spin on the patio. I'll get you into your seat." Then, he retrieved her wheelchair from the corner (it was very worn and cracked on the seat, Mel noticed, shabby-looking), and brought it to the side of the bed. Mel allowed him to lift her into it. Shamed that she enjoyed his touch, Mel looked away from him, toward the window, and the vase with the daisy. The daisy drooped—that was the end for it. Mel wondered how long it had been there, and who had put it there. Probably Hana.

John guided her down the hall, though she no longer needed his help. Mel saw some of the other inmates of the Center peeking out of their doors. They looked jealously at them. Quite a few were elderly. More than Mel had thought. She hadn't known how many there were during her blindness. She hadn't realized, although she could smell them, of course, always smell their terrible smell—death and decay and disinfectant.

When they reached the patio, John parked her in a sunny spot. A small bird, a linnet, Mel thought, flew past them, wings whirring. He pulled a packet of cigarettes from his shirt pocket, and a lighter.

"Come on," he said, shaking two cigarettes out. "Hana told me that you wanted to do this." He lit the cigarettes. Their red tips glowed—her visor showed a round ball of whitish heat around the tips. John put the filter of one cigarette to her lips.

The filter was hot. The smoke burned her nostrils. She put her lips around the filter and drew in a breath. Choking, horrible. Her arms flailed. Couldn't use the voiceboard…couldn't speak…coughing, spitting.

John threw both cigarettes down, crushing them beneath his foot, then whacked Mel's back. "Oh, no," he said in an agonized voice. "I should have known!"

The visor blurred. Mel's eyes were watering, and she was gasping for breath between coughs. What a horrible, vile taste, like swallowing burning coals! Her throat began to swell.

At last, she began to breathe more easily, and the coughing slowed to little hacks wracking her chest every few seconds.

"That's the worst thing I've ever tasted," she told him.

John knelt beside her, patting her knee. He nodded, his eyes full of regret. "Oh, God, I was so stupid," he said.

"No," Mel said. "I asked for it. But I like lobster better."

"Hana told me what else you asked for," he said. Before Mel could react, he'd leaned forward and had his arms around her. His lips brushed her neck. His voice, so warm and soft, whispering, right next to her ear. Mel felt her body trembling, legs jerking around. Stop it, she told herself, but it was hopeless. Her chest grew hot; she felt the flush all the way up her neck, working its way over her cheeks. "Sweet Mel," he said.

She managed to get her hands on the voiceboard, even John's body pressed against her lap.

"No," she said. "Please, John." How warm he was, how hard the muscles felt in his arms and shoulders. He smelled of John Player Specials and of some spicy cologne, and of his own clean, soft flesh.

He kissed her neck, gently. She glimpsed his face, eyes closed, moving in front of her, and though she closed her eyes beneath the visor, she still saw the patio, the canvas awning, the little bird flying over the cheap plastic furniture, as his firm, sweet lips touched hers. Not her mouth! She had seen the terrible teeth in the mirror; the misshapen lips, cracked and rough. What could she expect when she couldn't even stop herself from drooling, had to depend on others even to clean her teeth? It must be horrible for him to come so near. How could he?

"Why?" she asked.

His lips pressed tighter against hers, and his arms drew her close to his body, almost all the way out of the chair. Mel was afraid that she would explode with everything that was rushing through her; things she didn't even have words for. The patio wavered, her sight flickered, and she heard her heels rattling in the chair.

At last, he drew gently away, putting her back in the seat, and sat back on his heels. He was smiling, almost shyly.

"Hana said you wanted a kiss," he said. His voice was throaty and rough—a street-tough tone she'd never heard from him before.

Her hands fluttered over the voiceboard. At last, she made it say, "I was just saying that. I didn't really—"

"Yes you did," he said, putting his hand on her knee and looking into the visor, where her eyes should have been. As if he knew what she was thinking, he said, "The bloody thing covers your eyes. You have beautiful eyes, Mel."

She felt like he had stabbed her through her heart.

"Don't lie to me," she said.

His gaze was steady. "I've never lied to you," he replied.

She looked at his hand on her knee, where the ring glinted. "Yes, you have," she said, even though this wasn't exactly true, as she'd never asked him if he was married. She had always assumed that he wasn't.

He seemed confused at first, then he realized that she was looking at his ring. "Oh," he said. "That's what I had to tell you. Why I wasn't here last week. I got married."

"Last week?"

He laughed. "Yes. I should have told you. But it was really a last-minute thing."

Mel backed the chair across the patio. "Good luck to both of you," she said. "I'm sure she's very beautiful." She was thankful this time that the voiceboard droned mechanically. It could almost sound sincere. She didn't want John to know that she was foolish enough to care.

He stopped the chair with one hand, just as she was about to go through the open glass door into the Center. "She is beautiful," John said. "She's going to have my baby."

A cry came from somewhere deep inside of Mel. She masked it with a cough. Let him think she was still choked up from the cigarette. She would endure whatever she had to endure before he left, and then she would go back into her room. She would take away the voiceboard, and turn off the visor. When the cowboy counselor came and tapped her hand, she would not move. She would not jerk, so that he couldn't possibly imagine that she wanted to go on with it. She would wait until he tapped twice, then clench her hand tightly, with all her strength. She would let them think that the visual implants had damaged her. Somehow, she would get them to take the damn thing off. Tear it off herself, if she had to. She could make her hands obey, if she tried hard enough. Then, she would be blind again.

She wouldn't eat. Eventually, they would hook her up to machines, which would feed her. What was left of her body would waste away; then, real darkness.

John was talking, in the hard, street-wise tone she'd heard earlier from him. Mel refused to look at him.

"Alexandra and I have been together for a while. When she told me about the baby, it seemed like the right thing to do. My Da took off when I was just a kid. I'm not like that," he said.

"Good," Mel said, when he said nothing for a while.

John took her hand. Mel stared at the blank patio wall. Ugly gray bricks. She began to count them.

"Look, I'll never forget you," he said. "You've kept me going."

"Right," she said.

He squeezed her hand, then stroked her wrist and toyed with the bracelet.

"Take it away," she said. "I don't want it."

A wet drop hit her hand. John's voice, when he spoke again, sounded strange and thick. As if he was crying. It couldn't have been a tear, she told herself. Men didn't cry.

"No," he said. "It was for you. I thought you might be able to put it in the probe. To protect you when you go off."

"Take it," she repeated. "Damn you. I'm not going anywhere."

He tugged on the bracelet, but didn't remove it. "Oh, Mel," he said. "You've got to go!"

"Never," she said. "Go away. Take your cheap bracelet and go back to your wife." There—she had said it. Now, he'd leave.

He said nothing for a long while, then she felt his hand, lightly stroking her hair. No—she would not turn. She'd never look at him again.

"I did lie to you," he said, in a low voice. "That bracelet cost me a day's pay."

"Bully for you," she said. What a liar he was. It was just cheap beads, probably plastic.

"I had my eye on it for weeks. I had the fellow put it aside and I went after work to pick it up, the day I gave it to you."

Work? What was he talking about?

"I lied to you about what I do," John said. "I'm no viddy star. I work mornings at the Virgin store and afternoons I work at my step-dad's shop. Those were someone else's tunes you heard. Stuff I listen to for myself. Real musicians."

Mel drew in a sharp breath. Not a viddy star?

"My step-dad repairs guitars and sitars and such. That's how I know about them. Yeah, I play a little," he said.

Mel's fingers went to the voiceboard. "You should have said," she said. "You didn't have to pretend. I" she paused, moving her fingers tentatively back and forth. "I liked you for you."

Another tear fell on the back of her hand. "I wanted to impress you. When I first came, the nurses made a big show of saying I looked like a viddy star. It pumped me up a bit. When you believed them, I thought, why not play along? It went from there."

"You never told me why," Mel said.

"Why what?" She turned toward him, to see his handsome face once more. His eyes were swollen—yes, he had been crying.

"Why you came to visit. Someone like me."

"Oh, that," he said, shaking his head. He drew the back of his hand across his eyes. "Uh, well, I'm a Christian. It was part of my service to the church. Every two weeks. We all do something and this was my thing."

"Oh," she said, turning away. Of course. It would be something like that.

John seemed to realize her disappointment. He reached toward her, then drew back, as if he knew that touching her was the wrong thing at this moment. His face grew serious. "It became more than that," he said. "So much more. I mean, you're so brave. You're so much more than I'll ever be, Mel. I don't know how I can make you see that."

"I'm an ugly cripple in a chair," she said.

"No," he said, and he grabbed the chair, whirling her around. He put his hands on her face, then kissed her again, hard. Just as quickly, he drew back, then put his face beside hers, holding her shoulders tightly against him. Again, that intoxicating smell of his cologne and skin, the warm feel of his body. His hands hurt her shoulders, but she didn't struggle.

"You've got to go, Mel. You've got a chance to help everyone. You can't throw it away."

"How can you touch me?" she asked, feeling as though her heart was tearing itself in shreds.

His breath was hot, his voice fierce. "God, it's not what's outside. Look at me. Handsome, right? I'll never be anything. I'm just another working man. I'll live, I'll die, just like everyone else. But you've got it inside," he said, putting his palm against her chest, pressing down, toward her heart.

"John," she said. "John."

"You go on that trip," he said. "Get on the ship. Your body's nothing. Leave it behind."

Tears streamed from Mel's eyes into the visor, pooling around its lower edge. John moved his body, knocking the voiceboard to the patio. Mel heard it clatter, then a blinding colored light shot through the visor. Her body stiffened.

She heard John cry out, realizing dimly that she was on the patio, and she knew what it was—a seizure. She hadn't had one for years. She had thought they were long past.

All she could see was white, not black. Mel's body was jerking, out of control, and something hurt in her mouth, then came a strong, hot taste of copper. She heard footsteps, then Hana, crying for the other nurses.

"My God, I've killed her," John said in a terrible, choked voice.

"No, no, damn it! You dumb kid, it's the implants," came a twangy, American voice. The ISA counselor was there. Mel arms and legs stopped jerking—the visor flickered in and out. She was off the patio. Somehow, they'd gotten her back in her room. Time passed strangely during seizures, she recalled. Her senses were not to be trusted.

Then, the white changed, became a field of stars. Mel felt suddenly warm and calm, completely in control. It was she, floating, toward a whole group of stars. Above her, a beautiful, pinkish nebula. Below her, blank space. How much more she wanted to go to the nebula than down into the blackness.

How beautiful it was. Complete, ordered, everything in its place. And exciting also, because a star before her, a bare pinpoint of light, was growing brighter and brighter until she thought she could kiss it. She sensed things, felt things she did not know names for; only feelings, instincts, pictures in her mind. It was approaching. Closer and closer until she could see it was a small red thing, nothing like the sun that she'd known as a child, though she'd never seen that from above, nor from such a distance.

Could John see it as well? No, he was not there; she was gone, and so was he. They were very far apart. How easily her body moved, how elegantly, powerfully and simply. She was aware, dimly, of how delicate this body was, but still, so infinitely perfect and beautiful. Like the small red star—the stranger—which she reached out to with her senses of spectral analysis, of direction, and asked it how long it had to live, and how long it had known life. It opened to her like a flower, like the beautiful flower of a hibiscus which her mother had kept outside their house. So red, so perfect, with a bit of a flare like the stamen of the hibiscus flower, and she reached with her senses…and kissed the star… It was exciting and intoxicating, magic and eternity; mystery and wonder and within it like a seed, the evidence she sought, that yes, it was alive, here there could be life.

Then, someone, a flesh-and-blood person, touched her. Fingers pressing into her, and the star-flower shrank into itself. The warm blackness of space became white.

Faces appeared before her, hovering. Hana, her expression serious. John, his hand pushing his hair out of his face, eyes wide and frightened. The cowboy ISA counselor. The two technicians, standing behind the others. Someone took her hand. A finger tapped her palm, once.

It was her decision, hers alone. And she knew what John had said was right. Her body really was nothing. And oh…she had kissed the star. She did not know whether the vision had come from inside of her, or it had been something cleverly planted, perhaps something to make her want to go. She realized that she did not care, because she wanted to go now, more than anything else, because this was life—a new kind of life. It had been heaven to kiss John; but to kiss a star?

With all her might, Mel squeezed the finger.

The counselor laughed. "She's game," he said. "She's going."

Mel knew that she couldn't trust her voice, and beneath the visor, they could not see her eyes.

"What? Is she going to be all right?" John looked wildly from face to face, searching for answers. How Mel wished she could say something. She shook her arm, rattling the bracelet. Still, John didn't seem to understand.

"She's going to Epsilon Eridani, son," the counselor said to John. "In about three weeks."

Mel squeezed the counselor's finger again.

"Uh-uh-mmm go-ing," she said, looking up at John's face, relishing the expression of joy as it spread over his face. The words came out so easily. It was like something which had been holding her back had broken away inside when she had flown the heavens. Now her tongue and lips moved as she wished.

John, beautiful John. If she could not be normal, then she could have this other thing. And John had been right—no one else could have it. Only Mel. She didn't need to believe in Jesus, only in what he would do. He would not stay.

"I know what Jesus would do," she said.

John touched her cheek, smiling as he wept, his eyes silently questioning her.

"He would kiss the star," she told him.

For Julie M. Jones

Harden

Gillian Polack

I wanted to discover when werewolves and vampires came to Harden. I thought it was simply a matter of asking around, but no-one seems to know. Really. No-one seems to know. I find this hard to believe. No Aboriginal Australians have ever claimed to be either werewolves or vampires. This means that both species of almost-human beings came recently. If they came recently, there must be records.

I want to find out.

I found out when the honey shop in Harden opened. I went to visit and to ask some questions, given how famous Harden is for the preternatural. (Do I mean famous? No, I mean the other word.)

Every single local I spoke to last week was happy to tell me when Harden became the local centre for buying thirty-two types of honey. I thought this was because the people of Harden are so proud of their honey shop. Why they're proud of their honey shop and not of the fact that they have the highest proportion of vampires per capita in the whole damn Southern Hemisphere and the only farm anywhere run entirely by werewolves is a mystery. Yet they are. They have told me about the honey shop more times than I can count and they've not told me about the supernatural at all.

Wikipedia doesn't help. It informs me that Harden is near Canberra and the Riverina. This was why I started to research. Anyone can find Harden on a map and anyone from Harden knows that the main source of food for Harden's vampires is in Canberra and in the Riverina.

The vamps go on foraging expeditions. I know about this bit because, me, I'm a Goulburn girl and we are targeted by vampires who are tired of hitting on Canberra. Targeted in all kinds of ways. Sexual harassment as well as the drinking of blood.

The young vamps think they're so cool, because of the movies. They totally don't get that we don't want them. It's a source of ongoing tension. The police have a special speed dial number just for us, and we all eat garlic. We'd carry crosses if they worked. The only thing the crosses work for these days is to entice a vampire into saying, "Oh, so you support Hillsong. I can help you with that."

No-one talks about it in Harden. If pressed they say, "Young people deserve a bit of fun. What's in Harden except honey?"

The Harden wolves (sounds like a sports team, doesn't it?) protect their local friends. At full moon everyone local hides indoors. I was told about that. No problems. "Don't visit around the full moon. If you do, stay in the B&B the whole time." Not the hotels or motels. The vamps hang out in hotels and use motels to hook up with prey when they're not a-voyaging.

Harden looks so safe. I've been through it a dozen times and it looks…nice.

What I've told you so far was not hard to find, even though Wikipedia babbled about Hume and Hovell exploring. Wikipedia tells me about Murrumburrah and its railway station and that there is a second station for Harden itself so that trains don't stop at Murrumburrah.

Trains stop at Murrumburrah twice a week. Sydney to the Riverina via Murrumburrah. One stops an hour after dusk and one stops an hour before sunrise, in each direction.

Vampires, I discovered, get punch drunk when they're on human blood. The town of Harden issues regular warnings, "Locals should consider leaving their cars at home when visiting other towns."

The werewolves play rugby and will travel for games, except around the full moon. They always drive. They never take the train. The town survives because both wolves and vamps respect each other and play out-of-town for the most part. The vampires play with people (not just drink blood, other things, sometimes not so bad at all and sometimes terrifying) and the werewolves play with balls. There's a joke in there, somewhere.

All that is easy to find. Even the local paper (to stop publishing in two months' time) tells me this much. They even talk about the vamp games, when a young human finds it titillating enough. Vamps don't kill many people, so it's safe enough to talk and sometimes they score special points from tourists willing to go a little further. The local press talks about this as if it's a good thing.

I want the history.

My mother was from Binalong (lives in Canberra now, where the specialist lives). She doesn't tell anyone she comes from Binalong because when she does, everyone wants to tell her what they know about Binalong. Not the wheat silos. No-one ever tells her about the wheat silos. Nor the notorious road trip by a carload of teen werewolves heading to the big smoke for a match. That carload of idiot teens led to five werewolf babies nine months later.

Everyone wants to tell her about Johnny Gilbert. One of Ben Hall's gang. No-one talks about how many people Johnny Gilbert killed (even though it's written on his gravestone); they tell the family that he was part of Ben Hall's gang and that he died. No werewolves enter the story. The werewolf children are never mentioned, either.

My mother was one of them. She was the lucky one. Werewolf genes are regressive and she was first in a line. Her mother was bitten, and my grandmother is still locked up once a month by a community that can emotionally handle a serial killer, but cannot deal with the proof that grandma was raped. Every month that proof manifests and every month Binalong looks aside in shame.

The other four women are dead, but Grandma, she's a fighter. Her best friend committed suicide, and her worst enemy died in jail when she was caught trying to kill her child. 'Mutant!' she screamed at the world and that's when my grandmother started calling Mum 'Mute.' She thought it was funny.

She also thought it was clever, and it was. That nickname saved Mum's life for years. Acknowledging the past and mocking it shuts people up who want to give you a hard time.

I found this out in Sydney, the day I discovered that my father was also from Harden. Like my grandfather…and yet, not. Dad came to Sydney one day and met Mum. Mum said "This will never work." It took Dad three years of visits to persuade her to give it a go. It works because Dad lives in Harden and travels to Sydney every weekend.

He gets his bit of blood in the train on the way. There's always a tourist willing to play with a vampire who sounds like Crocodile Dundee.

There's something a bit odd about Harden. About why the vampires are there.

Packs of werewolves litter the NSW landscape. Most people don't know about them, but they're there. They're polite and are farmers, mostly, because it means they have animals and freedom to eat without public criticism. They pass as human, mostly. What happened in Binalong awhile back was an aberration. Even Grandma admits it was a one-off.

Those of us who have the other ancestry (manifested like my brother, who moved to London because he hates the Harden vamps and wanted to be shut of the whole family, or unmanifested like me) can find our people. Not that they acknowledge most of us as their people. They won't eat us, but they won't talk to us, either.

Flirting with humans is fine. Drinking from humans is everyday. Accepting human children means that one (or many) young men see humans as something other than food, and that is wrong. That's why Dad never moved in with us. Childhoods always feel normal, and my normal included hyper-senses and a Dad who we only saw on weekends and who slept all day in a very dark room. We told everyone he and Mum were divorced, because that was the most likely reason for the situation, given that our friends had divorced parents.

We tell everyone we're human, but that our blood smells like garlic to certain supernatural beings. We aren't (human) and we don't (smell like garlic) and it struck me last year that I had no idea when my ancestors came to Australia.

I want the history of Harden. My father and grandfather both came from there, so I'm a Harden girl, even if Harden doesn't want me.

I can't go up to people when I visit and say, "Are you my cousin?" I can't go into the pubs at night because it's not safe after dark. So I need to find out what I want to know using other means. Old-fashioned research when people won't tell you things.

I especially want to know why so few of the Harden vamps' descendants manifest. My brother was so angry when he found that most of the rest of us can pass. I was angry with him. At night he will wake up hungry for blood while the most I get is a bit of a desire for undercooked steak.

Also, what happens when you are a combination of werewolf and vampire? What happens when I have children?

Finding out where the information is held became much easier when we all shut down because of COVID-19. I can't go there personally, but that means I can't be rebuffed, either. I am ringing the library in Harden and the regional archives and someone very bored (again, COVID-19) is looking up information. I haven't said a thing about werewolves or vampires. I ask about all the farms and purchases up to the current family. I asked about newspaper articles or family history pieces about arrival from Europe. I don't ask where in Europe someone came from because I met a Scottish vampire last year, when I was on holiday, and we talked a long time and I discovered from my talking that his great-whichever uncles and aunts were buried (in Scotland) with bricks in their mouths. That was over five hundred years ago. I also discovered that vampires find me attractive in an ordinary way. They don't want to drink my blood. That was nice.

Thanks to the pandemic, I'm making progress. I know that the werewolves bought the farm in the 1850s, but probably arrived during the Gold Rush. I discovered the first vampire came in the Gold Rush. The archivist is clever and sent me to the National Library. He couldn't give me the information himself, he said. I guess that means he's a vampire, or has family that way inclined.

The National Library has so much stuff I can't get to yet. One day. In the meanwhile, it has Trove. All the newspaper reports. All the obituaries from all the papers. That's why I'm pretty sure the vampires came during the Gold Rush.

I need to find out more. Dad can't give me much, but has gone asking for more. If I can find the family names on the vampire side, I can do more. If I can find the date they arrived, I can do much more. How they arrived is a big curious thing, for these days vamps take supplements so they can deal with at least some day time. They can do normal jobs, as long as they're not out in the sun all day long. Back then, there was no science to help. The stories of coming in coffins are gross. Dad's as curious as I am about how our ancestors took the long voyage here. How many vampires died en route? Why did they leave? All these answers Dad has promised me.

He's allowed to find out about his ancestors. He's not allowed to have us as descendants. That sucks.

Though All the Mountains Lie Between

Jeffrey A. Carver

…In those days before the founding of the Guild, riggers lived with constant insecurity. Shrewd masters controlled them—often with subtle means, but controlled them nevertheless; and riggers then rarely supported one another against abusive masters. But if they suffered in the normal world, they found freedom in the net, in the dream by which they steered their ships, which their masters could never hope to share. The lucky rigger found a way to carry that freedom out of the net, to the other side of life…

—Jona'Jon'
Gazing Into Yesteryear, for ages 7-11

The starship moved quietly through the Flux, though its motion was invisible from the bridge, where Jael stood facing Mogurn. Only instruments told her of the ship's motion; she would see it for herself, more clearly, when she entered the rigger-net. She waited anxiously.

Mogurn's eyes were dark and stern. With his hands folded across his heavy chest, he studied her with those eyes, kept her frozen. "All right, Jael," he said, releasing her from his gaze at last. He glanced one final time over the thicket of instrumentation in the nose of the bridge, and then he indicated the rigger-station with a tilt of his head. "Go ahead and take the net," he said. "Don't tire yourself." With that he turned away, his robelike tunic spinning in folds, and he strode from the bridge. The door darkened to opacity behind him, leaving Jael alone in the ship's small control cell.

He doesn't trust me, she thought nervously, staring after Mogurn. Well, I don't care. She turned and made another brief inspection of the console, even though Mogurn had already done that with her, and then she climbed into the rigger-station, a couch recessed in a tight alcove on the starboard side of the bridge. She stretched out and relaxed gradually, staring at several mirrored monitors overhead as she tried to forget about Mogurn and think instead of the ship, of the Flux. She shut her eyes and let her neck settle against the neural contacts in the couch.

Her senses darkened and exploded outward into the rigger-net, outward from the ship, into the Flux. Into the streams of space. Jael opened her eyes to a vast and clear purplish sky; she floated like a seed high over a strangely glowing blue- and green-mottled land-scape. The net glittered faintly around her, binding her to the invisible ghost of a spaceship which it was her duty to guide. She spread her arms, and in the net her arms billowed outward as great wings, filling with a rising updraft of wind. Jael (and the ship) rose, soaring.

The landscape beneath her was an odd matrix of color, reflecting her mood. It was her own image, painted by her mind on the flowing canvas of the Flux, on the currents which carried her and her ship through the curved passageways of space among the stars, bypassing the endless light-years of normal space. The currents and tides of the Flux were objectively real, but it was her imagination, her thoughts and fantasies transmuted through the rigger-net, that detailed the realm through which she navigated.

Her feelings were quiet, now, and she flew silently through empty skies, daydreaming. She felt mildly depressed, neither happy nor actively unhappy, and she flew slowly, not even attempting to seek out faster wind currents. Hours went by, and she was content to float, to drift. Occasionally the landscape below shimmered and flared in response to tremors within her, aches which she kept unnamed. Certain longings she preferred not to allow expression; but whether she willed it or not, the landscape flared—now more and now less, sometimes with unfocused green fire and sapphire sparkles and sometimes with tiny billowing bloody plumes. The ache was always there within her and the landscape always responded to it.

She wished she could change the image somehow, drift away and leave the ache behind.

The com-signal chimed softly in her consciousness, and Mogurn's voice broke into her solitude. *Jael, what's wrong? The feedback out here looks poor.*

The landscape turned to brimstone and filled the sky with burning haze. She tried to control it, to cover her anger. *Nothing's wrong,* she answered. *Everything's fine.*

Are you sure? Mogurn's voice was low, disapproving. She envisioned him on the bridge, squinting anxiously, leering at her still form in the rigger-station. His voice was bodiless in the net, but physically he must be very near. She countered an urge to avoid him by retreating to the extremities of the net.

I'm fine, she said. The image was disintegrating, creating a potentially dangerous condition. She drew more energy into the net, trying to stabilize the image.

I'm depending on you, said Mogurn.

Jael didn't bother to answer. She thought hard a moment, searching her imagination, and then she focused on the angry horizon. The colors bled, and crimson sunset swelled over mountains to the northwest. Mountains...

The route through those mountains was actually the most direct to their destination, Lexis; but it was more dangerous, by all reports, than the skirting route Mogurn had ordered. Still, he had not absolutely forbidden her to fly in the mountains, and after all she was the rigger—he chose the images and the streams of the Flux to ride. Ultimately the choice was hers. The net sparkled as she grew excited —at the thought of danger, at the prospect of quickening the flight. She knew she shouldn't.

Abruptly she transformed herself into a mountain eagle, and she caught a new current and soared northwest, pulse racing, net glittering like diamonds in the Flux.

Sunset ahead. Twilight. Mountains jagged and black against a maroon sky, deepening into evening.

She scanned ahead with the edges of her mind. Would there be dragons? Riggers in the starports boasted of dueling with dragons along the Aeregian mountain routes. It seemed that there was a special quality of the Flux in this corridor which demanded mountain imagery and, sometimes, dragons. Many riggers believed the dragons to be living inhabitants of the Flux; others said they were just especially compelling images. Either way, it sounded dangerous; it sounded glorious.

A sense of quiet anticipation settled around her as she winged toward the mountains. She rather hoped that dragons might appear, to ease her loneliness.

The com-signal chimed again, chilling her pleasure. What now?

Isn't it time you came out? asked a bodiless Mogurn.

Is it? she replied, shivering in a sudden crosswind.

Six hours, Jael.

Six hours? she repeated, stalling.

What's wrong, Jael?

It may not be safe right now.

Not safe? Why not?

She spread her wings to catch a warm updraft. *Because*—and she hesitated, then said—*there may be dragons.*

His eyes squinted furiously, in her imagination. *Dragons? Dragons? The mountain route?*

Jael beat her wings furiously. *Yes.*

Find a stretch of safe passage. And then you come out and see me, Jael. His voice touched her like ice, and she stopped pumping. His anger made her tremble.

Yes, Mogurn, she answered, and the world grew cold with fear and loneliness. She did not want to face him, but she had no choice. Not if she wanted to receive the pallisp tonight.

Banking left, she flew parallel to the still-distant range, where she thought she could safely leave the net. But she stalled, gliding, watching the ominous peaks to her right, wishing that the fear and the loneliness would somehow subside, Finally she reluctantly set the stabilizers, the starship's sea-anchor in the Flux; and she set the alarms. Her senses melted back into her body as she withdrew from the net, and she opened her eyes, blinking, and looked around the rigger-cell and the bridge. Gloomy. Lonely. Nothing but instruments to greet her. She preferred it that way.

She climbed uneasily from the pilot-station and stretched. Her stomach said hunger, and her limbs said weariness. But Mogurn had said come immediately. Sighing, she left the bridge and went to Mogurn's cabin door; the ship Was only a small floater, and the compartments were tightly clustered, so it was a matter of a few steps. She pressed the signal fearfully. The door paled and she stepped inside.

Mogurn Was seated facing her, smoking. When she entered, he

rose and gestured for her to sit. She slid onto a narrow bench-seat; above and behind her an expensive crystal tapestry covered half of one wall. Mogurn exhaled sharp-scented smoke and frowned, studying the end of his long, tubular smoking pipe. "Jael, why did you disobey me?" he said.

Jael shivered, certain now that he would deny her the pallisp. "I meant no disobedience," she stammered, which was at least half true. He'd not forbidden her to rig through the mountains; he had only made it clear that he disapproved of that route, that in fact perhaps he was afraid of the mountains, or of the dragons.

Mogurn stepped closer, hovering over her, alternately blocking and exposing the light panel behind him. Jael squinted nervously. "Did I not say that I preferred the longer route, Jael? Was there some special circumstance you haven't told me of, some need to take the more perilous course?"

Was that fear in his voice? No; he was the master. Jael bit her lip. "I—was having trouble—the other way. But this way—I think the stories are just stories. Dragons! They can't be real."

"What is 'real' to a rigger?" Mogurn asked sharply. "What is in the Flux, or what is in the mind? Either can destroy us."

Jael nodded mutely.

"And, drunken sods though most of those riggers may be, one should never laugh at a rigger legend, should one?'

Jael winced. "No."

"Now, are we still close enough to our original course to turn back?" He exhaled another cloud of smoke, which drifted past her face to be sucked into the ventilators. She opened her mouth to reply in the affirmative, but something stuck in her throat. She shook her head. "We can't avoid the mountains?" he growled, and she shook her head again. Mogurn stared at her, smoking. After a long moment, he turned away.

When he turned back, he held a small, gleaming cylinder with a dull gray sphere attached to one end. "All right, Jael. It is time for your pallisp," he said. His eyes showed no kindness, but his words nevertheless sent a thrill of relief down Jael's back. Unhappiness and loneliness welled up out of her soul in anticipation.

At Mogurn's gesture, she bent forward and pushed her hair up from the back of her neck. Mogurn stood close beside her and lowered the pallisp until the gray ball touched the base of her skull. She felt the touch, cool—and then a warmth seeped into her from the touch, a warmth which encircled the ugly, waiting feelings of alienation, of fear, of anger, and which closed around those feelings like flowing blood, heating and soothing and transforming the emotions, stripping and softening shells of defense and filling her with love, with companionship...

The wave turned cold. Jael swayed with dizziness as a tide of paranoia rushed over her. The pallisp was gone. She sat up, blinking wildly, struggling to hold back tears. As Mogurn spoke, she could hardly see him through blurred eyes. "That's all for tonight, Jael. You must understand what obedience means, even for a rigger." Jael trembled, desperate with pain and frustration. Finally she steadied herself. Mogurn said, nodding, "Now, Jael, help me with my augmentor—and then you may retire."

Though dying to scream, she obeyed. Mogurn reclined and she fitted the synaptic augmentor to his head and adjusted the controls; and when Mogurn was reduced to a silent figure fluttering his hands or pawing himself with a blind-eyed grin, Jael backed away and fled to her cabin. The pallisp—lord how she wanted it, needed it to take the lonely bitterness from her soul and turn it into something warm, and she would almost kill for it, but only Mogurn knew how to use it and so she needed Mogurn, too. She stalked the tiny deck space of her cabin, brooding, and then she tossed and writhed violently in the sleep-field, unable to rest. Unable to stop thinking.

Unable to stop remembering.

Remembering... Dap, and the night and the dreamlink. Dap had been gentle and yet willful, telling her of the intimacies to be shared by riggers with the help of the dreamlink machine. And she had been young then—she was young now—and she had been seduced by his earnestness, his offer of friendship. Even now she could see his eyes, dark and earnest under silver brows, as he told her, "We'll be looking right into one another, and our souls will link..."

...They drove in a groundcar from the rigger hall to a cottage retreat where the dreamlink machine was located. They glided over the roadway in a gorgeous pink sunset. Jael steeled herself as they stopped, as they walked up to the retreat—a real house, not a multiplex—but Dap touched her arm, smiling. The gesture lent her enough strength to overcome her doubt and her suspicion; and she entered the house with Dap, moving about touching walls and banisters with nervous curiosity. In a small back living room, the dreamlink machine, a specialized type of synaptic augmentor, was set up—a half-silvered hemisphere which projected a golden glow when Dap turned it on. "We'll just let the field coalesce for a few minutes," he said. "Sit down and relax." He gestured to paired-off seats just at the fringes of the golden field.

"What's going to happen? How will I know?" Jael asked nervously, thinking to herself, he's your cousin good old Dap and why are you worried, he knows what he's doing. Dap smiled at her question and leaned forward to touch her hand gently. His eyes twinkled, and she thought he was amused by her naïveté, and perhaps being just a bit flirtatious.

"You'll know," he said. "It's gentle." He settled into his seat, looking relaxed but eager, and Jael realized she was worrying about nothing, after all. Nothing.

They talked idly, this and that about riggers and family, and Jael nearly forgot about the intensifying golden field in the room. Dap laughed, his eyes seeking hers, as he talked about his last flight—a three-system hop, fast and exciting, played in the net as skipping-stone islands in a tropic sea. It was a teamwork freighter flight with another rigger, and he hinted at the intimacy which underlay the teamwork. "It was the best part of the trip," he said, his eyes still seeking hers, holding her eyes a little longer than she wished them held. "My crewmate's gone out again," he added. "She left just the other day on a long haul. I miss her already. But I wouldn't give up that experience for anything."

Something in Jael choked silently, but she tried to contain it, to not betray her envy. There was a warmth around her, though, a suffused glow that somehow made it seem less important to hide her feelings. There was a gentle feeling of release in her thoughts, and suddenly as she looked at Dap, she no longer heard his words alone, but saw visions directly from his mind, across the widening dreamlink. She saw the woman he'd rigged with, the flights of fancy across space, the sly querying Interest he felt now toward her.

Feelings stirred in her heart which she couldn't control, and before she was aware of what was happening, thoughts and images rushed up out of her mind like a fountain, and spilled glittering into space, into the dreamlink: glimpses of her half-brother steeling himself against their uncaring father, unable even to reach to his sister. Jael herself at her father's closed door, suffering and wanting and needing. Rigging an occasional flight alone, too lonely to dare to seek companions. The images rushed out, and so too did her anguish. Before she could stop herself, she'd released it all, glimpses of herself that she'd never meant to let any person see.

In the dizzying energy of the dreamlink, the openness suddenly wrenched, tore—as Dap betrayed his dismay, that someone could release such staggering need. Betrayed his revulsion. Dap, who had promised understanding. Without a word Dap closed himself from the dreamlink, faded in the glow that now was a suffocating shield around a Jael who fumed with self-loathing and hurt. Dap no longer would look at her, and as she cried mutely in pain, he rose and left without her, left her there alone and desperate in the dreamlink field.

She made herself her own last audience: she let her pain dance in the field like threads of fire, tightening around her like a noose, choking her, and no one here to help—there never was, neither Dap nor her father—they forgot their promises and closed the door, one just like the other. She wanted to kill them both, and she was going to kill herself with this hate if she didn't do something to—

—control it—

—bottle it—

—which she did, wrapping it tightly around her finger and corking it back inside. And then when she was safe, while she was still sane, she turned off the dreamlink augmentor. And she returned to the hall where the riggers mobbed and brooded, looking for assignments. And a few days later she found Mogurn—

—who offered her a job. And the pallisp.

She started out of a brooding daze. Sleep was impossible. But insomnia was better than the cruelty of dreams. She thought constantly of the pallisp, which alone could soothe her anxieties and fears. A sophisticated electrostim, the pallisp was illegal except in the hands of a psych-med; it was terrifying addictive, just as Mogurn's synaptic augmentor was addictive. But the pallisp was Jael's only release. Except for the net.

She could go to the net now, she realized. There she could let her feelings go—shape them and play them out in images. It was perilous to let dark feelings loose in the net, but was it any better to keep them corked until they exploded? Mogurn would be furious if she went to the net now, while he was under his bliss-wire. But if she didn't do something, she would go crazy.

Leaving her cabin, she crept to the bridge. She climbed into the rigger-cell. The neural contacts touched her neck and head.

Her senses, electrified, sprang into the net. Into the Flux. The ship floated as a balloon-borne gondola in a nighttime sky, riding downrange winds. Jael let the breeze soothe her, and then she changed altitude, seeking higher crosswinds to take her to the mountains. The gondola swayed as she found the airstream she wanted. She set her sights upon the approaching range. A full, creamy moon sank slowly toward jagged black peaks, which looked like sullen teeth against the horizon. Backlighted by the moon, a blunt-nosed mass of clouds was moving out of the mountains toward her. Spooky. She liked it: darkness and gloom and eerily lighted clouds which looked like moving glaciers, or like bold angry pincers reaching out to shred the balloon...

The bag abruptly disintegrated. She caught at the air with her hands. For a moment she tumbled earthward, flailing, and then she controlled her panic and remade the image. The ghostly net shimmered and became a varnished glider, whispering downward through the air with her perched astraddle the fuselage. She leveled out, thinking: Take care! A rigger had to be careful of her images; dangerous thoughts could become real and could smash the ship into splinters, to drift forever in the currents of this strange reality, the Flux.

She let the wind soothe her face, let her feelings swirl ahead of her in the sky, in the emptiness between her and the clouds. They could hurt no one there. Time passed and she drew closer to the range.

The dragons stormed out of the clouds in random formation, like gulls out of a rain squall.

Jael stared into the moonlit night in astonishment. Dragons! Dreadful winged shapes, still distant, wheeled before the clouds. Sparks of red flame flickered. She could scarcely believe it; dragons weren't real—they were something from primal dreams, from legend, from racial fears and magical desires. But they were here in the sky right now, and she hadn't summoned them from her imagination—at least, she didn't think she had. Could they be real? Creatures which lived here in the Flux? Coolly nervous, she controlled the glider tightly.

The dragons grew in the moonlight. They soared and circled far off her wingtips. Three dragons broke from the others and spiraled in closer. She caught sharp glimpses of them as they swooped past her. One flew so close that its scales looked like polished pewter in the moonlight, throwing light back in subtly altered form, gray but not gray, as though banked fires lay beneath the surface of the scales. The dragon's head was rough carved and tipped with flaring, glowing nostrils, and its wings were serrated and broad, not narrow as Jael had pictured dragons' wings to be. Its eyes glinted. Another swept across her path, and then for a moment she lost sight, until she saw the three orbiting at a distance, as though she and her glider were hovering still in the air.

She held her course. What did one do when met by dragons? The old riggers talked in the bars of dueling—but what did that mean? These dragons looked capable of ruthless battle. Jael knew nothing of dueling and did not want to know. She wished she had come another way.

Are you afraid? she heard.

She looked around, frightened, thinking that Mogurn had awakened and was taunting her in the net as punishment. But the voice was not Mogurn's voice.

You are afraid, said the voice. *Shall we kill you now, as a kindness?*

With a start she realized that a dragon was speaking. She peered into the night and spotted a dragon alongside her whose eyes gleamed, betraying him in the night. The dragon edged closer. *What do you want?* she said hotly, fearfully.

The dragon's eyes flickered as it passed. The other two dragons retreated to join the rest, and the one remaining banked close by her, its eyes glowing brightly green. Turbulence buffeted Jael, and she fought to control the glider. *What are you doing?* she cried. *What do you want?*

Does that mean "No"? inquired the dragon, exhaling a cloud of sparks. It circled her. *You prefer to die in battle?*

What do you mean? Jael asked indignantly. *Who are you, anyway? What do you want—and how dare you speak to me that way?* She hunched low, pulled the net in around the edges.

Child! said the dragon. *One question at a time! You want to know who I am, and then—*

You haven't answered that yet!

Nor shall I. But you should not have given me so many questions not to answer. Do you think it's easy? Do you think you're the only rigger to come crashing through here looking for a fight?

Then it's true! You dragons are real!

The dragon sighed or snarled. *I never meant to tell you that! Duel, rigger!* It flipped in mid-air and bore down upon her, sparkling in the moonlight. It grew larger, larger...

Jael screamed. The glider shuddered. The dragon thundered and raked her with fire as it passed. *What are you doing?* she shrieked. Her skin sizzled, and flames crackled along the wings of her glider. Quickly she changed the image to a fireproof alloy glider. A flurry of snow cooled her skin and quenched the flood of energy in the net.

The dragon approached again, flapping its wings slowly. It eyed her suspiciously. *Your reactions were slow,* it said and moved off.

Jael looked after the dragon in astonishment. Suddenly it turned and streaked toward her in another attack.

Jael froze. She tried to make herself small. The dragon grew with terrifying speed. *Stop it!* she screamed.

Peeling off in surprise, the dragon circled warily. In the moonlit clouds, the other dragons looked like small dots, wheeling and cavorting. *All right,* said the dragon testily. *If you didn't want to duel, why did you come here?*

Jael was dizzy with confusion, fear, and anxiety. *I didn't expect you to try and kill me!*

What did you expect?

I don't know.

The dragon sighed impatiently and leveled off. He spoke in what seemed a mockingly measured and conciliatory tone. *Well, all right, then. Do you want to talk instead? I can see you're distressed, irritable—and who can blame you? I feel the same way myself sometimes. You want to just fly along and maybe chat lightheartedly? I promise not to try to kill you.*

Jael eyed him suspiciously. *Can we?*

Sure. The dragon tipped his head and winked. Jael nodded, but she felt uneasy. She decided to change her image; she became a winged pony and beat against the wind. *Very nice,* said the dragon, falling in beside her.

She did not answer. The night was changing, the clouds closing in. A moonbeam broke through the clouds to show mist swirling about a black and jagged mountain slope. *Do you know where we're going?* asked Jael.

Yes, said the dragon craftily—and suddenly it sideslipped and seized her in its talons. Jael's breath went out with a gasp. The dragon lowered its head, jaws gaping, as though intending to rend her with its teeth. Its hot breath washed back over her. Jael squirmed, twisted, and managed to roll forward just enough to kick with her hind legs. Her hooves caught the dragon squarely in the stomach and it wheezed, releasing her. Jael tumbled, beating frantically with her wings but losing altitude, headfirst, through the clouds. She glimpsed horrible sawtoothed slopes rushing to meet her. Frantic, she transformed herself to a hawk, warped her wings sharply, and pulled herself out of the dive. She spiraled back upward, squinting to evade the dragon.

Well done, the dragon said grudgingly, right behind her.

In a panic she looped up fast and came down behind it. She dogged its tail angrily, and warily. *Liar!* she shouted. *You promised and you lied! Is that a dragon's kind of honor?*

Of course.

What? she screamed. *Do you all lie?*

What the dragon did next she could hardly believe. One moment it was in front of her, and the next it was above her, and then behind, and it curled its wing around her like a net and scooped her earthward. She trembled and fluttered, a frightened bird, as they plummeted. The dragon lurched to a landing on a black outcropping of rock. It craned its neck to sniff her with smoldering nostrils and peer at her with green eyes. She puffed up her feathers and stared back. *You lied, and now you're going to kill me!* she squeaked.

The dragon seemed puzzled. *Of course I lied. Didn't they tell you before they sent you to duel?*

No one sent me! Jael cried. *I just came.* She choked in the dragon's breath. *Would you mind letting me have some air?*

Hissing, the dragon opened its wing. *I think you'd better show yourself as you really are,* the creature warned.

The world was wreathed in fog, but the night air revived Jael somewhat. *All right,* she muttered. Concentrating, she transformed herself back to Jael, a human girl, in the nexus of a ghostly neural-sensory net. Haloing the net was a shimmering ethereal spaceship.

Impressive, acknowledged the dragon. *I just wanted to see you, though, not your spaceship.*

She made the spaceship disappear. She stood lonely and frightened and cold before the dragon. *My name is Jael,* she said.

The dragon reared its head back and shrieked in dismay. Its cry reverberated through the mountains. *I did not ask your name!* it wailed. *Why have you given me your name?* It blew a great gout of fire into the night and screeched and scratched at the rock in distress.

What's the matter? Jael cried, covering her ears.

Finally the dragon quieted, rumbling and fuming unhappily. *Now I am obligated to give you my own name, and then I shall no longer be able to lie to you—or to duel!*

Jael scowled. *Never mind. I don't want to know your name.*

The dragon settled down glumly. *It is Windrush-Wingtouch-Highwing—Terror-of-the-Last-Peak.*

I don't want to know!

I suppose you may call me Highwing. I am the Sire of the four fastest—

You are a braggart, said Jael coldly. The dragon whuffled into silence. It shifted position awkwardly; the crag was crowded with the two of them. *I only want to be on with my flight,* Jael said. *You aren't helping me much.*

You didn't come here to duel with us? the dragon asked, in a wounded tone. Jael wondered if she really had hurt his feelings. Highwing watched her thoughtfully. *You are upset about something,* he observed. *And not just about me. Do you want to talk about it?*

No.

I have given you my name. You can trust me.

You? After you lied and tried to kill me?

That was when we were dueling. Before you knew my name. It was expected.

Not by me.

Uncomfortable silence followed. Highwing cleared his throat steamily. Some of the clouds broke and stars appeared over the mountains. Jael stared at them longingly.

Another voice broke the silence. *What's going on?*

Highwing peered around in confusion.

I'm flying, Mogurn, answered Jael.

Come out of the net at once, ordered Mogurn's bodiless, furious voice.

I can't. There are dragons. Jael glanced at Highwing. Please don't argue, she thought. It's both of our lives.

I'm disappointed in you. You get yourself out of trouble, and then you come and see me. Mogurn broke the link.

Highwing's dragon eyes glowed over his snout. *I see,* he said. *You must answer to someone on your spaceship. But you don't like it. Am I right?* His gaze bore into Jael. *Little Jael,* he said, *perhaps you had better come with me for a while. Perhaps I can help.*

She glared at him, startled by the suggestion. *Why? Never!*

I am your servant now, Jael, because we have exchanged our names, and you really must come with me. It is our duty to help each other if we can. The dragon sounded utterly earnest.

Why should I trust you? she shouted, stamping.

I am all you have at the moment, answered the dragon mildly.

Irrationally, Jael felt her anger subsiding. Some part of her wanted to go with this dragon—even though he'd tried to kill her. She squinted at him—at his huge unblinking eyes, at his great knobbed and finely scaled head. Certainly he had nothing to fear, and no need of tricking her. *I suppose,* she said cautiously, *you're going to promise not to hurt me. And I should believe that.*

No one can promise not to hurt, little one, said Highwing.

Jael was startled. The answer seemed honest. And at the moment, what choice did she have? *Not that I believe you,* she said, *but what did you have in mind?*

Climb onto my back. The dragon crouched low, and after a long hesitation Jael climbed up and perched astraddle his back, just in front of his wings. She held onto his neck. *Hold tight,* he said, and unlimbered his wings and sprang into the night air.

Jael clung, dizzy with confused emotions, with relief and fear. The wind whispered at her, and the movements of the dragon's powerful musculature soothed her. Instinctively she stroked his silken-hard scales. *I like to be scratched behind the ears,* the dragon remarked as he flew.

Abruptly she stopped. *Too bad,* she said coldly.

Highwing chuckled and banked so that she could see the landscape below. They were flying very low. Mountain landscape rushed by, jutting rock and dark ravines. He banked the other way, descending. She clung breathlessly. A valley spread open in the night. *Where are we going?* she shouted. The dragon belched a flame in answer.

They slowed and passed through a veil of mist. She felt a curious shifting, or twisting, of her time sense. Stars seemed to sparkle inside the veil, and she glimpsed dark stone walls sliding by. The veil shimmered and vanished, and in clear night air they glided into a fairyland valley. Highwing followed a trail of glittering dust strewn in mid-air, and below them, soft lights swung in the boughs of trees. Gossamer strands crisscrossed overhead, forming a continuing arch under which the dragon flew, barely fluttering his wings. *How do you like it?* he asked proudly.

Jael stared about in puzzled fascination. To the left, a waterfall spilled into a starlit pool, where several odd-looking creatures watered. *It's pretty,* she said, *but what are we doing here?*

Highwing craned his neck to look back at her. *Little one,* he said. *I wish I could remember your name. What was it?*

Jael, she said stiffly. Then she saw the twinkle in his eye. She flushed at the teasing, feeling—what? —anger? Perhaps—but despite herself she felt a trickle of warmth.

Little Jael, the dragon said.

Quit calling me "little"! Now that did make her mad.

Dear me, said the dragon. *Don't you know? I call you that as a measure of our friendship, little Jael.*

We have no friendship.

You say that now, large Jael. But we have come for you to see otherwise.

Jael hiked herself up to look the dragon squarely in the eye. *Hah!* she said. And then her gaze locked with the dragon's, and she seemed to fall into the depths of those glowing eyes, down a twisting spiraling pathway to the edge of another consciousness: a mind watching hers, almost as in the dreamlink field. But the consciousness she touched here seemed far deeper than any she'd encountered before, and she sensed that it was kinder, and that it observed her with interest but without malice or displeasure at what it saw. Catching reflected images of herself, she realized suddenly that the other saw beneath her surface, deep within her thoughts. She shivered, and her shiver resonated down the pathway and reflected back in a sympathetic chord. Astonished, she pulled free of the link, of the dragon's gaze, and she sat back blinking.

The dragon counted itself her friend and companion. He truly did.

But that was impossible.

What was she to do, then? She closed her eyes and thought. She stretched her senses back through the rigger-net; she felt the ship, the flux-pile energizing the net, holding her here in the reality of the Flux. Should she pull clear now, face Mogurn and explain her folly, suffer his wrath in hopes of forgiveness, in hopes of the pallisp, the dear pallisp? And then return, to modify the image if she could? But...Mogurn was very angry. He would never give her the pallisp now.

She could stay. Highwing had said he would bring her through, that he would help her.

She opened her eyes and said, *Well?* The dragon's nostrils smoked inquiringly. *This doesn't mean anything—but shouldn't we be moving on?*

The dragon turned to face forward again. *As you say, diminutive one.* Jael glowered, but before she could speak, Highwing added, *Look!*

The scenery ahead was different, starker and yet more magical— faceted angular rock faces, gleaming faintly, towering high, and here and there among the faces dim alcoves and caves. Jael felt a strange premonition. In those caves lurked dragon magic. She clung to Highwing in wondering apprehension. As the dragon wheeled slowly, picking his way through a maze of vaguely gleaming passageways, Jael again felt that curious twisting of time, as though each turn moved her backward or forward through years, or stretched seconds to infinity. Soon she felt quite disoriented.

Presently the dragon came to a landing before the entrance to a small cave. *Well,* he said.

Well, what? Jael rose up and peered in. The cave interior was gloomy, lighted by a single moonbeam piercing the ceiling. An enormous spiderweb spanned the back of the cave, shimmering in the moonbeam. The web seemed almost alive. There was a sparkling of light across its strands, and then a vertical rippling of cold fire. Jael watched, puzzled. The web danced with ghostly quicksilver, and suddenly stilled, and Jael found herself looking through a living window.

At Mogurn.

It was Mogurn at the spaceport, not on the ship. The background slowly fell into focus: the rigger dispatcher room in port. This was Mogurn the businessman; Mogurn the merchant, the thief. Mogurn the trader in illegal and immoral goods. He was talking with someone —a spaceport crew steward. Hanging onto Highwing's neck, Jael strained forward to pick up words from the window, but she could hear nothing. Both men smiled meanly at something Mogurn said, and the steward turned and pointed. A female rigger stood in profile, beyond them.

Jael trembled, recognizing herself half a year ago. She looked meek, frightened, lonely. Mogurn leaned toward the steward, grinning, and withdrew from his hip pouch—just far enough for the steward to see—the probe of the pallisp. The steward nodded, winking. They touched hands in farewell, and something twinkled between their fingers as they did so. Then Mogurn strode toward the rigger, Jael, standing bewildered in the lobby. And Jael, her stomach knotting, watched the younger Jael turn, startled at a sudden sensation of warmth, of companionship. Watched herself meet Mogurn, watched herself accept work—and watched herself surrender to the pallisp.

Jael's stomach fought back as for the first time she really saw the uncaring anticipation on Mogurn's face as he enslaved her with the pallisp. And for the first time she admitted to the rush of hatred that shook her when she thought of the man. Humiliation and anger rushed up in a torrent.

The dragon stirred as she wrestled with her emotions, trying to corral them, and she heard him say, *Shall I burn him for you, Jael?*

Yes! she cried, blinking tears, not even knowing what she was saying. *Yes! Burn him!*

Highwing lifted his head and breathed fire. His breath was a blowtorch, a leaping flame that engulfed the cave. The ghostly Jael vanished, and the ghostly Mogurn whirled in surprise—and screamed once before he died in the incinerating fury of the dragon's fire. Jael gagged at the dying sound of the scream, at the sight of the man dying in hellfire at her command. But when it was over, and the smoke cleared from the gutted cave which had held the image of the man she hated, she felt a sudden release, a bubbling up of joy and freedom, a rushing of cleansed emotions. And almost immediately, a backwash of weariness.

She scarcely noticed as the dragon carried her away from that place. Her thoughts were blurred, confused. Time strained and slipped by.

Gradually she regained both her strength and her wits as he dragon flew through the stark-walled and misty vale. *You took that from my own mind, didn't you?* she asked softly, stroking his scales to regain the feel.

What? he answered idly. He banked to the right and turned into a bowl-shaped dell and landed abruptly. Jael stared, frowning. The dell was a small, wooded place, in fading twilight. As darkness filled in, hundreds of gnatlike fireflies appeared, darting and corkscrewing through the glade like so many fiery atoms. Hundreds more joined them, and more still, until a cloud of whirling sparks filled a space beneath several of the largest trees. Jael was about to speak, to say *Stop—no more,* when the whirling sparks coalesced and from their midst emerged a man. Dap.

Jael's breath stopped. Dap looked as always, handsome and gentle, but—and this astonished Jael, who'd witnessed this scene before, but had never noticed—he was also frightened, anxious, putting forth a brave expression which hardly disguised his terrible insecurity. The sunglow of the dreamlink field came over him (and over an invisible Jael) and as the augmentor worked its magic on him, his discomfort became yet more evident. Images of Jael's memories danced about him like tiny sunbursts: her father opaquing doors as he retired with his women and boys, some not much older than Jael; her brother (before the groundcar accident that took his life, as he ran from his insane mother) wincing with the pain he never allowed out, though it tore him apart; her father ignoring, shutting out their pain, teaching them how to make walls but never windows.

All this Dap caught, in the swirl of memories among the fantasies, desperately lonely fantasies, rigger fantasies which Jael let free in the dreamlink. "Is all this true?" he asked, frightened at the enormity of her pain. And Jael remembered her answer well. "Only fantasies," she had lied, even as she tried to sweep them away, to hide them. As Jael watched Dap draw back from the unseen Jael here, she recalled the agony she'd felt, the abandonment. But the expression on Dap's face was fear, shame for his own needs and wants in the face of his helpless inadequacy. As she tried to cover, so did he. As she was frightened, so was he.

As he turned now to flee, Jael heard Highwing's voice, softly: *Shall I?* The dragon drew a deep breath.

No! she cried, startled. *Don't hurt him—don't burn him! I didn't know— I never realized!* Dap had fled out of fear, out of hurt. Perhaps even cowardice—but not hatred.

Highwing sighed, and the image and the cloud of sparks dissipated. *Did you remember it that way?* the dragon asked, rumbling.

No, said Jael. *No, I—*and she fell mute, remembering the abandonment she'd felt, thinking that Dap hated her, and remembering how she'd vowed never to let anyone touch her that way again.

Well, then, Jael—look up.

Reluctantly she lifted her gaze. For a moment she couldn't see what Highwing wanted her to look at, and then—in a sheltered aerie high above the glade—she saw a man.

Who is that? she asked, though a suspicion grew in the pit of her stomach.

Don't you know? Without waiting for an answer, the dragon sprang aloft and carried her to a perch near the aerie, where she could look across and see for herself. it was her father. He was a cold-eyed, stiff-limbed man, exactly as she remembered him. He gazed outward, apparently expecting a caller, but the angle of his stance suggested retreat, as though he refused to leave the shelter of the aerie. His eyes stared, his mouth curled with distaste, as when he'd wondered aloud why he'd saddled himself with two former wives, a son, and a daughter.

Kill him, Jael said softly, anger and loathing rising out of her heart. *Burn him.* The dragon did not immediately obey, and for a moment her anger flew at Highwing. *I hate him, I say—burn him!* And then she knew why the dragon hesitated. Not because he disapproved—but because her father was already two years dead, at the hands of a jealous lover. What point to burn him now? She cursed futilely, squinting at this man who was so hopelessly cold, so desperately alone, who had turned two wives against him and taught a son and a daughter how not to feel. *All right, Highwing—never mind. Maybe he suffered enough. I doubt it, but maybe he did. Now let's get out of here.*

The man vanished into the aerie as Highwing turned. He leaped, and they were airborne. *Little one—*

Let's get out of this place, dragon! Jael answered darkly, her mood blighted by anger. The dragon vented smoke from his nostrils in sympathy. That angered her further, and she struck his hardened scales with her fists. *Take me out of this accursed valley and let me finish my journey in peace.*

The dragon circled higher. He was silent for a time before speaking. *As you will, Jael. But when I take you out of these mountains, we will be near the place where I must leave you—and you will be near your destination. There I shall have to say good-bye to you.*

Too many images burned brightly in Jael's mind for her to respond to the dragon's sadness. As if she were concerned anyway. It was the damned dragon who had brought her here, pushed her nose in those memories, made them hurt—although, true, he had burned Mogurn to a crisp for her, in image if not reality.

Jael clung silently to the dragon as he beat his wings to gain altitude, as the lights of the valley fell away behind them. Images flashed brightly through her mind: her brother desperately gathering his dignity, unable to share his hurt even with his sister; Dap and the other riggers struggling with their own loneliness and fear; a rigger named Mariel who once treated her kindly; Mogurn in oblivion with the synaptic augmentor. She shook as feelings replayed in her mind faster than she could react to them, as memories of anger and pain and loneliness and frustration and hatred spawned a cyclone in her soul. Memories of a father who had loved no one, least of all himself. She scarcely saw the mountain peaks passing, dark and grim in the night, or clouds which muffled them and opened again, or the stars which gleamed like diamonds and then stretched peculiarly into lines...in response to the sensation of speed...in response to her fatigue in the rigger net.

In the faint roar of wind, she finally raised herself on Highwing's neck, understanding that she was exhausted, that she had been flying in the net for too many hours. *Where are we?* she asked, her voice straining.

On the way to where you wanted to go, said the dragon.

If I went away—to sleep—could you stay with my ship until return? The net sparkled, off color. She didn't even know why she'd asked that, but she felt a jab of pain, of loneliness. She didn't quite want to leave him.

I will be here, answered the dragon.

Sighing, Jael gathered her senses, materialized an image of the ship which was bound to her through the net, just a ghostly nose of the ship extending out of nothingness into the Flux, and she set the stabilizers astraddle Highwing. *I'll see you in a while, then,* she offered.

A plume of smoke. *Yes.*

Jael withdrew. Her senses darkened—and rekindled back in her own body. She climbed out of the rigger-cell and stood, weary, in the gloom of the bridge. She stretched once. Then she stole into the galley and ate ravenously, expecting an angry Mogurn to burst in at any moment. When she finished, and Mogurn had not appeared, she crept to his door and signaled. No answer. She paled the door and peered in. Mogurn was under the synaptic augmentor, his eyes rolled up into his head, a grimace stretching his mouth. His chest rose and fell slowly; otherwise he lay still. He hadn't been able to wait for Jael to help him.

Jael frowned, thinking reflexively of the pallisp, and then realizing that she didn't really need it just now. She could live without it while she slept. Turning, she went to her own cabin and fell almost instantly into deep sleep.

∞

She blinked; her dreams fled. Mogurn's voice startled her a second time, growling, "Are you being paid to sleep?" The anger in his voice was sharp, too sharp. She turned to look at him, standing just inside her door, and she pictured him cremated by dragon fire. "Make yourself ready and come see me in the galley,'" he ordered. Then he vanished.

Jael roused herself worriedly. Mogurn sounded unwell, perhaps unstable. Could that be a result of a synaptic overdose? She'd have to be careful—best to get back into the net quickly. And—strangely! — she was terribly anxious about Highwing. A queer ache settled in her chest when she thought of the dragon; it reminded her of the longing she felt for the pallisp. Or used to feel. At the moment, she didn't want the pallisp; she wanted to be with Highwing.

Head spinning, she went to the galley. Mogurn was eating, and under his baleful eye she dialed something for herself. As she began to eat, he spoke sharply. "Twice you've disobeyed. And you entered the net without permission, and put us in trouble with dragons. Are we clear of dragons now?" His voice sounded strained.

Jael swallowed. Highwing, burn him! she thought, wishing that the dragon could be here to obey. She chose her words cautiously. "We could still have trouble." Mogurn's eyes flashed. "But we are nearing the final current to Lexis. I should return to the net at once."

The shipowner squinted, his facial muscles tense. "You don't like me much, do you?" he said tightly. "You never did. But you like your pallisp well enough, don't you? And there is no man who can wield the pallisp for you as I do."

Jael held her gaze rigid, meeting his. I do not need a pallisp, she thought…not any longer. Nevertheless, she trembled under Mogurn's gaze. "There will be no more mistakes, Jael. No disobedience. No pallisp—until you have removed this ship from danger." Mogurn smiled queerly, triumphantly, and crossed his arms.

What a pathetic man, Jael thought—however cruel. What weapon did he hold over her now? She still feared him physically, yes, but—"I do not need your pallisp," she said aloud. Her throat constricted. "And now I must—"

"You *stay* until I command you to *leave!*" shouted Mogurn furiously.

An alarm on the bridge quailed, signaling changes in the Flux. Mogurn started, jerked his head around. "Go!" he said bitterly.

Jael hurried. If Highwing had left her…

When her senses sparked outward into the net, she found herself astride the dragon, flying in clear winds over low mountains. She trembled with relief. Two suns, pink and orange, were setting before her. The sky overhead was a sea of liquid crystal, and she knew at once that she was bound upward for that sea. *Greetings, small one,* sighed the dragon, snorting fire.

Jael hugged his neck, wanting to cry. *Highwing,* she said softly, *did you call me?*

The dragon pumped his wings slowly. *I wanted you to return,* he said. *I don't know if I called you or not.*

I knew it was time to come. Are we—are we almost at the end?

Of my range, yes, Jael. Dragons do not go beyond these foothills. I am zigzagging to go more slowly, but we are almost at the end. Do you wish me to fly straight?

No—please, no. Oh, Highwing, can't you come further with me? Or can't we go back? Even as she spoke, Jael knew that it was impossible. She had a ship to bring in, and even Mogurn was her responsibility. The currents of the Flux were inexorable; dragons could fly against them, perhaps, but Jael and her ship could not.

Sometimes friends must part, said the dragon softly.

And I made you leave, said Jael, half to herself, *when all along you were trying to help me. Just as you promised.* She was ashamed; tears wet her cheeks. *What will I do, Highwing? What will I do now?*

You will find others, said the dragon, *and I will still be here, thinking of you.*

Jael trembled and wept, and after a long time her tears dried. How could she dispel the terrible loneliness she felt already closing in upon her? The pallisp came to mind, and she turned it away. The price for that was too high, the comfort too short. No, Highwing's advice was best. However difficult, it was better than settling for the likes of Mogurn and the pallisp. Better than shelled-in emptiness.

Things will be different. Things will be better, she said, as though to the wind.

Highwing heard her and answered. *It will be different for me, too, little Jael. Never again will I duel a rigger without thinking of you. You, who have my name—and I yours.*

They flew in silence for a few moments. The lowest of the low mountains came into sight. *Highwing,* Jael said, *If I fly this way again, will I see you?*

The dragon breathed fire. *I shall be looking for you, little Jael, and so will other dragons. Cry, "Friend of Highwing!" and I will hear you, though all the mountains lie between us.*

Jael trembled with emotion. *Then let us fly high, now, and part in the sun,* she said, urging him toward the sky.

The dragon complied at once, soaring high toward the inverted lake of sunset crystal above their heads. Jael leaned with him into the wind, feeling it sting her cheeks and toss her hair, feeling the glowing radiance of the celestial ocean overhead filling her eyes and her soul. The two suns were setting now, but they threw their radiance in fuller color than ever into the sky. Channels opened in the clouds, and light poured through in great rays, washing over the dragon and Jael, and they flew up one of the beams, into the crystal sea, where colors shifted brightly and the currents of the Flux moved in streams and gossamer strands. And here, she knew, Highwing would leave her, for this was not a dragon's realm.

Highwing shivered, and she thought she heard echoes of weeping, and he blew a great cloud of smoke and sparks and a single brilliant, billowing flame. Jael caressed his neck one last time, and then extended her hands into space and turned them into great webs touching the streamers of light. *Farewell, Highwing,* she cried softly.

Farewell, Jael, said the dragon, and he wheeled and suddenly Jael was no longer astride him but in flight on her own, rigger once more. Highwing banked and circled around her, his eyes flashing, and he issued a long, thin stream of smoke in final farewell, and then he banked sharply and plummeted.

Jael looked after him, holding her tears, as he dwindled toward his own world. *Friend of Highwing!* she cried after him, and her voice reverberated gently down the sunbeams and perhaps she was only imagining but she thought she heard his laugh echoing in the distance below. And then she set her sights ahead and knew that the tears would flow and dry, for a while, and she looked in the shifting sky for the currents that would carry her to her destination star system, to the end of this voyage, to normal space. And she thought of how she would tell Mogurn that she was leaving his employ, and his pallisp, and she laughed and cried and turned her thoughts back to the sky.

Until I return, Highwing, she thought, and she saw the streamer she wanted and caught it in her webbed hand, and with her the ship rose high and fast into the current.

About the Authors

All of the authors are residents of Treehousewriters.com, *where you may find them blogging as they while away the pandemic in the company of crows.*

Jeffrey A. Carver was a Nebula Award finalist for his novel *Eternity's End*. He also authored *Battlestar Galactica,* a novelization of the critically acclaimed television miniseries. His novels combine thought-provoking characters with engaging storytelling, and range from the adventures of the Star Rigger universe (*Star Rigger's Way, Dragons in the Stars,* and others) to the ongoing, character-driven hard SF of *The Chaos Chronicles*—which begins with *Neptune Crossing* and continues with *Strange Attractors, The Infinite Sea, Sunborn,* and now *The Reefs of Time* and its conclusion, *Crucible of Time.*

A native of Huron, Ohio, Carver lives with his family in the Boston area. He has taught writing in a variety of settings, from educational television to conferences for young writers to MIT, as well as his ongoing Ultimate Science Fiction Workshop with Craig Shaw Gardner. He has created a free web site for aspiring authors of all ages at writesf.com. Learn more about the author and his work at starrigger.net, where a complete guide to his ebooks may also be found.

About "Dog Star," Jeffrey writes, "I'd been pondering for some time how to tell a story about dark energy, a concept so cosmic its effects felt only over billions of years as to seem impossible to tell in human terms. Somewhere in my unpredictable subconscious, this urge dovetailed with my fond recollection of a joke circulating on the internet: "How many dogs [name your breed] does it take to change a light bulb?" For the border collie, the answer is: "Just me. And while I'm up there, I'll bring that wiring up to code for you." (I once had a border collie mix, the smartest dog I've ever known. And yeah, his name was Sam. Jeez, I miss that dog.)

"The central conversation about dark energy was the first piece of the story that I wrote, though I didn't know yet that it was a dog asking the questions. I had to get that right, and clear, and conversational, and that was hard enough in itself. The next hard thing was figuring out how to wrap a story around it in which that conversation, and really knowing something about dark energy, would make a difference in the lives of the characters. I hope I succeeded. I realize the story is, in many ways, a throwback to the can-do, just give me a wrench and a place to stand, science-fiction stories of the 1950's. But that's okay—I loved those stories, and I don't see why they can't be updated to the Twenty-first Century.

"But I confess, I wonder along with Sam what were those astronomers thinking, when they named an invisible *something* that holds the galaxies together "dark matter," and a few years later, named another invisible *something* that pushes the universe apart "dark energy"? What *were* they thinking?"

Amy Sterling Casil was inspired to write science fiction because while she was growing up, Ray Bradbury spoke twice at her hometown library in Redlands, CA and his optimistic message stayed with her for life. Amy is an award-nominated science fiction writer who has published 44 books, hundreds of short stories, thousands of articles, and hundreds of textbook passages. Her mother Sterling Sturtevant was one of the first female animation art directors, an Academy Award winner who designed Mr. Magoo for UPA Studios in the 1950s. Amy is a past Treasurer of the Science Fiction & Fantasy Writers of America and founding Treasurer of the Book View Café Publishing Cooperative. She has also served as a high level development officer for major affordable housing and economic development projects in South and Central Los Angeles. Today she is a business consultant and fund developer working primarily for emerging and growing businesses in the U.S., Canada, and Mexico.

About "Smiley the Robot," Amy writes, "This is just a love story, and I've always been fond of it. Ron Collins liked it, too. I was to be named "Gia." I don't know why my mother changed my name when I was a baby, but she did. The name is somehow magical for me. This is like Harold & Maude. Or Smiley and Gia. Actually, it's inspired by my grandmother and is set in my hometown of Redlands. Some years from now."

About "To Kiss the Star," Amy writes, "I wrote this story inspired by my friend at Chapman University, Julie Jones. Julie was born with disabilities similar to the character of Mel in the story. I wanted to take an honest look at what it felt like to be in that chair. I spent about three weeks there. Julie remains my friend. She read the story and said it was truthful before I ever sent it for publication. It was nominated for a Nebula Award in 2002 after appearing in *The*

Magazine of Fantasy & Science Fiction. Only much later did Jim Blaylock point out to me the similarities between this story and *The Ship Who Sang*.

"I could never imagine you doing a story about a crippled girl in space and her cat," Jim said. Well, of course. In this story, there's no cat.

Leah Cutter tells page-turning, wildly creative stories that always leave you guessing in the middle, but completely satisfied by the end.

She writes mystery of all sorts. Her Lake Hope cozy mysteries have been well received by readers, who just want to curl up and have tea with the main character. Her Halley Brown series, revolving around a private investigator who used to be with the Seattle Police Department, leave you guessing at every turn. And her speculative mysteries, such as the Alvin Goodfellow Case Files—a 1930s PI set on the moon—have garnered great reviews.

She's been published in magazines such as "Alfred Hitchcock's Mystery Magazine" and in anthologies like "Fiction River: Spies." On top of that, Leah is the editor of the new quarterly mystery magazine: *Mystery, Crime, and Mayhem (www.MCM-Magazine.com)*.

Read books by Leah Cutter at www.KnottedRoadPress.com. Follow her blog at www.LeahCutter.com.

Doranna Durgin is an award-winning author whose quirky spirit has led to an extensive and eclectic publishing journey across genres, publishers, and publishing lines. Beyond that, she hangs around outside her Southwest mountain home training her dog pack for agility, tracking, and obedience. She says, "My books are SF/F, mystery, paranormal romance, and romantic suspense. My dogs are Beagles, my home is the Southwest, and the horse wants a cookie." Doranna is currently working on a sequel to *Wolverine's Daughter* (fantasy) and author editions of earlier fantasies. So many projects to choose from! Find her at changespell.com, or noodling around on Facebook.

About "In Search of Laria," Doranna writes, "For all the hard moments in this story, it's one that's meant a lot to me, and the ending is one that makes me feel that little blossom of hope."

Nancy Jane Moore is the author of the fantasy novel *For the Good of the Realm* and the *Locus*-recommended science fiction novel *The Weave*, both published by Seattle's Aqueduct Press. Her other books include the novella *Changeling* and the collection *Conscientious*

Inconsistencies. Her short stories have appeared in numerous anthologies and in magazines ranging from the *National Law Journal* to *Lady Churchill's Rosebud Wristlet.* In addition to writing, she holds a fourth degree black belt in Aikido and teaches empowerment self defense. A native Texan who spent many years in Washington, D.C., she now lives in Oakland, California, with her sweetheart, two cats, and an ever-growing murder of crows.

Twitter: @WriterNancyJane, website: nancyjanemoore.com

Pati Nagle has written more than twenty-five novels and two collections of short fiction, besides all the stuff that hasn't seen print. She was born and raised in the mountains of northern New Mexico and is an avid student of music, history, and humans in general.

Her fiction has appeared in *Asimov's Science Fiction, The Magazine of Fantasy & Science Fiction, Cricket, Cicada,* and in numerous anthologies, including those honoring New Mexico writers Jack Williamson and Roger Zelazny ("Emancipation" is from the former). Her fantasy short story "Coyote Ugly" was honored as a finalist for the Theodore Sturgeon Award.

Nagle writes fantasy, science fiction, historical fiction (as P.G. Nagle) and the popular Wisteria Tearoom Mysteries (as Patrice Greenwood). She lives in the mountains in New Mexico with her spouse and a feline muse.

Steven Harper Piziks was born with a name that no one can reliably spell or pronounce, so he often writes under the pen name Steven Harper. He lives in Michigan with his husband. When not at the keyboard, he plays the folk harp, fiddles with video games, and pretends he doesn't talk to the household cats. He also maintains that the most interesting thing about him is that he writes books. Most recently, he wrote the Books of Blood and Iron, a fantasy trilogy, for Roc Books.

Gillian Polack is a Jewish Australian speculative fiction writer based in Canberra, Australia. She was the 2020 recipient of the Ditmar (best novel, for her 2019 novel, *The Year of the Fruit Cake*) and the A. Bertram Chandler (lifetime achievement in science fiction) awards. She is an ethnohistorian with a special interest in how story transmits culture, both Medieval and modern. Her study of this will be released in 2022 (*Story Matrices: Cultural Encoding and Cultural Baggage in the Worlds of Science Fiction and Fantasy, Academic Lunare*). Dr

Polack's publications include ten novels, short stories, a monograph (*History and Fiction*, shortlisted for the William Atheling Jr Award for Criticism or Review) and various works of non-fiction. A list of her books can be found at gillianpolack.com/my-books.

About "A Plague of Dancers," Gillian writes, "St. John's Dance, St. Vitus's Dance, dancing pilgrims, choreomania, dancing mania, all these names described the dancing plague. The year it danced alongside the Black Death was one of the worst years in European history. Some districts never recovered. No one bothered to describe on parchment or paper the specific event that began in Yorkshire on St. John's Day, a year after the Black Death. Chroniclers, annalists, even the keepers of the small local records—none of them were interested. This means that it may have happened…or this story may be a complete fabrication."

Madeleine E. Robins has been a nanny, an administrator, an actor, and a swordswoman; has trafficked book production, edited comics, and repaired hurt books. She's also the author of the *New York Times* Notable urban fantasy *The Stone War*; *Daredevil: The Cutting Edge*; historical novel *Sold for Endless Rue*; and alt-Regency-noir mysteries *Point of Honour*, *Petty Treason*, and *The Sleeping Partner*. A native New Yorker, Madeleine now lives in San Francisco with an elderly dog, a husband, and a hegemonic lemon tree.

Deborah J. Ross writes and edits fantasy and science fiction, with over a dozen novels and six dozen short stories in print. Her work has earned Honorable Mention in *Year's Best SF*, and nominations for Lambda Literary Award, Gaylactic Spectrum Award, the National Fantasy Federation Speculative Fiction Award for Best Author, and inclusion in the Otherwise Award List, *Locus* Recommended Reading, and *Kirkus* notable new release lists. She has served as Secretary to the Science Fiction Fantasy Writers of America (SFWA) and the Board of Directors of Book View Café, and chaired the jury for the Philip K. Dick Award. When she's not writing, she knits for charity, plays classical piano, and hikes in the redwoods. She holds forth on life and writing (and the writing life) on her blog deborahjross.blogspot.com. You can also find more on her website deborahjross.com or in her newsletter.

"Unmasking the Ancient Light" was based on the life of Renaissance woman Dona Gracia Nasi, whose life was even more extraordinary, Deborah says, than what is here depicted here.

Judith Tarr's first novel, *The Isle of Glass*, appeared in 1985. Since then she's written novels and shorter works of historical fiction and historical fantasy and epic fantasy and space opera and contemporary fantasy, many of which have been reborn as ebooks. She has even written a primer for writers: *Writing Horses: The Fine Art of Getting It Right.* She has won the Crawford Award, and been a finalist for the World Fantasy Award and the *Locus* Award. She lives in Arizona with an assortment of cats, a blue-eyed dog, and a herd of Lipizzan horses.